Hidden Buddhas

ALSO BY LIZA DALBY

Geisha
Kimono: Fashioning Culture
The Tale of Murasaki
East Wind Melts the Ice: A Memoir Through the Seasons

Hidden Buddhas

a novel of Karma and Chaos

LIZA DALBY

with illustrations by Michael Hofmann

Stone Bridge Press • Berkeley, California

Published by
Stone Bridge Press
P.O. Box 8208
Berkeley, CA 94707
TEL 510-524-8732 • sbp@stonebridge.com • www.stonebridge.com

For more about this book, visit **www.lizadalby.com**, **www.hiddenbuddhas.com**, and **www.mayumimode.com**.

Cover design by Chloë Dalby incorporating artwork by David Mack.

Text ©2009 Liza Dalby.

Interior illustrations except map and on title page and part-titles ©2009 Michael Hofmann.

First edition 2009.

Printed in the United States of America.

2014   2013   2012   2011   2010   2009   10 9 8 7 6 5 4 3 2 1

LIBRARY OF CONGRESS CATALOGING-IN-PUBLICATION DATA
Dalby, Liza Crihfield.
  Hidden Buddhas : a novel of karma and chaos / Liza Dalby ; with illustrations by Michael Hofmann. — 1st ed.
     p. cm.
  ISBN 978-1-933330-85-3
  I. Title.
PS3554.A4147H53 2009
813'.54—dc22

                              2009025073

To Michael, Marie, Owen,
and especially
Chloë

According to Buddhist theology the world is suffering through a final corrupt era called *mappō*. As *mappō* continues, chaos will increase until the center can no longer hold. Then the world will end. In Japan, many believe that Miroku, Buddha of the Future, will appear and bring about a new age of enlightenment.

Hi sureba hana nari, hi sezuba hana narubekarazu
If hidden—a flower; unless hidden, no flower at all.

ZEAMI

Hidden Buddhas

THE HIDDEN BUDDHAS OF JAPAN

N

0		100		200 miles
0	100	200	300 km	

· hidden buddhas

temples

HOKKAIDO

Sea of Japan

HONSHU

Pacific Ocean

Seiryōji
Gyōganji
Kōryūji

Kashiwadera

Tokyo

Ōkannonji

Miidera

Kyoto
Nara

Fudō-in

Kōyasan

Hōryūji
Denkōji
Saidaiji

Kanshinji

SHIKOKU

Shidōji

KYUSHU

pilgrim route

The Hidden Path

IGNORING THE DULL ITCH of an inflamed flea bite on his ankle, the boy pressed his body against the cool plaster of the east wall, carefully staying out of sight. Crowds of worshippers had shuffled through the temple grounds until the gate was closed to the public at five o'clock. By now all the priests, including visitors like his grandfather, were supposed to be at the main hall for the evening service. The boy knew this, but just to be sure, he waited for the low rumble of sutra chanting to reach his ears. Pale pink flowering cherries trembled in a light breeze. Noboru did not know how much time he had before someone made his way back here to the hall where the temple's hidden buddha was housed.

This place, Kyoto's oldest temple, was once known as Hachioka-dera, Bee Hills Temple, but that name had faded and most people only knew it by its official name, Kōryūji, a temple belonging to the Shingon Buddhist sect. The compound was spread out with wide gravel paths connecting the venerable wood and plaster buildings and their precious population of sacred images. Among its trove of Buddhist deities, Kōryūji held a *hibutsu*—a "hidden buddha"—in this case a nine-hundred-year-old gilt wooden statue of Guan Yin. For one day a year, the lacquered doors enclosing the treasured image were opened, and worshippers allowed to view the serene visage of "the compassionate one who hears the cries of the world." Noboru knew there were hidden buddhas tucked away in temples all over Japan because his grandfather, a Shingon priest, was very fond of them. It almost seemed the old man's main interest in life was visiting temples when these *hibutsu* came on display. He knew precisely when and for how long each one was open to view. Two years ago he had started bringing Noboru along on his pilgrimages. Tonight the monks would close the Guan Yin back up in its black-lacquered sanctum for another year. Noboru looked around nervously. The area around the Hidden Buddha Hall was deserted. He heard the rhythmic sound of men's gravelly voices chanting sutras from the direction of the main building. Inhaling the fresh spring air, he glanced around one last time before ducking into the dark hall imbued with the deeply familiar musty odor of old wood and incense smoke.

Noboru Tokuda had been born in a temple. His father was a Buddhist priest, his mother the daughter of one. Sutras had been the lullabies of infancy and the soundtrack of his entire childhood. But Noboru's nostrils widened now, sensing an odor different from the ordinary temple smell. Not musty at all—ineffable and pure. Familiar, yet new. The delicate fragrance seemed to emanate from the statue of Guan Yin. He crept closer and sat on his knees, tucking his bare calves under his indigo cotton kimono. Hesitantly at first, Noboru formed his hands into the *mudra* gestures his grandfather had showed him earlier that day. The fragrance, rather like sandalwood and rare flowers, intensified. Concentrating deeply, the boy now made out a pale glowing penumbra around the statue. All his senses strained toward it. His grandfather had told him that if he indeed had the ability to comprehend the aura of a hidden buddha he would feel its effects on every sense.

The odor was the first thing he recognized, with no training at all. In fact, until today, he had thought everybody smelled it. This morning was the first time he had he even thought to ask. The old man stared at his grandson.

"You smell it?"

"It smells really good," Noboru replied. "Like incense but not incense. What is it?"

"It's the fragrance of the hidden buddha," said the old priest slowly. "But not everyone can smell it."

The possibility that his own grandchild had the ability filled him with relief and joy—followed by a twinge of trepidation. He must begin training Noboru immediately.

"It's a special talent that you're born with or you're not." Curious, the old man probed, "… besides the fragrance, do you see anything else about this statue? Or hear anything? Any other sensations?" Noboru hung his head. He had never paid close attention.

"No matter," said his grandfather. "Perhaps with practice." He taught the boy the ritual hand gestures of Shingon that were used in worshipping Guan Yin. "We'll continue tomorrow."

But tomorrow this hidden buddha would be closed up again. Excited by his grandfather's words, Noboru wanted to test himself before the *hibutsu* was hidden away until next April.

And now, alone with the statue, he found he could detect a glow! What about his ears? Was there any sound? He listened intently. A faint hum. Could it be his imagination? As he concentrated on the barely perceptible vibration, his hands dancing the mudra to Guan Yin, he became aware of a soft warmth on his skin. At the same time the hum became more audible—almost a high human voice, but vibrating like a koto string. Nose, eyes, ears, skin, tongue. The five organs of perception. Smell, sight, sound, touch, taste. All had engaged. A sweetness welled up in Noboru's mouth. It reminded him of the dark millet syrup his mother poured over rice dumplings. He felt tears of happiness squeezing the back of his eyes. The sixth element, consciousness, holding the five senses like a string through beads. Noboru, his senses, consciousness, the Guan Yin—melded without distinction.

The statue's serene full-cheeked face tilted up slightly, resting on one of its three right hands, elbow propped on knee. Another hand held the wish-granting jewel, as if giving it to him. It was already his. Noboru's mouth hung open, his eyes stared, unblinking. He could feel the statue offering him the wheel of the Buddhist law, balanced like a spinning toy on one of her left hands. He would devote his life to the Buddhist Truth. A lotus bud, too, held out. Compassion for the world—for him. His senses overflowed.

He had no idea how long he was suspended in this state, when, suddenly, the golden light wavered. The singing tone died away. The fragrance faded, and with its loss the warmth and sweetness dwindled away. All sensations ebbed into a dark emptiness that sucked Noboru's happiness, understanding, and love with it.

Panicking, he scrambled to his feet. Someone else was in the dim hall. He called out to his grandfather.

"Your grandfather's not here. Nobody's here."

Noboru whirled around, blinded by tears. The low voice belonged to a beautiful young woman. She, too, must have slipped into the building to pray to the statue. Her yellow skirt, fashionably cinched at the waist, seemed to glow in the fading evening light. She turned, glancing back briefly at Noboru before stepping outside.

"Wait!" The boy choked. Something terrible had happened. Even without understanding, he felt it. She was gone. His senses raw, Noboru now became aware of another odor. In front of the altar where the woman had been standing a lingering scent pricked his nose. It was like nothing he had ever smelled before—sharp, cool, insinuating. He had no words for it, but he would never forget it.

From the direction of the main gate, the great bronze temple bell rang once, sending its deep reverberations rippling through the balmy early evening air. Holding his head in his hands Noboru dropped down on the cool stone floor and wailed.

His grandfather, the head priest, and three disciples discovered him there. The head priest was angry. Someone had rung the great bell without permission. His suspicion immediately fell on the visiting priest's twelve-year-old grandson. Noboru's grandfather was already apologizing. He took the sobbing boy by the arm. The fact that Noboru was hiding in here, terrified, pointed to his guilt. What had gotten into him? But, then, he *was* only twelve…

The head priest was mollified by the older man's repeated bows and apologies. He gave Noboru a pro-forma cuff on the side of his shaved head. At that moment Noboru felt his grandfather stiffen, his bony fingertips digging into his shoulder. He looked up and saw that the old man was staring at the statue of Guan Yin. The head priest noticed nothing. He invited them to join the other monks for their evening meal before the ceremony of returning the *hibutsu* to its tabernacle.

"I need to talk to my grandson," said the older Tokuda. "We will be along. Please don't wait for us."

Figuring the boy was in for a private scolding, the other priests withdrew.

As soon as they were alone, Priest Tokuda squatted down in front of Noboru.

"What happened?"

"The bell…" Noboru began.

"The bell doesn't matter," snapped his grandfather. "The hidden buddha. What happened?"

Noboru told him about the effects on each of his senses. "Do you feel it too, Grandpa?" he asked.

The old priest nodded.

"But then it all went away," said Noboru. "I couldn't feel it any more. Not even the smell."

"I know." The old man's shoulders sagged.

Noboru trembled.

The priest watched the boy's reaction. It was remarkable. With the barest hint of training, the child had applied his abilities and felt the full power of this hidden buddha. Priest Tokuda needed no more proof that Noboru was meant to be his successor.

"I'm going to explain something to you," he said to the bewildered boy. "And I'm going to depend on you for help. Listen carefully. The hidden buddhas exist to protect the world. And over many, many years a few people have had the job of guarding them."

"Is that your job, Grandpa?"

"Yes. And one day it will be yours as well. Tell me, was there anyone else in the building?"

The beautiful young woman. Noboru's senses had been in such an over-stimulated state that he couldn't be sure now whether he had really seen her or not. He remembered hearing the temple bell, and then the priests crowding around.

"Someone—or something—is stealing the hidden buddhas' protective power," continued his grandfather. "Over the years, slowly killing them off. It always occurs when the statues are on display. That's when they're vulnerable."

Suddenly it dawned on Noboru why his grandfather wandered from temple to temple, always visiting the hidden buddhas that were briefly on view. He wasn't worshipping them, he was watching over them. And today, one had been destroyed right under his nose. Noboru had been there. This would be his job now too—to protect the hidden buddhas.

But he also realized that he had already failed. His throat tightened. How could he admit this? Definitely, a woman had slipped in to the hall while he was transfixed by the *hibutsu*. But until he understood more, he had better hide this fact. Next time, he vowed to himself, he would know what to do. His grandfather would teach him skills. One day he would find and confront her—he was sure there would be another chance.

"I'm not sure...I don't think there was anyone..." he faltered. Then, "Does the head priest know what's happened to this *hibutsu*?"

His grandfather jerked his head. "He knows nothing. None of them do. It's very rare, you understand—the sensations you have."

"What about my father?"

The old man shook his head. "He's a good priest, but he doesn't feel a thing." That had been a major disappointment. But it didn't matter now.

"Whatever is destroying the hidden buddhas sucks out their power so all that's left is the husk. The dead image. Most people can't tell, of course. The statue looks the same. Most of the hidden buddhas now are empty shells. I only watch over the live ones."

Noboru was still upset. He shivered. What, exactly, were the hidden buddhas protecting us from, he wanted to ask. He winced remembering that afternoon's experience of being uplifted to a plane of complete joy and then dropped into a dark void.

"Come on." His grandfather took him by the hand. "Let's get something to eat before it's all gone."

"But the hidden buddha?" Noboru turned to look at the image of Guan Yin.

"There's nothing we can do about this one. It's dead."

In the garden of career choices that sprang up in postwar Japan, modern-minded sons of Buddhist priests often chose to become businessmen rather than shave their heads. But it was obvious to everyone that Noboru Tokuda would follow his father and grandfather's calling. On school holidays, he traveled with his grandfather, viewing *hibutsu*, learning about Shingon. No one, of course, knew exactly what the older man was methodically transferring to his quietly serious grandson—or indeed that anything was being transferred at all. For his part, Noboru intuitively grasped the necessity of hiding the secret knowledge he was given.

Uninterested in sports, Noboru nevertheless had an athletic grace. His naturally Fuji-arched eyebrows were balanced by a square jaw that saved his face from being pretty. Throughout his teenage years, girls were attracted to him—and he enjoyed girls. He realized that he was not aroused by them, but he maintained a keen appreciation for the various ways in which they were beautiful. He could hear the hopes and desires hidden underneath the surface of their words, and so girls were inclined to share their confidences. When he appeared at graduation with the shaved head of a Shingon initiate, they all sighed. How old-fashioned.

By the time Noboru was twenty he knew all the gestures of mudra, and the sacred syllables of the mantras. He studied the life of Kūkai, Shingon's founder. But Noboru was also learning other things from his grandfather that his fellow acolytes had no idea were part of Kūkai's legacy. Every time a hidden buddha came on view he was given a chance to test his ability to sense its aura. His senses were trained to the point where he could read a *hibutsu* even when it wasn't on display, from behind the closed doors of its tabernacle. Allowing all his senses to vibrate in harmony with a hidden buddha became, for Noboru, the most blissful experiences of his life.

One morning in the middle of October, while looking into the nebula of dissolved bean paste of his breakfast soup, Noboru's grandfather was seized by the conviction that it was time for the young man's confirmation. The ritual he had to perform would be an initiation as well as the last test—the sign of whether Noboru was indeed meant to be his successor or not. If the youth passed—and he couldn't even know he was being tested—old priest Tokuda would then explain the final detail s of the enormous responsibility he would transfer to his young shoulders. Finishing the miso soup in one long gulp, he set the bowl down and told Noboru they would go to Mt. Kōya that weekend.

Kōyasan was the heart of Shingon—the mountain where, over a thousand years ago its founder, Kūkai, built an enormous temple complex and where he now rested in an Inner Sanctum, venerated by thousands of worshippers. Noboru had been there often, but he sensed today would be different from previous pilgrimages. The two shaven heads, one bristled white, one shadowed blue-black, joined the crowds bowing their respects at the Hall of Lanterns in front of Kūkai's mausoleum. In the late afternoon, as most people headed toward the parking lots, the two Tokudas hiked past the golden buildings and splendid tombs, farther into Kōyasan's cedar-forested slopes. Just before dusk they reached an old, seemingly abandoned temple at the end of an overgrown path.

Noboru felt slightly giddy breathing the rank, mildewed air inside. He waited while the old man felt his way around the back of the dark altar, looking for the mandala he would need. The older Tokuda had not seen it since his own initiation, when his teacher, Priest Zuichō, had declared that, of his seven acolytes, Tokuda was to be heir. Now he stroked his fingers gently across the joinery, feeling for an almost imperceptible latch. There. He reached inside the well-hidden compartment and touched the smooth paulownia-wood box holding the scroll of the Womb Mandala that had been used by Zuichō, and his master before him. It had been recopied every four hundred years, always an exact copy, stretching back over a thousand years to the one Kūkai himself had painted.

As he carefully unrolled the painting, Tokuda was flooded with memories of his venerable teacher. Zuichō had lived through the hard days of the late nineteenth century when the Meiji government, turning against imported tradition, had done its best to rip Buddhism from the fabric of Japanese life. For centuries, to be a monk was to be a vegetarian. Suddenly, bureaucrats told them to eat meat. They were discouraged from wearing clerical robes, and even celibacy was frowned on. "Get married if you want," priests were told. Zuichō remained steadfastly single, but his students all took wives. Tokuda's generation was the first in which Shingon priests had families in the temples.

Decades later, statues that had been buried away to keep them safe from the anti-Buddhist pogrom were dug up, temples were rebuilt, and Buddhism reclaimed its place in society—but things were never quite the same. None of his predecessors seemed to have had any problem finding a successor, but Priest Tokuda had reached a point of desperation. There had never been a hereditary connection in the long line of guardians. Succession was decided by ability alone—master to disciple, not father to son. This dearth of candidates was another disquieting sign. Even ordinary priests were starting to have trouble finding successors these days. Who would uphold the Law of the Dharma if priests all became salarymen? Tokuda's sole hope now rested on his beloved grandson.

When a *hibutsu* lost its power, inevitably catastrophe of some sort followed—war, flooding, fires, famine. The Great Fire of Meireki, which destroyed most of the city of Edo in 1657, killing a hundred thousand people, occurred just after the Amida *hibutsu* of Zenkōji temple went dark. The gruesome disaster catalog was part of the secret transmission Tokuda would need to teach his successor. The loss of a live *hibutsu* was the worst thing that could happen to the holder of the secret transmission. As it was, many guardians lived through their tenure never experiencing that trauma at all.

In the late nineteenth century, however, his own teacher Zuichō alone suffered the sudden demise of a dozen *hibutsu*—an unprecedented number. At least it was until Tokuda himself lost twenty-eight—including Kōryūji temple's Guan Yin. That one had been devastating—he felt the perpetrator must have been close by, and yet managed to slip through his fingers. He had been distracted by the sight of his young grandson sobbing on the temple floor.

It was clear that something dire was happening to the hidden buddhas, and the rate was accelerating. Tokuda's career as their guardian had been more frustrating than his master's, and it seemed likely that it would only get worse. The old man's fingers trembled at the thought of the burden he would transfer to his grandson. He would try to help Noboru as long as he could—assuming, of course, that the youth passed tonight's test.

In the waning light, he spread the large square mandala painting on the wide dais in front of the altar, and had Noboru sit facing it. Then he blindfolded him and placed a twig of woody anise in his hand. This much Noboru expected. The ritual was central to Shingon ordination. It echoed that performed by Kūkai himself when he received the teaching from his master in China. Master Huiguo had instructed the visiting Japanese acolyte to cast the twig onto the mandala. Kūkai tossed, and his twig flew true to center, landing on Dainichi, the cosmic Buddha. By this, Huiguo knew Kūkai would be his heir and he anointed him master of the teachings of Shingon.

Always, initiates prayed their twig would land in the center, on the cosmic Buddha, in an auspicious echo of Kūkai. Yet hundreds of other buddhas and bodhisattvas, painted different colors, in a variety of poses, peopled the mandala. One of these was the muscular, fanged warrior Fudō. Nobody prayed for their twig to land on the picture of Fudō. Yet, Noboru's twig had to. He didn't know it, but that would be the final sign. If he were meant to be the successor, the protector of the secret of the hidden buddhas, his twig would come to rest on the terrifying, sword-wielding Fudō.

Following his grandfather's instructions Noboru arranged the offerings, chanted the mantras, lit the ceremonial fire, and, aiming his twig in the direction of Dainichi, he tossed the anise a little too forcefully onto the mandala. He heard the old man suck in his breath. The twig had bounced off the center and skittered to the lower right. In the silence that followed, Noboru hesitantly untied the blindfold and saw that the twig lay squarely across the image of Fudō. He felt a stab of keen disappointment. Whatever this test was, he was sure he had failed. He saw an expression of elation as well as fear flit across his grandfather's face. That night everything was revealed. The mantle of protector of the *hibutsu* settled on the forty-first guardian of the unbroken line—twenty-one-year-old Noboru Tokuda.

In the tradition of esoteric Buddhism, Shingon is full of secrets. But the knowledge Noboru was given was unusual, even so. It had never been written down. The list of *hibutsu* was an oral tradition passed from one guardian to his successor, accreting layers of information with each generation. Not only the names of the previous guardians, but any hidden buddha that had lost its aura or been destroyed by war, fire, earthquake, or flood was also embedded in the litany that Noboru had to memorize.

During the early years of his training, Noboru often thought of the Guan Yin of Kōryūji. The figure of a beautiful woman with a cool steely smell seemed to mock him. Anger welled up, yet he still could not bring himself to reveal to his grandfather this failure hidden in his heart.

On the night of his initiation he was told how the hidden buddhas were put in place as a spiritual bulwark to keep the world from slipping further into the state of *mappō*—the degenerate final age that would culminate in the end of the world. A network of ritually infused *hibutsu* had kept the world safe for over a millennium. Yet, gradually over the centuries, and speeding up at an alarming rate, they were being deactivated, always when they were open to public view. When the last *hibutsu* had been seen by this destructive eye, the world would collapse on itself. *Mappō* would have reached its conclusion.

It was now quite dark, and the candles old priest Tokuda had lit had burned down to sputtering nubs. For a while they sat in silence.

"And then what?" Noboru asked.

One didn't need special powers of observation to see that the world was exhibiting signs of *mappō*. Nature disgorged earthquakes, hurricanes, volcanic eruptions, and floods. Within this tragic tangle of misery, mankind goaded human suffering with war, nuclear attack, genocide, and global pollution. *Mappō* was an old idea, enshrined in the cosmology of Buddhist thought. Noboru had no trouble believing it was real. The signs were clear enough. The auras of the *hibutsu* were real enough to him as well. The revelation for Noboru now was the idea that *mappō* and the hidden buddhas were intimately connected.

Noboru waited for his grandfather to tell him what the end of *mappō* would mean, but the old man seemed not to have heard his question. Instead, he handed him the flashlight he'd fished from his knapsack. Noboru shone the beam on the mandala while the old man rolled it up and put it back in its box.

"Here," he placed Noboru's hand on the cabinet behind the altar. "Feel this. It's the latch. When you choose your successor, you will have to open it." To himself, he wondered how many *hibutsu* would be left a generation from now. He thought about how best to answer Noboru's question.

"After *mappō*?" he finally said. "The world ends. Miroku, the Buddha of the future, is supposed to come. But, nobody knows what that means. It would be better not to find out, I think. Kūkai tried to save *this* world. The hidden buddhas were his plan for doing that. We are part of the plan."

Noboru decided he had to reveal his shame—the fact that he saw a woman in the hall at Kōryūji yet did not stop her. But first, he needed to know, "Grandfather, who is killing the *hibutsu*?"

On this precise point, the secret transmission had nothing to say. The job of the guardian had been simply to watch over the hidden buddhas and keep track. What caused a *hibutsu* to lose its power? Kūkai never said. His followers concluded that a person was responsible. Not an ordinary person, naturally, but a strong will that had embodied itself, reincarnating its way through multiple lifetimes, keeping a tally. Buddhist theology contains the idea of *akunin*, persons so irredeemably evil they can never reach enlightenment, no matter how many lifetimes they plow through. With the sharp increase of incidents in the nineteenth century, the elder Tokuda's master, Zuichō, came to believe that a particularly lethal sort of *akunin* was roaming the land, purposefully hastening the process of *mappō* by sucking the protective auras of the hidden buddhas. But he also thought that if this evil *akunin* could be caught in the act, the *hibutsu* might be saved. Consequently, he was always traveling, trying to attend every showing of the images he knew to be active. Watching.

"My teacher assumed this seer was evil, you see," said the older Tokuda.

"How could it *not* be evil?" Noboru asked. "If it's trying to bring the world to an end?"

His grandfather sighed.

"It's possible. But it's also possible it doesn't realize what it's doing. Perhaps it's caught in the clutches of some destiny it doesn't understand either—just like the rest of us. Reincarnation is not necessarily self-knowledge. Whatever is reincarnated, it's not thoughts, or even intentions. We are, all of us, a continuation of our ancestors' flesh, but I don't believe we reincarnate our ancestors' sins—or anyone else's. Our sins are our own."

"But destroying the hidden buddhas? Letting the world die? Isn't that a sin?" Noboru persisted. What about the beautiful woman he had encountered? Was she evil? Or just a woman? Once again he decided against mentioning her.

"Whoever or whatever is responsible—it must almost certainly be suffering, too," his grandfather replied.

They had gathered up their things and stepped onto the veranda covered in an encrusted layer of dead leaves. Outside, the light of a rising autumn moon, nearly full, cast shadows through the trees.

"It could be that the best way to conquer it is with compassion," he said.

Those words sank into Noboru's mind along with the content of the secret transmission.

PART ONE

From Outside In

Waiting for Miroku

IT WAS LATE OCTOBER. Philip Metcalfe had finished most of the classes for his advanced degree in Asian Religions at Columbia University. With the onerous foreign-language requirements out of the way, all that remained was settling on a thesis topic so he could immerse himself in the research that would yield him the Ph.D. But he was finding it difficult to decide on a topic. Buddhism interested him, and of all the locales and aspects of Buddhism he might choose to research, he was most drawn to Japan. He just had to come up with a subject narrow enough to master but wide enough that he could dig around in it for four more years without getting bored. Inspiration had better strike soon, though, because his advisors were becoming impatient.

Though he didn't need the class credit, Philip had decided to sit in on a survey course on Buddhism taught by Bertrand Maigny, a famous French scholar who had been invited to Columbia as a visiting professor. Since the course fulfilled a Humanities requirement, the class was packed with undergraduates. As usual, Philip slipped into the lecture hall early to get a good seat. To his surprise, the chronically late Professor Maigny himself scuffled in shortly afterward. He even gave Philip a nod of recognition. They had met, after all, although Philip had not sought him out. Philip returned the professor's nod somewhat more deeply, as if making a respectful Japanese bow. Should he say something? The professor seemed disinclined to chat. Immediately turning his back to contemplate the blackboard, he picked up a piece of chalk. The topic of today's talk was the sacred Japanese mountain called Kōyasan.

Bertrand Maigny had published scores of articles in scholarly journals, festooned with footnote upon footnote, argued with relentless logical clarity. He was the only Westerner to have burrowed deeply into the monastic life of Mt. Kōya, and was an expert on the Shingon sect of esoteric Buddhism.

It occurred to Philip now that he ought to read more of Maigny's work to see if it might inspire some ideas for his research. It would be stupid not to take advantage of his presence at Columbia.

For the first four weeks into the semester Philip learned nothing new. Maigny lectured broadly on the history of Buddhism's origins in India and its subsequent changes as it moved through different societies, gaining adherents across Central Asia, Tibet, and China. The eastward spread of Buddhism ultimately brought it to Korea and ultimately Japan. Philip knew all that. Today Maigny would talk about Shingon. Philip took out his pen to take notes for the first time. Finally, this should be interesting.

The hall filled with drifts of students. Professor Maigny began his lecture with a definition. Shingon was called "esoteric Buddhism," he said, because it held that absolute truth could only be transmitted from teacher to pupil *in secret*. Much of Shingon ritual involved secret hand gestures called *mudras*, the contemplation of world-diagrams called *mandalas*, and recitation of liturgical *mantras*. He wrote these terms on the blackboard. Although Shingon literally means "true word," the truth is available only to the initiated who had learned the secrets.

During the centuries of civil war that tore Japan apart and ravaged Kyoto time and again, said the professor, Shingon was overshadowed by new waves of Buddhist teaching that reached out to the suffering population. People were weary of secrets. He mentioned Jōdō, the "Pure Land" sect, that preached the compassion of Amida Buddha. All one need do is chant his name in order to be drawn up to heaven.

"The Pure Land sect is still the most popular in Japan," Maigny announced, adding, "this is an 'exoteric' tradition. Nothing secret here."

Later, there was Zen. "I shall not say much about Zen because you have a specialist here, Professeur Chernish, who is devoting an entire semester to it. Let me simply say that Zen's focus on meditation in action appealed in particular to the samurai. Westerners also seem to find Zen most congenial." (Harvey Chernish was the head of Philip's committee, and he was pushing Philip toward doing a study on the Zen temple Daitokuji.)

"Shingon did not disappear, but it has somewhat fallen into the background these days. It is not so well known outside Japan."

"There are still monastic buildings on Mount Kōya," Maigny told the students, "many of which are now—*comment on dit—auberges…*

"Inns," someone volunteered.

"Ah yes—inns, hotels…but in the eleventh century, there were nine thousand buildings on this mountain—temples, shrines, libraries, pagodas, monasteries. This was the spiritual center of Japan." He raised his eyebrows, surveying the crowd of students. "Women were not allowed on Mt. Kōya," he said, anticipating the rumble of whispers. "That's how sacred it was."

Philip rolled his eyes. Professor Maigny seemed to enjoy the murmurs of indignation.

"Most of the original buildings were destroyed by fire," he continued. "A few have been rebuilt. But more important than any building is the Inner Sanctum—originally a cave, and now a mausoleum in which Kūkai himself is interred. Monks bring trays of food there twice a day."

Philip looked up. Why would anyone bring food to a mausoleum? The other students were busy writing. No doubt they were filing this information under the rubric of strange Asian beliefs that might appear on a test.

Maigny described the Hall of Lanterns in front of the mausoleum.

"Hundreds of oil lamps flicker in the darkness in homage to Kūkai. Two of the lamps," he said, "are believed to have been burning continuously for over nine hundred years."

"Kūkai is also called Kōbō Daishi, which means the 'Great Teacher who Spreads the Law of the Buddha.' He entered his cave on the twenty-third of April, 835, shutting himself up in a state of suspended meditation," Maigny went on.

Philip again looked around to see if anyone else thought this turn of phrase odd. Perhaps it was just the professor's quaint English.

"His followers believe that he is still there, in the Inner Sanctum, awaiting the coming of Miroku, the Buddha of the Future," Maigny said. Well, thought Philip, that explains the trays of food. They think Kūkai is not really dead. Well, if Christian Scientists could put a telephone in Mary Baker Eddy's tomb in case death was just a cosmic mistake… This was pretty interesting, though. Definitely more compelling than the architectural history of Daitokuji. An idea began to take shape in Philip's mind that perhaps he should do his research on Kūkai. He felt a strange visceral pull toward "the holy man of Mount Kōya." Maybe Kūkai would lead him to his degree? Perhaps the old Frenchman would give him an introduction to some of the priests he knew. In any case, Philip could add Maigny's name to his proposal, and his other advisors would be relieved to see him launched. This could work. He turned his attention back to Maigny at the podium.

"Miroku, it is believed, will appear in the world once this corrupt age called *mappō* has run its course."

Maigny stopped to gaze at the sea of bent heads concentrating on writing notes. He knew that, to these secure and confident American students, the idea of *mappō* would have little reality.

"Of course, in times of great social upheaval, it is easier to see the signs of *mappō*," he continued. "Yet most Buddhists would agree we are living through this stage right now."

The volume of whispers rose again.

Maigny turned toward the blackboard.

The three ages of the Buddhist law

He wrote.

1—the age of correct law

"Beginning with the era of Siddhartha, the historical Buddha. A golden age when the Buddha's teachings were truly understood." He turned back to the board and scribbled,

2—the age of imitation of the law

"during this stage, the precepts of the Buddha are distorted, leading to..."

3—the age of decline of the law

"*Mappō*. The world is full of injustice, wars, famine, greed, and corruption. The center no longer holds."

A student spoke up, "What comes after *mappō*?"

Maigny put the chalk down. Dusting his hands, he squinted, trying to see who had asked the question. "How does *mappō* end?" he repeated. "Ah, *oui*—we would all very much like to know that. In fire? In ice? Your poet Monsieur Frost asks, *Avec un* bang? *Avec un* whimper?"

"Is this, like, the apocalypse?" another question from across the hall.

The usually placid students had suddenly come to life with this idea of *mappō*. A swell of low conversation passed through the room. Maigny waited for it to die down.

"*Apokalypsis*. Greek. It means 'lifting the veil'—revelation, literally. But you no doubt refer to the end of the world, yes? Armageddon in the Christian tradition? The Buddhist end of the world does not have such a well-planned program. The, the… four *chevaliers d'Apocalypse*? The return of the Messiah? And the judgments, the sorting of souls—to heaven with you. To hell with you." He pointed up with a beatific smile, and down with a scowl. The students laughed.

Maigny had now diverged considerably from his notes.

"No. In the Buddhist view, the world simply degenerates to a point where it can no longer sustain itself. That is *mappō*. No unholy monsters needed. No Gog or Magog. Evil—yes. There will be plenty of that—we humans are specialists in evil." Was he ranting? Maigny stopped to clear his throat.

"According to some calculations, we are now coming close to the end of *mappō*. But doomsayers have a way of tripping when they mention specific dates, no?" He tilted his head.

"So, Kūkai continues to wait—you know, like Monsieur Beckett's play? *En attendant Godot*? We are all *en attendant Miroku*."

Philip smiled. Maigny caught his grin in the corner of his eye.

Emboldened, another student raised a hand. "Is Miroku the Buddhist Messiah?"

Maigny was a bit unnerved at how the students had hijacked his lecture. Was this what his colleagues back in France had warned him about teaching in America? Again he waited for the voices to quiet before he spoke.

"Miroku is supposed to be waiting in a Buddhist paradise called the Tushita heaven. When the time is ready, he will incarnate on earth."

"Is Miroku a man?"

The question was from a girl.

Maigny knit his eyebrows. He had never considered this.

"Not necessarily…" he began. He was thinking of some of the earliest statues of Miroku found in Japan—they had a decidedly feminine aspect.

"Maybe Lady Miroku then?" the student shot back.

"Perhaps—why not?" Maigny gave a Gallic shrug. A ripple of laughter made its way through the lecture hall.

It was time to rope his talk back to the subject of Shingon. Maigny returned to the outline in his notes.

"But, do not think Shingon is just worship of a mummy," Maigny admonished at the close of the hour. "Shingon has been dismissed by many as full of mumbo-jumbo and secret ritual. Remember, though, its core belief is that a person can experience true reality in *this* life. In Shingon,

Buddha is neither a god nor a creator, but a symbolic pointer to the ultimate nature of things—which are themselves impermanent and without essence. Remember, too, these words of the Buddha:

If there is joy in the world
It comes from desiring others to be happy.
If there is suffering in the world
It comes from desiring myself to be happy."

A student raised her hand. "Could you write that on the board, please?" she asked.

It had been a lively class, and Maigny was exhausted.

The Water Child

DURING THE SPRING, WHEN OLD PRIEST Tokuda lay dying, his grandson Noboru never left his side. Two more hidden buddhas went dark in April.

"Watch for signs of *mappō*," were the old man's last words.

"What signs, grandpa?"

"Earthquakes…and plagues…" He briefly opened his eyes. "You know those. But others…strange things. Unnatural. Nature will change."

"The newspaper said it snowed in the Sahara for thirty minutes, yesterday," Noboru whispered to the old man. But his grandfather was beyond hearing. His predecessors only had to worry about Japan—Noboru had a window on the curiosities and catastrophes of the entire world. Were they all signs of *mappō*?

His grandfather died, and Noboru felt the burden of his mission settle like a harness over his chest. He resolved to follow his grandfather's plan of visiting each *hibutsu* as it came on public display. There would be times, especially in the spring and fall, when several came out on the same day. Noboru did his best, scurrying from one to another favoring the rare ones, of course, but keeping tabs on all. His special skills were honed to the point of second nature.

He could tell whether a *hibutsu* was alive or not even when it was wrapped up and sequestered behind the doors of its inner sanctum. He would stand, or—if there was room—sit, close to the image and begin to meditate. He recited the mantra for the hidden deity, then his fingers danced through the mudras. If the *hibutsu* were active, Tokuda could feel the quiet energy. To his ears it was a soft hum; to his eyes, a pale glow; and to his skin, a faint warmth. He smelled a fragrance of aloeswood, and the inside of his mouth turned sweet. If it had been stripped of its essence, then nothing but a cold dark absence met his efforts. A fire that had gone out. An egg that had died. He would not bother to re-visit that temple, for that *hibutsu* had effectively been killed and no longer formed part of Kūkai's protective net.

After much thought about how he was to make a living while carrying out his mission, young priest Tokuda eventually accepted a position at the Shingon Temple called Fudō-in in Kamakura, near Tokyo. Here he served as an assistant priest specializing in rituals for the dead unborn, called *mizuko*—"water children." The other priests were puzzled at his seeming lack of ambition to rise in the temple's hierarchy, but they saw that Noboru Tokuda had a definite rapport with the young women who had had abortions. Aborted fetuses were by far the most common *mizuko*, and the ceremonies commissioned on their behalf had become a rather lucrative source of income for the temple. The head priest of Fudō-in was happy to let this serious young priest with expressive eyebrows take charge of *mizuko* rites.

Tokuda usually caught a cold during rainy season. This year was no exception. Looking up from his paperwork in order to blow his nose, he saw two women walking toward the temple office. They came from the direction of the graveyard, a steeply tiered hill where row upon row of small stone images of Jizō crowded together. He could tell the women were not tourists. They appeared to be in their late twenties. One seemed to know her way; the other was hesitant. The confident one was shorter, slightly plump, with luminous skin. Not exactly beautiful, perhaps, but not without appeal. The second woman was taller, almost too slender, with shoulder-length blunt-cut very black hair. There were dark circles under her eyes and her skin was dull. Even so, she was more beautiful than her smartly made-up companion. He stood up.

"May I help you?" he inquired.

"Yes. Thank you." The shorter one responded. "My friend would like to make a donation for a ceremony for her *mizuko*."

"Yes, of course," Tokuda replied.

As he expected, the quiet one had had an abortion, and had come to assuage the feelings of the aborted water child.

He was drawn to minister to these women. They were suffering. An abortion might be necessary, but it was probably never easy. They came seeking to ease their guilt and sorrow, and he could help them. There was another reason he gravitated toward them. On his pilgrimages to check on the hidden buddhas, he often came across temples with special cemeteries for *mizuko*, and whenever he passed through one of these graveyards packed with tiny infantile statues, his senses prickled uncomfortably—as if a thousand muffled voices were trying to get his attention.

It was something he wished he could have asked his grandfather about. Were these small aborted souls connected with *mappō* in some way? Infanticide in times of famine was common throughout history—"weeding" was how the farming families thought of it. But the recent upsurge of abortions in prosperous Japan was not as easily explained.

Tokuda invited the woman to sit down. He noted her pallor, the shadows under her tea-colored eyes. Unmarried, probably. That's why she came with a friend instead of a man. He watched her through lowered eyes as she filled out the form.

Nagiko Kiyowara, he read silently when she handed him back the papers. Old-fashioned name. Tokuda made his way to a dusty warehouse where hundreds of small identical marble statues of the Bodhisattva Jizō were stacked. Each Jizō awaited its *mizuko*, just as each *mizuko* would be asked to wait for rebirth. In the sitting room, another unmother waited as well.

Each time Tokuda broke this sad triangle of waiting by performing one of these ceremonies, he felt as if he was midwifing the birth of a Jizō. In the womb, all fetuses are basically alike. Then they are born and slowly turn into individual people. Here in the warehouse, the Jizō statues were all the same, yet once installed in the cemetery, they became individuals as well. The features of some were worn smooth by weathering. Many wore red bibs. Others had hand-knit capes, plastic jewelry, and toys. The Fudō-in cemetery was quite a colorful place—like a nursery, Tokuda often thought.

A stack of pamphlets sat on a stand by the door in the waiting room. Tokuda picked one up for his latest client.

*Jizō Bodhisattva protects travelers and infants, including the still-
born, dead children, and aborted fetuses. By far the most numerous
of Jizō's supplicants are these small souls who have been turned back
before the door of birth opened for them. They are fated to wander
the netherworld on the desolate Riverbank of Sai with only the
compassion of Jizō for solace.*

Tokuda knew that the offerings of toys and candy women brought to
the cemetery were not so much for Jizō the Bodhisattva as they were for
the imagined child forced to live on the stony riverbank, watching in envy
as brothers and sisters passed over to be born. A writing brush and ink had
been laid out on the low table in the sitting room. Usually they cry now, he
knew. He turned his attention to the writing of Sanskrit phrases, noting that
Nagiko Kiyowara stared at the statue soberly and dry-eyed.

"I am connected to this thing now," she was thinking, "forever."

The women followed Tokuda to the cemetery where Nagiko's Jizō would
join the rank and file lining the hillside like a tiny crowd waiting for a train
that never comes. They bowed their heads as he intoned a sutra. Nagiko
ladled a scoop of water over the statue and then lit incense. Her friend
Satoko helped her arrange the flowers they had brought.

"It's not much different from visiting an ancestral grave," Tokuda
explained to them, "in terms of what you do."

Nagiko looked up at him gratefully. He was so kind. She felt his compassion wash away guilt and regret, as if she were the statue and he had
ladled absolution over her. At first she had resisted Satoko's suggestion of
this trip to Fudō-in, but Satoko had been right. Already Nagiko could feel
that the *mizuko* was soothed. Perhaps its tantrums would now stop. She
would be able to walk down the street without fear that a sudden cry would
stab her heart just as she stepped into a store. She would even be able to look
at a baby strapped to its mother's back without flinching.

Nagiko's thoughts turned to the unexpected whirlwind that had snagged
her in New York, torn apart her life, and dropped her back in Tokyo—in no
more time than it takes for a season to pass from plum blossoms to azaleas.
She was twenty-eight, a little stale for the Japanese marriage market. That
didn't bother her. Nagiko had no intention of marrying.

In Japan, she was considered tall. At five feet six inches, she was accustomed to looking men straight in the eye, even down on them. But in New

York, for the first time in her life she had felt cute and delicate. It completely changed her mode of relating to men. And she had gotten careless. She remembered the night. She had just finished her last project for the Manhattan-based design company that had hired her straight from Madame Morikawa's Paris atelier. Unfortunately, American clients had not been very interested in the unusual fabrics that were Nagiko's specialty, so she was being let go. It had been a depressing day, and she allowed herself to get a little drunk with an eager date.

Six weeks later, her last designs proofed and printed, she left her office cubicle for good, planning to take time to see the museums in New York. But, as she wandered through the gift store at the MoMA, Nagiko felt her knees melt. Trembling with a small wave of nausea, she made her way out to the street. Her period hadn't come, and now she realized why. So she would have an abortion. Knowing the nature of her indisposition, she was even somewhat relieved. She didn't need to go to a doctor to find out what was wrong. She just needed an appointment for the procedure.

But when she mentioned it to her Western friends, Nagiko discovered that Americans had strong ideas about abortion. She also found that in America women had had to struggle for something that Japanese women took for granted. Like a snail pulling in its eyestalks in the presence of salt, Nagiko withdrew into herself. It was time to go back to Japan. She arrived in Tokyo just as rainy season began.

On the third day after the abortion, her cramps had subsided, but Nagiko still felt limp as a raw squid. That night she was again awakened by a cry. Disoriented, she made herself lie back down on her single futon. She was not in her familiar apartment in Queens, she had to remind herself, but instead in a bare 2LDK Mansion unit hurriedly rented upon her return to Tokyo. Her friend Satoko stayed with her for two nights, but Satoko had gone home that afternoon. Now she was alone.

It was still dark. Nagiko heard the tires of a Lawson's delivery truck slosh through the puddles. Clear, hot May had been utterly smothered by damp gray June. Nagiko was not usually susceptible to rainy season blues, but she felt utterly vulnerable now. As a child, her classmates had called her *ochame*, tea-eyes. Girls with hazel eyes the color of green tea with toasted rice had the reputation of being tomboys, naughty and headstrong. She had obligingly fit the reputation. Her adult friends attributed her disarming frankness to the time she had spent living in Paris and New York. Now, though, Nagiko lay wilted, drained of confidence, conscious of a thin film of sweat coating her body.

She had dreamed she was underwater, swimming toward a receding shore. Something pulled her leg, dragging her back. She opened her eyes underwater and as her hair swirled around her face she glimpsed a tiny figure grasping her foot. Oh. It's the *mizuko*, she thought. The water child. She reached back to gently disengage the small fingers, whereupon it opened its mouth in a piercing scream.

She couldn't shake Satoko's suggestion that the cry was not a dream at all, but in fact the wail of the child that had been sent back. She pulled the terrycloth blanket up to her chin. "The symbolism of a water child is *too* obvious," she scolded herself. She had read Freud.

Nagiko got up to use the bathroom. Five steps took her from the six-mat room where her bedding lay on the tatami, across the living room, to the narrow linoleum-floored dining-kitchen area. 2LDK. Typical Tokyo space. Even her tiny New York apartment seemed luxurious in comparison.

House slippers, futon, sheets, and towels. Satoko had assembled all the basics. There was instant coffee in the cupboard, but Nagiko decided to walk down to the Ogawa coffee shop which offered "morning service"—a piece of thick toast with butter and jam, and a hardboiled egg—when you bought a five-dollar cup of strong coffee.

She peeled off her limp pink cotton nightgown and turned on the shower. She would have to make her career in Tokyo now. As the hot water streamed over her head, Nagiko's energy revived. She had connections at a handful of design firms. By mid-summer she would certainly have found a new job, decorated her apartment artfully, and ceased to think about the reason for her precipitous flight from New York.

Just then, over the rushing sound of the water, she heard it. The wail. A baby's wail. That afternoon she called Satoko.

"It happened again," she said softly.

"What happened?" said her friend, concerned.

"The cry," whispered Nagiko.

"You see, it's just as I told you," Satoko scolded her. "The *mizuko*. It's unhappy, naturally, at being sent back. It's haunting you."

"What should I do?"

"Apologize to it. Give it a memorial. Let it know you won't forget.

Someday it will get another chance." Satoko was definite.

"Why are you so sure that will work?"

Satoko went silent for a moment, then said,

"Because I did it myself."

"You had an abortion? When?" Nagiko couldn't keep the note of surprise out of her voice.

"Right after Yoji and I got married. We thought we'd wait a while before having children, and then, as you know…"

"Satoko, I'm sorry. I never imagined…" Yoji had been killed in a car accident the year Nagiko had been apprenticed to Mme. Morikawa in Paris.

"It's okay. These things are fated. The child would be fatherless now, if I'd had it. I'd still be living with my mother-in-law. It's much better this way." Nagiko apologized again. "What should I do?"

"We'll go to Fudō-in. Do you know it?—not too far from the Kamakura Great Buddha," said Satoko. "Now is the best time to go."

"Why is that?" asked Nagiko.

"Because…well, because the hydrangeas are in bloom…"

Satoko was an ikebana teacher.

"What a time to be thinking of hydrangea-viewing," Nagiko accused her friend.

She wasn't at all convinced that going to a Buddhist temple to commission some kind of rite for an aborted fetus was going to help anything. Yet in her current fragile state, maybe she should simply follow Satoko's advice. She'd think about it.

Now she put on light make-up and brushed her hair. Because the day was so gray, she decided to wear a brilliant red shirt. Like Parisiennes, Tokyo women do not venture out without makeup. Nagiko fell back into this habit quite easily—even after a year and a half in New York where people sometimes walk their dogs wearing down jackets over pajamas. Yet she had been perfectly comfortable in New York as well. A sudden wave of nostalgia for the storefront Greek cafés of Astoria washed over her. Her hand quivered as she opened the drab door of her new home. She would need to buy an umbrella. Then she turned back and took a black raincoat off the hook in the vestibule. She put it on, hiding the bright red shirt, and headed out the door.

The local merchant association of Kagurazaka had proclaimed a summer festival and closed the street to cars. Old-style street vendors hawked grilled corn and squid; trendy ones offered Belgian waffles. There was a wading pool filled with goldfish where children could try to scoop one up with a paper dipper before the paper dissolved.

Nagiko drifted along, noting the types of shops she might find useful in her new life in this traditional Tokyo neighborhood. Stationery store. Pharmacy. Bakery. A pottery store was having a sidewalk sale, so she bought a vase for 400 yen. On the next block she stepped into a florist shop with a display of delicate white bell-shaped flowers that looked like something she had played with as a child.

"Excuse me, what are these called?" she asked the shopkeeper. "We used to find something like them in the wild where I grew up. We called them 'firefly bags'."

The woman put down her snippers. "Yes, that's what they're called. They're related to Chinese bellflower. I suppose children used to trap a firefly inside and pinch the end of the blossom closed like a lantern."

"Yes, yes, exactly! But I've never seen them for sale," marveled Nagiko.

"Well, this is the first time any customer has known what they are. How many would you like?"

Nagiko hadn't been planning to buy any, but, she thought, why not? A flower arrangement for her apartment. So she bought two, each one twice the price of the new vase.

"Take these right home and put them in water," the woman said. "They'll wilt if you carry them around in the street for very long."

Nagiko left the store with her heavy plastic shopping bag dangling from her left hand, the delicate paper cone of bellflowers held carefully to her chest. Emerging from the cool flower shop, the sidewalk seemed even hotter than before. Men shuffled along in front of their wives. Mothers pushed toddlers in strollers. Children skipped from one sidewalk to the other, reveling in being allowed in the middle of the car-less road.

Nagiko was thinking about where she would put the flowers when suddenly she was startled by an unearthly cry. She gasped and looked around. Nobody else seemed alarmed. A woman with a baby strapped to her back was standing in front of a pharmacy, softly rocking from one foot to the other as she examined lipsticks on sale. Nagiko began to sweat. She hurried past the children scooping goldfish, their shrieks of triumph and cries of failure ringing in her ears. She didn't dare glance at the small wriggling creatures slipping through their paper nets back into the water. She found herself whispering as she stumbled along, "Please wait one more day. It will all be all right. Don't cry any more."

By the time she reached Lion's Head Mansion her red blouse was soaked. Now the rational inner voice which had been able to sneer at the obviousness of a dream of a water child, was no help. She needed to pacify this thing—anything to make it stop screaming. Breathing heavily, Nagiko kicked off her shoes inside the apartment and dropped the shopping bag at the edge of the kitchen floor. She discovered that the delicate white "firefly bags" had been crushed in her grip. She knew she had no choice but to go to Fudō-in to take care of this relentless *mizuko*.

Nagiko had never paid much attention to religion. Aesthetically, she liked the stained glass cathedrals of Europe, and regarded Buddhist temples as dank and boring. Yet, that day at Fudō-in, surrounded by blooming hydrangeas, lighting incense, listening to that good-looking monk intone a sutra—she felt the painful pinch of the *mizuko* relax its grip. It let her go. She was able to get on with her life. Monsoon season ended, and as the skies cleared so did her skin. Nagiko's energy returned and at the end of summer she found her dream job with the design company Kiji Enterprises, where she started as an assistant fabric designer. People saw her as bright and crisp. Those days, everyone wanted to know everyone else's blood type. Nobody was surprised that Nagiko's was O. Her outgoing efficiency was typical of a blood type-O personality.

Busy with work, she was almost able to forget the *mizuko*. The only time it crept back to her thoughts was during the oppressive June rainy season around the anniversary of the abortion. Every June she made a pilgrimage to Fudō-in with flowers and incense. Every year the number of Jizō statues had swelled. Her *mizuko* was no longer a newcomer. A small aborted army. Twice she saw the priest who had performed the ceremony for her. Nagiko didn't understand the Buddhist theology concerning where the *mizuko* was, or what it was doing. She could have asked the priest, but didn't. All she knew was that Jizō was watching over it and that was enough. The *mizuko* no longer troubled her dreams.

On the fourth anniversary, however, as she stooped to brush away a small heap of dead leaves that pooled in front of her Jizō, Nagiko suddenly pictured a four-year-old girl squatting on the riverbank of Sai, mournfully playing with pebbles. Her hand shook, dropping the stick of incense.

Mappō

EARTH, WATER, FIRE, AND WIND—the four elements of gross matter. Plus emptiness. The components of the world. Disaster can emerge from any one, and because they are all connected, feed off the others. The great Kantō earthquake of 1923 was even more deadly because a nearby typhoon swept through Tokyo, creating firestorms. In three days, earth, wind, and fire united, killing 140,000 people. That was just after the Unrakuji *hibutsu* had gone dark. Most horrible of all were the atomic bombs that descended from the sky in 1945. Under Tokuda's grandfather's helpless eye, more *hibutsu* lost their power during the early years of the war than at any other time in history.

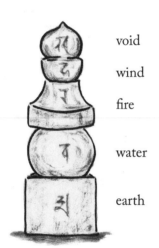

void

wind

fire

water

earth

Priest Tokuda occasionally recognized a woman who returned to the cemetery for an anniversary, but not one of them ever tried to talk to him about their water children. What was there to say? He could hardly keep up with the new additions. The *hibutsu* were constantly on his mind as well. In 1979, a number of rare *hibutsu* came on display simultaneously. He exhausted himself running from one to the other, only to discover that the place he just left had been depredated.

Twice he thought he sniffed the mocking silvery odor of the bewitching young woman, like an evanescent whiff of an old handkerchief suddenly plucked from a forgotten pocket. Was she still alive, he wondered? Now a middle-aged maven with too much makeup, carrying a Louis Vuitton handbag? He continued to watch for manifestations of *mappō*. A magnitude 7 earthquake in southern Italy? A tsunami in Nice, France? A British schoolgirl who sneezed for a thousand days straight? All were out of the ordinary—but were they signs?

In New York, Bertrand Maigny was just emerging from the elevator at Kent Hall.

"Professor Maynee—"

The friendly secretary of the department called to him on her way to the copy machine. "There's a student waiting to see you in front of your office," she said brightly.

Merde. Only ten minutes past ten, he thought to himself. A week ago someone had complained that Maigny routinely showed up fifteen minutes late for his lectures. His colleague Harvey Chernish had taken Bertrand aside to fill him in on the rules of punctuality expected in an American university.

"Ah, of course," he conceded. He had made a point to be early for his lecture yesterday. And even though students rarely came to his office hours, he was supposed to be there at the posted time. *Merde.*

"… and another thing…" Chernish suggested that when Maigny used the word "esoteric" he should be aware that American undergraduates might take it in a rather different sense from what he intended.

"There is *ES-oteric* tradition and there is *EX-oteric* tradition…" Maigny held up his hands, bent back at the wrists. "Very basic. This is not clear?"

"Yes, yes," Chernish had soothed him. "But young Americans think 'esoteric' means something, well, mysterious—or possibly having to do with sex."

"*Hah…vraiment?*" This was news to Maigny. Well, he hoped he had taken care of that too.

Turning the corner to the long hallway of offices, Bertrand Maigny saw the dark-haired graduate student who had smiled at his attempted joke in class. He had met him, along with a half dozen others at a wine-and-cheese party when he had first arrived. The wine had been forgettable, so had the cheese, and unfortunately, also the students. This one had milk-pale skin, almost black hair, and dark blue eyes—his face was memorable, but his name was not. The young man scrambled to his feet and made a perfectly proper Japanese bow.

"Professor, my name is Philip Metcalfe. I'm really sorry not to have come to see you sooner. We met in September."

Maigny raised his eyebrows ever so slightly as he unlocked the office door.

"*Entrez,*" he said, indicating a battered wooden chair for Philip. He hung his jacket on a hook behind the door. "I can tell you have been studying Japanese," he remarked dryly. "No one who doesn't know Japanese would introduce himself with an apology like that."

"Right. Sorry." Philip apologized again.

"You will get along just fine in Japan," said Maigny, as Philip reddened. "One needs that apologetic frame of mind to accomplish anything. When in doubt—apologize! All doors will open. But you know that, obviously. How many years have you spent in Japan?"

"Two years of high school in Yokosuka. My father was in the military," said Philip, trying to make his reply sound unapologetic. "And I just tried to absorb all I could."

Maigny looked at him. "Well," he said, "you seem part Japanese already. *Alors.* What brings you to my humble office this very bright morning?"

"I hoped I could discuss my thesis topic with you," said Philip, ignoring the faint sarcastic edge to the professor's query.

"*Bien sûr.* And what might that be?" Part of his teaching duties involved advising students, but so far none of them had taken him up on it.

"Well, I was thinking, I'd like to write my thesis on Kūkai," Philip said hesitantly.

"Anything in particular...about Kūkai that interests you?"

This boy has eyes like the sea, he observed, watching Philip fidget. A rather shallow one, though.

Maigny gazed mildly, fingertips tapping gently under his chin.

"Umm, well, I was hoping you might be able to help direct me toward something," he replied.

"Do you read classical Japanese?" Maigny asked.

"Pretty well," said Philip. "There are some texts I would have trouble with, but..."

"I should hope there would be texts you would have trouble with," observed Maigny. "There are many I can barely understand myself. What about Chinese? Do you read it?"

"Yes."

"Sanskrit?"

"Yes."

"German? French? Russian?"

"Yes, yes, and no." Philip was flustered. Columbia was notorious for its burden of language requirements, but he was not aware of any Russian Buddhist scholarship.

"Ah, I make the joke about Russian," chuckled Maigny. The subject is too soft for *les Russes*. "Hmmm. Well, you're adequately prepared. There's just one problem…"

Philip started to say that languages came easily to him, but stopped. It sounded like an apology.

Maigny looked at Philip. What he wouldn't give for an assistant with those linguistic skills. But he needed someone with intellectual passion. Someone who could help discover the last pieces of the puzzle of the hidden buddhas that had obsessed him for years.

"Just one problem?" repeated Philip, waiting for Maigny to continue.

No, decided the professor, this was not the apprentice he was waiting for. What a fool he was to think that he would find someone in New York. In America. Wasn't that the real reason he had accepted this post? To look to the wider world for his intellectual heir?

He pulled his mind back to this graduate student sitting expectantly in front of him.

"Yes," Maigny answered evenly. "The problem is that there is nothing more to say about Kūkai."

Philip was taken aback.

"Japanese scholars have researched and recorded everything about his life. There are great blanks in what we know about most ninth-century historical figures. But not Kūkai. There is, if anything, too much detail." Maigny softened his tone.

"Although I suppose it would be useful for someone to sort through it all and come to a point of view on what has basis in fact and what is legend," he added. "It might be a bit tedious, but probably worth doing. A lot of translating, annotating."

Philip looked crestfallen. Was there no chance that his thesis research would be anything but tedious?

"What about a study of Shingon in modern Japan," he ventured. "I mean, do people really think Kūkai still lives, or will literally come back to life one of these days?" He was hoping to engage Maigny on the subject of yesterday's lecture, when he had felt as if the holy man of Mt. Kōya had pulled a string and he had felt the tug.

Maigny shrugged. "Plenty of people believe that Christ will rise again," he replied. "There is no limit to the literal-mindedness of believers in any religion. And yes, some people think that Kōbō Daishi will open his eyes when the time is ripe for Miroku to appear. But that is hardly the most interesting thing about Kūkai."

The conversation was starting to encroach on Maigny's obsession. Everyone knew Kūkai, and scholars knew about *hibutsu*; but no one had ever suggested a connection between Kūkai and the hidden buddhas before Bertrand Maigny started thinking about it. By his calculation, there were about one hundred fifty *hibutsu* scattered in temples around Japan. They were definitely odd. No other Buddhist culture hid statues in this way. Not Chinese Buddhism, not Thai, not Tibetan. Only the Japanese. Yet, it fit a pattern. Over the course of years he spent in that country, Maigny had noticed how Japanese seemed to prefer the covered to the open, the glimpse rather than the complete view. A full moon was most beautiful when partially obscured by clouds. If everything had to be explained, you were a child or a fool. A hint should suffice, or as the expression went, "By hearing one thing, you understand ten."

The most interesting thing about Kūkai, Maigny had begun to realize, was this phenomenon of hidden buddhas, and it finally dawned on him that Kūkai must have masterminded their creation. The question of how he did this might or might not be historically verifiable, but it was not nearly as interesting as the question of why. Why were there hidden buddhas at all?

"What *is* the most interesting thing about Kūkai, then?"

Maigny was brought back from his reverie by Philip's straightforward question. No, this was hardly the person in whom he could confide. But he would help him anyway.

"Yes, Shingon is fascinating," he said, redirecting the conversation. "Believers purify their souls with fire rituals, and gain spiritual merit by pilgrimages. I definitely think it would be more interesting for you to do your thesis on Shingon in modern Japan. I'll be happy to give you a letter of introduction to people on Mt. Kōya."

Philip was now totally bewildered. Concrete guidance was what he had come for, but he couldn't help feeling that he had missed something. The most interesting thing about the sainted Kūkai—what could it be? He stood up and thanked Maigny for his advice. He made sure to shake the professor's hand warmly, without apology.

After Philip left, Maigny propped his elbows on the desk and sank his head into his hands. There had been a freak tsunami in Nice, of all places, and his housekeeper Annette's nephew had been one of the people drowned. Horrible events like this made him think of *mappō*. In fact, *mappō* was never far from Bertrand Maigny's thoughts—it explained so much.

He had first gone to Japan after the liberation of the Nazi death camps from which his wife Charlotte had not emerged. He knew the Japanese military had committed atrocities that vied with Nazi horrors he had witnessed personally. Yet somehow he found it more tolerable to live in Japan than Europe. On Kōyasan he immersed himself in the study of Shingon Buddhism. After twenty-five years he returned to his hometown of Brest where the Université de Bretagne Occidental gave him a professorship. And this year, to his initial surprise followed by an over-hasty acceptance, he had allowed an invitation to teach at Columbia to bring him to New York.

Maigny's thoughts began to wander. He wondered what his housekeeper was doing now. Maybe she had brought her two-year-old granddaughter Gabrielle with her as she cleaned the house and later cooked duck legs in their own fat, in a *confit de canard*, to tuck away for his return to Brest. His cranky Pekingese, Kookai, was not fond of toddlers, but Gabrielle would learn not to tug his tail.

Maigny waited another twenty minutes till noon, just to make sure no more students turned up. At precisely twelve o'clock he closed the office door and, dreaming of duck, went out to find some lunch.

Pachinko

PHILIP HAD NOT BEEN BACK to Japan since his father had been stationed at the Yokosuka Naval base. Living in that American military bubble hardly qualified as experiencing Japan, but the surrounding countryside beckoned, and fourteen-year-old Philip itched to explore it. A widowed housekeeper who came once a week sometimes brought her teenage son Ichirō along to the Metcalfes' house, in the hope of improving his English. Philip latched on to him and wangled permission to tag along to Yokohama and even Tokyo at every opportunity. They rode the trains, hiked around the harbor, and watched Japanese television. Philip's tastebuds were introduced to *ramen*, *tonkatsu*, and sweet bean buns. He even managed to pick up a passable Japanese accent. It was clear he had an ear for language. Through her son, the housekeeper invited Philip to visit their home in Yokohama. It was Philip's first time inside a real Japanese house. He was served a meal of pickled, chopped, roasted, and stewed items that he mostly could not identify. He learned that sashimi was raw fish. Pinching the lid off a covered bowl, he found a cup of clear soup in which nestled a trio of clams hiding under seaweed. It reminded him of a tiny tidepool. He tried everything, and was sorry to see the plain white rice that ended the meal.

After dinner, as they were watching television, Philip became aware of a mumbling sound in the next room, separated from the two boys by only a paper sliding door. He nudged Ichirō. It sounded like his mother was talking to someone.

"That's just my mom talking to my dad…" Ichirō said, sliding the door open. She sat facing a large black cabinet with a burnished golden interior. A spiral of smoke rose from a stick of incense. Philip could see a small statue, a miniature version of the one in the Buddhist temple his class had visited on a school field trip. There were black and white photographs, and a plate with a banana and tangerine arranged on the lower shelves.

"That's my dad…" Ichirō pointed to the picture of an expressionless young man in an army uniform. His mother bowed toward the cabinet and turned to her son. She didn't appear upset with him, but Ichirō hastened to slide the door closed. It was time to take Philip home.

Their wordless interaction, the mysterious cabinet, the photograph of the dead father stuck in Philip's mind. Japanese seemed to communicate without outwardly communicating—as if they all were privy to secrets that outsiders couldn't share. Philip wondered if he would ever be able to break the code.

Just before his father was to be relocated back to California, Super Typhoon Anita crashed into western Shikoku. That hurricane was the first in a string of uncommonly fierce storms to batter Japan that year. Philip had been eagerly awaiting summer vacation because the family planned to visit Kyoto before they left Japan. He was hugely disappointed when his parents decided to cancel the trip because of the terrible weather. They went directly back to California, and Philip entered San Anselmo High School in September.

That was also the summer Noboru Tokuda learned that a *hibutsu* image of Fudō from a temple in Narita had been lost. The local people of course had no idea that anything had happened to their famous Fudō statue. Noboru had gone to check this *hibutsu* by himself. It was opened to viewing only once every three years. He should have felt its live presence immediately. When he did not, he hoped against hope that it was his failing, not the statue's. Desperately meditating in the main hall until the priests told him he had to leave, Noboru finally gave up and accepted the truth—this *hibutsu* was dead. He dreaded breaking the news to his grandfather. Narita was in the news for other reasons, too. Government plans to build a new international airport had unexpectedly run into a quagmire of opposition. Conservative farmers were joined in the rice paddies by radical students, and together, these unlikely comrades blockaded the bulldozers. Noboru's ailing grandfather watched the riots on television, mourning the demise of Narita's hidden buddha and wondering if there was some connection to the mayhem. The typhoons that summer were ferocious and early, but the construction of Narita International went ahead.

That had been thirteen years ago. Philip's attraction to Japan had not weakened a bit since then. The more he studied, the more paths beckoned. The written language with its complex roots in Chinese was an endless puzzle that whetted his curiosity. For him, Japan was a paradise of discovery. His parents did not share his fascination. They had not enjoyed their expatriate years there. Where Philip saw puzzles to solve, they saw a confusing lack of candidness. They liked their world frank, straight, and open. Japan could not have felt more alien to them.

Two days after Philip passed his last exam, he was packed and on the plane. He couldn't wait to dive into Japanese life as an adult, with his newly-honed language skills. Finally he would get to see Kyoto. He had told his advisor that there were enough Westerners studying Zen—he wanted to work on Shingon. Professor Chernish shrugged and acquiesced—Philip did have a point about Zen.

With his letter of introduction from Bertrand Maigny, Philip could approach any Shingon priest in the country. He established himself at Unmonji, a training temple in Kyoto, but he also traveled, gaining access to temples where treasured scraps of Kūkai's calligraphy were hoarded like jewels. He interviewed priests and believers, immersing himself in Shingon texts to try to understand the intentionally difficult teachings. Though actual Shingon adherents were few, Philip found that everyone in Japan venerated Kōbō Daishi.

Most Japanese were Buddhist, at least if asked. But—as he wrote to his mother and father in California—most people didn't think about it much. "It's rather like us—Catholic by default," he wrote, scandalizing his mother, who was now somewhat worried about the state of her son's soul. Philip's relentless pursuit of this foreign religion was not something she approved of.

"Aren't there any Christians in Japan?" she asked. Philip wrote that recently church weddings had become fashionable. "Here, people celebrate births with visits to a Shinto shrine, weddings at a Christian church, and funerals at a Buddhist temple. Buddhist priests are mostly funeral specialists." He was being a little glib, but it wasn't far off the mark. A death in the family was practically the only time anyone thought about religion.

His mother worried even more.

As he learned about the variety of Buddhist denominations in Japan, Philip came to see the peculiarities of Shingon more sharply. He climbed Mt. Kōya, sharing a bag of chips with some wild monkeys who swooped out of the underbrush like bandits at a bend in the road. In one of the many temples on the forested slope he saw a Shingon priest light a mound of thousands of prayer sticks into a crackling, purifying blaze. Flames and smoke shot up toward the temple's dark ceiling as dozens of worshippers watched the priest pour water from an array of brass bowls, his hands forming the mudras, as he chanted the mystic syllables of a *goma* ceremony.

"The fire of wisdom," it was explained to him. "It is meant to burn away doubt and confusion in your heart."

Glancing around at the faces of the people who brought their worries and pain here for unction, Philip understood how the fiery metaphor might work if you imagined it sweeping through your body and mind, turning your cares and sorrows into smoke. Watching the undulating flames, he could feel the power of the ritual himself.

Back at Unmonji, the training temple where he lived with a dozen acolytes, Philip sat in on lessons. Shingon priests had to learn Sanskrit in order to write out mantras on amulets and charms for their future parishioners. Philip quickly saw they were taught set phrases by rote memorization. When the young monks in training realized Philip had actually studied Sanskrit grammar, they either sought him out or avoided him—depending on their feelings about Sanskrit. The one exception was Kōji. Kōji hated Sanskrit, but he was curious about this outsider who had worked his way into their midst. He couldn't imagine why anyone would submit to the rigors of Shingon training if he wasn't forced to.

Short and lumpy, nearsighted, and bucktoothed, Kōji Kon was a "temple brat." He knew he would eventually inherit his father's temple and become head priest whether he studied hard or not. He treated his stint at Unmonji as an ordeal. He had to do it in order to get his credentials, but otherwise living at Unmonji was an inconvenient distraction from his true interest—pachinko. Every chance he got, Kōji sneaked off from the monastery, making his way to the pinball parlors of downtown Kyoto. If his winnings were moderate, they would be followed by a snack of Korean-style barbequed innards. If he had a real streak, he might buy a wad of pornographic *manga*. He found Sanskrit utterly wearisome. But he liked Philip.

The first time he inveigled Philip to come along on one of his sorties, Philip asked him point blank, "Gambling, meat, and women—does your father know about this?" The students were supposed to be vegetarian during their training.

"He used to do it himself," said the young man airily. "It's an antidote. To all the tofu."

"Pachinko Mandala!" cried Kōji whenever his flipping thumbs brought down a cascade of metal balls.

Kōji entered a state of altered consciousness whenever he sat down in front of one of these glittering boxes. Philip preferred to flick the thumb-lever more slowly, just to watch each ball careen down through the wing flippers and bounce off the bells and columns before disappearing into the void. Every so often a ball dropped into a winning hole that returned a rush of additional steel balls.

Harsh light filtered through a haze of cigarette smoke, illuminating the clattering cacophony. There was no socializing. Each player was absorbed in the action of his box alone. When Philip asked Kōji a question during a session, all he got in return was a grunt.

If Kōji wasn't winning fast enough, he would abruptly get up and look for a different machine.

"What's the difference?" asked Philip.

"Oh, they're all different," replied Kōji, squinting at an individual machine. "I'll let you in on a secret. This is what you're looking for." He pointed to a set of two pins positioned directly above the main scoring slot.

"See that pair of nails? They're called the *inochi no kugi*. Everything depends on them. If they're adjusted too close, your balls will bounce out. If they're too low, they won't slow the speed enough for the balls to drop where you want. You're looking for high and wide."

Inochi no kugi—the nails of fate. Philip looked for high and wide, but could see no difference in any of the machines he examined.

"It's a subtle thing," explained Kōji, tapping his chubby fingers together at the tips of his ragged fingernails. "When you're experienced, you'll know."

Philip hoped he would never be experienced enough to judge the pachinko nails of fate. He felt a headache building. At nine p.m. the hall was no longer quite so packed. A few high school students with fuzz darkening their upper lips. Why weren't they home studying for their college entrance exams, Philip wondered? They played with an air of guilty thrill. Laid-back young men with real moustaches—college students. Once accepted to a university, they could afford to relax. They played as if killing time. Office workers in cheap suits—young ones, older ones. Laborers in jodhpur-like work pants. An occasional middle-aged housewife. Aside from the fact that there were no young women, the pachinko parlor contained a fairly repre-sentative slice of Japanese society.

Philip tried to understand the appeal. His thumb ached. His eyes watered from the smoke, and the constant noise drove every sensible thought from his brain. Maybe people came to the pachinko parlors in order *not* to think? Observing the blank faces fixed straight ahead, each to its own, it occurred to Philip that perhaps Japanese came here to be alone. There were few places in Japanese society where one could do that.

Finally Kōji accumulated a bucket full of metal balls. He stubbed out his cigarette. "Let's go."

Philip was more than happy to leave. He added his handful of winnings to Kōji's bucket.

"Thanks," said Kōji gruffly.

"Now what?" asked Philip.

Kōji exchanged the bucket of balls for prizes—three ballpoint pens, a tissue holder, a cigarette lighter, and a glass ashtray. It looked like junk to Philip. He followed Kōji out the door, down a nearby alley. Kōji went up to an unmarked window in a dingy wall. A hand emerged to take his prizes. A moment later the hand came out again with some bills.

"Hungry?" asked Kōji, gradually becoming talkative.

"Sure," said Philip. "But I'm not so keen on pig innards…"

"Potstickers, then? *Ramen?*"

"That sounds better."

"Okay, I know a place."

They had been playing pinball in a huge neon-enhanced pachinko emporium on Kyoto's main street, Kawaramachi. Kōji pulled a knitted watch cap over his shaved head. He started walking toward the Kamo River, two blocks east. Philip followed.

"Aren't we going to get in trouble for this?" Philip asked him.

"You? You can't get in trouble for anything," replied Kōji. "And I'm used to it. But don't worry. I'm watching the time. We'll get the last bus back." Kōji was confident. He knew this routine. He ducked into a narrow alley threading through the sides of buildings. It opened onto a quieter, willow-lined street.

"This is nice," said Philip, looking around.

"Yeah," agreed Kōji. "C'mon, I'll show you someplace cool."

He continued across a small bridge to an even skinnier street—too narrow for cars. A few bars, restaurants and discreetly lit signs showed it to be some kind of expensive entertainment district. Men in business suits, ties askew, tottered along, accompanied by women in evening dress or kimono. Just in front of Kōji and Philip a wooden door slid open. A young apprentice geisha bobbed out on perilously high wooden sandals. Philip was dumbfounded. Kōji poked him in the ribs.

"Cute, huh?"

The maiko ignored the two scruffy young men. Clutching her basket purse, she clattered down the street, avoiding eye contact, intent on her destination—another teahouse fifty yards ahead. The tourists on the street parted like the wing levers of a pachinko machine as she passed through on her beeline.

"My Dad used to come here," said Kōji. He held up his hand with the little finger extended.

Philip didn't get it.

"You are pretty ignorant for somebody who's so smart," complained Kōji genially. "That's the mudra that means you've got a woman."

"Thanks for the religious education," said Philip.

"Yeah, it's a good thing you've got me as your teacher," said Kōji. "Secret transmission."

"I feel perilously close to enlightenment when I'm with you," Philip retorted.

"Okay. Here's the place." They ducked under the short *noren* curtain stretched over the entrance of a cheap Chinese restaurant.

Kōji spent his pachinko takings on their meal.

After weeks of vegetarian fare, the greasy potstickers were delicious. Burned just the right amount, oozing meaty juice through the cracks in their doughy seams, they went down easily with a few beers.

Kōji was an enigma to Philip. He took every opportunity to wriggle out from under the monastic rules. He did not seem interested in his studies. Yet in a few years he would be presiding over a temple, conducting funerals, chanting sutras, and performing fire purifications. He would be an acting Shingon priest. He knew it, his father knew it, and the teachers at the monastery knew it. Nobody, least of all Kōji himself, ever seemed to question whether this is what he ought to be doing.

"So, your father kept a geisha mistress?" ventured Philip. "Is that what you meant by...?" He repeated the hand gesture Kōji had made.

"Keeps," replied Kōji through a mouthful of dumpling.

Philip was scandalized. And he was getting worried about the time.

Pointing to his watch, "Shouldn't we get going?" he said to Kōji.

"Yeah, yeah. Would hate to miss four a.m. meditation." Kōji was full of beer, slightly belligerent. They stumbled out to the street. By the time they slipped back into their rooms Philip's stomach was uneasy with its unaccustomed cargo of meat and alcohol. He didn't know how Kōji managed. He lay uncomfortably awake on his futon until he was able to disgorge the whole mess on a run to the toilet. After the purge he felt better and lay down quietly. Sometimes he joined the monks at their earliest meditation session, but it was not required. He thought he'd skip it today. Poor Kōji.

Philip was a glutton for knowledge and it was easy to indulge his passion here. He reveled in the intricate details of the mudra hand gestures, the rich iconography of the mandala paintings, and the calligraphy of the Sanskrit mantras—all of the stuff Kōji was oppressed by. He filled notebook after notebook with diagrams indicating which mantras were associated with which of the numerous deities of the Shingon pantheon. He sketched maps of the mandalas to identify all the different buddhas. He was even allowed to film the *goma* fire ritual.

Yet the more information Philip gathered, the harder it was to see how he would turn it into a dissertation. During the day Philip distracted himself by study. Another book to look up, another statue to view. After his last rambling report, Professor Chernish had chided him to sharpen his focus if he wanted to stay on schedule for his degree. Still, he was getting better at meditation. His knees had stopped aching from bending them into half-lotuses, and his mind occasionally cleared like a still pool. But sometimes at night, lying awake in the stillness, doubts buzzed like mosquitoes. Even Kōji knew why he was at Unmonji. Why was Philip there? Researching his thesis seemed like a tunnel into which he could wander ever deeper without coming to the end.

Finally, Philip decided to focus on modern followers of Kūkai. His research told him that the most important way for a believer to relate personally to Kūkai was to go on a pilgrimage of eighty-eight temples strung around the perimeter of the island Shikoku. It was an arduous hike. Even for the fit it took about two months to navigate some of the mountain paths and rocky coastline of the route. Many pilgrims were elderly. Some rode a bus part of the way, but a surprising number did the "pure walk" precisely for the physical and spiritual challenge.

Most people embarking on this expedition thought of their pilgrimage not so much as homage *to* Kūkai as a journey *with* him. *Dōgyō Ninin*—one discipline, two people—carved in Sanskrit and Chinese characters on their hiking staves, was the pilgrim slogan. Even if you were making the pilgrimage by yourself, you were not alone. Saint Kūkai would be at your side at each step.

Since settling in Kyoto, Philip had filled notebooks with research, observation, and sketches. At the end of every week he re-read what he had done, made a condensed version, and sent it—not to Harvey Chernish, but to Bertrand Maigny. Now back in France with his spoiled Pekingese, Maigny had not asked for these reports, but he read them, occasionally sending a short response. Philip now wrote to say he was thinking of making the Shikoku pilgrimage. Did Professor Maigny have any advice?

Although he seldom replied with much specific comment, Maigny sent a short letter. "By all means," he wrote. "Don't take a bus. And keep a journal." He had made the pilgrimage himself, thirty years earlier. In wealthy modern Japan, Maigny knew that pilgrims could choose austerity as a novel contrast to their everyday lives. When he himself had trudged the circumference of Shikoku, austerity had not been a matter of choice. "One more thing," he wrote, "take many *bandelettes* for your feet." Philip figured Maigny must mean Band-Aids.

"Don't do the pilgrimage in summer," Philip's Japanese friends advised. "Too hot. Not winter either. Do it in the fall, or spring." But Philip went in June, partly because once he made the decision he wanted to get started, and partly because that was when Bertrand Maigny had gone. Philip began his journey at Mt. Kōya. Some of his fellow students, including Kōji, were doing advanced training there. They encouraged him.

"We'll see you back here in August," they said, thumping him enthusiastically on the back. "You must come back to Kōyasan. Show Kūkai you made it."

Philip promised he would. He bought an official staff. "Now it's just me and Kūkai." He donned the uniform of the traditional pilgrim: a white thigh-length cotton jacket with a narrow purple cotton scarf draped over his shoulders.

"White is the color of death, you know, so this is your shroud in case you don't make it," Kōji told him. He gave him straw sandals and a woven straw hat as a present.

"Let me guess," said Philip. "My coffin?"

The others laughed uproariously. "Your walking stick is carved so it can serve as your grave marker, too."

Shingon humor. Philip stuffed half a dozen notebooks, five pens, and three envelopes full of Band-Aids in his pack. He was given a set of white paper amulets called *ofuda*. He was to leave one at each temple he visited.

"Your calling cards," said one of the young priests.

One must follow protocol, Philip saw, even on the road to enlightenment.

Pilgrimage

IN THEORY, ONE CAN BEGIN the Shikoku pilgrimage at any one of the eighty-eight temples, but Philip saw no reason not to start at number one. He arrived in Shikoku's port city of Naruto along with about two hundred other pilgrims. The first eleven temples were practically a picnic stroll—one after the other, as you headed west along the flat banks of the Yoshino River. During the first two days, pilgrims struck up conversations with one another, coalescing into friendly groups, dispersing according to their walking speeds. Day three was a different matter. Getting to Temple 12 entailed a hot, dusty, five-hour struggle up and down hills. After depositing his *ofuda* card and getting his journal stamped at the temple office, Philip sat exhausted on a stone bench. He watched several dozen bus pilgrims swarm in, get their booklets stamped, then buzz away again. His fellow "pure walkers" gradually straggled in, not so convivial now, and trickled away to their lodgings. Philip did likewise. The blisters were starting.

By the end of the first week, he had made it to Temple 22. When he first decided to do the pilgrimage, Philip thought he was in pretty good shape—twenty-seven years old, trim, and fairly strong. But now his quadriceps quivered, begging him to stop climbing hills. And the blisters...he had only ten bandages left from his original hoard.

At the end of the week, as usual, he wrote out a copy of his journal to send to France. Philip always tried to tell Maigny about the interesting things he had discovered, taking care to remove any hint of doubt or complaint. There was really no one else to write to. He knew his parents disapproved of this "Buddhist stuff." Nora, his former girlfriend, had just gotten married—and she wouldn't have been interested anyway. At Columbia, Professor Chernish had never said anything overtly against Philip's choice of dissertation topic, but Philip could tell that Chernish was miffed when had not leapt at the chance to work on Daitokuji. It was hard not to be discouraged now. Philip was alone, tired, and his feet throbbed. The room was hot and there was a hole in the mosquito net.

He was coming to the end of the first stage of the pilgrimage. It had been much more difficult than he expected. A number of people he met early on seemed to have dropped out, or climbed on a bus. According to pilgrimage lore, this first stage of the journey was called "awakening resolve." Philip pondered what that meant, finally deciding that he would resolve simply to finish because he had started it. At the same time, he was bothered by doubts about writing a thesis that nobody outside his committee would probably ever read. Should he persevere in that too, just because he started it? Rubbing insect repellent on his face, Philip crawled under the mosquito net and fell asleep.

Back home in Bretagne, Maigny read the notes Philip sent. "The young man is waking up," he thought to himself. He pushed back his chair, displacing the sleeping Pekingese, and shuffled over to a low bookcase where he pulled out a tattered journal and an old woodblock-printed map. Thumbing through the journal entries, he wrote down some numbers and did a calculation. Then he plucked a fresh blue aerogram from his desk drawer. He addressed it to "the American pilgrim," in care of the Green Dragon Temple where he knew Philip should arrive in about ten days.

By July, Philip had gotten into the rhythm of his trek. He would crawl out of his bedding as soon as it became light, wash, put on fresh socks and his now not-so-white jacket. Every third day he shaved. He headed off for the next temple. By now the routine was automatic. Pass under the temple gate guarded by scowling warrior statues. Leave a coin. Enter the sacred space of the grounds. Cleanse mouth and hands at the stone basin in the courtyard. Enter the main building to pay respects to the deity enshrined there. Recite that deity's mantra. Offer your *ofuda* card. Philip usually tried to make a sketch if there was enough light. Finally, he went to the temple office to get his souvenir book stamped.

He arrived at Number 36, the Green Dragon Temple. From his map Philip could see that he would need the rest of the day to get close to Number 37. He ticked off the steps efficiently, ending up in the office waiting for the priest to stamp his journal. As Philip thanked him and reached for the booklet, the priest looked hard at his face. When he saw Philip's dark blue eyes, he said, "Oh!"

Philip was used to this. There had been fewer than a dozen foreigners to ever make this pilgrimage. But he was astonished when the priest added, "I have a letter for you."

"Is this you?" he asked, pointing to the envelope.

"Yes," Philip answered when he saw Maigny's name in the return address space. "But how..."

The monk shrugged. "The sender must be very knowledgeable."

Philip took the flimsy letter out to a shady spot under a camphor tree and set his pack down. He pulled out his Swiss army knife and carefully sliced open the blue flaps.

Dear Philippe,

I have read your notes with much pleasure. The key to the first stage of the pilgrimage, Awakening Resolve, is, in my opinion, simply to stay alert. You can't proceed to the next stage unless you are awake to the possibility of learning something you didn't expect. I think by now you have entered the next stage, no? You are well along in An Ascetic's Training?

But you might think about the fact that even with the Spartan conditions you submit to, you still get warm dry lodgings every night, breakfast and dinner included. Not so very long ago the pilgrims who traveled this route had no coffee shops, no nylon raincoats. After passing Temple 35, you will be awake whether you intend to be or not. You will be more aware—of your actions, more aware of the people you meet, aware of the insects that bite your arms, of the dust that settles on your hat. By this time you are no longer just existing, you are living.

The pilgrimage is more than simply walking from one temple to the next. Life is more than just getting by day to day. You have eight hundred more kilometers to walk while you contemplate this. Despite today's luxuries, it is still possible to discipline yourself. The first stage, simply being awake, is the hardest.

Yours,
Bertrand Maigny

Philip read the letter several times. If he wanted to reach his lodgings by dinnertime, he'd better get going. He picked up his pilgrim's staff with its inscription. "One practice, two people." Reading it now, "three people," he thought, folding Maigny's thin blue aerogram back along its original creases and tucking it into his pack.

Some of the temples were bunched so closely it was possible to visit two, three, or more in a day. Others were widely separated. Today he would have to scramble down a mountain path, head along the southern Shikoku shore, cross a rocky beach, plod along a highway gassy with truck fumes, to end up in a town called Kubokawa where he had read there was a guesthouse. This would put him within hiking range of Temple 37 tomorrow. The sun beat down, but the path hugged the coast and was cooled by sea breezes. His feet were tough now. People gave him fruit, cookies, and soft drinks as he passed through the towns, gaining merit through their little gifts to the wayfarers. Philip accepted them gratefully. He had no trouble finding the guesthouse, as it was the only one listed in the pilgrim's guidebook. The problem was, it was full.

The woman who ran the hostel apologized. She had had to turn away another pilgrim who had come by half an hour earlier as well. If Philip wished, he could go to her sister-in-law's house, a five-minute walk, where she had directed the other pilgrim. Her relatives had an upstairs room, and they welcomed lodgers, if Philip didn't mind sharing a room.

"Wait," she said. She bustled back into the house and returned a few minutes later with three substantial rice balls wrapped in seaweed. She gave them to Philip. "Shall I call?"

"Please," said Philip. He had become comfortable in accepting unplanned changes in his itinerary. Maigny was right. He was awake to things in an entirely new way.

The woman called out to a little boy who had been trying to remain unseen while staring at Philip from behind a doorway.

"Ki-chan! Show this esteemed pilgrim the way to Auntie's house." She pulled the protesting child out by his arm.

"Not again!" he complained, embarrassing his mother.

"Hush your mouth," she told him.

"But I just went!" He looked up at his mother with panic. "I can't speak English," he hissed loudly.

"What? Do you think I can?" said his mother with a snort.

"That's all right," said Philip quickly. "Really. Just tell me how to get there. I'll find it."

Realizing that this odd foreign pilgrim could speak Japanese, the little boy suddenly changed his tune.

"No, no! I'll take you!" he shouted. "You'd get lost."

Relieved, his mother went back in the house to phone her sister-in-law to expect another guest. "What's that? No. No need. I gave him food already."

"Retsu go!" said the boy, hopping from one foot to the other. That exhausted his English. Chattering in Japanese the rest of the way, he led Philip to the gate of his aunt's house and announced in a loud voice, "Auntie! Uncle! I've brought the American pilgrim!"

Philip tried to give him a coin, but the boy refused to accept it.

"No, no—I should give *you* a coin," he protested, knowing the etiquette for treating pilgrims.

"Okay," said Philip. "Give me a coin."

Now the boy turned quiet. He didn't have a coin. Philip quickly reached into his pack and slipped a hundred-yen coin into the boy's hand just as a woman came out to open the gate. Making sure his aunt saw him, the boy ostentatiously presented Philip with the money, turned, and ran home as fast as he could.

"I hope you don't mind sharing a room," said the woman, leading Philip up a steep, narrow staircase. "Here's the toilet," she indicated a door as they passed, "and the bath is downstairs. I'm sorry everybody has already taken their bath, but the water is still hot if you're interested."

"Thank you," said Philip. "I am."

She called out "Excuse me" and slid open the door to a large room. Another pilgrim, just back from the bath was arranging his things in the corner.

Perhaps early forties, tanned, with close-cropped hair, the man moved with a quiet authority that made him seem taller than he was. Looking up, he said, in perfectly pitched English, "Welcome!"

"Thanks," said Philip, surprised. "Philip Metcalfe. Pleased to meet you."

The man extended his hand, "Jun Muranaka. Likewise."

The old woman smiled innocently at the international flavor her simple house had acquired. She bowed and left these two pilgrims to their incomprehensible conversation.

"Don't mind me," said Muranaka. "Go take your bath. You need it."

"Do I smell that bad?" asked Philip.

"You do."

Philip set down his pack, hat, and staff in the opposite corner of the room. He noticed that Muranaka had a bundle of rice balls just like the one the woman at the hostel had given him.

"Care to dine together later?" he asked.

Muranaka looked at Philip's identical dinner and laughed.

"Sure."

Philip pulled a nylon case of toiletries out of his pack and headed downstairs to the bath. On his way past the old couple, who were watching television, he asked if it might be possible for the two travelers to have a pot of tea.

By the time Philip had scrubbed, washed his hair, soaked, shaved, and soaked again, it was dark. Fireflies glowed and blinked in the garden. Philip reveled in the feeling of being clean all over.

Back upstairs, he tapped on the doorframe to alert his roommate.

"Come in," called Muranaka.

Their sleeping mats had been laid out at the edges of the room. A low table was now set up in the middle. Roasted sardines and pickled cucumbers sat beside the rice balls the two had brought with them. There was the pot of tea, and in addition, a ceramic flask of saké.

"Wow," said Philip. "You must really rate."

"Actually, it's because of you," the man replied. "The auntie seems quite smitten with you. She brought in all this stuff, asking me questions about why an American would be doing the pilgrimage, and who are you, and are you married, et cetera. She was very disappointed when I told her I didn't know a thing about you."

Muranaka poured a cup of saké for Philip, who returned the favor. "Call me Jun," he said.

"First alcohol I've had since the start of the trip," remarked Philip. "This is quite possibly the best saké I've ever tasted."

"Is that so?" said Muranaka. "Abstinence is the best condiment, I guess. I can't imagine that our hostess is in the habit of serving high-grade saké."

When they had eaten enough to take the edge off, Philip said, "So where are you coming from? Are you walking? I haven't seen you at any of the temples so far."

"Yes, walking," replied the older man. "But I'm doing the circuit in reverse. I started at Temple 88."

Philip recounted his own reason for being in Japan, and his study of Shingon which had led him to undertake the pilgrimage. He himself was an odd pilgrim; he sensed that Muranaka was unusual as well. Men in their forties were at the peak of their careers. This was not the time they would choose to spend two months on an arduous pilgrimage. It was clear, too, that Muranaka had been educated abroad.

"University of Chicago. Economics, 1966."

They finished the saké. Jun Muranaka gave Philip an abbreviated rundown of his life history. "…made a success of a small business, sold it to a big company, said goodbye, and then got asked to join a government task force. Problem: figure out how to develop a high-tech infrastructure to get people to move out of the big cities back to rural areas."

He took a noisy slurp of tea. "—and get more people to be entrepreneurs. Japanese have got to start taking the initiative. An American professor has written a book about Japan being Number One—have you read it?"

Philip had not.

"All the businessmen are flattered by this book," said Muranaka. "But it's got no more substance than 'a passing dream of a spring evening'."

"Tale of the Fall of the Heike?" Philip recognized the allusion.

"Exactly…or a bubble, as the economists now say."

"And your pilgrimage?" asked Philip.

"Just clearing my mind," said Muranaka. "Before stepping into the swamp of consulting."

Philip had a thought. Perhaps he could test his questionnaire out on Jun. At Professor Chernish's prodding, he had come up with a batch of questions designed to reveal a profile of people who undertook the pilgrimage. He had yet to give one out.

"Sure," Muranaka agreed, "but is it okay with you if I stretch out?"

He lay down on his futon while Philip read out the items on the questionnaire.

"It's anonymous," said Philip.

"Of course," said Muranaka. "Japanese are quite used to surveys, actually.

Consumer research, schools, government—everybody does surveys. We're well trained. Shoot."

Philip checked off boxes as the other pilgrim answered.

"Age?"

"42."

"Sex?"

"No, thank you.

"Ha. ha. Home?"

"Tokyo."

"Traveling alone? Or with a group? If a group, how many others?"

"Dōgyō Ninin—just me and Kūkai."

"First pilgrimage?"

"No."

"If not, how many times have you done the circuit?" Philip read.

"Why don't you just have a blank space for the number of pilgrimages?" suggested Muranaka.

"Good point." Philip made a note.

"Why don't you make it simple?" said Jun. "One page. Give them a stamped envelope with your address. Just ask people to fill it out when they've completed the circuit. You can ask what motivated them, and whether that changed by the end. Age, sex, where they're from. Let them give their name and address if they want."

"I hadn't thought of that. Do you think they would?"

"I think so. They'd be flattered that a blue-eyed pilgrim was interested in their story." Muranaka raised himself up on one elbow.

"Watch out for the old ladies. They'll give you phone numbers too."

"Thanks," said Philip. "Enough." He put his questionnaire away. Turning off the light, he stretched out on his futon.

"Do you know the Canterbury Tales?" asked Muranaka suddenly from across the room.

"Sort of…" answered Philip. "You've got a bunch of pilgrims traveling along. They stop for the night at some grungy inn…"

"And they tell tales to entertain one another." said Muranaka. "So you've entertained me with your questionnaire. Now I feel I ought to give you a tale as well."

"Please do," said Philip.

"Do you know *Kōya Hijiri*, the tale about The Holy Man of Mt. Kōya?"

"You mean Kūkai?"

"No. This is a different holy man. It's a story by Izumi Kyōka. Early twentieth-century Japanese gothic novelist. Rather famous."

"I don't know it," said Philip.

"It's slightly creepy," continued Muranaka. "Might give you a chill…"

"That would be good. It's pretty warm in here," Philip responded.

Enlightenment

"IT'S A STORY WITHIN A STORY—begins with two travelers, an old priest and a young man, being thrown together at a lodging house."

"What a coincidence," remarked Philip.

"Oh, everything is coincidence," replied Muranaka. "Surely you've figured that out by now. And they aren't ready to sleep so the older man tells the other a strange tale that happened to a young priest he knew.

This priest was complaining about a traveling salesman he had to share a room with at an inn—we've got the same traveling salesman jokes in Japanese, you know—and he was disgusted by the way the salesman flirted with the maids. What a letch, he thought. He left early just to avoid him, but the guy passes him on the road. Farther on, where the road forked, a farmer told him he saw a traveler go up the mountain path earlier. 'You don't want to do that,' he said. 'People get lost and die up there.'"

"So now the priest was conflicted. Can you guess what he does?"

"Goes the other direction, presumably," said Philip.

"You'd think, wouldn't you? But no—he decides to take the mountain path in order to warn the salesman, even if he is a creep. In fact, it's precisely *because* he has angry feelings toward the man that he feels obliged to save him. Interesting, don't you think? If the other guy had just been a stranger, he wouldn't have bothered. But they have a connection, even if it's a crummy one.

So off he goes up the mountain. And soon he comes to a meadow full of snakes. He panics, but somehow manages to get through it. Beyond the meadow is a dark forest. He goes in. Suddenly he feels something heavy plop onto his hat. He thinks it's some kind of fruit. But it's cold and slimy and clings to his fingers. There are more of them. Leeches. He's covered with leeches—on the back of his neck, his chest, his legs. The tops of his feet are covered with them."

"Uck," interjected Philip, "enough with the leeches."

"But these are the leeches of the apocalypse," said Jun. "People might think the end of humankind comes in a blast from the cosmos, or the seas rising up to swallow the planet. But this priest is suddenly sure that the destruction of mankind lies in these black leeches. Yet he flailed on, scratching and rubbing, until the suffering was so unbearable he felt he couldn't continue."

"Are you still awake?" Jun asked.

"I'm listening," replied Philip. "Are you done with the leeches yet?" He had been reminded of Professor Maigny's lecture on the subject of *mappō*.

"Yes, actually. Just at the point of totally giving up, the priest caught sight of the moon rising in the sky. He had reached the far edge of this terrible forest. A cool breeze was blowing. For the first time since the plain of snakes he thought guiltily about the salesman. Suddenly he heard the whinny of a horse and figured there must be a village or at least a mountain hut close by. He came to a woodcutter's cottage.

He called out and a voice answered from inside the hut. A beautiful voice. A woman's voice. The priest was not reassured by this. What would a woman be doing in this forsaken place? Maybe there was some grotesque serpent spirit lurking inside the hut, its voice mimicking that of a woman.

Then she appeared—a graceful young woman with a voice as clear as a mountain stream. The priest was relieved. Not a serpent. She offered to take him to a river back behind the house to bathe. And this made him nervous again.

Just then, an old man came out from behind the house. The woman asked 'How's it going with the horse?' He laughed. 'Oh, I'll get a good price for this one, all right.'

"There's something strange about that horse, isn't there?" asked Philip. He saw that Muranaka had lit a cigarette and was blowing smoke at a mosquito.

"Oh yes. Quite strange."

"At the stream, the priest started to wash the leech bites on his arms, glancing over at the woman whose kimono had come partially untucked.

'Here now,' she said to him. 'You'll get your kimono all wet. Take off your clothes and have a proper bath. Come on. I'll wash your back for you.'

She stripped off his robe in one swipe. The priest had never been naked in front of a woman before. She put her beautiful white hands on his back, massaging with her delicate fingers, working her way from his shoulders, down to his flank and buttocks, massaging, massaging..."

"Jun?"

"Yes?"

"Um, is this a set-up for a traveling salesman joke?" Philip suddenly wondered if Muranaka was leading him on.

The lit tip of Muranaka's cigarette bobbed up and down in the dark. He was laughing. "Ah, yes—whatever happened to that traveling salesman? Don't worry about him for the moment. Are you sleepy? Shall I stop?"

Philip wasn't sleepy but he didn't feel like being strung along for a dirty joke.

"You know," said Muranaka, "right at this point in Izumi Kyōka's story within a story, the old priest breaks off and warns his roommate about salacious content. He says he hopes he won't get over-stimulated hearing these details lying there in the dark."

"It's okay," said Philip. "I think I can stand it."

"Well, then," continued Muranaka, extinguishing the cigarette. "You might expect that the priest would be getting all hot and bothered. But no. He feels like he is being enveloped by some kind of flower. He is totally absorbed in this ecstatic dream, when suddenly he loses his balance and falls flat on his ass in the water.

"But the woman just says calmly, 'Don't worry—there's no one around to see us.' Muranaka stopped talking while he lit another cigarette. "And what do you think happens now?" he asked Philip.

"The priest loses his virginity? I don't know. What?" This was turning out to be a very strange tale. What was the point?

"Just then a couple of huge bats came flying out of a cave on the river bank. Angrily, she tells them to go away.

"The priest is now confused, but he resolves not to break his vow of chastity by even touching this goddess-demon-woman. Yet climbing back up the ravine, he stumbles on the decrepit suspension bridge and grabs her hand. Suddenly it was as if he was floating.

"Okay, now I *am* getting sleepy," yawned Philip. "Can you cut to the end?"

"Of course," said Muranaka. "You know, this is the point in the story where the travelers are distracted by the innkeeper tramping down the hall to use the toilet. I guess the old priest was a better storyteller than I am, though. Because his roommate hates the interruption, and is eager to hear the rest."

"Oh, I'm eager to hear the rest," groaned Philip. "Please, continue…"

"The woman tells the priest how lonely she is. She asks if he wouldn't give up his holy pilgrimage to spend his days on the mountain with her.

"He is tempted. She tells him to decide by morning and goes back to her room. In the middle of the night he is awakened by noises outside."

"Is this the scary part?"

"I suppose so. It's as if all the animals of the forest have converged upon the hut. The priest grabs his rosary and begins to chant the *Heart Sutra*. Over and over, he recites it until finally dawn breaks, and all is quiet. He slips out of the house, walking without break till noon, when he collapses near a waterfall just outside a village.

He has escaped the clutches of the seductress, but he hasn't. All he has thought about, with every step, is how he can return to her. He is ready to give up his pilgrimage, his spiritual life, everything. Gathering mountain mushrooms, collecting firewood, snuggling next to the fire—he imagines their life together. He realizes his religious austerities have given him no superiority over ordinary people—he was subject to lust just like any man. Since he's a sinner anyway, why not chuck it all and go back to her?

He is just about to turn around when somebody walks up to him from the direction of the village.

'Well, well, if it isn't the young priest…'

It was the old man who had led the horse down from the mountain. He now carried a huge carp, still moving its tail though threaded through the gills with a straw rope.

'Still thinking about her, aren't you?' he said. 'Don't deny it—I see it in your eyes. Let me tell you something,' the old man continued. 'I was amazed to see you come back from the river with her last night.'

'What do you mean?' the priest asked.

'In your human form, that is,' the man said slyly. 'You clearly have a strong will and firm resolve. That must be what saved you. Anybody she's ever taken down and bathed and caressed in that river ends up turned into a cow or a horse. Or a toad. Or a bat. Or some other creature that strikes her fancy at the time.

'The salesman…'

The old man chuckled. 'He was a lecherous one all right. He turned into a horse immediately. And now I turned the horse into money, and turned the money into this carp. It's her favorite food.'

The priest stood up quivering, his body covered with sweat.

'Take my advice young man, and continue on your way as quickly as you can. It's a miracle she spared you—perhaps she felt pity.' The old man gave the priest a tremendous thump on the back, then headed toward the mountain, the carp twitching on his shoulder."

The room was silent.

"Is that the end?" asked Philip.

"Well, that's the end of the priest's story. And then the two travelers go to sleep and the next day the narrator watches the old priest disappear off into the mountains." Jun moved around, plumping his buckwheat-husk pillow.

"Just like us, huh?"

"Maybe. The point of the story, I think, is that sometimes enlightenment comes when you least expect it."

"Do you think I'm looking for enlightenment?" asked Philip.

"Well, why *did* you come on this pilgrimage?"

Philip hesitated. "I'm not sure any more."

"Maybe you should fill out your own questionnaire..." Philip heard him slap a mosquito. "Everybody lusts after something," he continued. "And it usually catches them by surprise. Like that priest. He thought he was immune to sexual attraction. He felt so good after conquering his fears—the snakes, the leeches, the suspension bridges—and then he was almost undone by a passion he didn't recognize."

Now the mosquito that Jun missed came whining around Philip.

"Lust comes in many flavors," sighed Muranaka, "even lust for knowledge. And it can turn us into beasts."

Nirvana

THEY SLEPT LATE. Philip's dreams crawled with bats, toads, and horses. Muranaka had joked about salacious content, but Philip's imagination was bothered more by leeches than lust. They were still asleep when the auntie came tapping at their door with breakfast. Embarrassed to be thought lazy, both of them shot out of their futons. She left the food outside in the hall. As they finished up the usual rice, soup, and pickles, Philip said, "I'm almost halfway now. Since you're coming from the other direction, you're ahead."

"Are we racing?" asked Muranaka, crunching a bright yellow pickle.

"I was just thinking I might see you again at Temple 88. You'll stop there again to close the circle won't you?"

"Yes, but I've done most of the hard ones and you've got that terrain ahead of you. Here, look at this map. From where we are now…" he pointed to Temple 37, "we both go here today, and then try to make it to the next one by tonight. The temples on this stretch are the farthest apart of the whole route. You'll go on to Number 38, Ashizuri—way out on this little bluff overlooking the sea." Jun's finger indicated the place on the map. "And I follow the same road you took yesterday to get to Green Dragon Temple."

Philip realized that Muranaka would finish well before he did.

"So, can I give you a questionnaire to take along?" he asked.

"Sure. Write down your address. I'll mail it to you when I get back to Tokyo. Ashizuri is the highlight of the entire circuit," he added, "—for me, anyway."

"Why?"

"A couple of reasons. You'll see when you get there."

They paid the old woman for their meals and lodging and set out for Temple 37, Iwamotoji, the Temple at the Foot of the Cliff.

"You said this is not your first pilgrimage…" Philip said to Muranaka as they hit their stride.

"No, it's not…I did it the first time when I was five, in the normal order. With my mother and my aunt in 1944."

Philip's ear snagged on the date. 1944 was during the darkest days of the war. Where was Jun's father at the time, he wondered? But he said, "So you've been to Iwamotoji before…"

"Yes," said Muranaka, "this temple is unusual. It has five main statues. All the others, as you know, have only one."

"Five!" Philip exclaimed.

Muranaka looked at him. "You sound so surprised."

"I've never heard of *any* temple with five main deities," said Philip. "And also—well, I've been trying to sketch them all as I go," he explained, "but I missed the last one. It will take me all day to sketch five. Who are they?"

"The usual suspects," said Muranaka. "There's even a little song about them. People come to this temple to pray to all five in one go. Let's see, it goes something like: 'Fudō to thwart the evil eye, Guan Yin for good luck. Jizō will watch the kids, Yakushi to reveal the truth, and Amida for salvation.' All five installed by our friend Kūkai, of course."

"Damn," Philip muttered. "But now that I've missed one anyway, maybe I should just forget it."

Muranaka stopped and looked at Philip. "Well, that would depend on why you're doing the drawings in the first place, wouldn't it?" he remarked.

"What do you mean?"

"Like the priest in the story. He figured that since he let the woman wash his back, he was no longer pure. He might as well give up everything and go back and fuck her…"

"Wait a minute…"

"Yes?"

Philip was about to protest the comparison, but he stopped. Why *was* he sketching the images?

"Just think about it," said Muranaka mildly. They walked on together, silently, their steps falling into the rhythm of a practiced stride.

They arrived at the temple gate in an easy half hour's walk. Still silent, Philip followed Muranaka. As they headed to the main building of the compound, Muranaka pulled Philip's sleeve.

"Look, the striker pole for the bell hasn't been tied up. That means we can ring it."

All of the temple compounds had one of these open-walled belfries sheltering a huge suspended bronze bell. At most places though, the pole used to strike it would be knotted up to prevent the bell from being rung.

"Technically," said Muranaka, "you're supposed to ring it when you arrive at *every* temple—to announce yourself."

"To the monks?" asked Philip.

"No, to the buddhas," replied Muranaka. "But with all the pilgrims coming through, I bet the monks get tired of the constant ringing. They tie up the pole. Maybe it's the townspeople who get sick of it—I don't know. But this temple is sort of out of the way, so let's do it."

"After you," said Philip.

Muranaka grabbed the rope attached to the log and gave it a few trial swings. Then he pulled it back to its furthest reach and let go. The bell resounded with a deep bong that rippled outward in waves. Muranaka held the rope to prevent the log from damping the bell on the rebound. Almost forty-five seconds passed before the reverberation died away.

They walked over to the main hall of the five deities and lit sticks of incense. They placed small orange candles on the metal pins of the candle rack, and lit them as offerings to all dead souls. The last thing was to put their pilgrim's calling cards in the silver box on the opposite side of the hall. Philip pulled out one of the white slips he had prepared at the beginning of the journey. He was shocked when Muranaka reached into his robe and brought out a silver one. White *ofuda* were for first-timers. If you had done the pilgrimage more than four times, you used a green one. More than seven times, they were red. Light blue or silver meant that Muranaka had done it anywhere from twenty-five to forty-nine times. Muranaka saw Philip's surprise.

"Someday I suppose I'll have gold ones," he said with a shrug.

Philip was speechless.

At this point Philip was not able to say exactly why he was on this pilgrimage—except that despite blisters and doubts, it felt like what he should be doing now. He couldn't, however, imagine doing it again. What could possibly have prompted his companion to repeat it over and over? Muranaka had not tried to hide his previous pilgrimages, exactly, but he hadn't volunteered to explain them either. Philip felt chastened. Some of his earliest memories of Japan were of the way people kept things in. Americans were always keen to confide their thoughts. We crave instant intimacy, he thought. He wondered if Jun felt that, too, judging Americans to be shallow? He didn't feel he could ask.

As they left the dim interior of the main hall, they tossed coins into the offering box. Turning to face the deities, they recited the *Heart Sutra*. Philip had it memorized, but his voice was a squeaky accompaniment to Muranaka's deep chant. At least that's how it sounded to his own ears.

Just before they turned toward the temple office to get their journals stamped, Muranaka asked him,

"Would you show me the sketches you've done so far?"

Philip was still feeling sensitive, but he said "Sure." He opened his pack, taking out a black notebook full of detailed, shaded pencil drawings.

"Very nice," said Muranaka. "Just like explorers' drawings of the natives in the days before cameras."

"It helps me notice all the details when I draw them myself," explained Philip, ignoring the dig. "I know I could just take a picture, but this way I think I see more."

Muranaka nodded. "That's what I was trying to get at," he said. "Before. When I asked your reason for drawing."

"I'm no artist," Jun continued, "but I wonder what you could do if you tried to, somehow, absorb the essence of the statue, and sketch it more impressionistically. Say, look at it—*really* look at it—for five minutes, then do a one-minute sketch."

"I suppose I could try that," said Philip.

"Well, I'll leave you to your drawing, then," said Muranaka. "I probably should be getting along. Don't dawdle. You want to leave before one-thirty."

Philip knew they had to go their opposite ways, but there was so much he now wanted to ask Jun. "I'm sorry we're not going the same direction," he stammered. "Is there anything you think I ought to watch for in the places coming up? Be sure not to miss?" He was hoping to prolong their camaraderie just a bit longer.

"Well, Temple 86, Shidōji, has a *hibutsu* that's due to be displayed on July 16. It's an eleven-faced Guan Yin, the only hidden buddha on the entire 88-temple circuit—if you're interested in that kind of thing. Townspeople do a special festival dance for the occasion. It's one of those cultural events the government has declared to be 'an intangibly priceless bit of traditional foofaraw'—or however all that is put in English."

Today was July 8. Only a week away. Philip asked, "Can I make it to Temple 86 in time? How long is this hidden buddha on display?"

"Ah, good point. Probably not. It's opened one day, closed the next." Muranaka stood up. "Good luck on your journey," he said. "I hope you find what you didn't think you were looking for. I'll see you in Tokyo—we'll go have a beer."

Philip stood as well. "Goodbye, Jun. Thanks."

"I told you Ashizuri is the high point of the circuit…when you get there tomorrow, go out to the lighthouse on the point."

"Okay, I will…"

"And say a prayer."

"For?"

"My mother. She threw herself off the cliff. When I was five. Popular spot for suicides, you know."

Muranaka turned around and strode out through the temple gate. Philip watched him go, mouth agape. When he had finally disappeared from view, Philip looked down at his watch. One o'clock. Okay, he thought to himself, five minutes per image. He was surprised at the results, so different from his painstaking earlier sketches. Dead detail had given way to lively impressions.

Philip had long legs. Determined now, he hit a powerful stride and maintained it, reaching Temple 38 well before dark. Luckily there were accommodations at the temple itself. Leaving his pack in the pilgrim's dormitory he went briskly through the required rituals in the temple, and then wandered out toward the lighthouse at the tip of the cape.

As the sun set, he stood at the cliff edge looking out to sea. How many Japanese had been lost sailing off from this point in search of the Pure Land of Guan Yin, he wondered? The Potalaka Palace of Guan Yin, as described in scripture, was thought to be just over the horizon from Ashizuri point. Some people loaded boats with provisions and sailed off into the void. If they wanted to get there even more quickly, they jumped to their deaths from the cliff. A cool breeze arose, giving Philip a shiver. He imagined a five-year-old boy standing where he stood now, then coming back year after year to this terrible spot. Perhaps his father had been killed in the war? He remembered his promise to Jun and said a prayer for both of them.

Philip got an early start the next morning. Maybe, if he kept up the pace, he could finish in a week. It wasn't that he wanted to get the marathon over with more quickly—he was intrigued by Muranaka's mention of the *hibutsu*. Wouldn't it be great to write to Maigny that he had gotten to view the only hidden buddha on the 88-temple tour? Anybody could plan to be at Shidōji on that particular day. But to have it work out that way on his pilgrimage? Even better.

He plotted out his route to maximize the number of temples he could get to in a day. On his way to Temple 45, he climbed to the top of a mountain ridge with spectacular views over the forests and valleys. The day was clear and he could see all the way to the distant Inland Sea. This leg had taken three days from Ashizuri. But from this point the temples were clustered more closely. He thought he could tick them off at a rate of six or seven a day. The walk to Number 45, Iwayaji "Rock Roof Temple" was exhausting, though. From the mountain ridge the path plunged down through a thick forest ending at the base of a cliff. The temple was built right up against the rock.

All the temples on the pilgrimage route had stories attached to them. Some were plain historical records of their founding; others were riddled with legend. Philip took notes. The Rock Roof Temple's story was that it was given to Kūkai on his original pilgrimage by a female mountain hermit, perhaps a shamaness to the native gods. Kūkai is supposed to have carved two figures of the guardian deity Fudō—one in wood for the temple altar, and one in stone, in a cave behind the building. To worship the latter image was to worship the mountain itself. He sketched quick impressions of both statues. Later he ate a meal of rice mixed with barley and some stewed gourd shavings. As soon as it got dark he went to sleep in the pilgrim's communal hall. He decided to get his journal stamped in the morning.

At dawn, just as the other pilgrims began to stir, Philip packed up his things with practiced efficiency. Holding his now-frayed straw hat, he crouched outside the office waiting for the priest to come open up. He would give him another letter to mail to France. From here, he thought, every step would be taking him closer to his destination rather than further from his starting point. Yet it also hit him that his destination and his starting point were one and the same. It was only the words attached to them that made them appear opposites. When he wrote about the things he had experienced, he had to label them with words, but was his journey today really so different from yesterday's? Weren't the blisters of the first week and the calluses they had hardened into connected? What if he did the pilgrimage in reverse? Or repeatedly? They were all the same journey, Philip realized.

He kept to his rigorous schedule, managing to arrive at Shidōji on July 17. The famous folk dance was over, but the *hibutsu* of the eleven-faced Guan Yin was still on view.

Philip had become a connoisseur of images of the eleven-headed avatar of Guan Yin. He enjoyed drawing its variations. Guan Yin figures of this

type wear a crown of smaller heads. Usually they hold a vase with a lotus in their left hand, a string of rosary beads in their right. Yet, Philip marveled, despite the demands of the iconography, each one had its own personality.

The eleven-headed Guan Yin at Shidōji was life-sized, carved from a single log. The arms, robes, and even the rosary were all of a piece. Behind the silky-looking plain wood of the figure, an elaborate full-body gold-painted mandorla of curling clouds glimmered in the shadows. Philip spent a long time gazing at it from different angles. Like a Noh mask, the figure's expression seemed to change depending on the angle from which it was viewed.

By now, Philip had seen hundreds of Guan Yin statues. Technically a bodhisattva rather than a full buddha, Guan Yin is an enlightened being who postpones its own entrance into Nirvana in order to help all living things. "Many ways to help, thus many forms," was how one of the Unmonji priests had explained the rich variety of images of Guan Yin, the "One Who Perceives the Sounds of the World."

Staring at its subtle smile, Philip began to hallucinate that its wooden mouth was moving. "Touch me…" the statue seemed to be saying. His head began to throb. Must be the incense, he thought, feeling dizzy. He put his notebook away and stepped out of the main hall into the bright courtyard. He had to sit down. He had really pushed himself to get this far in one week, and the effort suddenly caught up with him. He felt slightly nauseated.

Because of the exhibition of the *hibutsu*, all the pilgrim accommodations were taken at Shidōji. Philip didn't think he could make it to Temple 87, so he asked about inns for pilgrims in the nearby town of Sanuki. Probably all full, the priest at the office told him. "Why don't you take the bus to Temple 87?" he suggested. "It's just a twenty minute ride. They've got room for 100 pilgrims there. I'll call ahead for you."

Philip was floored. He was almost to his journey's end. Two more temples to go. He had walked the entire way. Take a bus now? He thanked the monk, then he picked up his staff and started walking.

He arrived at Temple 87 in a little under three hours. Along the way his head cleared, helped by a cup of coffee with double cream and lots of sugar. He bought a bread bun with red bean jam filling at a convenience store and nibbled it on the way. He was beyond a second wind. Time melted away. He was reminded of the story of the priest struggling back up the mountain from the stream—*he took the woman's hand and suddenly it was as if he was floating*. Philip, too, felt like his feet were hardly working, yet they propelled him along easily. Before he knew it, he had arrived.

After the eleven-headed Guan Yin *hibutsu* he had viewed at Shidōji, the statues here appeared rather ordinary. Still, he lit incense and a candle, dropped his card in the box, and chanted the sutra. He had his journal stamped, and then wandered behind the main building where he discovered a trail. In the temple woods Philip felt the quiet presence of the spirits of nature that the ancient Japanese celebrated before the great religion of Buddhism led them to codify their own practices into a system as well—as Shinto, the Way of the Gods.

By now it was dusk. Philip was not floating any longer. His feet felt like lead. He trudged back to the dormitory, ignoring the attempts of other pilgrims to be sociable. Mechanically, he removed his hat, jacket, pants, and socks. He splashed water on his face, washed his feet, and then crawled onto the futon. The bedding smelled of mold. That was the last thing he remembered until he awakened in an empty sunlit room the following morning, after everyone else had left. An annoyed-looking junior monk was waiting impatiently to sweep the quarters.

The walk to Temple 88 took what was left of the morning. Kūkai 's walking staff was enshrined here. Many pilgrims left their walking sticks here as well, but Philip decided to keep his rather than abandon it to the huge collection. The trek back to close the circle at Temple number 1 was long, and he would miss his "third leg" if he gave it up now. He wondered if Jun had already come and gone. Given Philip's accelerated schedule, they were probably not so far apart after all.

Philip kept his eye out for someone with Muranaka's compact muscular stride, but he didn't pass a single pilgrim coming from the other direction. Temple 1 was full of chatty beginners eager to start out. Philip felt immensely older. He used this opportunity to pass out his revised shortened questionnaire. People clamored for them, and the folded sheets were all distributed within five minutes. "Jun was right," he thought. "People love it when you want to know their stories."

He stayed at an inn in Naruto that evening. He had a proper bath, an excellent fish dinner, and a comfortable room. The next morning he climbed aboard the ferry off Shikoku and, still in his pilgrim's wear, headed back to Mt. Kōya where his fellow Shingon students, and of course Kūkai, were waiting.

Kōji was the first to notice the unusually tall, gaunt pilgrim with the filthy jacket who strode into the young priests' quarters. He sauntered over to see what the man wanted. When sunburned hands removed the hat to reveal Philip's shaggy head, Kōji did a double take.

"Philip-san! What are you doing back here so soon? Dropped out?"

Philip merely grinned and reached into his pack for his pilgrim's journal. He flipped its pages under Kōji's nose—all 88 stamped pages.

Kōji was not easily impressed, but this had the desired effect.

He put his hands together in mock prayer and bowed to Philip.

"You're the MAN," he said. "So—any words of wisdom for the rest of us?"

"Form is emptiness," said Philip.

Kōji rolled his eyes. "Yeah, yeah…"

"Emptiness is form."

"Come on!"

"I highly recommend the trip. What can I say? It's not the destination, it's the path?" Philip took a swig of the cold barley tea Kōji had brought out. "You've just got to do it some time. You'll see."

"I will if you'll come along."

Philip laughed. "I think I'll wait a while," he said. "Hey, Kōji—do you know anything about hidden buddhas?"

"Why?"

"I saw one on the trip. Temple 86 has one, an eleven-faced Guan Yin. Pretty amazing."

"Yeah, my Dad's temple in Maizuru has one, too. A thousand-arm Guan Yin. It was last shown in 1933. Supposed to come out once every 50 years."

Philip looked up with interest. "That would be next year, then" he said.

Kōji shrugged. "Supposed to be, I guess, but I haven't heard that they're showing it."

"Tell me more," said Philip.

"It has a surrogate—a lot of the *hibutsu* do. They put a substitute out on the altar so the old *hibutsu* doesn't have to do any work, you know."

Philip was fascinated. He couldn't wait to write to Maigny.

"So, what does the substitute look like?"

"In our case, exactly the same. A thousand-arm Guan Yin. Supposed to look just like the hidden one."

"Is there always a stand-in?" Philip asked.

"Not always," Kōji replied. "And if there is one, sometimes it's a copy and sometimes it's totally different."

"Is this all written down somewhere?" Philip asked, his mind racing ahead.

"Dunno. I'll ask my Dad," said Kōji. "Why this big interest in *hibutsu?*"

Philip didn't feel he could tell Kōji about the surreal effect the *hibutsu* of the eleven-faced Guan Yin had had on him. But he again sensed that compelling surge that had struck him at Maigny's first lecture. His instinct told him that here was something worth studying. He turned to Kōji.

"The whole idea of hiding an image behind closed doors—it's pretty strange, when you think about it. I mean, a Buddhist image is made to be seen and worshipped, right? That's its whole purpose—especially in Shingon. It can't possibly be that those images were carved in order to be shut away. No other Buddhist culture hides images away like this."

Kōji had never considered this before. "Is that true?" he asked. "Hidden buddhas are only in Japan?"

"I'm pretty sure," said Philip, "but I know who to ask."

Before he removed his pilgrim's jacket for the last time, Philip hiked over to Kūkai's tomb to pay his respects.

"I'm back," he said simply. He left his walking staff there and feeling strangely light, made his way back to the monks' quarters. He'd left an overnight bag with a change of clothes here before he embarked on the pilgrimage. Now he stripped off his ragged pilgrim gear and bundled it into a garbage bag. It was beyond salvage. He showered, changed into clean slacks and a shirt, and sat down at Kōji's desk. He took a blank aerogram out of his pack.

> *Dear Professor Maigny,*
>
> *I'm writing from Mt. Kōya where I'm just back having finished the pilgrimage. I followed your advice. I did not take a bus and I kept a journal. Thank you for your letter. I had some bleak moments, but your words really helped. I did sketches of many of the statues. Someday I hope we get a chance to sit down together and compare our journals. I was lucky enough to be at Temple 86 when their hibutsu was on display.*

(He decided to make it appear as if this were a lucky coincidence rather than make a point about the effort it cost him to get there on time.)

> *It was an eleven-faced Guan Yin, as I gather a good many of the hidden buddhas are. I have developed an interest in this particular iconography,*

(He erased that, as it seemed like something you'd write to a thesis advisor. Then, he reminded himself, that's exactly what Maigny was. He reworded it:)

> *I have become fascinated by this form of Guan Yin. And further, I would like to know more about the hidden buddhas. One of my colleagues here has asked me if it is true that* hibutsu *are exclusively Japanese. I said that I thought so, but would appreciate anything you could tell me about them. For my thesis, I think rather than write about the meaning of Shingon in modern Japan, I would like to investigate these hidden buddhas.*
>
> *I am greatly in your debt for any advice you might have.*
>
> > *Most sincerely,*
> > *Philip Metcalfe*

Kōji came slinking outside the door of his room just as he was finishing his letter to Maigny.

"You're leaving for Tokyo tomorrow," he said. "How about one last night of pachinko? We'll go eat barbequed eels after."

Philip was game.

Syzygy

NOBORU TOKUDA WAS WORRIED. He had been nervously cataloging disasters of earth, water, fire, wind, and space whenever he discovered that another hidden buddha that had once enlivened his five senses no longer did. In February, a Japan Air Lines flight crashed into Tokyo Bay under suspicious circumstances. The captain was one of the first to bail—telling rescuers who plucked him from a lifeboat that he was an office worker. But it turned out that, prior to descent, he had deliberately reversed the engines in an attempt to destroy the aircraft. Tokuda had the uncomfortable feeling that this was exactly the way the seer of the *hibutsu* was operating—in secrecy and denial.

A month later, he read in the newspaper that all nine planets had aligned on the same side of the sun in a highly unusual configuration known as a syzygy. Was that a portent? If so, was it bad or good? Indifferent? Tokuda felt a maddening compulsion to see meaning in anything out of the ordinary, but he was losing his sense of what was ordinary. How was one supposed to judge? Mudslides in southern Japan killed almost three hundred people in Nagasaki. That was unprecedented—but was it something else as well? He wished there was someone he could talk to about how to interpret the strange tragedies. His grandfather had been clear about his mission, but Noboru was starting to flounder. Meanwhile, the numbers of water children consigned to the care of Jizō continued to swell.

Were those who knew the reason for the existence of *hibutsu* simply cogs in the machinery of Kūkai's plan? It was a miracle that the line of succession had actually been able to continue for so long without a broken link. There were no backups, after all. What if the line *had* been broken, and nobody knew what the hidden buddhas were really for any more? Would that even make any difference? The trouble with being the single repository of a secret tradition was there was no one you could talk to.

Now it was nearly August. Philip had just moved to Tokyo to begin writing up his thesis. On one particularly hot and muggy afternoon he decided to take a break and go browse the English floor of the air-conditioned Shinjuku Kinokuniya Bookstore. Paperback bestsellers, about six months behind the curve, were stacked on a table near the window. These were for homesick expatriates. On another table were the English-language books popular with Japanese readers. He saw two copies of Harvard professor Ezra Vogel's *Japan As Number One* which had come out with great fanfare a couple of years ago. Oh yes, he remembered—Muranaka had mentioned it. Of course it had been translated immediately, but many Japanese could read English well enough to read it in the original. Maybe he should take a look at it?

At that moment a woman stepped up to the table from the other side and reached over to pick up one of the two copies. Philip noticed her delicate fingers and the gauzy white fringe on the dark blue of her sleeve—it reminded him of the frothy spume of an ocean wave. He opened the other copy and glanced through the chapter headings. He could see from the subtitle why Japanese were so pleased with it—*Lessons for America.* Yet Muranaka had been somewhat cynical about it as Philip recalled.

He glanced over at the woman standing across the table. She had done the same thing—leaf through the contents, and she looked up at the same time. Philip's eyes met hers, and he blushed. She had those rare hazel eyes known as tea-eyes in Japanese.

"Should I buy it, do you think?" she asked him in flawless English.

"I was just wondering the same thing," Philip stammered in reply.

She put the book down.

"A friend of mine was just talking about it," he continued.

"What did he say?" asked the woman. She wore light makeup and her blunt-cut thick black hair swung back from her chin as she lifted her head. Philip caught a faint scent of an unusual perfume.

"About…?"

She smiled. "About the book…"

"Oh. Um, he said the idea of Japan as Number One was like *a passing dream of a spring evening…*"

"*Fall of the Heike?*" she murmured.

That had been Philip's response.

"Very good!" he started to say, then stopped, embarrassed. Who was he to praise Japanese for knowing their own literary heritage. "I mean, yes, the beginning of the Heike…" he was floundering now. "*The proud and boastful shall not last…*"

"*It is all just the passing dream of a spring evening,*" she finished the quote.

They both laughed. Other shoppers glanced over. Philip put the book down as well.

"Perhaps I can live without it," he said.

"I'm sure you can," she agreed.

Neither of them spoke. Then they both did.

"Sorry…"

"No, what were you going to say?"

"Nothing…I…" Philip cleared his throat. "Are you in a rush? Would you like to have a cup of tea or something?"

Nagiko looked at her watch.

"I guess I could…sure."

The oppressive heat in Bretagne that summer reminded Bertrand Maigny of Japanese summers. He was not feeling well, although it was not his throat or his liver or anything he could directly point to or take a tonic for. Kookai was suffering too. There was no air-conditioning in the old stone farmhouse Maigny had redone as his home. Usually the thick walls kept the interior pleasantly cool, but the sun beat full bore day after day. Even nightfall provided little relief. The Pekingese panted as it sought out the tile bathroom floor where it splayed out unhappily under the porcelain sink. Bertrand and Kookai took their walks shortly after dawn, then spent the rest of the day in the darkened library with an old electric fan stirring the languid air.

At noon, Bertrand scuffed out to the mailbox and back. What was this? An aerogram from Japan…Metcalfe most likely. He turned it over. *Ah, oui…*Still on the pilgrimage probably. He set the mail aside until after lunch. Maigny thought of summers in Kyoto where people drank hot seaweed tea to cool off. The hot beverage made you perspire, and the perspiration cooled you off. The tea was salty, and so replenished your body's electrolyte balance—or something like that. Maybe he could get young Metcalfe to send him some seaweed tea from Japan. Praising Annette's kitchen skills with a kiss of his fingers, he disappeared back into his study.

There he opened the letter from Philip. Finished the pilgrimage, did he?

That was awfully quick. Maigny read on. Temple 86, the hidden buddha—well, if he got that far he must have finished the entire route…

> *For my thesis, I think rather than write about the practice of*
> *Shingon in modern Japan, I would like to investigate these hidden*
> *buddhas.*

Bertrand Maigny forgot about his liver and took a deep breath. Then he fetched a handful of sheets of onionskin paper, inserted one in his old typewriter and began to type. Annette came in with his pot of tea. Maigny didn't notice.

It was getting dark. Annette became concerned. The professor had been typing without a break since after lunch, showing no sign of quitting for dinner. She tapped on his study door.

"Professor?"

"What is it, Annette?"

She pushed the door open slightly. "I thought perhaps you might like to rest a bit. It seems to be cooling off—there's a bit of a breeze outside now…"

Bertrand Maigny looked up at the clock. Good heavens—she was right. No wonder his fingers were getting stiff.

"Thank you Annette." Yes, time to stop, catch his breath. It was good to finally be writing some of these things down. Kookai followed him outside as he walked meditatively around the stone wall enclosing the garden. Maybe it would be better to point him toward the evidence, let him chew over it a while, and then bring up his theory. Yes, that was better. First, the map. And he would send Philip the list of all the hidden buddhas. We'll see what he makes of that, thought Maigny. Philip had probably already started digging up a bibliography at the National Library, but he would send him references as well.

But Philip had not gone to the National Library. He hadn't accomplished much of anything really, since he couldn't get the woman he had met at the bookstore out of his mind. They had stepped into a café in the Odakyu building, where she ordered coffee jello, and Philip had sweet bean syrup poured over a mountain of shaved ice. She was so sophisticated, she made him feel like a teenager…no, that made it seem like she was putting him down. She was actually very nice—it was his own fault that his tongue tripped all over itself. She didn't have a card, but she wrote down her name. And she gave him her phone number. Maybe it wasn't hopeless. He would call her. What should he say? Hidden buddhas receded from his mind and when he looked at his sketch of the Shidōji Guan Yin, all eleven faces turned into the face of Nagiko Kiyowara.

Just as he was despairing of pulling himself together—to either forget her and get back to work, or to call her—he received a printed invitation with a handwritten note from Jun Muranaka. "That's it," Philip thought in relief. "I'll ask Jun for advice."

Muranaka was hosting a special awards dinner to honor the kind of entrepreneurs who he felt were the hope of the future for Japan.

"Sorry to be sending this so late," said the scribbled note. "I misplaced your address. Hope you can come. Give a call." Philip called Muranaka's office immediately.

"Mr. Muranaka is out of town. He's gone to New York, getting back the day of the dinner," his secretary said. "But I'm sure he will be delighted to hear that you will be there. I'll let him know when I fax him his messages tomorrow."

Philip decided he would wait to call Nagiko until after he had a chance to consult with Muranaka. And what was "fax" anyway?

The dinner was at the Chinese restaurant at the top of the New Otani Hotel. Philip fetched his only suit from the dry cleaners and put on a clean white shirt. This was his upper limit of dressy. It would have to do. He bought a tie. His pilgrim's sunburn had faded to a ruddy tan, and his dark hair was only slightly in need of a trim. He looked better than he realized. Teenaged girls giggled and whispered to each other when he walked by, and middle-aged women on the subway noticed him with lowered eyes. He was a *gaijin*, but a non-threatening one. Not huge, not red, not hairy. He moved gracefully. They could tell by his body language that he understood Japanese. He inspired daydreams. Philip was totally unaware of the effect he left in his wake.

He took the elevator up to the top floor.

"I'm sorry, but tonight the restaurant is closed for a private function…"

Philip fished Muranaka's invitation out of his pocket.

"Oh, I'm sorry. Right this way…"

Philip followed the maître d' into a large ornate room. It was a buffet-style event, with small tables set up around the edges. Philip did not expect that he would know anyone and he was right. Except for a small group of women who huddled together at one of the corner tables, everyone was a gray-suited male. A fog of cigarette smoke rose to the ceiling. This was crazy, Philip realized. There was no way he could have a private conversation with Jun even if he could find him.

Philip wandered over to the buffet where a Japanese chef in a French toque was serving delicate Chinese shrimp dumplings. Where was Muranaka? Filling his plate, he wandered back into the crowd, thinking that he would leave after he had eaten a bit. Ah, he was coming in now. Philip remembered he was just back from New York. Maybe his plane had been delayed. He must be exhausted.

He didn't look it, though. Clear-eyed and energetic, Muranaka moved through the knots of people, greeting and being greeted. Philip joined the flow, and finally Jun caught sight of him.

"Philip! Glad you could make it." He pulled him toward the trio of men to whom he had been talking, and introduced him.

"Those look good…" Muranaka eyed the plate of food Philip was carrying.

Philip offered it to him.

"Thanks. It's hard to get anything to eat at these affairs…" He wolfed down three dumplings.

Just then a phalanx of waiters came through the doors carrying folding chairs. They set them up in the middle of the room. A microphone was brought to Muranaka, who took it as he gulped down the last shrimp.

"Catch you later," he said to Philip. Microphone in hand, welcoming everyone, Muranaka moved toward the dais at the front of the room. People stuffed the last bits of food in their mouths, looking around for places to unload their dishes. By the time Muranaka reached the speaker's table the plates had all been whisked away, and everyone had found a chair. Displaying none of the usual stiffness of Japanese speechifying, Muranaka launched into a talk about the importance of the individual entrepreneurial spirit to Japan's continued success as a major player in the world economy. Clearly he had given this pep talk before.

He started out talking about Japanese inventors of the late nineteenth century who had pushed the modernization of the country in the Meiji era.

"Everyone knows about Kokichi Mikimoto and how he made the oyster reveal the secret of making pearls. But how about the organic chemist Umetarō Suzuki, who first isolated vitamin B1? Or my own personal hero, Jōkichi Takamine—the man who discovered how to produce pure adrenaline?"

Several people in the crowd laughed.

"But not everyone is an inventor," he stressed. "Japan's great strength has lain even more in those who see the potential of what others have first discovered."

One by one, the awardees were called up to the table. There was a man from Toshiba who was responsible for pushing the company to develop and market fast, small, cheap facsimile copiers.

"Toshiba didn't invent the fax machine," said Muranaka, "but it saw the potential in this technology and made it available to a lot of people. What good is a facsimile machine unless you have someone who can receive your fax? I predict every office and home will have one of these things in five years."

A young man from Sony was summoned. He had not invented something called optical-digital data-storage technology, but he was preparing to mass-produce it as the latest and highest quality form of musical reproduction.

"These little circles will replace records and tapes," predicted Muranaka, "compact discs."

More clapping. Half a dozen more attendees were called to the dais and given awards.

Philip marveled at Jun's social dexterity. In his mind's eye he tried to lay the image of this suave businessman over that of the pilgrim he had met in July. Jun was working his audience now, and it responded like an eager pet. He was coming to the end of the list.

"We all know that some parts of Japanese culture may never be accepted in the wider world—*manga*, for example. Now there's a hybrid form that foreigners will never appreciate…"

The men in the audience laughed. They had all been besotted with those thick weekly comic books in high school. Certain things were obviously not for foreign eyes.

"But there are some artistic hybrids that Japanese entrepreneurs are now taking back to Europe and America, garnering great praise. I cannot claim any knowledge in the field of fashion design, but our last awardee has received great acclaim both at home and abroad. Will Miss Nagiko Kiyowara come forward please."

Heads craned as chairs were scraped aside in the corner of the room where the small group of women were clustered. Philip felt himself turn scarlet as a maple leaf. Time slowed down. He saw her smile and dip her head to her wildly clapping companions as she rose from her chair. The silvery ruffles of her sleeves glistened like a school of fish caught in the spotlight. She glided up to the main table and bowed to Jun who caught her hand and shook it. As Nagiko turned to acknowledge the applause of the audience, her eye fell on Philip, and her smile widened.

When Nagiko had lived in Paris, she discovered she had an extraordinary effect on Western men. Japanese men might be intimidated by Nagiko's cool independent streak, but Western men were attracted to it like bears to honey. Yet, in the end, most of them had only been interested in a glamorous Asian accessory to complete their self-image. By the time she got to New York Nagiko had become thoroughly wary of their overtures. Even now, her social antennae bristled whenever she met a foreign man who seemed attracted to her. But this was Tokyo, not New York, she had to remind herself—it was not as if being a Japanese woman was exotic here.

Until tonight she had almost forgotten about the earnest young man she had met at the bookstore last week. She had deliberately not given him her business card, writing her name and phone number on the napkin instead. She had meant it as a personal touch, and was a tiny bit disappointed when she hadn't heard from him. Now, as she stood here basking in the light of flashbulbs, holding this award that had dropped so unexpectedly out of the heavens and would certainly give her company, Kiji, a tremendous shot of free publicity, there he was in the audience, looking at her with a rapt expression. And though she would hardly have thought it possible, she was even happier.

As the party tapered off and people began to leave, Muranaka came over, Philip in tow.

"Let me introduce you to a friend..." he said.

"I believe we've already met," said Nagiko, as Muranaka raised a puzzled eyebrow in Philip's direction.

The Pillow Book

SPRING AND AUTUMN WERE THE most dangerous. The *hibutsu* tended to come out at the same time tourists did—when the cherries bloomed in springtime and maples reddened in the fall. Summer and winter gave Tokuda some respite. During one frantic April when he was younger, he had asked his grandfather why Kūkai hadn't simply buried the *hibutsu* away somewhere? They would have been safe, their protection guaranteed.

"But if they were buried, they would have been forgotten. They need to be connected to people," the elder Tokuda said, "…connected to the priests. In their own way, the *hibutsu* are alive—they need the incense and the offerings. Kūkai solved the paradox by making sure they would be displayed rarely, and on different schedules. It would be very difficult for anyone to see all of them."

"But not impossible?" asked Noboru.

"No, not impossible."

Tokuda no longer knew what he was supposed to be watching for, but he grew jumpy around attractive middle-aged women. She would now be in that stage where certain women can be called *iki*—suspended between innocent youth and indifferent old age. Such women are experienced, but keep the depth of their experience hidden. He had replayed the memory of the Kōryūji Guan Yin many times in his head, imagining different outcomes. What if he had yelled for help? Or followed the woman? If she was human, he should have been able to catch her. Now that he was an adult, he was sure, if the chance arose, he could. But what, exactly, was he supposed to do then? The secret transmission was only a list, not a directive. What was its purpose in an age when the *hibutsu* were dropping like ripe loquats in June?

"Whatever happens," his grandfather had said, "we are part of Kūkai's plan."

An uneasy thought crossed his mind. Was it possible that trying to save the *hibutsu* might actually be interfering with Kūkai's plan? Maybe they were *meant* to wink out, one by one, their job done, having slowed the process of *mappō* just enough? Perhaps the job of those who knew the *hibutsu's* secret really was simply to stand witness, nothing more. The point was arguable—had there been anyone for Tokuda to argue with.

On this September evening, perched on a high stool at a tiny tempura restaurant, Nagiko turned her face away from Philip who was squeezed on the next stool so closely their shoulders touched. She dabbed her nose and forehead with a square of powdered blotting paper. He noticed how her curtain of hair swung down, effectively hiding her face while she performed this task. He thought everything about her beautiful.

Nagiko was preparing a series of fabrics inspired by the seasons. For spring, she named the translucent organza-like textile *akebono*, "dawn." The cloth, opaque in flat light, shimmered when the model moved out of shadow into sunlight. Loose wisps of purple thread trailed from the edges.

Her summer piece was called "fireflies." If asked what summer meant to them, most people would talk about a day at the beach, but when Nagiko closed her eyes and thought of summer, she thought of night. A moonlit summer night was nice, but even more so if moonless and dark. Away from city lights, fireflies would be drawn out. This fabric she called *hotaru* was a blend of silk and cotton in a solid color, with a pattern of white spots reserved from the dye in a process that involved tying off small pinches of cloth over cotton swabs. Her staff complained at the labor-intensive effort of creating the fireflies, but Nagiko insisted. It was the kind of thing that would sell in Japan to ladies who recognized an old-fashioned technique once used for fine kimono fabric. She admitted that foreigners might not appreciate the difficulties behind such a simple design, but she knew some would. The ones who did sought out precisely this kind of understatement. Her clientele. Nagiko had by now risen to head designer at Kiji.

The third in the series represented autumn. Nagiko ended up naming it "wild geese." This fabric was tightly woven pale blue raw silk with rust-colored attenuated V-shaped guillemets woven in widely spaced, almost random patterns that could be seen as a connected line of geese appearing like specks in the distant sky.

"But if it's a pattern, how can it be random?" Phillip asked, as Nagiko described her new series. "Pattern means precisely *not* random, doesn't it?"

"Of course it will have to repeat at some point, but it's not obvious," Nagiko replied.

"Ah, I see. But I rather like the idea of random pattern, come to think of it. It's oxymoronic."

Nagiko's English skills had sharpened once she started going out with Philip, but this word threw her.

"Opposite words stuck together in the same phrase—jumbo shrimp. Or, my favorite—act natural."

Nagiko still didn't quite get it, but resisted the urge to fall into speaking Japanese. Philip's Japanese was very good, but Nagiko made speaking English a condition of their relationship. Philip acquiesced. He did not lack for opportunities to polish his language skills, and he would do anything to please her.

"Can we order some jumbo shrimp here, I wonder?" Philip scanned the handwritten items on the wall of the tempura restaurant. "What's the fourth one? What's for winter?"

"In the snow country, where I grew up, I loved waking up early on a winter morning and rushing to look out the window to see if there was fresh snow. We completely miss that in Tokyo. Even if it snows, you can never get up early enough to see it unspoiled."

"Let me guess," said Philip. "It's called *yuki*."

"Not exactly. It's tan and white wool. I call it *muragie*—I don't know what you'd say in English. Like the ground when the sun has melted part of the snow off in patches. Is there a word for that?"

"Hmmm," said Philip. "Snow splotches? Not very poetic, I'm afraid."

Something about Nagiko's description of her new designs felt familiar. Philip tried to remember where he had seen or read those images before. It escaped him, and he let it go, distracted by the delicate plate of tempura-fried lotus root the chef placed in front of him. When Nagiko excused herself to go to the ladies' room, Philip's thoughts returned to the blouse for spring. Of course! "In spring it is the dawn"—the opening phrase of the tenth-century classic *Pillowbook of Sei Shōnagon*. The author's very first entry in that miscellaneous collection of little essays was a list of her favorite aspects of each season. In spring it is the dawn. Definitely. Did summer include night? Philip thought it did. Fireflies too. And and geese for fall evenings? Frosty winter mornings? It all sounded right. He would check. When Nagiko slipped back into her seat beside him, Philip asked her,

"Have you ever read the *Pillow Book*?"

"We had to read sections of it in high school for literature class," she said, "Why?"

"Do you remember how it starts?"

"In spring it is the dawn. Every Japanese knows that," she said. "But nobody remembers what comes next."

"How about summer nights with fireflies?" Philip asked.

"Hmmm. Now that you mention it..." said Nagiko, "That could be it, yes. Curious. I should go back and read it."

"Yes," replied Philip. "You might find some surprises."

She asked him about the year he had lived in Kyoto and about Mt. Kōya. As he described those days to her, they seemed to Philip like a long-ago dream.

"Kyoto is so beautiful," he said. "Have you spent much time there?"

"I go on quick business trips, mostly to work with weavers and dyers," Nagiko replied. "And of course, when I was in eleventh grade, my whole class went in the spring for a school trip." She let Philip take the check. She would have preferred to pay since she knew he was eking by on scholarship money, but she was sensitive to his pride.

"But I can't really say that I know Kyoto."

"How about in the fall? Ever been there in autumn?" As they left the restaurant, Philip had an idea.

Nagiko shook her head.

"I have to go back to Kyoto in a couple weeks," he said. "Some research. Why don't you come along? I could show you some really wonderful things..."

"Like some of those hidden buddhas you're studying?" Nagiko asked.

"If you like," he said. "I was thinking more of maple leaves, though."

"Well, I'll think about it. Perhaps I can get away."

The idea that she might consider coming on a trip with him gave him a pleasant feeling.

"Philip?"

"Yes?"

"Where shall we go?"

"You mean in Kyoto?

"No, here. Tonight."

"It's nice out, do you want to walk for a while? I don't really know many places, like bars or anything…"

"Okay, how about, there's a place in Roppongi, a new hotel—it has a really charming bar, lots of atmosphere…you can be my guest this time."

She tucked her arm into his.

As far as Philip was concerned, this was fine. He would be happy just to walk around Tokyo all night with the soft pressure of Nagiko's arm against his side.

The Roppongi Marquis Hotel was on a quiet side street just up a short slope from the bars and restaurants of this expensive international district. The cab let them off at the modern red and gray entrance planted with timber bamboo.

The bar was on the third floor. A hostess showed them to a corner table with a comfortable couch. A jazz trio played on the other side of the room. Philip and Nagiko talked about New York, trying to figure out if there were places where they might both have been at the same time and might even have unknowingly seen one another.

Nagiko excused herself, and Philip let himself sink back in the soft gray comfort of this room designed to soothe. He was slightly lightheaded. When Nagiko came back, he smelled the scent he had noticed the first day they met.

"What is that perfume?" he asked, sniffing her shoulder.

"Do you like it?"

"Very much. It reminds me of something…"

"What?"

"That's the thing. I can't put my finger on it. It's familiar in a funny way, but I can't say from where. Is it French?"

Nagiko laughed. "Hardly," she said. "It's a traditional kind of body incense, called zukō. My grandmother used it. My mother didn't like it— reminded her of old clothes stored in cupboards, she said. Anyway, it's got sandalwood, camphor, cloves—the same sort of stuff that's in incense. It probably smells like temples to you."

"Yes—exactly!" he said, "Well, not exactly. It's not smoky—but yes, there is something about it that…"

"I think most men might be turned off by something that smells of temples," said Nagiko.

"Mmmm. Not me," replied Philip.

Nagiko brushed her hair off her cheek. "No, you're strange that way." She smiled at him.

Tokyo in October. Philip had never felt so alive. Now he truly understood the intense Japanese preoccupation with spring and fall. A September typhoon had swept away the last remnants of summer, leaving crisp dry days with bright blue skies. It was as if all his senses had awakened. On his pilgrimage, Philip had gradually learned how to pay attention. He came to understand what it felt like to be aware instead of self-absorbed. Maintaining the same awareness in Tokyo was a lot harder. Yet being with Nagiko put him in a state that he had never felt before. When he tried to describe it to Jun, the older man listened for a while, until he finally stopped him and said,

"Philip...this is called 'being in love.'"

"Oh," said Philip. Then, "Any advice?"

"None whatsoever," said Muranaka with a shrug, "enjoy it while it lasts."

Although Nagiko teased Philip about his interest in the hidden buddhas, she was gradually becoming interested. Professor Maigny had sent a fat envelope with a detailed list of all the temples he knew had hidden buddhas. He included a map of Japan with red dots indicating their locations. His theory was that the pattern on the map itself formed a kind of geographical mandala, with Mount Kōya at its center. Maigny wondered whether the pattern itself might be meaningful. Since the "eternally meditating" Kūkai is at the heart of Mt. Kōya, Kūkai himself, logically, could be considered the ultimate *hibutsu*—one that is never shown.

What the implications of this observation were, Maigny did not say. Philip was eager to engage him further. He wrote to ask him Kōji's question whether *hibutsu* are unique to Japan. Maigny's response came on sheets of onionskin rather than his usual thin blue aerogram.

> *There is,* he wrote, *a Chinese version of the word* hibutsu, *but it is not the same thing as what you find in Japan. In the Tang era in China, each day of the month was assigned a "secret buddha"— rather like a patron saint. But this custom died out. In any case, the*

Chinese concept was somewhat abstract, whereas the hibutsu *in Japan are quite physical, and quite individual. I encourage you to view as many of them as you possibly can while you are there.*

Yours,
Bertrand Maigny

p.s. If it is not too much trouble, when you are in Kyoto next, could you purchase a small packet of seaweed tea, and send it by air? I am afraid it would absorb moisture and get musty if it were sent by sea mail. Merci.

Nagiko was coming to Philip's apartment for the first time. When he invited her, Philip vowed to make an entire gourmet dinner on his hotplate.

"You must come, even if just out of curiosity."

"Well, okay," she agreed. "To see a graduate student cook something other than instant ramen or curry rice on a hotplate would be a novelty."

Philip liked to cook. He regarded his single burner as a challenge. It almost felt like cheating that the rice cooker was on a separate plug. He bought beef, vegetables, and red wine at a specialty grocer in the morning and began preparing them for boeuf bourguignon in the afternoon. By evening, his tiny apartment smelled like an authentic bistro. He opened the sliding glass door to his three-foot square balcony, only to have the neighbor who was watering her bonsai collection on the adjoining balcony inhale the aromas and ask wistfully what he was making for dinner.

The door buzzer sounded. Philip took one more look around. Spotless room, low table (otherwise known as his desk) now covered with a white cloth and candles, a bottle of Burgundy (more expensive than the one he had used for cooking), salads composed and resting in the refrigerator next to the grapes, which had already been washed. A fat disk of odorous Epoisses cheese, which most Japanese would find totally repugnant—but that he was sure Nagiko would appreciate—sat on the counter, its creamy soft interior slowly relaxing into its brandy-bathed rind.

He buzzed her in to the lobby, then jammed his feet into a pair of broken-backed tennis shoes to walk out to the elevator.

She carried a wrapped bouquet of chrysanthemums in various colors.

"Hi," she said. "Sorry to be so late."

Philip led the way along the outside corridor to his door, which he had propped open with a boot.

"This is it. Pretty small, I know..."

"No smaller than my place," she remarked, removing her shoes and setting them at the edge of the step up to the kitchen.

"Really?" said Philip.

"And much neater," she remarked, taking in the setting Philip had gone to such pains to prepare. She sniffed the air.

"What have you made? It smells wonderful. I am back in France!" She moved toward the pot simmering on the single burner. "May I?"

"Of course..." Philip lifted the lid with a flourish. It did smell good, he had to admit. She remembered the flowers.

"Here let me put these in water. They're like carp, these chrysanthemums—they can live a long time without water. Still, might as well perk them up. Do you have clippers?"

Philip didn't.

"That's okay, I'll just slice their stems with the chef's knife. Vase?"

He didn't have a vase either. She arranged them in an empty teapot. He poured two glasses of wine.

Nagiko sniffed the air again, until her eye caught sight of the salmon-colored round of cheese near the sink.

"I don't believe it!" she turned to look at Philip. "I didn't think it was possible to find Epoisses in Tokyo. Where did you..."

"Loved by Napoleon and Louis XIV both," he said.

"And me," added Nagiko. "How could you possibly have guessed?"

"You have good taste," Philip said.

"I think I have good taste in men, anyway..." she replied. She noticed Maigny's map of Japan marked with red dots lying spread out on top of the bookcase.

"What's this?" she asked. "Japan has measles?"

Philip looked up from the savory pot he was slowly stirring. "Oh, it's more *hibutsu* stuff from my professor in France. He's mapped out where all the hidden buddhas in Japan are."

"That's interesting," mumbled Nagiko, picking up the map. "It looks like there are some right around Tokyo. What a surprise." She was suddenly and uncomfortably reminded of Fudō-in. What would Philip think if he knew about the *mizuko*? She saw no need to bring it up.

"We should talk about what we're going to do in Kyoto..." she said instead.

"You mean you can come?" Philip leapt up to refill her wineglass. He had resigned himself to the probability that she'd be too busy. "That's great!"

Nagiko hadn't actually decided until that moment, but seeing Philip's enthusiastic face, she was glad she'd agreed. She needed a vacation.

Drenched in Love

THEY HAD RESERVED SEATS on an early bullet train leaving Tokyo Station. Nagiko pulled the collar of her coat tightly to her throat as October wind whipped down the stairway to the train platform. Shielding her eyes from the dust-laden eddies that gusted capriciously off the tracks, she looked around for Philip. There would only be three minutes for passengers to board when the train pulled up.

She caught sight of his dark brown hair, bobbing toward her above a sea of shiny black. "Nagiko!" He waved his hand. She waved back, noting that several people glanced over to see who would respond. For a moment she saw herself through the eyes of the middle-aged businessmen beginning to queue between the yellow lines. Nagiko shrugged it off. She was confident that Philip wouldn't do anything as gauche as try to take her hand or hug her. He had been in Japan long enough to understand how to behave. He stopped in front of her and dipped in a proper bow.

"Kiyowara-san. *Ohayō gozaimasu.*"

Nagiko smiled and bowed back. The businessmen who a moment ago had satisfied themselves that as men of the world they could judge the relationship of a pair of strangers at a glance were confused. And then everyone forgot these half-conscious perceptions as the train came gliding heavily along the track to its appointed roost. With a hiss, doors slid open and they boarded.

"Have you had breakfast?" Philip asked once they had found their seats and gotten settled.

"No, there was nothing in the house, not even coffee," she replied. "Besides I like egg salad sandwiches for breakfast."

The sleek-snouted bullet train picked up speed as it passed through Tokyo, overtaking boxy local commuter trains. Soon it was speeding past row after row of identical apartment blocks called Mansions. In the past, one could have gazed over broad plains, maybe catching a view of Mt. Fuji in the far distance if the day was clear. But modern Tokyo simply sprawled on, low and endless.

The door at the end of the compartment opened and the coffee-and-ice-cream girl, dressed in a starchy pink and white uniform, bowlegs in bobbysocks, pushed her cart along the center aisle, proclaiming her goods in a ritualized sing-song voice that seemed to emerge from the back of her throat. Nagiko stopped her and purchased two coffees.

Now the train was gliding past green fields and vegetable gardens with long undulating strips of blue plastic insulation covering tender cabbages and young radishes. Every so often a cluster of houses or a temple would come into view and then disappear. As she sipped her coffee, Nagiko gazed at the unscrolling countryside. Then, there it was, like a painted backdrop tacked up on the sky—

"Look, Philip—Mt. Fuji!" she plucked the sleeve of his shirt.

"Unreal," he said. "The Japan Tourist Bureau should be commended for such an amazing piece of outdoor art."

Mt. Fuji had a new snowcap, gleaming pristinely over a single cloud that hovered humbly beneath its summit. As they watched, Fujisan, too, passed from view.

Philip noticed how they were never out of sight of buildings, yet little mountains stuck up out of the plain, wooded and green, apparently untouched by cultivation. He pointed this out to Nagiko.

"I love that about this country," he said. "No matter how modern everything seems, pockets of the past are hidden everywhere."

The door between train cars hissed open again, and the pink-and-white girl was back, this time with a tray supported by straps around her neck.

"Sandwiches. Box lunches. Tea."

Philip waved her over and bought Nagiko a dainty box containing six fingers of sandwich—invariably two ham-and-mustard, two cucumber, and two egg salad. Then he bought another box for himself.

"Here, I'll trade my egg for your cucumber," he said. "It's too long till lunch."

"Okay," said Nagiko, unwrapping the wax paper lining inside the box. "This reminds me of grade school." She could feel herself starting to relax, and she was grateful to Philip. It was not possible to be casual with her colleagues, or with the men in her business. Even as Nagiko's assistants looked to her for direction, they expected her to remain somewhat aloof. Most of her classmates were now married, deeply embedded in the scholastic needs of their children. Nagiko had no hobbies. She worked like a man, paying little attention to anything but her job, designing fabrics. But men at least had the after-hours, the cozy bars and elegant clubs with attendant hostesses, where they could unwind. A feeling of freedom washed over her. She realized she hadn't felt like this since she left New York. She put her head on Philip's shoulder and allowed herself to fall asleep.

She was on vacation for the first time since—she couldn't remember when. Best of all, she could share someone else's world and someone else's obsessions—Philip's world, his enthusiasm for beautiful things, even his fascination with those strange hidden buddhas. The maples of Kyoto's gardens awaited. She was looking forward to viewing them with Philip more than she dared admit.

They arrived at Kyoto station. Philip hailed the taxi driver in his best Kyoto accent and asked him to take them to the Tawaraya Ryokan. Nagiko was stunned. This famous inn was one of the oldest and most expensive in Kyoto.

"Philip!"

He smiled. "I'm really looking forward to this."

She opened her mouth to say something, but he interrupted.

"No, I've never been there before. But a friend of mine told me this would be the best place to bring a special person—someone who would really appreciate it." (Cackling when he realized why Philip asked him about a nice inn, Kōji had told him about the Tawaraya. Philip had decided against introducing Nagiko to Kōji on this trip.)

They left their bags at Tawaraya in the center of the city, then walked toward the eastern hills, crossing over the Sanjō Bridge, heading to a tofu restaurant Philip knew. They sat outside on a low platform with a gas jet built into the table, where Philip ordered the specialty casserole of tofu and vegetables. When the waitress brought the pot, she naturally handed a pair of cooking chopsticks and spoon to Nagiko. But as soon as she left, Philip took over.

"Allow me," he said.

Nagiko smiled. "You really like to cook, don't you?"

"I do. I don't understand why Japanese men aren't more into it."

Snowy fresh tofu, sliced scallions, three kinds of mushrooms. They ate slowly.

"Are you tired?" Philip asked.

"No, I'm just unwinding," said Nagiko. "Ever since I won that award your friend Muranaka dreamed up it's been pretty intense at the company. Visitors to the office, interviews, lots of new orders…I'm not complaining, but it's been kind of frantic."

"Let's walk over to Nanzenji," said Philip. "Have you ever seen the rock garden?"

"The famous leaping tiger rocks? No, I've never been there. Are there maples too?"

"Of course."

They left the restaurant and walked south toward Nanzenji.

"Any hidden buddhas here?" Nagiko asked.

"No," said Philip. "They're not really a Zen thing. They seem to be found pretty much only in the esoteric sects, mostly Shingon. I've been trying to figure out what happened to start this tradition of hiding buddhas in Japan. It's got to have something to do with Kūkai, I'm sure. Buddhism was already established in Japan before Kūkai, but there don't seem to have been any *hibutsu* before him. But it's not as if Kūkai told his followers to start wrapping up statues. I'm guessing now that…Nagiko, are you really interested in any of this?"

Philip knew that once started talking about his obsession he could go on indefinitely. Kōji would listen to him for only so long before yawning a huge mock yawn and pretending to fall off a chair. He knew Nagiko would not be so crude, but he was afraid of boring her.

"No—it's fascinating," she protested. "I never learned anything about Buddhist history, and I've kind of gotten interested in it recently in any case. Before I met you, even…"The *mizuko* briefly floated up in her mind.

"Okay, well stop me if you're bored. So, I've been trying to figure out what was going on at that time…"

"Excuse me, Philip, what century are we talking about? I'm really hopeless at history…"Now Nagiko tucked her arm into his as they strolled down the narrow side streets toward Nanzenji.

"Sorry. Early ninth century. One thing that happened then was that this huge wave of Buddhism came in from China and Korea. At this point

Buddhism started to put down deeper roots in Japan. Much of that was due to Kūkai. In Shingon there is one supreme cosmic Buddha..."

"Sorry, which one is that?"

"Dainichi, the Sun Buddha. And the idea is that the whole universe and everything in it is a manifestation of this supreme cosmic Buddha."

"So all the other buddhas, and bodhisattvas like Guan Yin and Jizō are manifestations of the Sun Buddha?"

"Everything is. Every action, every thought, every word. Everybody. You, me, Bob Dylan, that Maltese terrier across the street over there. Everything."

Nagiko laughed.

"And," continued Philip, "this meant that the old Shinto gods could be considered manifestations of the supreme Buddha, too. Shinto deities and buddhas got mixed together around this time..."

"Ninth century..."

"Right. This was fine with Kūkai. He encouraged it. But the upshot was that things inherent to Shinto were blended into Buddhist rituals."

"Like what?" Nagiko was beginning to see a connection.

"Well, right around this time you start reading about statues with miraculous powers—healing powers, in particular. And you find that these images had been carved out of special trees that themselves had magical power. The trees were especially big, or especially old, or had been struck by lightning, or something. What does this sound like to you?"

"It sounds like the kinds of trees that in Shinto you would mark off with sacred ropes," said Nagiko.

"Exactly. The Shinto focus on the sacred spirit of natural objects now gets folded into the creation of a Buddhist image. And there's something else about Shinto..."

"Yes?"

"Ever go inside a Shinto shrine?"

"Of course."

"What do you see?"

"What do you mean, what do you see?"

"What does it consist of? A statue? A painting? An image of a Shinto god? Or what about the household shrine? I'm sure your family had one tucked up on a high shelf near the kitchen when you were growing up?"

Nagiko pictured her grandmother's house in Kanazawa. "Well, there's that little cabinet with closed doors..."

"Precisely," said Philip. "In Shinto shrines, the holy image—whatever it is, a mirror, or whatever—is hidden behind the doors of that little cabinet. It's powerful precisely because it's hidden. Or the amulets you get now. They are little wrapped packets are they not?"

"Usually, yes…"

"Ever unwrap one?"

"It never occurred to me."

"Of course not," said Philip. "You would feel very strange doing that. It would be sacrilegious, wouldn't it?"

Nagiko thought about it. It was true, she couldn't imagine opening up one of those amulets.

"There's nothing in them," said Philip.

Nagiko looked at him in surprise. "You opened one?"

"Several. Out of curiosity. Hiddenness is the whole point. If opened, there's nothing—the power simply vanishes. This Shinto idea that the deepest spiritual power is hidden is very strong…"

"Oh, you mean, just like…"

"The hidden buddhas," Philip nodded. "I think that was why you start finding *hibutsu* after Buddhism absorbed all those Shinto gods."

"What does your professor say about this?" Nagiko asked him.

"I haven't written him about it yet," said Philip. "I'm still sort of thinking it through. But it's kind of exciting…" He threw his head back. "God, you must think I'm a total weirdo. We don't need to talk about this."

They had arrived at the entrance to the gardens of Nanzenji. Nagiko called Philip's attention to a huge leafy maple that was still totally green except for a single bright red leaf.

"Look at that," she said. "A weirdo leaf…" then, "Look how beautiful it is." She squeezed his hand.

"So," she continued, "tomorrow we're going to Nara to see this *hibutsu* at the Saidaiji temple, right?"

Philip nodded. "If you're still interested…"

"Want to tell me about it?"

"Oh, let's have it be a surprise."

The crowds had thinned now in late afternoon as tourists hurried back to waiting buses. Philip looked at his watch.

"Let's try one more. There are so many temples here, so many gardens, yet people all crowd into just the famous ones. Here, for example…"

They had slipped down a side street and through a small temple gate. No one was there. They bought their entrance tickets from an impassive old woman who reminded them tersely that the garden would close in twenty-five minutes.

This garden had a wide pond with a low slab bridge that broke into individual steps as it neared the other side. Philip crouched down at the center of the bridge and extended his hand out over the water. Immediately a swarm of huge carp came thrashing up from the edges of the pond. They thrust their monstrous heads right out of the water, smacking noisily. Nagiko was reminded of the carp at Fudō-in. At the same time it occurred to her that she could think about the *mizuko* and not be bothered by it any more. She could even talk about bodhisattvas and not feel guilty.

"They think you have food," she reproached Philip. "That's mean…"

"But I do…" he said, reaching into his pocket and pulling out one of the train sandwiches that he had wrapped in a paper napkin.

"You've been carrying that around since this morning?" Nagiko was incredulous.

"You never know when you'll meet a hungry carp," Philip said calmly, breaking off tidbits and dropping them precisely into the gaping mouths. "Here, want to try?"

Nagiko shook her head. Then she laughed. Just as they were retracing their steps toward the entrance, they saw the old woman lumbering around a corner of the building, obviously coming to shoo them out. Luckily she had not seen Philip feeding the carp. Instinctively they inclined their upper bodies in a walking bow as they headed to the gate without slowing their steps. They could almost hear her silent harrumph as she bolted it after them. On the street Nagiko giggled. Philip poked her in the ribs as she danced away from him, pushing his hand back. He caught up to her and put his arms around her waist, swinging her around.

"Help, help!" she gasped, still laughing.

"Up for walking back?" he asked, "or shall we get a cab?"

"Let's walk!" she exclaimed. "Do we have time?"

"Just depends on how long you want to steep in the tub before dinner…"

When they arrived at the Tawaraya, their things had already been taken to the room. Philip had expected a small room, cozy and old-fashioned. He was amazed when their hostess slid open a door to a broad expanse of tatami mats, facing a lovely private garden. A single low table with two large square cushions was all the visible furniture. Tawaraya's mostly Japanese clientele, even very wealthy people, came from small houses crammed with all manner of stuff. In fact, the wealthier they were, the more likely their living rooms would be bursting with expensive objects. For them, the ultimate luxury was empty space.

A maid brought a pot of tea with some Kyoto-style dry sweets. Nagiko poured them each a cup as they sat quietly.

"Why don't you go ahead and take a bath before dinner?" Philip offered.

Nagiko emerged forty-five minutes later with damp hair, wearing the dark-blue and white cotton yukata supplied by the inn.

"I'm sorry I took so long," she said, touching Philip's shoulder as she glided barefoot past the table.

"That's okay," he said. "I'll take a quick shower now, and soak after dinner."

Philip came back in ten minutes, also with damp hair, also wearing the inn's trademark yukata. They heard movement outside the door. A voice called, "May I bring in dinner?"

Nagiko set the cushions on either side of the table as Philip called out, "Dōzo!" The maid slid open the door, reached back for the footed tray she had brought, set it down in the room, closed the door, then picked up the tray again and brought it to the table.

"It's the Kyoto way," whispered Nagiko. "Not terribly efficient, but it's considered manners." The maid bowed. Then she set out two pairs of chopsticks with tiny ceramic pillows to rest the tips on, two skinny beer glasses, and saké cups. She opened a large bottle of beer and poured for each of them, Philip first.

"I'll be back with the appetizer course," she said with a bow. Then she reversed her way out of the room, tray down, door open, tray up, tray down, door closed.

"Is she going to do that every time?" marveled Philip. This was his first formal *kaiseki* meal.

"Of course."

"But aren't there about twenty courses or something to this dinner?"

"I don't think quite that many..."

"But still…a lot. Whew."

"Yes, it's very hard work being so proper."

"And she makes it look so effortless—down, up, down, up, down…"

"Philip!"

"Sorry…it's kind of mesmerizing."

Nagiko remembered her grandmother showing her the proper way to enter a traditional-style room when she was a little girl. It was a skill that Nagiko had never had to use in her adult life. Of course you saw this kind of thing more in Kyoto, where traditional architecture was so prized, and people preserved the old ways. It would never have struck Nagiko as funny until she saw it through Philip's eyes.

The maid came back with a tray containing four pairs of small dishes. Now aware of the woman's movements, Nagiko had to look away and bite her lip to keep from smiling. Philip, in contrast, watched gravely as she arranged the plates in front of them, announced the ingredients in each, then refilled the beer glasses. Again, she left them alone.

"So, what is all this again? I'm not used to such fancy fare…"

"This one is squid pickled in the stuff that settles at the bottom of the cask when you brew saké."

"Ah," said Philip.

"And this is eel with black sesame sauce," she said picking up a dish in the shape of a maple leaf. "And this, I believe she said smoked salmon with okra and salmon caviar."

"I once had an argument with a friend who insisted that *okura* was a native Japanese vegetable," said Philip, thinking of the stupid things he used to argue with Kōji about.

"And here we have radish and cucumber shreds with chrysanthemum petals," said Nagiko. "It's pretty, isn't it?"

"Yeah, that one I could probably make," said Philip.

"Well, *bon appetit…*"

"*Itadakimasu…*"

They nibbled their way through each tiny portion, savoring the delicately different combinations of flavor and texture.

"I would love to be able to cook like this," said Philip, dabbing at the last shred of eel. "Maybe someday I'll take a *kaiseki* cooking class…do you suppose that's possible?"

"If you do, I think I would marry you," replied Nagiko.

"Well," said Philip, "That settles it."

Nagiko laughed and rolled her eyes. The maid came back, sliding the door open again.

Kaiseki was served in courses that reminded Philip of the movements of a symphony. They had now finished the prelude. The next course was the "raw" movement. It consisted of sashimi-sliced halibut with grated radish and a drizzle of citrus sauce. This was followed by the grilled course, which in this case had two parts: a long rectangular plate bearing a charbroiled headless freshwater trout, its belly full of tiny eggs, garnished with a pen of ginger shoot. It was accompanied by a round black dish displaying six roasted ginkgo nuts skewered on pine needles.

The simmered course followed. Each time, the maid removed the dishes that were empty, although she left them if even a single morsel remained. The simmered items were presented in bowls, one lidded and one open. The open bowl was meant to be room temperature.

"Soy-simmered mountain yam, mushrooms, greens," she announced.

The lidded bowl was hot.

"Miso-simmered duck with wheat gluten and scallions. Specialty of the Tawaraya. For autumn."

They ate.

"How many more courses are there?" Philip asked Nagiko.

"I think one more, plus the rice course, and maybe dessert," she said. "Are you getting full?"

"Well, I am, but I could also go on like this all night, I'm afraid..." he said. "My God! This is fabulous!"

"It is," she agreed. "And so are you...thank you..." She leaned over the table and kissed him.

The door slid open again, and the maid averted her eyes as Nagiko quickly sat back on her cushion.

"Beef with white miso sauce," she said, placing a square celadon plate in front of each of them.

"Scallops with tomato vinegar." This on a dark brown round plate with a small lip.

"This must be the vinegared course," whispered Nagiko.

It was finally followed by the course technically called "the meal"—in other words, rice. They had been eating for three hours, but at such a leisurely rate that they did not feel at all stuffed. The last course was announced—

deizaato, the maid called it. A sorbet of Japanese crystal pear with an Italian amaretto cookie, if they would like. It was the first time they had been given a choice all evening.

"Yes, please," said Philip. He asked her if the dessert course was part of the original *kaiseki* sequence.

"No, it's not," she replied, clearing off all the remaining dishes. "But people nowadays seem to want it so we make one up."

"Nagiko?"

"Of course!"

The sorbets appeared—pale snowballs beginning to puddle in frosted footed cups of dark green glass. The amaretto cookie was the color of pear skin. Philip dragged his cushion to Nagiko's side of the table as they ate the icy essence of pear, pressed side to side.

"Here, you take this last bit," she said suddenly, and as Philip turned toward her, she scooped up the last bite into her mouth and then pressed her mouth against his. Cold sweet pear melted into a warm lingering kiss. Philip dropped his spoon, and reached around Nagiko's back. He started to slide the cotton yukata off her shoulders.

"Excuse me…" The maid was back to move the table and spread out the bedding.

Coughing and shuffling, Philip and Nagiko drew apart and straightened out the sashes on their yukatas.

"*Chotto matte kudasai*," Philip called, giving Nagiko a chance to neaten her sash. He tried to appear nonchalant.

Nagiko stood up.

"Let's go to the bath," she said. "You didn't have a chance to take a proper soak. And this time, I can scrub your back."

They slept late, a novelty for both of them. Nagiko rolled over on top of Philip and began tickling his eyelashes with the tip of her tongue.

"Oof," he groaned, then flipped her over and pinioned her wrists to the futon while he attempted to do the same to her. She thrashed her head from side to side trying to avoid his tongue.

"You know," she said breathlessly, trying to distract him, "you have incredibly long eyelashes. I wish I had eyelashes like yours…"

"Really?" said Philip. He lifted his head back.

"Yes," said Nagiko, trying to wiggle out of his hold and keep him talking.

Both their yukatas lay crumpled somewhere in the tangle of sheets. "Long, curly eyelashes—just like a girl…"

She squealed as he clamped his arm across her waist.

"Just like a girl, you say?" He rubbed his sandpapery cheek down the side of her face and neck as she struggled to evade the stubble. "Take it back!"

"Ow, stop…not like a girl…"

Philip was now curled around Nagiko from the back. He buried his nose in her hair, "You smell so good," he murmured, and she relaxed as he softly ran his hands over her breasts and down her body. "So soft," he continued to nuzzle his fingers further into her damp crevasse. "So melty…"

She sighed.

"Mmmm, just like a ripe Epoisses cheese…"

"You are the funniest man I've ever met," laughed Nagiko, turning around and straddling him. "I thought it was supposed to smell like fish…"

"Cheese, fish—it's all good," gasped Philip, as he grasped Nagiko's slender hips and pulled her down.

They lay side by side, breathing slowly. Philip glanced at the clock.

"Yipes, breakfast will be here in ten minutes. We'd better find our robes…"

Breakfast was elaborate but, unlike dinner, it came all at the same time. Two maids padded up to the door with a cheerful *Ohayō gozaimasu*, each bearing a lacquer tray with seven dishes of different colors and shapes, all with intriguing tidbits of fish, egg, seaweed, and vegetable. They put them down and with practiced efficiency folded up the bedding and moved the table back to the center of the room. Nagiko was taking a shower. Philip sat down as one of the maids arranged the trays. The other came back momentarily with a wooden container of rice and a pot of tea.

"Shall I serve the rice?" she asked.

"That's okay—we'll serve ourselves," Philip told her.

She bowed and left the room, leaving Philip to contemplate the art form that was their breakfast and marvel at the fact that he could feel hungry again after last night's feast. Nagiko returned to find him peeking under the lid of the covered bowl of miso soup.

They took a local train to nearby Nara, a city even older than Kyoto, full of Buddhist temples, including Tōdaiji, the "Great Eastern Temple" with its famous huge seated Buddha. Tourists all headed to Tōdaiji, but Philip and Nagiko were headed toward Tōdaiji's much less famous twin, the "Great Western Temple," Saidaiji.

"So now will you tell me about the hidden buddha we're going to see?" asked Nagiko.

"Sure. It's the Buddhist love god."

"Come on. There's no such thing."

"You really don't know any of this stuff?" Philip asked her.

"I've only been to a Buddhist temple once, for my father's funeral when I was eleven."

"But aren't you from Kanazawa? Home of the famous Ninja temple?"

"Well, yes," she admitted, "but that's just a tourist attraction now. Okay, so I've been there, too. And, let's see, I've been to Kamakura..." her voice trailed off vaguely.

"The Great Buddha of Kamakura," said Philip. "You know, I've still not seen it. It's such a cliché of Japan, I expect it will be kind of a let-down when I finally do."

"It might surprise you," said Nagiko. "When I went to Paris and saw the Eiffel Tower for the first time, I was really thrilled. Of course it is the cliché of Paris, but to actually see the real thing after all those pictures—well, it's like your brain is primed to experience it. Maybe it's the same with these hidden buddhas, you know?"

"How so?" Philip asked.

"Actually, I guess it would be the opposite. When you see something all the time, ever notice how you stop seeing it? Like artwork on the walls of your living room—after a while you just forget about it. I mean, you'd notice if somebody stole it, of course. But it just stops registering, if you know what I mean."

"Sure. That's what so great about the *tokonoma* in a Japanese room, where you change the paintings all the time. Or flower arrangements..."

Nagiko smiled as she thought of her friend Satoko's passionate hatred for silk flowers. "They don't die," she had said. "That's the problem with them..."

"So, these hidden buddhas of yours—because they aren't on display all the time, people really look at them when they are. It's a great idea, I think." Nagiko remembered an old saying. "Do you know the expression *'kakusu mono wa mitai?'*"

Philip laughed. "The hidden thing is the thing we want to see? No, I never heard that. Pretty good…"

Nagiko had a sudden inspiration. "It's like in a nudist camp—when everybody is naked, nothing is erotic. But as soon as you start hiding things, they become interesting…"

"I've noticed that," said Philip. "Although naked can be pretty erotic, too…" He ran his finger along the rim of her ear.

"Aren't there any hidden buddhas in Kamakura?" Nagiko asked, changing the subject.

"Not that I know of," said Philip. "At least there weren't any on the list my professor sent me."

"Okay, so who is the Buddhist Cupid we're going to see?" asked Nagiko.

"It's one of the mystic kings. Aizen."

Nagiko fell forward in mock disbelief. "Aizen! You're kidding!"

"Nope."

"The god of love? Are we thinking of the same person?"

"Using the term loosely…"

"Three eyes? Six arms? A lion in his hair? Red skin? Fangs…"

"Bow and arrow," said Philip. "Just like Cupid…'Aizen'—think about it, it means 'drenched in love'…"

"But, but…" Nagiko floundered.

"See, you do know something about this," Philip beamed.

"Well, everybody knows when you say Fudō or Aizen, it's those demon guys who guard the temples…but, god of love?"

"Yes, exactly. Fudō is another. In Shingon, Fudō is in charge of spirit or mind—subjective knowledge. He has the sword that cuts through ignorance. Aizen is the physical world and objective truth. Together Fudō and Aizen represent all of reality, as embodied in the Great Sun Buddha, Dainichi—whose great big statue is the one sitting over at the other temple, by the way.

"Oh," said Nagiko, "Is that who that is…you know, Philip, this is all rather complicated…"

Philip sighed, removing his arm from her shoulder. "Not everybody shares my fascination, I know…"

She stroked his hand. "It's just a lot to remember. But it's interesting—really." She grazed her fingers over his cheek, across his lower lip.

"So, how does Aizen get to be the god of love? Personally, I find those sweet little Italian putti a lot more appealing."

"Well, I think it's because Aizen is the force of eros, the way the Greeks thought of it. The energy of desire, which also happens to be the life force. Aizen is supposed to convert physical passion into spiritual awakening."

"I see…" said Nagiko.

"Oh, stop," said Philip. "You were going to make some smart remark, weren't you?"

"Well, I could see how one might…but I won't," she added hastily.

"You see, what's so interesting about Shingon," Philip went on," is this whole emphasis on the non-duality of body and mind. I think this is what has absorbed Professor Maigny all these years—the idea that, when truly understood, nirvana is not something separate from the reality of the world—it *is* the world. That's the understanding that Fudō represents. And 'enlightenment' doesn't mean getting rid of passion, it means truly understanding its energy. That's what Aizen is."

Nagiko didn't say anything.

"I have a friend," said Philip, "who tells me that Aizen is especially worshipped by the geisha because he saves people from the pain of falling in love."

"Is it painful?" asked Nagiko, turning to him and holding his hand more tightly.

"It could be," said Philip slowly, "very painful, I should think…"

The statue of Aizen stood in its own building, separate from the main hall. They stepped inside. To their surprise a tea ceremony gathering of about thirty people was in progress. They skirted their way around the group, which at this point was noisily socializing rather than appreciating tea. When they got to the altar itself, they saw the doors of the shrine opened to reveal a surprisingly small figure of Aizen sitting on a lotus blossom that looked more like an artichoke with its top cut off. The Aizen was very red, and very angry looking.

"If you ask me," muttered Nagiko, "he looks like the god of little boys who throw tantrums..." She turned to Philip, expecting him to mock scold her, or at least smile at her joke, but his eyes were closed, and he seemed a bit unsteady on his feet.

"Philip?"

He put his hand to his forehead. "My head...I don't feel so..." He started to waver.

Nagiko grabbed hold of him. "Philip!" The panic in her voice caused people nearby to look over.

"Is everything all right?" someone asked.

Philip was leaning heavily on Nagiko now, and she felt her knees buckling under his weight.

"No," she called out, trying to stay calm. "Can somebody please help me take him outside?" Two older men stood up and got on either side of them. Together they propelled Philip's legs toward the entrance and down the steps. They managed to seat him on a bench.

"Maybe we should call a doctor, Miss?" they said to Nagiko, eyeing Philip, who still hadn't opened his eyes. She thanked them but said she thought he'd be fine in a few minutes of fresh air. They assumed she meant he had a hangover, so they didn't insist. Several curious heads could be seen looking out from the hall.

"Philip? Are you okay?" She whispered.

"I'm okay." He opened his eyes to a squint. "Sorry...I don't know what... my head just suddenly felt like it was being squeezed from the inside..."

"Just take it easy," Nagiko stroked his head. "We can sit here for a while."

An old woman emerged from the building carrying a bowl of thick green tea. She came over to them and directing her remarks to Nagiko, said, "Let him drink this, it will help."

"Thank you..." Nagiko put her head down toward Philip's ear.

"Philip? Can you drink?

"I think so." He took the bowl in two hands and sat up slowly. Nagiko's hands fluttered anxiously nearby in case it seemed he would drop the teabowl. But he didn't. On his last sip, he even lowered the bowl and ran his forefinger and thumb over the rim where his lips had touched. The old woman laughed appreciatively—the *gaijin* knew tea ceremony rules! Wait till her friends heard about this! With a bow, she took the bowl and scuttled back up the steps.

"What is it?" asked Nagiko, clutching Philip's hand. "What happened?"

"I'm not sure," he said, rubbing his eyes. "I'm better now…"

He coughed. "Wow, that tea is thick," he croaked. "Do you suppose you could find some water somewhere?"

"Sure. There's a vending machine just over by the main temple. I'll run over and get a bottle. Will you be okay? I'll be right back." Nagiko seemed relieved to be able to do something.

"Yeah, I'll be fine," Philip said with another cough.

She stood up, fumbling for her purse. Philip watched her walk toward the main hall, the hem of her black skirt twitching with each quick step. She turned around anxiously to look at him, so he smiled at her and waved. She was almost running now. The pain had disappeared the same way it had come on. And then she was back with a bottle of chilled water, unscrewing the cap, holding it out.

"Thanks." Philip took a long drink. "I'm much better now. It was probably just all that unaccustomed physical activity…"

He sounded better. Nagiko sat down next to him, trembling a little.

"Philip…"

"Here, want some water?" he offered her the bottle.

He saw that her lip was quivering.

"Nagiko…"

She burst into tears. Philip put his arms around her until, after one last hiccup, she became quiet.

He thought that he didn't want to be saved from the pain of falling in love.

A Dog Is a Dog

THE HEAD PRIEST OF FUDŌ-IN KNEW that his assistant Tokuda liked to travel, especially in the spring and autumn. He was aware that Tokuda's parents were getting older, and as their only child, he was obliged to visit them often, but unfortunately, April and October were also two of the busiest months for *mizuko* clients. Really, did he have to be away so much right at this season? Perhaps he was a little too fond of viewing cherry blossoms? He broached the idea that Tokuda might postpone his trips to less hectic times. Tokuda listened politely, wordlessly, to the head priest's not unreasonable request, but as the older man finished talking, relieved at the lack of resistance, Tokuda said,

"It's impossible."

The head priest was taken aback. No offering of extenuating circumstances—not even the regretful sucking in of breath that would indicate a perception of inconvenience. No explanation at all. Well, he could hardly order him to stay put—what if he left Fudō-in? Most of the *mizuko* clients came here through friends' referrals, and the grave and handsome priest Noboru Tokuda was definitely part of what attracted them.

"If you'll excuse me, then..." Tokuda bowed, and the mystified head priest acquiesced.

Tokuda had six *hibutsu* to assess—three in Kyoto, two in Shiga, and one in Nara.

Philip and Nagiko said goodbye at Tokyo Station. It was late afternoon by the time he got back to his apartment. Philip glanced through the mail as he waited for the elevator. Some bills, a thin letter from his mother in California, a thick one from Professor Maigny. Dragging his feet, he nodded a greeting to his bonsai-keeping neighbor, then undid his double locks, dropped his bag, and mechanically put the kettle on his only burner to make tea. He was trying to mentally gear up for the long letter he planned to write Maigny about his idea that Shinto concepts of hidden divinity had been responsible for the origin of the *hibutsu*. Not tonight, though. He was exhausted. He read his mother's letter over quickly. All was fine back in San Anselmo. Was he okay? They missed him. Love.

He hadn't written and was feeling guilty. Tomorrow. Now Maigny. Philip carefully slit the envelope open and took out several thin sheets of paper, typed single-space.

> *Dear Philippe,*
>
> *The air of autumn is finally breaking the summer heat but I confess at this time of year I miss the maples of Japan. I hope you are enjoying them. I have read your accounts of the temples you have visited. I wonder if you remember back in my office in New York when you first came to me for advice? I mentioned something about Kūkai. Perhaps you may have felt that I was holding something back.*

Philip took a sip of his tea. He remembered very well. "But that's not the most interesting thing about Kūkai…" Maigny had said, trailing off into some reverie as Philip waited for him to continue. He hadn't continued, though. Philip was suddenly not tired any more.

> *I feel it is time that I revealed to you my thoughts and frustration in trying to pull together my life's work on Shingon. You may indeed be the person who can best build on what I have deduced over the course of my career.*

It had not been easy for Maigny to write this letter. It brought back memories of his first trip to Japan after the war. He was not much older than Philip was now, but he had been a shattered man. His mother and father, his wife, had all been murdered at Auschwitz-Birkenau. He felt there was nothing for him back in France—or in Europe, for that matter. Since there was nothing compelling him to be anywhere, he chose Japan. The reason was simple yet profound. He saw a map of Japan sprinkled with swastikas. Disgust turned to fascination when he learned they were the map icons of Buddhist temples. The swastikas that had been seared into his soul under the Third

Reich spun the opposite way as a Buddhist symbol, as if they had the power to undo the horrors he had experienced.

Once there, as many foreigners do, he gravitated to Kyoto, and in Kyoto he discovered Zen.

Looking for something to quiet his tormented soul, he attached himself to a Zen master. He tried meditation but found it agony to just sit, struggling with his own mind. When he closed his eyes in stillness, an image of his terrified mother rose up. The last time he'd seen her when she was forced on the train, his father sobbing, helpless.

"Let thoughts arise, but do not hold on to them," the *roshi* said.

The thoughts kept returning though. Charlotte's face, thinner and thinner, and then she was gone—but not from his thoughts. After six months of this, Maigny asked his teacher,

"How does Zen explain something like the suffering of the Jews in the holocaust?"

To which the Zen master replied,

"A dog is a dog."

Maigny smiled ruefully at the memory. A very Zen answer, of course. But he was ignorant enough to be insulted and he left the temple in a fury. He could do without Zen. For centuries Zen masters had trained the samurai with techniques of meditation—but to what purpose, Maigny asked himself. Was it not primarily to enhance their concentration so that they could kill or face their own death without faltering? To encourage them to be absolutely dedicated and act without thinking? The sword, which had always been a Buddhist symbol of cutting through delusion, became, for some samurai, a literal bloody weapon. He concluded that Zen had supported the sort of blind obedience that fed right into the imperial war machine. Well, Maigny had had enough of blind obedience. Their gardens were lovely, but in the end, he had found nothing in the Zen temples that he wanted to pursue. That was when he discovered Mt. Kōya and Shingon.

In Shingon, words and ritual were keys to truth—not, as in Zen, hindrances to it. By proper use of the ritual process a person could participate in the body of ultimate truth. This, he realized, was the meaning of the statues, mandalas, and mantras. They were aids. As he studied Shingon, Maigny felt something stir beneath the layers of disillusionment that lay over his heart like so much dust. Buried in the debris of his memories was some tiny germ, barely alive, of a desire for knowledge. That germ quickened.

In Shingon, every sentient being was considered a microcosm of the cosmos. This followed from the logic of universal similarity. As Kūkai himself wrote, "the ultimate truth of the Buddhist law cannot be conveyed in words, yet without words it cannot be manifested. The ultimate reality is beyond form, but by taking form it is comprehended." All phenomena were words—to be understood as letters in a world-text.

Bertrand Maigny stayed at Kōyasan for twenty-five years. He did not become a Shingon priest, nor even a believer in the usual sense of that term. As a historian of religion, he saw that one of the most important aspects of Shingon was its manner of transmission. Teachings were passed from master to apprentice over years of training. This training included studying the texts, learning the ritual gestures and the visualizations of meditation. But there were also secret oral traditions passed from master to disciple. And here his education abruptly ended. He was bewildered. Perhaps, after all, he had been too much an outsider to be allowed to receive any secret oral tradition. Because he was a foreigner? Or perhaps because he was a scholar? After the years he had spent in Japan, Maigny took this as an insult. He argued with his teacher—later, he deeply regretted his words—then he returned to France.

As he sat in his study now, trying to compose a letter to Philip, he relived the trajectory of his experience in Japan. He had been angry and bitter, but then, amazingly enough, once back in France, the bitterness drained away and he discovered that he was content—and this contentment took him by surprise. In Japan he had lived at a tight pitch, always making the effort to understand, never quite fitting in. And then finally, after all those years, he relaxed. It occurred to Maigny that it was almost as if his teacher knew that by cutting that tie, by denying him that last bit of knowledge, he was in fact giving him the greatest gift. By the time Bertrand fully realized this, though, his teacher had passed away. Maigny had not been back to Japan since.

Well, he could hardly write all this to Philip. The main issue now was the hidden buddhas. Unpromising as the young man first appeared when they met at Columbia, he had also been drawn to Japan, and then to Shingon, just as Maigny had. And now, on his own, he had come to an interest in the hidden buddhas. Maigny typed:

> *The point is, Philippe, that the ritual function of many of the icons*
> *of Shingon is not documented because it is only preserved in the oral*

tradition, passed from masters to worthy adherents. Herein lies the secret of the hidden buddhas, I am convinced. I have already sent you the map I have worked out to show the location of the hibutsu *all over Japan. I believe they form a geographical mandala with Mt. Kōya at its center, and it all goes back to Kūkai. For what possible reason, you will wonder?*

Precisely the question, thought Philip, his tea getting cold. He realized that Maigny was writing things that he had never made public.

As a scholar, Bertrand Maigny had reached a dead end. Historians needed texts. Without texts, how could you begin to analyze anything? But things could be texts too, if you knew how to read them. The hidden buddhas themselves must be secret texts, Maigny thought. How to read them, though? He pondered everything he knew about Kūkai.

Maybe it was not enough for Kūkai to have grasped the truth of the world—it made sense that he had a plan for transmuting that knowledge into action. Kūkai could see that the world was beginning to descend into chaos—that the age of *mappō* had already begun. Perhaps he foresaw the disasters that lay ahead not only for Japan, but for all mankind. He would have tried to devise a way to slow it down, if not halt it entirely. Maigny wrote:

Kūkai is credited with many impossible miracles, as you know from your pilgrimage. There is simply no way he could have carved even a quarter of the images attributed to him. Yet I think he did something even more miraculous. I think he instructed one of his disciples to keep some sacred images hidden until the time was ripe for the Buddha of the Future to appear. In other words, the hidden buddhas are Kūkai's legacy—a bulwark against the world's total dissolution into chaos. If you look at my map you see that they encircle Mt. Kōya in a protective ring, with Kūkai's tomb at the center.

It had occurred to Maigny that his epiphany regarding the hidden buddhas contained echoes from his own religious tradition. The Lamed Vav, for example. In Jewish legend, thirty-six "hidden virtuous men," were said to bear the suffering and sins of the world. When one of the thirty-six died, God would choose another to take his place. Not famous people, or saints—

no, these guardians were obscure. Rather like the *hibutsu*, it seemed. And if there came a time that thirty-six worthy men could not be found, then, well—God would wash his hands of the world. Would that not be *mappō*?

As for the creation of the sentient images of the *hibutsu*, did that not recall the famous golem, the figure of clay brought to life by secret incantations? the Hebrew word truth, *emet*, inscribed like a mantra and slipped under their clay tongues? *Shin* "true" *gon* "word." Had Kūkai made something like hidden golems, making sure they would be maintained by Shingon spells in the temples where they lived? Maigny did not know how far to push the analogy. In the lore of the Kabbalah, the creation of a golem was considered dangerous to its creator. Was it possible that the *hibutsu* were dangerous? Maigny sighed. There was so much he would have liked to know.

He continued his letter to Philip:

> *Of course I don't believe Kūkai's mummy still lives in order to reawaken in some crude literal sense—that is not necessary. By establishing a line of secret transmission, Kūkai's words and knowledge would continue to live. By staying hidden he thought they would retain a mysterious power. If what I have surmised about the purpose of the hidden buddhas is true, how can one pretend to understand Kūkai and the meaning of Shingon without knowing this?*

Bertrand Maigny came to the end of a page, scrolled it out of his Olivetti and reread what he had written. Did it sound foolish? He was a proud man, especially about his scholarship. But he tried to imagine himself in Philip's position. He was surprised when Philip wrote that he wanted to change the focus of his research to the hidden buddhas. "I wonder what Chernish will say to that," Maigny thought. His own position on Philip's committee was just a courtesy. Professor Chernish was the one Philip would have to convince.

And then, in the back of his mind appeared a nagging thought. Suppose Philip *were* to be successful in proving what Maigny had failed to find evidence for? Then Philip would be the one to publish and receive credit for it. Maigny recognized that thought and was ashamed. He put one more sheet of paper into the rollers of the Olivetti.

> *So, Philippe, what I am offering you is a chance to pick up this*

thread that I fear I am unable to follow to its source. Should you truly wish to make a meaningful study of the hibutsu, *in my opinion you must seek out this hypothetical secret line of transmission. I cannot guarantee success—after all, I have failed myself. But you seem to have some sort of intuitive sense that I lack, which may just be the key to succeeding where I have failed.*

If all this seems ridiculous to you, I will understand. I'm sure you have many questions, and I doubt very much whether your advisor will approve such an intellectual wild goose chase. I would hate to cause a rift or delay your progress in obtaining your degree.

With fond regards,
Bertrand Maigny

Philip read Maigny's letter over in its entirety one more time. He knew something about secret transmissions in Shingon. Kōji had told him that even now at Ishiyama Temple there is a famous secret box that has been handed down from each abbot to his successor since at least the middle of the tenth century. No one besides the head priest has ever seen what it contains. Kōji also told him about the forbidden heretical branch of Shingon— the Tachikawa school, or so-called "left-handed tradition" that was all but stamped out in medieval times. From Kōji's snickers Philip deduced that this must have been a tantric sect that equated sexual bliss with spiritual enlightenment. Secrets—Shingon contained its share.

So the idea of a line of secret transmission was hardly far-fetched—even one stretching directly back to Kūkai. But a secret that encompassed all the temples harboring *hibutsu*? One that was never once mentioned in the popular or scholarly literature? Philip could well understand why Maigny had not published his theory.

Philip didn't want to think about *mappō* right now. He was already starting to miss Nagiko. It was late though, so he resisted the urge to call her. What should he say to Maigny? He had also put off writing to Professor Chernish even to tell him that he no longer wished to write about Shingon in modern Japan and had become interested in the hidden buddhas instead. Tomorrow. All of these things he would deal with tomorrow. Philip stripped, showered, pulled out his folded futon, and crept into it.

Hall of Dreams

FOR THE REST OF OCTOBER Philip was somewhat paralyzed. Maigny's letter had taken the wind out of the sails of his own hypothesis about the Shinto origin of the *hibutsu*. An occasional questionnaire from a pilgrim would arrive in his mailbox, reminding him that he still hadn't written to Professor Chernish. Now that the extraordinary offer from Bertrand Maigny had fallen into his lap, he was even less keen on telling Chernish what he was up to. Finally he made the non-decision of pursuing both. He would write his original thesis for Columbia just to get his degree, even though his heart was no longer in it. Choosing his words carefully, Philip finally wrote his reply to Maigny.

> *Dear Professor Maigny,*
>
> *I was stunned by your letter and honored that you chose to confide your ideas to me. Your theory took me completely by surprise. I still don't really see the implications to which you refer, but I am very curious and eager to hear more. Naturally, I have grave doubts as to whether I can succeed in discovering something that you yourself were unable to find, but I am more than willing to try.*
>
> *By the way, I think it is probably wise for me to pursue the question of the* hibutsu *separately from my dissertation research. My own habit of procrastination has been a blessing for once, as I have not written anything to Professor Chernish about my interest in the hidden buddhas.*
>
> *Incidentally, this weekend I plan to go back to Nara, to view the famous Guan Yin of the Hall of Dreams, which is having its autumn airing. I take it this may be the most famous* hibutsu *of them all.*

*I hope you are well and please do not worry yourself about my
dissertation.*

Respectfully,
Philip Metcalfe

Philip tried to get Nagiko to come along, but this was high season in
the fashion world.

"You can tell me all about it when you get back," she said. "The designs
will be on their way to the weavers, out of my hands."

"Do you know anything about this Hall of Dreams Guan Yin?" Philip
asked her. "It has a very strange history. One of the oldest *hibutsu*—and
longest hidden."

"Isn't that the one that was opened for the first time by that American
art collector in the nineteenth century? What's-his-name?"

"Fenollosa. Ernest Fenollosa, along with his student Okakura Tenshin.
Yes, their mission was to make a record of Japan's most important works of
art. Fenollosa somehow convinced the Meiji government to let him unwrap
this *hibutsu* that hadn't been seen for almost a thousand years. The priests at
Hōryūji were terrified that something terrible would happen if they opened
it. They all ran and hid."

"So he had to do it himself?"

"Yes. He was the only one who dared. He wrote that it really stank, too.
Nine hundred years of dust, mold, and cobwebs—actually, worse than that.
Insects had gotten in, and rats had come after the insects. And then snakes
had come after the rats."

Nagiko shuddered. Then she thought about all that seventh-century
silk. She wondered what had become of the fabric.

"You know," said Philip, "Its halo is not attached to a back support—it's
pounded right into the back of his head with a huge long nail."

"Sounds like voodoo…" said Nagiko.

"Yeah. Sure you don't want to come?" Philip coaxed.

"Of course I want to come," she nudged his shoulder. "I just can't do it
now. When is the next time this dear thing comes out of the closet?"

"They bring him out of hiding every spring and fall now," said Philip.
"We could go in April if you like. See the cherry blossoms too."

"Okay," Nagiko agreed. "Are you sure you're going to be all right?

Remember that last *hibutsu* you saw…you had a pretty bad reaction."

Philip laughed. "I'll take it easy this time."

Philip stopped in Kyoto first where he tried to convince Kōji to join him.

"Come on," he pushed. "You've never seen it, right? It's the most famous *hibutsu* in the country. You should be ashamed of your ignorance…I appeal to your sense of pride as a Japanese."

"You and your goddamn *hibutsu*," grumbled Kōji.

"Yeah, the base of the lighthouse is dark," said Philip, quoting the standard proverb applied to those who never bother to see the sights that lie closest to home.

"That's right," said Kōji. "And maybe it likes it that way…"

"You're hopeless," Philip gave up.

When it appeared Philip was through begging, Kōji finally gave in. "Okay," he said. "For you—I'll go…"

"Great!" Philip enthused. "You won't be sorry. This will be amazing, I promise."

"And we'll go drink till our livers burst afterward," added Kōji.

"It's a deal," replied Philip.

The next morning Philip went to fetch Kōji only to find that he had been confined to his room for sneaking out once too often.

"What!" Philip exploded. "Kōji, how could you?"

Kōji was exceedingly sheepish. "Sorry," he said, not looking Philip in the eye. "But I promise I'll go next spring. Truly I will. You'll come back for that won't you?"

Right, I'll be back with Nagiko, thought Philip. He still had a hard time imagining introducing her to Kōji.

"Okay. Fine," he said. "Dumb ass. Your loss." He'd looked forward to investigating this hidden buddha with Kōji's disparaging humor at his side.

"Here, take this." Kōji thrust something into his hand.

"What is it?" Philip was unmollified.

"A flashlight. It's going to be pretty dark in that hall. So you can see better."

Philip tried it out and then put it in his pocket.

"Thanks."

"Don't mention it."

Philip cuffed him on the head. "Idiot."
Kōji grinned.

Once again Philip took the train to Nara. He sighed. Kōji would have
been good company but he wished even more that Nagiko were along. He
changed trains and got off at the Hōryūji station from which it was a ten-
minute bus ride to the immense temple complex with its unusual octagonal
building called the Yumedono, "Hall of Dreams." Philip had expected more
people, but found only five or six visitors milling about. Despite the many
posted No Smoking signs, an old man with nicotine-stained fingers was
sucking on a filterless cigarette, puffing it down to the end before grinding
it underfoot at the bottom of the steps. He turned and said something to
Philip, who was so bowled over by the man's foul breath that he couldn't
understand him. The man shrugged.

A knee-high wooden barrier barred the open bays. Visitors had to
peer in from the perimeter. Inside the octagonal building stood a smaller
octagonal structure—the container in which the image resided, cocooned
away from the world. Now its south-facing door was open, revealing the
life size image of the Guan Yin. But what an odd one. It appeared to be
a portrait of a person—thought to be Prince Shōtoku Taishi. Hōryūji was
his personal temple, built next to the palace grounds, which was eventually
turned into his mausoleum. The prince himself had been transformed into
a bodhisattva.

Philip had been brought up Catholic. He found himself reminded of
the golden sunburst monstrance that holds the consecrated host, an elaborate container for something holy, yet imbued with what the Italians called
terribilità. Yes, that is what emanated from this statue—*terribilità*. Its huge
hands held a sphere emitting waves of flame. Philip wished Kōji were along
to prick the spookiness. He stared at the face—the narrow eyes, broad nose,
and wide lips reminded him of portraits he had seen of the Meiji emperor.

Well, it wouldn't be surprising, Philip continued to muse, since the Japanese believe their imperial line has been unbroken for two thousand years.
Family resemblance. He walked slowly past the open bay, waiting for his
eyes to become accustomed to the gloom. A couple of high school girls
approached, and after much whispering and poking at one another, pulled
out a small flashlight and played it tentatively over the statue's robes. Philip
remembered Kōji's present. He took it out and shined its circle of light

on the floor—it was much stronger than the penlight the two girls had used. Did he dare blast this beam of modern illumination onto the statue? Would that be sacrilege? In situations like this Philip tended to be excessively polite—even though he knew that, as a foreigner, he would be given leeway to do things Japanese would be far too shy to attempt.

He glanced around. The two girls had scurried away. The old man with the rank tobacco breath was mumbling to himself. A middle-aged couple wandered by, and there was a trim looking fellow, late thirties perhaps, with head shaved bald like a priest. He was wearing slacks and a windbreaker, however, and stood to the side gazing off in the distance. Philip clicked the flashlight and scanned the beam across the statue's face.

Immediately he clicked it off again. None of the photographs he had seen of this famous image prepared him for the visceral quiver of dread that rippled from his belly up to the hairs at the back of his neck. In pictures, this Guan Yin might appear beatific, but in person, and from this angle, Philip felt he had been issued some kind of silent existential threat. It wasn't that he felt malevolence directed toward himself personally, but rather that he had looked at a face that had seen into the Infinite—and not found it nice at all. It was that imprint of terror that reflected back in the glare of his flashlight and that chilled his ribs.

As Philip stumbled backward, he narrowly missed bumping into an impeccably dressed woman who had been standing just behind him. He had been oblivious to her approach. Taking in Philip's discomposure, she graciously waved off his apology before turning away and disappearing behind the angle of the octagonal shrine. Philip noticed that she didn't pause to look at the disquieting statue at all. He didn't blame her—he didn't feel like looking at it again either.

He shook his head, aware of the lingering breath of her perfume. Just then, the shaven-headed man he'd seen in the courtyard came up the steps, his eyes darting about as if searching for something. He stopped abruptly, frowning when he saw Philip.

Philip assumed he was about to be scolded for the flashlight, and tried to unobtrusively slip it back in his pocket. The man was focusing intently on the statue—nevertheless, Philip apologized.

At the sound of his voice, Tokuda looked up. He eyed Philip warily, remembering that the forced opening of this powerful *hibutsu* had been directly due to interference by a foreigner. What was this guy doing here?

"You are interested in this statue?" he asked. From Philip's polite apology he cold tell the young man's Japanese was fluent.

"Yes," Philip replied. "I'm interested in hidden buddhas. This is my first time to visit the Hall of Dreams."

"Really?" one of Tokuda's elegant eyebrows lifted. "So you know that this Guan Yin is said to be a portrait of Shōtoku Taishi?"

"So I've been told…"

"And you must know then, how it was not shown for a thousand years…"

"Till Mr. Fenollosa said 'Open up in the name of Art'…yes."

"And?" Tokuda paused, "So, what do you think?"

Philip looked at him, trying to decide whether to be honest or polite.

"To be honest," he began, "I find it rather terrifying."

"As well you might," Tokuda sighed. "This *hibutsu* should never have been opened."

Now Philip was curious. "Why do you say that?" The man appeared to be a priest, though he was not dressed as one.

Aware of Philip's eye bouncing between his shaved head and his windbreaker, Tokuda said, "Yes, I'm a Buddhist priest."

"Off duty?" inquired Philip, indicating his clothing.

"Special duty," he replied. "I'm very interested in the hidden buddhas myself."

"Really!" Philip exclaimed, introducing himself. "My advisor is a famous French professor who has studied them. Bertrand Maigny…perhaps you've heard of him? He lived on Mt. Kōya for twenty-five years."

Tokuda shook his head. "I'm afraid I'm rather ignorant of the scholarly world. My interest is not so much academic…" He thought a minute. "But I did hear about some foreigner who was on Mt. Kōya for a long time— maybe it was this same man?"

"It must have been," said Philip. "But why did you say this *hibutsu* should never have been opened?"

"It doesn't help anything to have so many people come stare at this statue," said Tokuda, surprised at how easy it was to talk with this foreigner.

"But it's an official National Treasure," Philip pressed. "You can't say people shouldn't be allowed to view their artistic heritage?"

"Is it such a great work of art, then?" Tokuda replied. "Is it surpassingly beautiful? Surpassingly inspirational?"

"Well, it's incredibly well-preserved," said Philip. "From being wrapped up for so long."

Tokuda sniffed. "It's called the Guze Guan Yin...you know what *guze* means I suppose?"

"Savior of the world?"

"That's right," said Tokuda, "Not monkey on view."

"You know," began Philip, "Speaking of saving the world, my professor has come up with an interesting theory of what the *hibutsu* are all about."

Now Noboru Tokuda stiffened.

"Really?"

Philip hesitated a moment. Was he authorized to go blabbing about Maigny's theory to someone he didn't know? But wouldn't it be interesting to get the reaction of someone in the Buddhist establishment? Why shouldn't he take the initiative now anyway, if he were going to help Maigny? He decided to plunge ahead.

"Well, he thinks that the location of all the hidden buddhas form a mandala centered on Mt. Kōya. And he thinks that they were all set up in a system arranged by Kūkai..."

Tokuda's knees went weak.

"Is this common knowledge in foreign countries?" he interrupted. Was it possible that this long-shrouded secret transmission had an exposed back-side outside of Japan?

"Oh, no," said Philip. "He's never published it—he doesn't have the evidence."

Tokuda calmed down slightly.

"So why does he think this?" he asked carefully.

"He thinks there must be a secret line of transmission of this knowledge going directly back to Kūkai. He also thinks that it might still continue, even now."

He broke off, and glanced at Tokuda, noting that the priest appeared uncomfortable.

Philip tried to backtrack. "I guess it sounds a little far-fetched...I'm not really sure of everything that's involved."

Tokuda looked around. The smelly old man had shuffled off for another cigarette. Three older women, chatting among themselves, were walking toward the Hall of Dreams.

"Tell me everything your teacher said. I'm very interested."

"Really? Do you think he's on to something?" Philip was relieved that the priest did not seem to think the idea idiotic.

It was now dusk. Noboru Tokuda walked with the young American out to the Middle Gate, where they parted. Then he turned back to the Hall of Dreams, his head reeling. This was the last day of his vigil. They would be closing this *hibutsu* back into its cabinet this evening, and he could return home to Kamakura. But now he was trying to digest the things Philip had told him.

It's unbelievable, Tokuda muttered to himself. This must be yet another sign of how far things had deteriorated. Someone else had deduced the secret of the hidden buddhas. A foreigner, no less. But he didn't know everything. And this French professor had no evidence—he was just guessing. Yet his guess was awfully close. Although he could not know the mechanism. Today he had suddenly thought he smelled a hint of that odor memory which was lodged deep in his brain—the sharp cool scent that had pierced his senses when he was twelve. It was maddening that the irritating presence of the tobacco-sodden old man had almost completely masked it. Then, following his nose right up to the image's octagonal shrine, he stumbled upon this odd *gaijin*. At least, the "Savior of the World" Guan Yin still retained its mysterious power. Like a doctor taking a pulse, that much Tokuda had been relieved to ascertain.

Of all the government-sanctioned anti-Buddhist attacks in the 1880s, Priest Zuichō had believed the forced opening of the Hall of Dreams *hibutsu* was the Meiji government's biggest mistake. The Guze Guan Yin was still powerful, all right. Even non-believers could feel its eerie presence. Even *gaijin*? It had never occurred to Tokuda that the hidden buddhas might also have an effect on non-Japanese. But now, after meeting Philip Metcalfe, he realized that it was stupid of him not to have considered that. Japan now included the world.

Tokuda felt very alone. He was thirty-eight years old and had no idea who his own successor would be. One of his main responsibilities was to continue the line. Unless he got married and had an heir pretty soon—all very unlikely—he would have to find someone. In fact, even if he did have a son, what was the chance of the kid becoming a priest—let alone having the ability to sense the *hibutsu*? He returned to Kamakura with a deep sense of foreboding.

Karma

PHILIP GAVE NAGIKO A KEY to his apartment, even though he had still never seen hers. It was a little awkward that she had never invited him. What was she hiding, he wondered? He didn't realize that no one ever visited Nagiko's apartment. Even though she always emerged from Lion's Head Mansion looking like a page from a magazine, the apartment itself was a squalid tangle—like the reverse side of a piece of intricate embroidery. To Nagiko, revealing her living quarters was more intimate than revealing her body. But finally she felt the time had come to make the gesture. Too embarrassed by her lack of cooking skills to invite him to dinner, she devised a casual ruse to bring him by. She said she had forgotten the tickets for a Noh performance they were going to see, so they needed to go by the apartment.

"It will be a half hour detour," she said. "Sorry about that."

"No problem," said Philip. They took the subway to Kagurazaka and walked to Lion's Head Mansion.

"Shall I wait down here?" he asked.

"No silly, come up. You've never seen my place, have you?"

In the casual remark—of course she knew he'd never been there—Philip immediately recognized the offer of a new level of intimacy. He had sensed dark little pockets in Nagiko. Her living situation was one of them. He wasn't expecting anything luxurious, but he *was* taken aback at the overwhelming amount of stuff she had crammed into this tiny space. Fabric swatches, books, papers and notes seemed to have bred and multiplied. His apartment with its meager furnishings appeared roomy in comparison.

"It's a narrow little hovel, but welcome," said Nagiko.

"That sounds so odd when you say it in English," Philip replied.

"It's just a reflex," said Nagiko, pursing her lips. "Where did I put those tickets?" She pulled a cushion out from under a low table, and pushed it toward him.

They were going to see a performance of *Dōjōji* at the National Theater.

"I would say it's a way of deflecting criticism before it can arise," Philip mused. "This Japanese habit of downgrading yourself in front of others. It's supposed to pull the rug out from under the disapproval people might otherwise feel—like a puppy rolling over to expose its belly, you know?"

"Hmmm, I never thought of it that way," said Nagiko. "Ah, here they are!" She pounced on an envelope. "But in this case, it's true. It really is a narrow little hovel."

"This is obviously the den of a highly creative mind…" Philip had been trying to think of something nice to say.

"Oh pooh. It's a rat's nest," she replied. "I know it. Would you like tea? We have a little time…"

"Sure," said Philip. "You've never made me tea before."

"Are you doubting my ability?" Nagiko asked, stepping over him to reach the kitchen.

"Your ability to make tea? Yes."

Nagiko brought over a stack of old-fashioned books with hand-sewn dark blue bindings. She cleared a space on the table and set them in front of Philip.

"What's this?" he asked.

"Noh texts," she answered. "My grandmother loved Noh theater."

Philip looked through the volumes. "According to my professor, if you want to see the best example of the Shingon world-view in practice, you should watch Noh," he said.

"Did you ever read Zeami on the art of acting?" Nagiko asked him.

"Isn't he, like, the Shakespeare of Noh?" Philip said.

"Yes, he wrote a lot of famous plays, but he also wrote something that every artist should remember—'if you hide it, it's a flower; if you reveal it, it is nothing.'"

"Hide what?" Philip looked up.

Nagiko smiled. "Nothing," she said. "There. I've revealed it."

Philip shook his head, then he paged through one volume after another until he found the text for *Dōjōji*, the play they were going to see. Nagiko had already told him the story. The bell scene is famous, she had said. As well as the deranged dance the main character performs before she transforms from jealous woman into serpent demon.

"For Noh, this is a pretty action-packed play."

"I'm trying to remember what else my professor said about Noh." Philip took a sip of the tea Nagiko had set in front of him. "Mmm—brown rice tea."

"Sorry, it's just the common stuff," Nagiko replied.

Philip smiled to himself, reminded of his first meeting with Bertrand Maigny. The professor had said he apologized just like a Japanese. "They apologize when it doesn't matter and don't when it does."

"Why are you smiling?"

Philip looked up from his tea cup.

"Your eyes are just like brown rice tea," he said. "So—jealous woman turns into demon. What else is new?"

"On that score? Nothing is new," said Nagiko, shaking some slightly stale rice crackers into a bowl. "Deranged women are the biggest theme in the whole Noh repertoire."

"What about love stories?" Philip asked.

"Not in Noh—well, I can think of one, maybe. But it's still put in the category of 'deranged women' plays."

Philip looked puzzled.

"—because the state of being in love was considered deranged."

As Nagiko cleared the cups away, Philip looked around, wondering where she slept. He didn't see any open space wide enough to spread a futon. Now he understood why they stayed overnight at his place or at a hotel. He couldn't imagine sleeping here. But he understood that she had opened up a guarded part of herself by allowing him to see it, and for that he was grateful.

Nagiko came and went freely to Philip's apartment. One afternoon in mid-December she had been meeting with a client in Shinjuku when she was suddenly gripped with fatigue. Rather than beat her way back to the office, she called him. She was so close, maybe she would just drop by his place and rest a while. No answer. She was trying to decide whether to go home when she remembered he had given her a key. She would just go stretch out for a bit and wait for him. He was probably at the National Library, or maybe just shopping. Perhaps this would be a good time to tell him what she had begun to suspect over the past week while he was away looking at *hibutsu*.

She pressed the buzzer in the lobby to see whether he had returned in the time since she called. Still no answer. She went up to the third floor and looked down the hall. Good, his nosy neighbor was nowhere in sight. She let herself in. The bare simplicity of his rooms was refreshing. Like a monk's cell, she thought.

Maybe she would benefit from sweeping away some of her own clutter. Philip's quiet neatness appealed to her. He was a good influence. He brought out a tenderness that she wasn't even aware she had lost until she met him. She liked the person she was around him, and with this serene foothold, she felt more creative than ever.

After returning to Japan from New York, Nagiko had sacrificed various parts of herself to feed her desire to design fabrics. She had known since childhood that she wanted to be an artist, and that fabric would be her medium. For her, fabric enveloped all the arts—the colors of painting, the textures of sculpture, the chance to take traditional techniques and use them to weave new expressions. Best of all, the cloth thus created could be touched, felt, and worn. It could be wrapped, folded and draped. Her clothes were soft and flexible, like living creatures. Her fabrics were poetry, patterns from chaos.

Anyone would say she had been successful. She was recognized and respected. She had ceased thinking about romance. Who would want a thirty-two-year-old bride who couldn't even cook? Her closest male friends were gay. She was not interested in affairs with married colleagues. She had simply closed off the romantic part of her heart. If that was the sacrifice, so be it. Looking at her married friends, she felt no envy What still excited her most was pattern, texture, color. This was her life until she met Philip. The only way to describe what she felt now was a karmic link. How else could you talk about a connection where so many pieces just fell into place naturally? The link was already in place, opening out like a tightly furled bud beginning to bloom with its own logic.

She opened the cupboard and found a heavy foil bag of good-quality green tea. As she waited for the kettle to boil, she glanced through the books on Philip's shelf. Books on Buddhism, mostly, but also a volume of Hume's *An Enquiry Concerning Human Understanding*, a recent edition of works by Jean-Paul Sartre, and some English translations of classic Japanese literature, including a Penguin paperback of *The Pillow Book of Sei Shōnagon*, written almost a thousand years ago. It had come up in their conversation a while ago, and she had meant to look at it.

"Read it in English," Philip had said, "it will be easier than the original." He was right about that. Nagiko had been bored to tears by the way the classics had been taught in high school, and managed to do the bare minimum of literature classes in college as well. The thing that had interested her most about *The Tale of Genji* was the multi-layered robes worn by the court ladies. She found the Shining Prince himself totally without appeal, and the ladies he seduced, with one or two exceptions, insipid.

Nagiko skipped the introductory material, looking for the first page where the author rhapsodized over some of her favorite things. Ah, here was the well-known first line:

> *In spring it is the dawn that is most beautiful. As the light creeps over the hills, their outlines are dyed a faint red and wisps of purplish cloud trail over them.*

> *In summer the nights. Not only when the moon shines, but on dark nights too, as the fireflies flit to and fro, and even when it rains, how beautiful it is.*

> *In autumn the evenings, when the glittering sun sinks close to the edge of the hills and the crows fly back to their nests in threes and fours and twos; more charming still is a file of wild geese, like specks in the distant sky…*

Nagiko heard the kettle whistle, and hastily set the book down, her face flushed. Philip had been right—she had totally lifted the concept for her *Saisons* line from *The Pillow Book*! She filled the teapot and went back to read the beginning of the last paragraph:

> *In winter the early mornings. It is beautiful indeed when snow has fallen during the night, but splendid too when the ground is white with frost…*

She snapped the book shut. This was too embarrassing. Why had no one else pointed it out? Was it possible her clients hadn't noticed? Did they take it as a veiled reference? To have copied it on purpose would have been clever, but to do it unintentionally—that was simply stupid. She flipped through the pages. Here and there were Shōnagon's notoriously idiosyncratic lists: presumptuous things; squalid things; adorable things—the vignettes, the musings. What more might she find? Broken spider webs spangled with dew that no one else thought remarkable...a pair of tweezers that was good at grasping a hair...to wash one's hair, put on makeup, perfume, a beautiful robe—even if no one else will see it—these preparations produce such an inner pleasure...

It was as if she were reading her own diary. Nagiko could have laughed and said here was a woman after her own heart. But the parallel was too uncanny. She heard the rattling of keys in the door.

Philip, carrying a bag of groceries, held the door with his foot as he struggled out of his shoes. He noticed Nagiko's burgundy leather high-heeled boots in the entry.

"Hello?" he called.

"Hi," she responded. "I'm here."

"Nagiko..." Philip poked his head around the corner. "When did you get here?"

"Just a while ago. I was in Shinjuku. I was feeling a little unwell, so I came by for a break. I called, but..."

Philip padded into the room. "Are you okay?" he asked. "You look really tired."

"I'm okay," she said.

"How about some tea?" Philip asked. Nagiko winced. She had forgotten about the tea. Too late. Philip was already in the kitchen.

"What's this?" he said, lifting the teapot full of over-steeped bitter liquid.

"Sorry," said Nagiko, "I forgot it."

"Never mind. I'll make another pot." He noticed the book on the table in front of her.

"You found *The Pillow Book*? Pretty interesting, isn't it? Did you look at the first section—weren't we talking about its influence on some of your designs?"

Nagiko sighed. "Do you believe in reincarnation?"

"Of an individual, you mean?" asked Philip, just coming into the room with a dish of rice crackers.

"Of course," said Nagiko, somewhat puzzled, "what else?"

"Well, if you mean the Buddhist idea of the endless cycle of rebirth, that's one thing. If you mean do I think a particular person who is alive now could have the same soul, remember the same experiences—essentially be the same person as someone who died long before—then no. At least, I don't think so."

"My friend Satoko thinks she is a reincarnation of Cleopatra," said Nagiko.

Philip almost dropped the dish.

"Cleopatra? Satoko? Come on…" Philip had met Satoko when Nagiko brought him along to an ikebana exhibition. He had amused Nagiko by the skill with which he charmed her friend with his Japanese manners.

"Satoko says whenever she sees pictures of the pyramids, she has this feeling she's seen them before."

"Well that would be true every time except the first, wouldn't it?" said Philip. "Look, I like Satoko fine. She's very nice—and I know she's a good friend. But Cleopatra? I don't think so…does she have urges to dissolve pearls in vinegar?"

Nagiko smiled. "Okay, maybe that's farfetched. But surely you've come across other people who believe they've been reincarnated?"

Philip was well acquainted with the matter-of-fact way Japanese talked about reincarnation. He had always dismissed it as one of those funny ways Japanese had of creating identities for themselves—donning a pre-formed personality the way you might put on a beret to show you were an artist, or wear kimono to show you were a lady of refined traditional taste. Reincarnation was a cool metaphor, but he had never taken it seriously. Philip turned to his bookcase and pulled out the volume of Hume. He opened it to a bookmark.

"What's that?" Nagiko asked.

"Here. Listen to what this Scottish philosopher has to say about personal identity—

> *… we are nothing but a bundle of different sensations, succeeding one another with inconceivable rapidity and in a perpetual flux and movement.*"

Philip closed the book.

"Hume thought the whole idea of personhood itself is a fiction. We are simply a wave of perceptions, rising and falling away. The interesting thing is, this is very close to the original Buddhist position regarding the impermanence of the self. A group of elements come together briefly to form a consciousness, but then scatter like a wave breaking into foam. So technically, there is nothing to reincarnate."

Nagiko blinked, "But…"

"I know. That's not the popular understanding of Buddhism, especially in Japan. And yes, I've met lots of people who think they are reincarnations of somebody. Why do you ask?" Philip went back to the kitchen to pour the tea.

"Whoa…I let it steep too long…"

"I'm a bad influence," said Nagiko.

"I'll just add some hot water, it will be fine." Philip came back with two steaming cups.

"Personally, I like to think of reincarnation as DNA. Elements of information coming together, 'incarnating' into a person, being sustained briefly, scattering. Are you your great-great-grandmother reincarnated? Well, in a way, yes, but you are also a unique individual. It's like pattern replication—with infinite form and variation."

He set the cups down. "Okay, so who are you a reincarnation of?"

Nagiko was not sure she could explain the eerie sensation she got from looking through *The Pillow Book*. At this point she was afraid to read through the whole thing. And she was afraid Philip would laugh.

"There's something strange about this book," Nagiko began. "I mean, unless I am a reincarnation of Sei Shōnagon, then I am some sort of plagiarist."

"Show me," said Philip pulling a cushion around next to Nagiko. "You mean your seasons designs—spring dawn, summer fireflies? Were those in fact in there?

Nagiko nodded. "Down to the last detail."

"But you said yourself you had read it in school," Philip pointed out. "Consciously you may have forgotten, but deep down you remembered even though you forgot the source." He looked at her stricken face.

"Hey," he said, and put his arm around her. "It's not something to worry about. She's not going to jump up from the grave to sue you…"

"But that's not the only thing." Nagiko felt her voice catching in the back of her throat. "Every page I open to…I feel like it's something I could have written, or something I experienced…"

Philip tried to soothe her. "That's the power of great literature," he said. "People can really connect with it."

Nagiko was tired, and her stomach was upset. Perhaps this was not the time to tell Philip, after all. She let him fix her rice with tea and pickled plums, draw a hot bath, and then later wrap her up in a flannel yukata and tuck her into his futon. He lay quietly curled around her.

Philip was aware of Nagiko's little twitches and sighs as she slept. He had told her he did not believe in the reincarnation of personal identity, backing it up with an overkill of philosophical comment. Yet it struck him now that in his rant about reincarnation he had also shoveled a pile of dirt over whatever Nagiko had been trying to tell him.

Fretting, Philip finally dropped off to sleep. He woke to clear cold December sunlight. Nagiko had gotten up and made instant coffee and toast. She was sitting on a chair at the little kitchen table looking tousled, no makeup on her perfect skin. She was watching him when he finally opened his eyes.

"Philip?" she said.

He yawned and stretched. "What?"

"I have to tell you something. I meant to tell you yesterday." Something in her voice made him sit up.

For the past week Nagiko had experienced a dip in energy, as if her batteries were getting weak. When this lethargy was accompanied by a bout of seasickness on the subway, she recognized the feeling. For the next three days she went back and forth to work in a daze, mechanically going through the business matters that were laid on her desk, all the while conscious of a new kind of hidden creativity that had begun to sprout in darkness.

This was not a good time to have a child, obviously. She owed her successful career to the painful experience of sending the *mizuko* back once before, but could she possibly send it back again? The *mizuko* had been quiet for a long time. But perhaps it had only been biding its time. Plus, it was no longer anonymous—it was someone she had visited, brought flowers to, lit incense for, even cajoled and argued with. Yes, she told herself, but the *mizuko* was also someone Philip didn't know about. How would he react? Philip had been brought up Catholic, after all.

Nagiko was quite sure he would do the responsible thing, if it came to that. He would take her to the clinic, attend her convalescence, be supportive—Nagiko was certain. But what if she said she didn't want an abortion? How would he react then? Luckily Philip had been away for a few days, off visiting a *hibutsu* in Narita that was one of the few on display this December. She had some time to sort out her emotions.

She had resolved to tell him as she waited in his apartment. But that was before she got sidetracked by *The Pillow Book*. The sense of deep familiarity—evident even through the lens of a translation—was so unnerving Nagiko couldn't concentrate. That night she fell asleep, dimly aware of Philip's body curled around hers like a mitten.

She dreamed she was walking along the stony banks of a river. At first it was cold under a low gray sky, a wintry breeze kicking up tiny waves on the water's surface. She shivered. Then some rays of sunlight started to poke through the clouds. She was walking quickly, hands in pockets, hugging her coat close. She heard a babble of voices ahead. At a bend in the river she saw a group of young children on the other side. Playing? Fighting? She couldn't tell. A small figure wearing a pink sweater crouched at the edge of the river just ahead. As she approached, it turned around. A girl with black hair and dark blue eyes. Nagiko stood stock-still, as if paralyzed. The child regarded her seriously, then went back to the pile of rocks she had been playing with. She placed one more on top of the little edifice and turned back to Nagiko with a smile.

"*Kaa-san,*" she said. Mother.

Nagiko woke with a jolt that sent her elbow straight into Philip's ribs. He murmured in his sleep, rolling over without waking. Nagiko lay there quietly thinking for almost an hour until winter morning sunlight coldly brightened the room. She crept out of the futon, tucking the top quilt carefully around Philip's shoulders. Shivering, she looked around for a robe. She didn't see anything but a thin plaid blanket which she folded into an uneven triangle and draped over herself as a shawl. She made some instant coffee and a piece of toast and waited for Philip to wake up.

Finally his eyes opened. She gathered her resolve.

"Philip?"

He was groggy. "What?"

"I have to tell you something. I meant to tell you yesterday."

He was wide awake now and he sat up. Nagiko took a deep breath.

"I think I'm pregnant," she said.

Philip just looked at her, speechless.

"In fact, I am pregnant," Nagiko went on, looking straight at him, blinking back tears from the effort.

"Nagiko…" Philip scrambled out of the futon, not quite disengaging himself from the sheet that had wrapped itself around one knee. She was sitting tightly folded upon herself, legs crossed, arms crossed, anxious and cold, her hair falling over her eyes. Philip grasped the dangling foot.

"Cold…" he murmured, rubbing it tenderly. "Will you marry me, Coldfoot?"

"What…?" Nagiko had built up such a hard fortress of mental resolve she couldn't believe she might not have to retreat behind it. She looked down at Philip's dark head bending over her foot. He was exhaling his warm breath onto her instep. She wove her fingers into his hair and raised his head.

"Please," he said. "Would you? I was afraid I'd never get the courage to ask, but I've thought about it so many times…" He pulled the tangled sheet off his ankle. "I would have proposed more elegantly, but…"

He took Nagiko's face in his hands, "Please marry me, Nagiko Kiyowara. We have a connection. I felt it from the first time I met you…and now the connection is more real than I could possibly have dreamed."

Nagiko threw her arms around him. Her tears melted the fortress she had not needed. They carried away the stones of pain and guilt that the *mizuko* had dropped in her heart for five years. How could she have thought Philip would have wanted something other than what she wanted? She cried for doubting him. She cried for relief. She cried for happiness.

"Hey, why are you crying?" said Philip gently, kissing away her tears.

They decided to get married in February. That would give Philip's parents time to plan for coming to Tokyo. After the initial shock of hearing for the first time that her son had a girlfriend, now a fiancée in Japan, Philip's mother got around to asking him if Nagiko was Catholic.

"No, Mom, she's not," he told her in a rare long distance phone call.

"Well, that simplifies things," said his mother after a long pause. "Catholic weddings are so complicated. Will it be a Buddhist wedding?"

That threw Philip. He supposed there was such a thing, but he had never run across one.

"In Japan, the only legal way to marry is to get your license at City Hall," he said. "So that's what we're going to do. And a reception party."

Philip saw no need to tell his mother about the baby at this point. He wanted her to meet Nagiko first. Aside from Satoko, they decided to keep the pregnancy a secret from everyone. There was one other complication. His advisor Harvey Chernish was going to be in Japan in February, so naturally he would have to be invited. That meant Philip would need to throw together something that looked like the beginning of a thesis before then. Luckily he had collected a sheaf of filled-out questionnaires from the Shikoku pilgrimage.

Wedding planning began. They enlisted Satoko to take charge of the flowers. Philip overheard her ask Nagiko something about Kamakura, and his ears pricked up. He still had not seen the Great Buddha on the hillside there.

"Who's going to Kamakura?" he asked, coming over to the table where the two women were addressing invitations. Nagiko turned red.

"No one," said Satoko curtly. "Why do you ask?"

"I just heard you mention Kamakura, that's all," said Philip, backing off. "I've never been there."

"We should go," said Nagiko quickly. "I'll take you."

Satoko glanced at her.

"…to see the Great Buddha."

"Oh, and we should go to Fudō-in while we're at it," said Philip. "There's a famous eleven-faced Guan Yin image there. It's huge—supposedly the biggest wooden statue in Japan. I'd really like to see that."

"Yes, of course," said Nagiko smoothly.

"You really should wait until June," said Satoko.

"Why?" Philip asked.

"Because…because then the hydrangeas will be in bloom…" Satoko floundered.

"But I'll be eight months pregnant by then," said Nagiko. "I'll probably hardly be able to walk."

Philip tried to imagine Nagiko with a huge unwieldy belly. He couldn't.

"Okay, I'm off to the American embassy to get something called my sworn-affidavit-of-competency-to-marry document. See you later, ladies," said Philip, grabbing his coat.

After Philip had gone Satoko asked, "Are you going to tell him?"

"Mmmm."

"You're going to tell him about the *mizuko*?"

Nagiko put down the card she was folding. "Why not? It doesn't seem right to keep a secret like that now."

"Well," said Satoko. "I wouldn't. If I were you. I mean…are you going to take him to the cemetery? Why not wait till after you're married…"

Nagiko cocked her head sidewise to look at her friend.

"You think he'll want to call it off if he knows? Is that it?"

"Men can be funny…" Satoko said briskly, gathering up a pile of invitations and tapping them together like a pack of playing cards. "You just never know. Things are so good for you right now—why look for trouble?"

Nagiko sighed. "I have to tell him. But it will be fine. I'm sure."

"I hope you're right, for both of your sakes," said Satoko. "And you should tell him to find out his blood type while you're at it. I can't believe he doesn't even know his own blood type…"

"He's probably an AB just like you," teased Nagiko.

"You think so?" said Satoko. "That would be good. Goes well with O."

The Great Buddha

ON A COLD GRAY SATURDAY in January, Philip and Nagiko took the train to Kamakura. It had snowed the previous night, although none of it stuck to the ground. Just outside the train station they noticed a few dark red plum buds straining to burst into flower, now covered in caps of soft wet snow. They took a taxi to the temple of the Great Buddha first. The huge bronze image sat lotus posture, by itself, in the middle of a wide stone courtyard. It had once had a building over its head, like its fellow Great Buddha in Nara, but the last wooden structure here had been washed away by a tsunami some 700 years ago. Since then the massive figure had stolidly braved all the elements—today cupping snow on its meditatively held thumbs, each the length of a large child.

Nagiko had a small camera. Philip had brought his sketchbook. Depending on the angle from which one viewed the Great Buddha, its demeanor changed drastically. Regarding it straight on from the front at about twenty paces the image radiated an unearthly calm. But if you walked up close, examining it with an artist's eye, you could see that the head and shoulders had been cast disproportionately large in order to create the illusion of symmetry.

"Maybe this is where you would have first seen it when you entered the building…" said Nagiko, moving back and forward till she found the spot where she decided the huge figure of Amida looked right.

"That would be my guess," replied Philip. "But look here. If you come over to this side, from here, he just looks weary—hunched over from the cares of the world…you almost feel sorry for him from this angle." He hooked his arm in Nagiko's and brought her over to the spot from which he was sketching.

"You're right," she said. "All that responsibility…"

"And from the back. Those open panels at his shoulder blades—like he's trying hard to sprout little wings…"

Nagiko laughed at the thought of this massive Buddha suddenly being able to fly away.

"So, how about some hot ramen, then on to Fudō-in?" said Philip, blowing on his fingers now stiff from drawing in the cold.

"Ramen?" Nagiko's stomach turned queasy at the thought of Chinese noodles in oily soup. "Well, ramen for you, okay. I think I'd rather have something lighter."

"Udon in broth? Soba?"

"Udon, maybe…"

"Okay. We passed a bunch of places back by the station. Can you walk? Or shall we take a cab?" Philip was extraordinarily solicitous of Nagiko these days, as if he had been entrusted with a fragile jewel.

"Sure, let's walk," she said. "Actually, we'll pass right by Fudō-in. Let's go there first, then have lunch."

"If you're sure you'll be okay. Aren't you supposed to be eating crackers or something every three hours?" Philip had been reading hints on quelling the nausea of early pregnancy.

"I'm fine…really."

He pulled a cellophane-wrapped packet from his coat pocket.

"Here. Biscuits. You should eat a couple."

Nagiko felt like a child being force-fed a snack to prevent crankiness. But she ate the cookies Philip placed in her palm.

They walked slowly, enjoying the rare snow and the quiet of being away from Tokyo. Philip held Nagiko's arm firmly tucked inside his, lest she should slip on the icy stones. She wore flat-heeled fleece-lined boots at his insistence, rather than something more fashionable.

Nagiko still hadn't decided how she would tell Philip about the *mizuko*. She was counting on sudden inspiration to strike when they got to Fudō-in. They had now reached the main gate with its towering lopsided pine tree. Today, laden with snow, it was even more formidable than Nagiko remembered. She had never visited the temple at this time of year. It looked quite different under the picturesque frosting.

"Oh. I forgot about all these steps," said Nagiko as they reached the path leading up to the main buildings. The Jizō cemetery was halfway up, on a leveled out plot of the hillside.

"I thought you'd never been here before," said Philip.

Maybe this was the time to tell him. She started to say something, but Philip was in a mood to tease.

"Or maybe it was in a different lifetime?"

It did seem like it was a different lifetime.

"Philip—let's take a rest here for a minute." She pointed to a nearby stone bench.

"Of course. Are you feeling all right?" suddenly he became serious.

"It's fine. I just get tired quickly. Maybe I'll have another biscuit—are there any more?"

He sat down next to her and dug into his pockets.

Sitting there, Nagiko began to panic. Philip had not given any weight to her careless remark about the steps. But the thought of trudging right past the small Jizō statue where she had brought flowers and incense every year, and now pretend to ignore it…Why hadn't she listened to Satoko? This had been a terrible idea. Philip looked at her.

Nagiko forced herself to take slow deep breaths. She smiled at him reassuringly.

"You know, maybe I'll just sit here and rest. I don't feel up to climbing that whole mountainside right now—but you should go up…it would be silly for you to come this far and not see the main temple. I'll wait for you right here."

"Definitely not," said Philip. "I'm not leaving you here alone."

Nagiko scolded him. "Now look. Don't go acting like a mother hen. I'm telling you it's fine."

Philip looked crestfallen. "Have I been smothering you?" he asked.

Nagiko pulled off one of her gloves then one of his. She slipped her naked hand in his. "Never," she said. "No one could ever make me happier. But I'm perfectly capable of taking care of myself for half an hour." She squeezed his hand. "Now run up and see your big Guan Yin."

"Okay," he said. "I won't be long." Philip kissed her lightly on the forehead then sprinted up the stone steps.

"Be careful!" Nagiko called out after him. He turned and waved.

It felt good to run. Philip had lost some of the hard muscle from his pilgrimage, but he still had fair stamina. He turned and waved once more from higher up, then he disappeared over the top.

When she was sure he had gone into the temple compound, Nagiko stood up and quickly moved along the same path, following the familiar steps part way up to the Jizō section. She picked her way resolutely through the narrow pathways over to her own statue.

"Now see here," she wanted to say, looking down at the smooth marble head, "you are warm and safe now. You don't even live here any more, so I haven't brought you anything…" She spread her hands over her belly. "You are coming home with me, and I'm not coming back here again." She didn't even ladle water over the Jizō. That would not be kind on such a cold day. Though no one else was there, Nagiko glanced around then turned and walked back down to the bench to wait for Philip. There was no need to tell him any of this she decided.

A beautiful snow-clad vista had opened up to Philip when he reached the top. He took a quick jog around the bell tower and the observation platform before heading toward the temple's main image. He had a nostalgic flashback to his days on the pilgrimage. Inside the gloom, a tall glimmering gold-painted image of his favorite icon, the eleven-faced Guan Yin, stood holding a staff and a vase. It was haloed by a full-body nimbus, also gold.

Even though he knew Nagiko was waiting for him below, Philip could not help stopping to chant the *Heart Sutra* at the door of the building. So what if the few people wandering about the courtyard were surprised at a *gaijin* intoning a sutra like a monk. Just as well Nagiko hadn't come up. He would have felt self-conscious. He bowed once more toward the interior of the building, then turned back. A man stepped across his path. Philip felt himself being appraised. He returned the man's glance. Something about him was familiar.

"Metokafu-san," the man said.

"Yes, I'm Metcalfe…"

"Tokuda," said the priest. "We met at the Hall of Dreams in Nara."

"Of course," said Philip, now remembering the eyebrows. "But what are you doing here?"

"I work here," said Tokuda. "Today you see me in my working uniform." He indicated his monk's robes.

He fell into step with Philip who had continued to move toward the stone stairway. "You sounded like a priest yourself just then…"

"The sutra?" Philip was a little embarrassed. "I did the Shikoku pilgrimage last summer, and seeing this magnificent Guan Yin just kind of brought it all back. One gets into a habit you know, especially when all the right elements are there."

"I can understand that," said Tokuda. "Are you leaving? I'm heading back down myself..." They walked together down the long series of steps leading back to the lower garden. As they passed the Jizō cemetery, Philip waved his hand at the legion of small stone statues.

"This is kind of interesting," he said.

"Yes, the *mizuko*," replied Tokuda. "That's primarily who I minister to these days."

"Water children?" said Philip, turning his head to look at the priest, "whose are they?"

"They have many mothers," said Tokuda. "Stillborns, aborted fetuses..."

Nagiko saw Philip coming back down the stone pathway, but strangely, he was not alone. It looked like he was walking with a priest. She stood up and shaded her eyes, straining to see. Philip caught sight of her and waved. The pair approached the bottom of the steps, still talking as they walked toward the bench. With a lurch, as if the bottom of her stomach had given way, Nagiko now recognized the priest.

Philip couldn't believe his luck in running into Tokuda again. The man had shown interest in Maigny's theory. He would be a great sounding board for discussing it. Obviously today was not the time to really get into it with him—Nagiko was waiting on that cold bench in the garden. It was time to get some warm soup into her—but he let Tokuda know that he wanted to pursue it. The priest seemed very interested. They made plans to meet in the middle of the week. Philip would come back to Kamakura by himself.

They came up to Nagiko who stood there as if frozen. Philip put his arm around her and introduced her to Tokuda.

"This is my fiancée, Nagiko Kiyowara," he said proudly.

Tokuda bowed, without a flicker of an indication that he had ever seen her before.

"*Hajimete o-me ni kakarimasu*," replied Nagiko, using the politest Japanese phrase for being introduced to someone for the first time. For a fraction of a second their eyes caught.

Tokuda was unnerved. He had had one client that morning—a worn-down looking woman in her early forties who had come dragging a chain-smoking uncommunicative husband. They had been here before. After taking care of them, setting up a new Jizō next to an older one, Tokuda walked up to the main temple to clear his head. He gazed across the snow-dusted mountains down to the city and the curve of the beach. Snow had muffled the usual babble of human activity. And then a clear, unusual voice rang through the cold air. It was someone reciting the Heart Sutra. Tokuda looked around. In front of the Guan Yin hall stood a tall young man—not Japanese, judging from his long legs—head bent, singing out the sacred syllables. The deeply familiar chant, usually mumbled together like a wave rolling over pebbles, sounded odd enunciated so strongly.

Tokuda couldn't help turning toward the sound. The chanter was coming to the end now. *Gyatei gyatei haragyatei…* When the young man turned around and started walking away, Tokuda made sure to cross his path. Even more odd, it turned out to be that foreigner whom he had run into last November, the one with the flashlight. He had been kicking himself that he had not gotten the young man's address at the time. Now, he hailed him, and the young foreigner remembered. Not only that, he seemed extremely glad to see him again. Something further he wanted to talk about regarding the hidden buddhas.

He said his fiancée was waiting for him in the deserted garden below, and he had to get back to her, but suggested he come back to Kamakura by himself so they could talk more. Tokuda had walked down the hill with him, only to find that the fiancée was a beautiful woman he had met before. He realized that Metokafu could not have been the father of her *mizuko*. He probably did not know about his fiancée's earlier abortion, either. Yes, he could tell that from the swift, petrified look she had given him, and the way she introduced herself.

Ah well. These things were always complicated. No need to get involved. He was good at keeping secrets. He just hoped she wouldn't come up with a scheme to prevent the young man from coming back alone because she was afraid the priest would "turn the light on in the closet" by letting a word slip about her *mizuko*.

Until meeting Philip, Tokuda had more or less convinced himself that his responsibility to the hidden buddhas consisted of watching and keeping record. Despite Priest Zuichō's idea of actively trying to catch the creature who was killing the *hibutsu*, wouldn't there have been specific directives in the tradition itself if that had been a necessary part of the training? Nothing had happened to any hidden buddha last year, further convincing Tokuda that he should simply stand by and observe. But then, like a spider attuned to any little movement in its web, he had suddenly felt a tremulous ripple through the entire web of hibutsu in October. He didn't yet understand the feeling, but he was quite sure he felt it. And now here was this foreigner again, dropping practically in his lap. This could not be coincidence.

The Nails of Fate

NAGIKO HAD SEEMED RATHER UPSET after their trip to Kamakura. Philip attributed her mood to the fragile emotions of early pregnancy. He had read about that in a book for prospective fathers. "A woman's psychological state can be easily upset by the surge of hormones. Expect bouts of tiredness, irrational cravings, sudden headaches, tears." He decided not to tell her about his plan to see the priest, Tokuda. They were going to meet the day after Jun Muranaka had invited him to dinner.

"Boys' night out," Jun had said. "Do you know why we don't have bachelor parties in Japan?"

Philip suspected a joke, but Jun was serious.

"In America, you're expected to do things with your wife after you're married. A bachelor's party is the last chance to be with just the boys. But here in Japan—every night is boys' night out."

Philip realized with some embarrassment that he didn't even know whether Jun was married.

Nagiko had presented him with a custom-tailored suit from an expensive new menswear designer who was one of her clients. The suit for Philip was of lightweight Merino wool, seaweed-green so dark it was black in all but bright sunlight, with a tiny undulating stripe of slightly thicker worsted that gave the cloth texture and drape. The suit was narrow cut, with four buttons (Of course you must never button them, Nagiko instructed Philip) and narrow rolled lapels. The trousers were plain, straight, and absolutely the most stylish thing Philip had ever put on. Nagiko paired it with a yellow shirt ("Really?" Philip had been doubtful) and a chestnut brown necktie with a pattern of what looked like pale pink and green sea anemones waving in a pool of black dots. ("Trust me," she had said.) It was smashing. When Philip tried it on for the first time in the designer's atelier, Nagiko looked proudly at him as if he were a piece of artwork.

"Beautiful!" she exclaimed. The designer himself came in and made little applauding gestures. Philip blushed—which she found more endearing than if he had peacocked around the room.

He felt self-conscious dressing up like this without Nagiko at his side, so tonight he substituted a plain white shirt and striped tie. Still, when he walked into Jun's downtown office, the first thing Muranaka said was "Nice suit. You've come up in the world."

"It's Nagiko's influence," mumbled Philip.

"I figured," replied Muranaka. "She's quite amazing…now tell me again how you two met…did you tell me before?"

Philip had briefly mentioned the encounter at the bookstore, but now he went into the details of how they had both been looking at the same book—

"I only picked it up because *you* had talked about it," said Philip. "*Japan as Number One.*"

"So you're telling me I was your go-between?" asked Muranaka genially.

"I guess you were. I might not have had the nerve to call her again if I hadn't met her at your awards dinner the week after."

Jun picked up a camelhair overcoat and scarf, then stopped to give his secretary some final instructions about his schedule. The young woman nodded efficiently at everything he ticked off his list, but all the while she couldn't keep her eyes off Philip. This was not lost on Muranaka. He propelled Philip out the door.

"Are you sure you're ready to settle down?" he nudged when they were in the elevator. "You seem to have quite an effect on the ladies."

"Cut it out, Jun…" Philip said in mock exasperation. "Yes. I've found the one for me. I'm sure."

The elevator stopped four times, picking up smartly dressed secretaries and older businessmen on each floor. The young male employees never left work this early. They had to prove their organizational macho by staying late in the office. At least now, after their bosses had gone, they could finally get some work done before they, too, headed out to bars and clubs to unwind with professional hostesses.

Like an elegant greenish-black crane, Philip towered over everyone in the increasingly crowded box making its way to the ground floor. Jun grumbled as they emerged in the lobby.

I feel like a plank walking with a nail," he complained.

"Because I stick out, I'm the nail? As in 'the-nail-that-sticks-out-gets-pounded-down'? The *deru kugi*?" asked Philip.

"Nah. You stand out in a good way. Nobody's looking to pound you down—you're not Japanese. Lucky for you. I guess in that sense, I'm the *deru kugi* around here—I feel pretty pounded upon these days."

They were standing on the street now, in front of office buildings streaming with people. "I should have had my secretary get a driver," said Jun as cab after occupied cab drove by. "The subway will be unbearable at this hour."

"Where are we going?" asked Philip. "Can we walk?"

Muranaka turned and looked at him. "Of course! We're just going to Akasaka…let's walk. We'll be pilgrims again!"

They set off in the direction of one of Tokyo's pricier entertainment districts. At one point they cut through an alley with neon-flashing pachinko parlors on both sides of the street. The familiar ching and clatter of little steel balls reminded Philip of Kōji. He would never walk into one of these places on his own.

"Ever play pachinko, Jun?" he asked.

"Everybody in Japan has played pachinko," his companion replied. "This is part of the problem."

Philip wondered what problem he was talking about. Jun seemed to have aged since he saw him last, even stooping a bit as if he was conscious of a looming weight—or maybe it was the psychological pounding he had referred to earlier. Philip tried to lighten things up.

"So, speaking of nails, have you figured out the *inochi no kugi*?" Philip asked him.

"Oh God—not you too? I hope you haven't been wasting your time trying to second-guess pachinko machines?"

"No, it gives me a headache," Philip confessed. "I have a friend who's really into it, so sometimes I keep him company. But frankly, I just don't understand the appeal."

"You restore my faith in mankind," said Jun. "Pachinko will be the death of us one of these days."

Though he had no taste for pachinko personally, Philip didn't see how it could be as bad as Muranaka seemed to hint. An innocuous, if mindless, diversion for when you just wanted to put your mind on idle. If you could stand the noise and the cigarette smoke, what was the harm?

"Really, Jun, aren't you going a little overboard?"

"No. Not a bit. Let's get out of here, I really can't stand it." They reached the end of this street. When the noise of pachinko was no longer audible, Muranaka spoke again. His hands were stuffed deep in his pockets and he was scowling.

"Were you in Japan four years ago when a young Japanese couple disappeared while taking a stroll along the beach?"

Philip shook his head.

"There was not much news coverage even in Japan, so I'm not surprised," continued Jun, "but that wasn't the only time. Other people started vanishing—all along that stretch of the coast opposite Korea."

"What's that got to do with pachinko?"

"The government hasn't wanted to get involved, but they were kidnapped by North Koreans."

Philip was still mystified.

"I presume you know how pachinko works? With the winnings?"

Philip remembered accompanying Kōji down an alley where he turned in his armful of cheap prizes for cash.

"I figured there was something kind of shady about it," he admitted.

"More than shady. Welcome to the dark side of the economy. Gambling is illegal in Japan, so technically those places can only give away 'prizes'— cigarettes and candy and stuff. You get your cash in the back alley. But what the parlors give out is piffling compared to what they take in.

"You mean—yakuza?"

"Of course. Utterly riddled with yakuza, through and through. But I estimate that somewhere between a third and a half of those parlors are run by North Koreans, and that's where all their profit goes."

"To North Korea?" Philip was incredulous.

"Exactly. Without Japanese pachinko money, the North Korean economy would sink like a stone."

"Unbelievable…"

"If only," said Jun grimly. "North Korea is a black hole, but it's up to something. These kidnappings are very worrisome. The foreign ministry is getting concerned—they've asked me to help them come up with a plan… sorry, I'm not in a position to talk about the details—but pachinko is part of it. Drives me crazy."

They had been walking quickly, and didn't feel the cold any more. Jun stopped in front of a sleek new building complex housing a number of expensive restaurants.

"This is it."

They peeled off their coats inside the overheated lobby, and took the elevator to the top floor.

"French *kaiseki*," Jun said. "I thought it would be the sort of thing you'd appreciate—French food in Japanese style."

"Great!" said Philip, as the maitre d' showed them to their table.

Philip saw Jun gradually relax in between the tiny, exquisite courses. Appetizers of foie gras studded with jewel-like orange salmon roe, dollops of lobster mousse nestled in hearts of artichoke, were followed by a fragrant consommé served in a lidded lacquer bowl.

"This makes so much sense," Philip marveled. "*Cuisine française a la Japonaise*—a marriage made in heaven."

"May yours be the same," said Jun, raising a glass of Sancerre.

"I feel like such an idiot not having asked you this before," said Philip, clinking glasses, "but I don't know anything about your wife, or family."

Jun took a long appreciative sip from his wineglass then put it down.

"A wife, yes. Masako is her name. No children," said Jun. "House in Mejiro. A dog—my wife's dog, cocker spaniel…"

"How did you and Masako meet," Philip asked, genuinely curious. Jun had never spoken of her.

The waiter collected their soup bowls, replacing them with timbales of asparagus.

"Arranged marriage. My aunt and uncle took on the responsibility. Found a nice girl from a respectable family. Everybody was happy."

"Excuse me, but you don't sound so happy…"

"Well, it's been seventeen years. It was just one of those things. She came to Chicago with me, but she didn't like it very much. She didn't feel safe walking out of the University Apartments—come to think of it, she didn't feel safe *inside* the apartments. Hyde Park was a pretty brutal place back then. When we got back to Japan I promised her she'd never have to travel with me again—so she didn't. We each live our separate lives. But it works, for us. We'd never think of divorcing. We Japanese don't have the same outlook on marriage as you romantic *gaijin* do. Start out with low expectations, then you can only be pleasurably surprised if it's better than that."

Philip didn't know quite what to say. Jun, too, realized this was not the sort of thing he ought to be saying on this occasion.

"Artists excepted," he added hastily. "You and Miss Kiyowara are clearly on a different level from most of us. You know the expression *go-en ga aru*? To have a karmic connection with someone? I don't know much about how karma works, but there are people you see sometimes who just seem to fall together, despite the most improbable circumstances, almost as if they are acting out a script they have already rehearsed a hundred times."

Philip nodded. He finished his glass of wine.

"I think it's rare," continued Jun, "but it happens. And those people are very lucky." He paused. "We're going to a private club in Akasaka after this, so I hope you told her you wouldn't be back till late."

"Yes. Of course." Philip lied, thinking of what he actually had said.

(When he left the apartment, he kissed Nagiko and told her he would be back by ten o'clock. She laughed. "I'll be amazed if I see you before two a.m.," she had said.)

They floated down to the lobby in a warm winey fog. Outside, the cold air slapped them briskly enough that they hastily struggled into their coats.

"It should start getting warmer pretty soon," Jun stamped his feet. "Anyway, where we're going is not very far."

Ten minutes later they were standing in what looked to Philip like some ultra-fashionable designer's living room. Small groups of men and women clustered on sofas and around tables. The men were Jun's age or older, the women were mostly in their twenties, knockouts, without exception. One, a little older, hair up in a simple chignon, and wearing kimono, came over as soon as she saw Jun. She pretended not to take in every detail of his young companion.

"Muranaka-san! We haven't seen you for so long! How are you?" She waved one of her companions over—a long-haired beauty in a glamorous low-cut velvet dress. The four of them sat snugly together at one end of a curved sofa. The kimono'd woman cried, "Introductions!" Then before Jun could even speak, she laid her hand on his arm and asked if he wanted the usual.

"Bourbon," said Jun. "Philip?"

"Fu-wi-ri-pu," the other girl tried to pronounce with a little hiccup, breaking into giggles.

"Uh, sure—bourbon is fine," he said. Internally he was saying to himself so this is one of those hostess bars…interesting…"

"This is Umeko," Jun introduced the woman who had taken charge of them. "She is an Akasaka geisha. This is her bar. This is my friend Philip Metcalfe—we met on the Shikoku pilgrimage last summer."

This elicited a great deal of interested cooing from both women. Umeko pulled an elegant business card from her obi, handing it to Philip with both hands, as if it were a precious tidbit. She introduced the other girl as Erika, a newcomer who had just started hostessing three weeks ago. Erika looked around for her evening purse to give them a card as well, but she seemed to have left it at another table. She giggled again. Umeko narrowed her eyes slightly.

"Umeko is a great dancer," said Jun. "Don't you have a performance at the National Theater coming up in March?"

She lowered her eyes modestly.

"You know I do. You bought all those tickets…"

"Philip, remind me to give you a couple for yourself and Nagiko."

"Who's Nagiko," interrupted Erika with a little pout, putting her hand on Philip's arm.

"Philip's getting married next month," said Jun. "To Nagiko Kiyowara…"

"The designer?" asked Umeko.

"Yes," said Philip, somewhat relieved to have Nagiko's presence introduced to the conversation.

"Is this one of her fabrics?" asked Umeko, fingering the sleeve of Philip's suit.

"It is," he said.

Erika ran her hand over his thigh. "It's ve-e-ry nice," she whispered in his ear, her head almost resting on his shoulder now.

A waiter brought a tray of glasses, ice, and a bottle of Maker's Mark.

Umeko poured three glasses. Straight for Jun, on ice for Philip, and diluted for herself. She pointedly did not pour one for Erika, who was soon summoned away to another table despite her protests that she wanted to stay with Fu-wi-ri-pu-san. Another waiter came by with two plates of something dark, sliced very thin. Jun frowned.

"What's this?" asked Philip, always curious to try something new.

"Umeko—is that what I think it is?" Jun did not sound happy.

Umeko was startled. "Oh! I'm so sorry!" She immediately called the waiter back and whispered something to him.

Philip was bewildered. "What is it Jun?"

"Whale," scowled Muranaka. "It beats the hell out of me why some people insist on Japan's god-given right to eat whale." He said this in English.

Umeko apologized profusely for allowing it to be served. Had she realized Jun was coming tonight she certainly would have taken it off the snack menu. It was just that she had so many older clients who asked for it…

Jun calmed down. "It's okay," he said, patting her arm. "I'm not blaming you. It shouldn't even be available for sale, in my opinion. It's not worth it. The rest of the world just points to Japan as monstrous for killing whales." he paused. "And it doesn't even taste good!"

Philip regretted that the waiter had scooped up the dish before he had a chance to even try it. He was definitely on the side of sparing the whales, but since it was too late for this one anyway…"

Muranaka looked at him.

"I know what you're thinking," he said. "No."

Philip grinned sheepishly.

Around one a.m. Jun asked Umeko to call a car for them. Philip had been trying to explain Maigny's theory of the hidden buddhas to Jun, Umeko, and another pretty young thing named Urara who had slithered in beside him after Erika left. When Jun looked discreetly at his watch, Umeko called the waiter over to the table to snap a picture with her new Polaroid.

"Cheezu, everyone…"

She waved the damp square gently back and forth to dry the chemicals before giving it to Philip. He thanked her but then immediately forgot it on the table as they stood up. The women accompanied them out to the street. After many fond farewells, Jun managed to push the loquacious Philip into a cab. All the way home Philip marveled to Jun about how interested the two women had been in the hidden buddhas. They hung on his every word. Who would have thought such an esoteric subject could be so engrossing? He felt he had been absolutely inspired. Jun listened in silence until just before the car pulled up to Lion's Head Mansion when he let out a big guffaw.

"You're such an innocent, Philip," he laughed. "That's their job! To make us feel brilliant! Give my best to your bride…"

Philip slunk into the building, somewhat deflated, but glad to be heading for bed. He was surprised to find that Nagiko had waited up, even though she had fallen asleep in the chair. He gently led her to the unrolled futon. Then he took off his suit and carefully draped it over the chair she had vacated, He rolled into bed beside her.

"Whew—you smell like bourbon..." she mumbled groggily before falling back asleep

The next morning Philip woke with a throbbing head. Nagiko was up, making tea.

"Just stay in bed for a while," she said. "You don't have anywhere you have to be today, do you?

Philip groaned. He remembered his appointment with the priest in Kamakura that afternoon. Right—but he was not going to tell Nagiko about that. He hoped he wouldn't have to lie directly because he was sure he would botch it. Instead, he asked her what her schedule was.

"I'll be fine..." he said with a wince. "What about you? What are you doing today?"

"Office. As usual. You want some tea with milk?"

"Oh, yes please..." Philip sank back on the pillow, relieved.

"And tonight I have to go out to dinner with that guy from Spiff, the new home furnishings store—remember?"

Even better, thought Philip, sitting up. "Okay, I'll fend for myself," he said. "Don't worry about me."

"Worry about you getting fed?" she asked, bringing a mug of milky English tea. "Never." She set the mug down and massaged his forehead. "Was it fun? Did Muranaka-san take you to a club?"

"Yes. And yes. It was interesting..." Philip took a long slurp of tea. "What kind of name is 'Urara'?"

Nagiko rolled her eyes and gave his hair a little yank.

"Owww...you made me spill... Hey—they knew your stuff. One of them asked me about my suit."

"Glad to be of service..."

"Come on, you're not jealous are you..." Philip rolled over and grabbed the hem of Nagiko's bathrobe. He tugged several times. "Please don't turn into a snake demon," he pleaded.

Finally she untied the belt letting the robe slip completely off. At the last tug it tumbled onto Philip's head as she walked naked to the shower.

After a hot shower and two more cups of tea, Philip left the apartment at noon. On the train he dozed off, daydreaming about the previous evening's dinner. He was meeting the priest at the same garden bench where they had taken their leave the weekend before. The fickle early February weather had turned warm overnight and the weekend snow had now totally vanished. A warm breeze carried the vernal scent of newly thawed mud. Philip was early. He wandered along the pebbled path that meandered back by a pond. Quince had burst forth and the plump fists of plum blossoms seemed ready to explode. He looked at his watch and turned back toward the bench.

Tokuda was standing there. He had on a pair of extra high wooden garden *geta* to keep the hems of his robes out of the mud. Philip apologized.

"Not at all," said Tokuda. "Let's go over to my office." He stopped. "Unless you'd rather...have you eaten?"

Philip realized that even though he'd been thinking about food all morning, he hadn't actually had any. "I could eat something, now that you mention it..." he said.

"Let's do that, then..." Tokuda changed direction.

He led Philip down the street to a tiny storefront with a hand painted sign, *Casa Rosa*, in the window.

"Mexican?" exclaimed Philip. "In Kamakura...?"

The restaurant was empty. As they sat down a young Japanese man with long hair tucked back in a ponytail appeared from behind the curtain separating the dining area from the tiny kitchen.

He nodded a welcome.

"*Habla español?*" he asked Philip hopefully.

"*Solamente un poco*," Philip apologized. Tokuda smiled. It sounded authentic to him.

"What will it be?"

"The special," said Tokuda.

"Same," added Philip, although he did glance through the menu, amused at the thought of tacos in Kamakura.

He had decided to go ahead and tell Tokuda everything he knew. Philip recognized that if he wanted to gather anything of interest to Maigny he was going to need help, and this curious priest seemed like a good place to start. Right at the moment, however, with a steaming cheese-filled tamale placed under his nose, he wasn't quite sure where to begin.

Tokuda helped him out. "So," he said, carefully stripping the cornhusk wrapping off his tamale, "you said your teacher thinks the hidden buddhas were Kūkai's idea…"

"Although he has no textual evidence," interjected Philip.

"Yes, no evidence. So then, why…"

"Well, he thinks perhaps Kūkai arranged for the hidden buddhas to be set up in all those temples—to protect the world…"

"What?"

"To protect the world…from ending…from *mappō* rushing to its end. My professor suspects that Kūkai regarded the hidden buddhas as a brake on *mappō*."

Tokuda had told himself beforehand that he would remain unruffled no matter what Philip said, but this was unbelievable.

"And how does he think they do this?" he managed to ask.

"He thinks it's by keeping their protective power hidden. It must be that when they are on display, they are vulnerable."

Despite his vow to be calm, Tokuda almost choked, although he disguised it by pretending to cough on a pepper. He reached for a glass of water.

"But that doesn't make sense," he spluttered. "If it was Kūkai's plan to protect the world with secret images, why didn't he just hide them away somewhere safe?" It was a logical question, one he once asked his grandfather.

"If they were buried, they would have been forgotten. Kūkai might have solved this problem, according to my teacher, by making sure they were displayed only rarely, and all on different schedules."

"I see," Tokuda said quietly.

"And he believes there must be secret knowledge of this system that has been passed down from master to disciple over time."

Tokuda was nodding as he listened. "Yes, that's what you said before."

The waiter now came scuttling over to their table bearing two platters. Tokuda seemed to be lost in thought.

"But tell me what your professor thinks is happening with the hidden buddhas."

"That's where he's stuck," said Philip. "If only he could find evidence of a secret transmission, he would be able to answer that. How they are supposed to protect the world…and I guess, as you say, what Kūkai thought was driving *mappō*."

By force of habit, Tokuda's instinct was to hide his knowledge. Until now, that had been easy, because nobody had ever known enough to inquire. But now he had to carefully decide what, if anything, to reveal. At the same time, he felt he had to draw out everything Philip knew.

Maybe the thing to do was hide in plain sight? How would this young American react to Zuichō's theory he wondered?

He gazed directly at Philip.

"So the hidden buddhas are vulnerable, he thinks. Has he considered the possibility that there is a force of evil that is going about systematically viewing them, draining their power?" Tokuda asked. "As a student of Buddhism, surely you know about the *akunin*?"

Philip nodded, squinting to remember. *Icchantika* in Sanskrit. Beings of such darkness and delusion they could never reach enlightenment, no matter how many times they reincarnated. It was the closet thing in Buddhism to a theory of evil.

"You mean, what if there is an *akunin* who has been working over the centuries to overcome the system of safeguards Kūkai put in place…trying to push *mappō* to its ultimate conclusion?" Philip asked.

Tokuda nodded, and Philip had the sudden feeling that they were no longer talking simply about theory.

"You mean…" he probed, "You mean, like, if *mappō* was real?"

"That is a given. Are there not signs everywhere that *mappō* is real?" Tokuda replied coolly.

"But, reincarnation?" Philip pressed. "Are you saying that maybe it's some person's destiny to bring the world to an end?"

"Destiny?" Tokuda put down his fork. "What is destiny?" Destiny does not belong to an individual. Destiny is the pattern that holds us. Life is interconnected on all levels—all acting and reacting like threads shuttling back and forth. Very few of us see the pattern because we *are* the pattern…"

Philip wasn't sure how to respond. "What about Kūkai? Do you think he understood the pattern?" he asked.

"I think that, yes, Kūkai understood. But I'm not sure we can follow," Tokuda said. He had been afraid he wouldn't know how to talk to this young *gaijin* about these things, but it was not difficult at all. He felt everything he said fell on sympathetic ears.

"Look at it this way," said Tokuda. "Realistically, all the sciences tell us that the earth had a beginning and that the earth will have an end, right? And all religions, too. Things come into being and they dissolve. Can we influence this process? Maybe. Can we stop it? Of course not. Kūkai would never have tried to thwart *mappō*—to somehow heroically 'save' the world from the inevitable. But perhaps he did try to influence it, long after his bodily death, to try to ensure that the rhythms and patterns of the world worked their way to their proper end. *This* is what destiny meant to Kūkai."

"So the hidden buddhas…?"

"… maybe they've been protecting us from ourselves," said Tokuda.

Neither of them had touched their food, and now the waiter came toward them anxiously, wiping his hands on a dishtowel.

Tokuda saw him coming, and picked up his fork. Philip took the cue and began shoveling rice and beans onto a spoon.

"This is great," he said heartily, "I haven't had Mexican food since I left California. This is really *autentico*…"

Reassured, the waiter went back to the kitchen. "*Gracias*," he said, "take your time."

When they were alone again Philip suddenly asked, "Are you married, Tokuda-san?"

The priest shook his head. "Why?"

"Nothing…I'm getting married in two weeks, and I was just wondering…that is," Philip wasn't sure exactly what he was trying to say. "It just kind of changes the way you think about things, you know…having a family…"

"You mean, thinking about things like the future?"

"Exactly."

They finished their meal at *Casa Rosa* and walked slowly back to Fudō-in. Philip didn't know what to do. Not only did this priest Tokuda seem to think Maigny's theory was reasonable, he appeared to believe it was actively real. Tokuda was struggling too. What was he to make of what he now realized they shared? For the first time since his grandfather's death, he was not alone in his knowledge. What would Philip's reaction be if he were to confirm that indeed there was a secret line of transmission? It was starting to dawn on Tokuda that, crazy as it seemed, perhaps he was talking to the person he ought to make his successor—or even his partner.

Nowhere did it say the person had to be Japanese, or a priest, or even male for that matter (although any of those qualifications would have been self-evident to his predecessors.) The main thing that gave Tokuda pause in bringing Philip into his confidence was whether or not the young man would have the ability to "read" the images. Techniques could be taught, but you had to have an inborn ability.

Tokuda remembered Philip's visceral reaction to the Hall of Dreams Guan Yin. That was promising. He must probe further, he decided. He asked Metokafu about other hidden buddhas. What was the first *hibutsu* he had laid eyes on?

"It was on the Shikoku pilgrimage," Philip told him. "I heard about the hidden buddha at Temple 86 when I was halfway around, and decided I had to see it. The timing wasn't great—it was only open for two days, and I really had to push myself to get there in time."

"And?" Tokuda knew that this image was still powerful.

"Well, it was beautiful, of course," Philip began, "but I think I must have exhausted myself getting there because I almost lost it right there in the temple."

Tokuda pressed, "What do you mean?"

"Oh, you know—I felt kind of woozy, like I was going to faint or something."

"Did anything like that ever happen at another *hibutsu*?"

"Now that you ask," said Philip, "yes. At Saidaiji in Nara."

"That little Aizen?"

"Right. I went with Nagiko—that is, my fiancée. She had to drag me out of there…"

Another active *hibutsu*, Tokuda noted to himself.

"Any others?" he asked

Philip listed the other hidden buddhas he had visited with no ill effect. All of them were among those Tokuda knew to be either decoys or deactivated. Perhaps this was coincidence, but Tokuda didn't think so. He decided he would reveal certain things to Philip now. He did not need to say anything about making him a partner yet. That could come later.

They had reached the temple. The grounds were deserted in the pale late afternoon light.

"Let's walk up to the top. I have to ring the evening bell," Tokuda said. "In fact, if you want to, I'll let you ring it. You've had experience with these big bells, I imagine."

Philip remembered the temples on the pilgrimage. Whenever the striker hadn't been roped off he would take the opportunity to let loose the deep reverberation of the temple bell. He loved it. The sun was setting over the mountains behind Kamakura as he swung the pole back and released it to hurtle toward the thick bronze bell.

"What if I could give you evidence that your teacher is right?" Tokuda suddenly said. "That there has in fact been a line of transmission preserving the knowledge of the hidden buddhas over many generations?" They were now in a shabby sitting room—Philip was sitting on the very sofa where Nagiko and Satoko had sat on their first visit to Fudō-in. The room smelled faintly of cigarette smoke.

"Well, that would be great…but what could you show me that would be evidence?" asked Philip.

"There is no physical evidence," said Tokuda. "It's all here." He tapped his shaved head.

"What? You know the secret transmission? How is that possible?"

"Because, at this moment, I am its keeper."

Philip was speechless.

Tokuda continued measuring out this conversation that no one had prepared him to have. "Your teacher must be a very wise man. Everything he has deduced about the hidden buddhas is true. It is a system set up by Kūkai in order to 'put the brakes on' *mappō*, as you so colorfully put it. The images have to be both hidden and exposed, just as you said."

Tokuda got up to turn on the light in the darkening room. "But, the thing is…the hidden buddhas have been losing their power…"

Philip's head began to swim. So Maigny had guessed right about the *hibutsu* and Kūkai's mission at the heart of Shingon. But did Maigny think it was real? What was Philip supposed to do with these confidences that Tokuda was handing him? Time seemed to collapse. He felt as if he were in a net that had laid its first string over him at Maigny's lecture. More strings had pulled him to Japan, to Shingon, and eventually to the hidden buddhas and this priest, Tokuda. He was completely enmeshed. Maybe it *was* real? Okay, he didn't have to believe that, but right now he had better engage this priest as if it were. If *mappō* were real…and then it hit him, of course *mappō* was real. The signs were everywhere. "So…what are you doing about it?" Philip finally managed.

Tokuda flinched. "Watching," he said guardedly.

"Just watching? But aren't you supposed to be protecting them? Isn't that the point of the secret transmission?"

Tokuda got up and paced to the other end of the room. Here he had thought Metokafu would be thrilled, grateful for this unprecedented revelation. But instead, the first thing he did was echo Tokuda's own buried fear. What are you doing about it? Tokuda turned around to face Philip who was sitting on the sofa watching him intently. He would play the devil's advocate.

"*Mappō* is a natural process," he said carefully, relying on the line his grandfather had taught him, and which he had used to comfort himself whenever another *hibutsu* died. "You might think that whoever is picking off the *hibutsu*, one by one, is doing it with the intention of destroying the world—but *that* is the premise that lacks evidence."

Philip sounded skeptical. "Bringing *mappō* to a close—bringing life to an end—if that's true, you don't think that's evil?"

"What I meant was, whoever is doing it may not be conscious of their actions." Although Tokuda spoke sharply he could hear in Philip's voice the same question he had long ago asked his grandfather. It was almost as if he were arguing with himself.

"But what does it matter whether it's conscious or not?" Philip objected. "And fine, we can leave 'evil' out of it. But if it brings down the world?" He too was standing now, facing Tokuda.

"Isn't that all the more reason to prevent it? If a child is about to carry a lighted candle into a room full of gas fumes, isn't it your duty to restrain it? Especially since you know what will happen, and the child doesn't? Do you really think Kūkai would have created a body of knowledge to be passed along simply in order to *observe* this process?"

Tokuda winced at Philip's words. He felt like a heavy rock had been lifted away and he could see his own thoughts brought to light, like pale grubs unaccustomed to the glare of full attention. These were the very thoughts that Philip now enunciated, clearly, to his face—the same way he spoke out the syllables of the *Heart Sutra* in front of the Guan Yin hall, pronouncing each syllable as if its meaning were precious.

"So, how many of the *hibutsu* are still standing?" asked Philip. "Do you know?"

"Yes. There are twenty-one left."

Philip sank down on the sofa. "Out of the one hundred fifty that

Professor Maigny recorded on his map, there are only twenty-one that work?"

"Yes."

"And the rest?"

"Empty shells."

"How do you know?" Philip demanded.

Tokuda was humiliated. He had arrogantly thought that he would parcel out bits and pieces of the knowledge as it suited him, and here he was, being interrogated like a criminal. What did he know, and how did he know it? A secret tradition twelve-hundred years old, handed off one to another, ending up here, in him, but having somewhere along the way lost its meaning. Unless he could figure out what to do with the knowledge, he was merely holding a tawdry old basket of secrets that were of no use.

He sat down across from Philip.

"I will tell you everything," he said quietly.

Philip had started out curious, then he was confused. Then he was astonished. But now he was angry. Each emotion had washed over him like a tsunami. He felt extraordinarily clear-headed. This was real. For the first time in his life his intellectual knowledge, his instincts, and his heart aligned in one purpose—he had a huge stake in the future, and he was determined to protect it.

Tokuda told Philip the way he had been taught to recognize whether a *hibutsu* still retained its power. He described the way each of his five senses received the messages—and he also told him that the sixth sense was one he had to be born with. Philip probably had this sense also, judging from the completely untrained physical reaction he had experienced at the "live" images he happened to visit. Philip knew immediately which ones he meant.

It was quite dark out by the time Tokuda had finished answering all of Philip's questions.

"Won't your fiancée be worried?" he asked.

"When she hears that *mappō* is real? I imagine she would be...I don't plan on telling her, actually."

"No, I just meant, if you were late for dinner..." Tokuda was by now utterly drained. He felt terrible.

Philip relented. He could see that this had been extremely difficult for the priest. He stood up. "Look," he said, "Why can't we take this on together? You yourself said that even one live *hibutsu* could prevent *mappō* closing in. Whoever is viewing them has to catch every last one, isn't that right?"

Tokuda nodded.

"So I'll help you watch over the remaining twenty-one. If one of those goes down, we'll catch whoever is doing it—conscious or not—and we'll keep him away from the rest. And after us, we'll have others to help. I'm going to be a father—there will be another generation."

Philip was standing behind Tokuda now. He put his hand on the priest's shoulder.

"Think about it, all right? I'm getting married in two weeks, then we're going on a honeymoon to Hawaii. I'll be back the first week of March—a month from now. We'll figure out a plan then. What do you say?"

Tokuda took a deep breath. "All right." This meeting had not gone at all as he had expected. But just maybe he had found the way to carry out his mission.

Consciousness

PHILIP MADE IT BACK BEFORE Nagiko got home. He found a scribbled message by the telephone. "Mr. Chernish called. In Tokyo, wants to see you. Staying at International House. Please call."

Oh great, Philip thought. He looked at his watch. Ten o'clock. Should he call now? Ugh. Might as well get it over with. He dialed the number.

"Professor Chernish? It's Philip Metcalfe."

"Ah, Philip! How are you? Haven't heard from you in a while."

"Fine, thanks. Yes, uh, things have been a little hectic…I'm hoping we'll see you at the wedding week after next."

"Yes, of course. I'll be there. Do you want me to make a speech? Be happy to…"

"Thanks, that's very kind…"

"But Philip, we need to get together to talk about your thesis."

"Right. Could we possibly do that after the wedding, though…"

"Look, Philip, I haven't got a lot of time in Tokyo. I know things are busy for you now, but it would really be a good idea to talk sooner than that. I'm free tomorrow afternoon…around three o'clock? If you could swing by International House, I could see you between three and five. How's that?"

"Great…" said Philip.

"Okay, see you tomorrow." Chernish hung up.

Philip kicked the wastebasket.

Briefly he thought about blowing Chernish off. Then he considered telling him the truth—that he had completely lost interest in his original thesis topic. The alternative of letting him know what was really going on was not even an option. Yet if he were to unmoor himself from his official university ties, not to mention his scholarship money, it would be impossible to stay in Japan. No, he had to come up with something he could throw Chernish just to get him off his back. It was maddening. He needed time to think, time to write to Maigny. The last thing he wanted to do right now was cobble together a bogus progress review for Professor Chernish. He sighed. Looked like he would be up all night.

Nagiko came home a little after eleven. She found Philip in a terrible mood. He could say nothing about the momentous understanding he had reached with Tokuda, so he ranted about the unfortunate necessity of meeting with Professor Chernish.

"But he sounded like such a nice man on the phone…" Nagiko had no idea of the spot Philip was in.

"Well, he's not particularly nice, and I'm going to have to stay up all night plus every minute until three o'clock tomorrow afternoon to come up with something," said Philip. "In fact, I'm going back to my place now. All my books are there. I'd just keep you up in any case." He lifted his coat off the hook and began putting on his shoes. "I'll see you for dinner tomorrow night, okay? I'll be done with Chernish at five then I'll come back here. Come home early if you can…I'll need a drink by that point."

Nagiko looked at him with dismay. "Really? It's past eleven…you have to leave now?"

She stood at the entrance in her stockings. Philip, shoes on, ready to leave, gave her a long kiss. Tomorrow night he could tell her everything.

By midnight Philip was back in his Shinjuku apartment. He made himself a bowl of intensely caffeinated whipped green *matcha* tea. Then he pulled out his typewriter and got to work. He had read all of Harvey Chernish's books and articles. He knew exactly how his mind worked, and he knew what he had to do.

By seven a.m. he had an outline, a list of hypotheses, a bibliography, and an introduction typed out. He was starving. The only thing in the pantry was instant ramen. He cooked two of them, and went back to typing. Nagiko called. He reassured her in a cheerful voice. He had now broken through the main problem, and could easily talk with Chernish for two hours. In fact, he realized, he had more than enough material, since once he fed Chernish a few questions, the professor was likely to take up most of the time talking himself. That was fine. Philip was beyond shameless. He threw together a matrix for analyzing the results of the questionnaires. He would bring those along too.

At one o'clock he took a brief nap. At one forty-five he showered and changed his clothes. Then he packed all of his papers into his backpack and headed off to International House. Philip felt pretty positive, considering how bleak things had looked last night. He emerged from the subway at Roppongi, in front of the pink-and-white striped awning of the Almond Confectionery where he briefly considered buying a box of cookies for Chernish, and then mentally laughed at himself. "God, you've been in Japan too long…" He headed up the hill toward International House.

Philip was about to cross the street into the long driveway when he suddenly felt a black wave welling up from somewhere behind his eyes. He stumbled, and he did not see the Mercedes driven by the Singaporean ambassador's new driver.

The driver did not see Philip either, until a sickening thud made him mash his foot on the brake. This was it. He would be fired. Maybe sent to jail. His wife would leave him. His family would be shamed. Where did this guy come from? He hadn't seen him at all. These thoughts pelted through the driver's panicked mind in the six-second breath he inhaled before opening the door.

Philip lay sprawled on the driveway in front of the car's front wheel. His right leg was twisted at a strange angle and blood had begun to seep from somewhere, slowly darkening the fabric of his jacket. He was unconscious. The backpack he had been carrying lay ten feet away, spilling papers over the ground. The hysterical driver was punching the buttons on his two-way radio to no effect. Finally an elderly gardener took in the situation and notified the front desk. It was ten minutes after three o'clock.

Harvey Chernish was working on an article for *The Japanese Journal of Religion* when he heard the siren of the approaching ambulance. The wail got very loud then it stopped. He glanced at his watch. That damn Metcalfe was late. He got up to stretch, walking over to the window that overlooked the drive. A knot of people stood surrounding the front of a black limousine. Someone must have been hit. Yes, they were moving him on to a stretcher. Looked nasty…

Chernish continued to watch the driveway drama another minute, thinking that perhaps Philip might be among the group of onlookers below. He would have to ask him the details. Suddenly an uncomfortable thought occurred to him and he decided he'd wander down to the lobby. People were buzzing around talking about the accident. Police were trying to find someone who could identify the victim. One officer held the damaged backpack, and another had scooped up the various papers that had fluttered out onto the street. Chernish approached the policeman holding the backpack. He asked to look at the contents, but by now he knew what he would find. A glance confirmed it.

"I know this person. He is my student. He was coming here to meet me this afternoon," Chernish told the police.

"Does he have family here? Any contacts you know of?" There was the fiancée he had spoken to yesterday, but Chernish knew little about her.

"Well then, you had better follow us to the hospital," said one of the officers.

Harvey Chernish left the hospital at seven. He had been able to leave a message back at I-House for the person he was supposed to meet, but now he needed to go back there since he'd left Philip's phone number in his room. He should also call the American embassy and fax the department at Columbia so that someone could contact Philip's parents. What could he tell them at this point? Philip had a broken leg, a snapped collarbone and some minor internal injuries—this much was revealed by the X-rays. He had probably sustained a concussion as well. In any case he was still unconscious. There was no reason to think he would not recover, however. The injury did not appear to be life threatening.

Since he had identified himself as Philip's *sensei*, the police had given Chernish all of his belongings for safekeeping. Chernish glanced through the papers. He had been feeling annoyed that Philip had communicated so little about the progress of his research this past year, and he suspected him of going off the deep end with his pilgrimages and such under the influence of that Frenchman Maigny. But here it seemed he had made a fair amount of progress after all. Chernish felt guilty about his uncharitable thoughts. But now he had to call the fiancée. They had spoken in Japanese yesterday. Did she speak English? He couldn't recall. Better look up how to say "concussion" in Japanese just in case.

Nagiko had gotten home by five-thirty. She was worried about Philip and wanted to be there when he returned. She didn't understand why he had to suddenly work so hard to prepare something for his professor. Hadn't he been working steadily ever since she knew him? She was feeling bad that she understood so little about his intellectual interests. Well, tonight she would get him to explain it to her. Next week his parents would arrive in Tokyo.

Nagiko was clearing time from her schedule to be able to take them around, but she knew that by the time they appeared, the days counting down to the wedding would become a blur. She would not be able to have any serious quiet time with Philip till they got to Hawaii on their honeymoon. She would wait to announce her pregnancy and put up with her colleagues' ribbing until they got back to Tokyo in March.

How annoying! It was now eight o'clock and not only had Philip not come back, he hadn't even called. She half-heartedly tried his apartment, not expecting to find him there. He had probably gone out drinking with his professor. That's what graduate students did, after all. That was fine—it almost certainly meant that whatever difficulties Philip was having with him would now get worked out amicably over beers. But still. He should have called. Was he going to turn into a Japanese husband after all? Nagiko was becoming indignant.

The phone rang. This had better be good...she thought.

She hung up after talking calmly with Professor Chernish. Then she started to shake so violently she had to bite her sleeve. What should she do first? Philip's *sensei* had given her the details of the accident and the name of the hospital. There would be forms to fill out, doctors to talk to.

At Aoyama Hospital she steeled herself as the nurse opened the door, then pulled back the curtain. Philip's head was not bandaged, and his face looked so peaceful Nagiko couldn't believe he could be badly hurt. She tentatively pulled down the sheet. There were gauze bandages on his arms, and his broken leg had already been set. She could see bruises on his sides. This would make for an awkward honeymoon. Yet his breathing was even. She pulled a chair next to the bed and stroked his face. It seemed like he should open his eyes any minute. She willed him to open his eyes.

She was concentrating so hard that Nagiko did not notice when the doctor entered the room. The man cleared his throat and spoke, jolting her back to her surroundings.

"You are this man's fiancée, is that right?" the doctor asked.

"Yes," Nagiko whispered.

"But you have no legal relationship at this point..." he continued.

Nagiko remembered the document Philip had gone to the American embassy to obtain. She wasn't sure what the doctor was implying.

"Tell me what's wrong with him."

"He was struck by an automobile, and that is the cause of the fractured bones, skin abrasions, and some internal bleeding," said the doctor. "But the more difficult question is why he has not regained consciousness."

Nagiko suddenly saw that what had at first reassured her, his seemingly peaceful sleep, might not be a good sign. "You mean he has not been awake at all?" she asked.

"He has not. There is no x-ray evidence of a concussion, although we are assuming that he has had one. We will need to do more tests. For that we will need a family member's authorization…"

"I see. And I don't count as a family member yet…"

"Unfortunately not." The doctor was apologetic. "Perhaps you could obtain his parents' signatures?"

"Give me the forms," said Nagiko. "I will translate them and fax them tonight." She did a quick calculation of the time difference between Tokyo and California. She should call Philip's parents now. As soon as the nurse brought a copy of the consent form Nagiko stood up and put it in her purse. She touched Philip's cheek as she spoke to him.

"I have to go now and take care of some things. I'm going to call your Mom and Dad. Don't worry. I'll take care of everything. It's going to be fine, I promise." She decided to assume that Philip could hear and understand even if he couldn't respond.

"I'll be back as soon as I can," she said. "Maybe you'll be awake then." She bowed to the nurse and hurried out of the room.

By the next day a number of things had been set in motion. The caterer called about the menu for the reception. Philip had been in charge of all that, but obviously he was in no shape to choose between grilled chicken livers or skewered mushrooms. Satoko advised her to call the whole thing off, but Nagiko felt that would be tantamount to admitting Philip's condition was serious.

"I don't need to decide that today," she told Satoko. "Let's just wait a day or two, after they've done the tests. After he wakes up."

She had faxed the forms to Philip's parents and was now waiting for them to be returned. Finally her assistant knocked, bringing in a fax from California. She looked at it. It was not the form she had sent. Instead, it was a short letter. Philip's parents had not given their permission for more tests. They were coming to Japan to fetch him back to the United States for medical treatment. Philip's father was arranging emergency medical transport from Yokota Air Base. They asked Nagiko to meet their flight arriving tomorrow evening at Narita.

Nagiko collapsed back into her chair, feeling like the breath had been knocked out of her. Since Harvey Chernish had called last night, she hadn't eaten a thing except a piece of dry toast early this morning. Her assistant hung outside the door, worried. Now the girl timidly poked her head back into the room.

"Are you all right," she asked, alarmed at Nagiko's pale face and the deep shadows under her eyes. "Can I bring you some food? You really should eat something…"

Nagiko wondered for a moment if the girl had guessed her condition. Then she realized that word of Philip's accident had been passed around. She thanked her and said yes, maybe she could order her an *oyako donburi* from the carryout place they always used. The girl didn't think twice that Nagiko ordered parent-and-child on rice. Chicken and egg is always called that.

Philip continued to sleep. Nagiko brought his parents directly from the airport to the hospital at their insistence, even though she had suggested they stop at their hotel first, just to check in and drop off their luggage. They had brought very little. It was obvious that they were not planning to stay long.

James Metcalfe was tall like Philip, but heavier. He moved with the deliberate gait of someone used to getting his way. When he stood up, the stiffness of his jaw radiated down his whole body. Philip's mother Linda, in contrast, wobbled on the verge of melting. Her once-blonde hair, now sandy brown with bleached highlights, fell in short curls over blue eyes that were squinty from weeping. She was about the same height as Nagiko, but whereas Nagiko struck people as tall, Linda Metcalfe seemed like a compact model of some larger, now lost, original.

The three of them stood awkwardly around Philip's bed in the cramped space of the tiny hospital room, waiting for the doctor. Philip's mother was crying softly. When the doctor came in, Nagiko translated the same information he had given her the first day to her soon to be mother- and father-in-law. There had been no change. The doctor was clearly insulted that he had not been allowed to do further tests. Nagiko did not relay the scope of his annoyance to Philip's parents. She had assumed she would accompany them on the flight back to California, and was just now absorbing the realization that they were planning to take him back alone.

"He will have much better care at home. Of course you realize that. We all want to do the best we can for him. You must fly to California as soon as he regains consciousness," his mother said.

"But—I want to come, too," she finally blurted out. "I want to be there when he does…"

Philip's father cleared his throat. "There's no clearance on this military plane for non-related persons," he said gruffly. Nagiko wondered whether she should tell them she was pregnant. She looked at Philip's mother, who had been avoiding looking at her, and felt a chill curtain ripple across her heart. She decided she wouldn't say anything.

"We will of course call you the moment he shows improvement," Linda Metcalfe said. "Maybe you two could get married at our church in San Anselmo—that would be so nice…"

By now Nagiko's emotions were close to shutting down. She forced herself to smile and nod to Philip's mother, but later had no recollection at all of what she had said.

Palaka

THE WEDDING DATE CAME and went. Jun Muranaka called to offer condolences. He asked Nagiko to let him know if there was anything he could do. He didn't know she was pregnant.

Spring passed into May, and the weather turned hot. Nagiko was short of breath during the day, and at night the restless unborn child kicked and somersaulted and pressed a foot unremittingly under her ribs. Although she had made no official announcement, by now her condition was obvious. Nagiko started to interview Filipina maids for a nanny to live in the apartment. Two more months to go. Philip's parents had not called. Finally Nagiko called them, only to learn that there had been no change. "We'll let you know…" Linda Metcalfe said. "The doctors say the longer he continues like this, the less hope there is." Nagiko hung up helplessly.

By the time rainy season enfolded Tokyo, Nagiko felt ready to crawl out of her skin. She was always on the verge of tears. Her body no longer belonged to her. She had tried to salvage inspiration by coming up with a line of maternity fashion, yet she had refused to allow herself to be photographed modeling any of the outfits. She claimed modesty, but in fact she was still debating whether or not to tell Philip's parents about their imminent grandchild. Their silent hostility was daunting. If Philip didn't recover, Nagiko was not sure she would tell them at all. This was her secret, to reveal or not, in the manner of her own choosing. By now Nagiko had allowed herself to think "what if…" Even, what if he didn't recover…

As the famous blue hydrangeas of Kamakura came into bloom, Noboru Tokuda hoped against fading hope that Metcalfe would contact him. He had been expecting to see him in March when he returned from his honeymoon. Tokuda had cautiously called his apartment three times in April, each time fearing Philip's new wife would pick up the phone, but he had never gotten an answer. He called once in May, but the number had been disconnected. Tokuda didn't know what to think. His last hope was that Miss Kiyowara would come to the temple in June as she had done for the last five years. He did not leave Kamakura the entire month, watching. But she didn't come.

Tokuda had been thinking hard since that revelatory meeting in which Philip's outburst had shattered his lone singularity. His nagging worry about choosing a successor had suddenly evaporated. If not a successor, he would have a partner. Over the centuries during which transmission of the secret knowledge had jumped from person to person like a synapse firing down the line directly from Kūkai, there had never been a partnership. It had been master to disciple all the way. Perhaps the urgency of the current state of affairs permitted—no, required—a different approach? If the secret knowledge had any meaning at all, didn't it make sense to push past the forms and try to grasp its essence? What was the alternative? To simply watch as the remaining *hibutsu* were snuffed out one by one? Was that the ultimate outcome Kūkai had planned? This was, Tokuda now realized, unthinkable.

Tokuda went over everything his grandfather had taught him, including the commentary that had barnacled on to the core knowledge. In particular, he mulled over the theory that an *akunin* might be stopped if caught in the act of willfully killing off the *hibutsu*. It was a theory that had never been tested. Tokuda had been the only one to actually witness a dying *hibutsu*. His own secret, since that day twenty-seven years ago, was that he had let the woman escape.

Now it was more important than ever to watch each hidden buddha.

Everything Philip had said made sense. The two of them. This was a real mission now, with real consequences. Tokuda felt resolve coursing through his veins, energizing his very being.

Now, where was Metcalfe?

On July 23, Nagiko gave birth to a girl. Satoko came to the private maternity hospital every day. As godmother, she had consulted fortunetellers about a name, finally settling on Mayumi. The baby was extraordinarily pretty except for a slight malformation of her fingers and toes, which were connected by thin webbings of flesh. The doctor said it was not uncommon and could easily be corrected surgically.

"It's a stage in the growth of the fetus. Usually the digits differentiate at about the sixteenth week of development. Occasionally they don't, resulting in syndactyly—but it's quite easy to fix so don't worry about it," he reassured Nagiko.

She looked at Mayumi's tiny webbed fingers opening and closing and was reminded of a little frog. What had happened during the sixteenth week of her pregnancy to have caused this? She counted back and realized with a shock that that would have been right about the time of Philip's accident. Hesitantly she asked the doctor if he thought there could be a connection.

"None at all," he declared. "Total coincidence."

She was unconvinced. She remembered Professor Chernish's phone call, how the bottom of her belly seemed to drop, how her insides clutched and froze. How could this state of shock not have an effect on a baby growing in the middle of it? Perhaps Mayumi reacted by ceasing to develop for a period? And then when she started to grow again she had missed a particular window?

On the second day after giving birth, Nagiko's milk came in. She awoke with a fever and painfully swollen breasts. The baby's mouth bumped against her rock-hard flesh, unable to latch on. Mayumi wailed. Nagiko felt like sobbing too. As the nurse went through a well-rehearsed litany of the benefits of breastfeeding for mother and child, Nagiko's heart sank. She knew she could not manage that. Mayumi would have to transition to a bottle as soon as they left the hospital. During the day, Josefina, the placid Filipina nanny who had four children of her own back in Manila, would be in charge of feeding her.

Nagiko's room filled with flowers and presents from well-wishers. Satoko helped with visitors, snipped out the dead blooms from the flower arrangements, and held the baby while Nagiko cried. Mayumi cried too—constantly. It was unnerving, all this sobbing. Satoko asked the nurse what she could do about it, but the nurse assured her that feeling blue was a normal part of the post-partum process. On the afternoon of the fourth day, Jun Muranaka came by, carrying a teddy bear and a monstrous bunch of intense yellow sunflowers. He greeted Nagiko with the shy hesitancy of a man totally unaccustomed to being around infants.

"I just found out..." he began awkwardly. "I mean, I didn't know that you were..." He stopped.

At Satoko's urging, Nagiko had forced herself to put on makeup and dress nicely for visitors in the afternoons. She had washed her hair that morning. Looking in the mirror, she was surprised at her own glowing skin. The great waves of emotion that had reared up and swamped her since the birth had begun to recede. She felt like a small tropical island that had been battered by a fierce hurricane and survived.

Now she smiled at Muranaka. "I'm sorry. I should have said something…"

"No, no. I completely understand. You had a lot of things to deal with, clearly…" He glanced at the sleeping baby. "Does Philip know…"

Nagiko looked at him without lowering her eyes. "I really meant to tell you. The truth is, he doesn't know anything. He has not woken up since the accident."

Muranaka let out his breath sharply. "I'm so sorry," he said.

"At this point, we would have to hope for a miracle," said Nagiko, looking away, "but it doesn't seem too likely. I've pretty much given up."

"I see."

Just at this moment Mayumi stretched her limbs out like a starfish and opened her eyes. Muranaka peered at the baby.

"Oh, she's got Philip's eyes!" he exclaimed.

"All babies have dark blue eyes," Nagiko said. "They'll change."

Muranaka said nothing about the curious fingers. "What is her name?"

"Mayumi," said Nagiko, explaining the characters Satoko had chosen to write it.

"Mayumi Metcalfe?"

"Someday, maybe," said Nagiko warily, "but for right now it's Mayumi Kiyowara."

Muranaka was struck by Nagiko's combination of softness and determination—not to mention how forlorn yet beautiful she looked. He could understand why Philip had fallen so totally in love. It seemed cosmically unfair.

"You know," he said, "I don't know if Philip ever mentioned it, but I consider myself to be something of a go-between for you two."

"How so?" asked Nagiko. "—wait a minute, let me guess. You told Philip about *Japan as Number One*? And that's what made him pick up the same book I was looking at… is that it?"

"Yes, but not only that. There was the awards dinner where you met again. Philip told me he had been planning to get my advice on how to ask you out. That was his real reason for going that night—and then, there you were. So, luckily I wasn't put in the position of giving advice on something I know nothing about…" Muranaka joked lamely, one eye on Mayumi who had screwed up her tiny red face and was showing signs of getting ready to wail.

Nagiko stood up and walked over to the cot to pick up the baby.

"I'm not very good at this yet," she said to Muranaka as she gingerly slipped her hands under the whimpering bundle. "But somehow, I suppose, we'll manage."

Afraid that Nagiko was getting ready to feed the baby, Muranaka made hasty excuses, and stood up to leave. Satoko came back in the room, and he put his business card on the table.

"If there's anything I can do, please don't hesitate," he said. "If it's all right, I'll call you in a month, just to check on how you're doing." By now Mayumi's wails reverberated off the walls as Nagiko bounced her in her arms to no effect. Satoko led Muranaka out.

After three more days trying to follow the instructions and helpful hints for nursing, Nagiko gave up. The pain of that wolfish little mouth clamping down on her sore nipples was excruciating. She had Satoko call a car to fetch them home where Josefina waited. From the moment Nagiko placed Mayumi in Josefina's arms, the baby quieted. Nagiko began binding her breasts with cotton strips the next day, and Mayumi went on formula.

"Little *palaka*," Josefina called Mayumi, crooning as she cradled her on her wide bosom.

"What does that mean?" Nagiko asked her one day.

Josefina reddened.

"Tell me."

"Frog…," Josefina mumbled. "But, cute frog…"

Nagiko frowned. She would have to ask the doctor when that operation could take place. First a water child, now a frog. Mayumi continued to be colicky, which Nagiko blamed on herself for not breastfeeding. Strangely, she still dreamed of the *mizuko*. She saw a four-year-old child shed its clothes and jump into a river where it metamorphosed into a tadpole then gradually changed into a baby—a baby with webbed hands and feet. She would be awakened by a cry—and it would not be the *mizuko* this time, but a very real Mayumi, howling in hunger or stomach cramps, or who knew what. Sometimes Nagiko thought it was sheer perversity. She lurched out of bed to give Mayumi a midnight feeding, letting Josefina sleep till 5:00 a.m. when she took over.

Her newly recurring dreams of the *mizuko* made her think of the priest Tokuda. It occurred to her that maybe she ought to take Mayumi to Fudō-in one of these days. She had once been scared that Tokuda would reveal things to Philip, but that was no longer an issue. Maybe there was even something she ought to have done about the Jizō figure after Mayumi was born. She had no idea about these things, and neither did Satoko. As it was, though, she was too busy and too exhausted to take Mayumi anywhere.

Tokuda's hopes faded. He had no choice but to continue his lonely rounds, keeping track, looking for anything suspicious, without knowing what suspicious was.

Perception

IN DECEMBER THE SHOPPING STREET near Nagiko's apartment was hung with tinsel garlands, glittery Styrofoam snowflakes and plastic bells. Every time she went out Nagiko was reminded how much she disliked the combination of red and green. It hit you in the eyes like a one-two punch. Josefina was about to leave for Manila to spend Christmas with her own children. Nagiko faced her first week alone with Mayumi.

On the morning of December 23, the phone rang. Nagiko had been changing a diaper, and was holding the receiver jammed between her shoulder and chin as she cleaned her hands with a baby wipe.

"*Moshi mosh…*" she mumbled.

"Hello? Nagiko? Hello?" It was a woman's voice.

"Hello," she said clearly, taking the phone in her hand, "yes this is Nagiko…"

"Nagiko, this is Linda Metcalfe. Philip's mother…"

Nagiko felt an icy clutch in her stomach. She glanced at Mayumi, who seemed quite content, for the moment at least, to lie on her back kicking her feet in the air.

"Hello, Linda," she said, turning away from the baby and covering the mouthpiece as soon as she had spoken. This was the first time either of the Metcalfes had called her. "How are you?"

"Oh my—I'm not used to this international dialing. There seems to be a delay on the line…hello? We are fine, thank you. I'm calling because I have some wonderful news."

Nagiko felt a rush of blood to her head. Her heart started pounding. She snagged a kitchen chair with her foot and pulled it toward the phone.

"Hello? Are you there?"

Nagiko sat down, "Yes," she said. Mayumi hiccupped.

"It's Philip. He's woken up."

"He's...conscious? He can talk?" Nagiko's head spun. She had stopped allowing herself even to think of this possibility.

"Yes. He can talk, interact, he's sitting up..."

Nagiko hardly dared respond. "Can...can I talk to him?" she asked.

"He's still at the hospital," said his mother. "He's very weak, of course, and they still need to do some more tests..."

"More tests? What for?"

There was a pause at the other end of the line.

"Hello?" Nagiko repeated.

"Yes, I can hear you. It's that, well, there's something still a little strange about his memory..."

"His memory? What do you mean?" Nagiko felt like the balloon of her heart that had suddenly been sent soaring now turned into a boulder, hurtling back to earth. Her voice turned wary. She might as well get straight to the point. "Does he remember me?" she asked bluntly. She knew the Metcalfes had never been keen on the idea of their marriage.

"We'd like you to come, so we can find out," said his mother.

Just then Mayumi let out a screech.

"There's interference on this line," Nagiko said. "Let me call you back." She hung up the phone and looked blankly at Mayumi who had managed to flip herself over onto her stomach. She was pumping her arms and legs as if she were a small airplane trying to take off.

Nagiko sat lost in thought, and when the phone rang again she jumped.

"Hello?" she answered, uncertainly.

"*Moshi moshi? Na-chan?* It's me. What's the matter?" It was Satoko. She could tell immediately that something was up.

"I have to go to California," Nagiko said. "Right away." She told her about the call.

On the floor, Mayumi's strenuous efforts were getting her nowhere.

"Okay, let's think about this," said Satoko calmly. "I bet you can get a ticket for the day after tomorrow. It's Christmas, so the flights won't be full. Then come back on New Year's Day—again, not so many people will be flying."

"But Josefina has gone home."

"You're not going to take Mayumi?" Satoko sounded surprised.

"No. Definitely not. There is still some problem. I don't understand exactly yet, but I can't possibly take the baby."

"So, leave her with me," said Satoko.

"You'd really do that?" asked Nagiko.

"Sure. Mommy for a week—it'll be fun. I'd like to. Really. Satoko insisted. "You get your ticket today. Get your stuff packed. Tomorrow you can bring her to my house."

Nagiko could see that Satoko was enchanted with the idea of being fairy godmother for Mayumi for a week. And just as she had predicted, she had no trouble getting a seat, even at such short notice. She pulled out a suitcase and began to pack. Buried in the back of her underwear drawer was the expensive black lace nightgown she had bought to take to Hawaii. It was still in its box. She lifted it out—almost weightless it was so filmy. It wouldn't take any room, but should she bring it? She hesitated and then finally folded it into a tiny square and slipped it in.

The next day Nagiko bundled Mayumi into a stylish fuzzy jumper with mittens and attached hood, and took her to Satoko. In this cold weather she could cover up Mayumi's hands and feet and not feel embarrassed by her deformity. Heads turned as Nagiko and Mayumi passed by—such a beautiful baby with those big round eyes and extraordinarily long eyelashes. One had to look closely to see that her eyes had remained dark blue, even darker than Philip's. Her fine-textured glossy black hair peeked out of the hood in wisps around the perfect petal-soft skin of her rosy face. She did not have the funny ash-pale hair that "half" babies often had, and no one looking at her now would think she was not pure Japanese. She looked like a doll come to life.

Nagiko felt strangely light, traveling with only herself to worry about. She bought three different international fashion magazines for the plane. Settling down in her seat she tried to remember what Philip's mother had said exactly. He's woken up. He's talking and interacting. There's something a little strange about his memory—what could she have meant by that? On the other hand, they had asked her to come as soon as possible. This must mean that they thought there was a chance that seeing her could help. Nagiko tried to concentrate on her magazines, but the French models blurred into the American ones, and all the international luxury goods ads were the same anyway. She drank two glasses of wine and fell asleep.

She arrived in San Francisco on Christmas morning, the same day she left. Emerging from customs, she caught sight of Jim Metcalfe's solid figure wearing a pale blue cardigan sweater, standing back from a crowd of Asian families eagerly pressing forward awaiting friends and family. His dark hair looker a little grayer than Nagiko remembered, but then, she had no doubt failed to notice a lot of things when they first met.

"Hello, Jim," she waved at him. She had stopped trying to call them Mom and Dad. He shook her hand awkwardly when she emerged from the barrier gate, and they walked over to the baggage claim, trading the usual polite questions and responses about the flight.

It was easier for Jim Metcalfe to talk without having to look directly at Nagiko, so keeping his eyes on the road straight ahead, he told her the sequence of events. One morning last week the nurse had come into the room and found Philip awake, coughing, trying feebly to pull out the various tubes attached to his body. He was confused and disoriented, asking for water. The nurse immediately called the doctor in to examine him, then notified Jim and Linda. By the time they rushed over, Philip was propped up on pillows, eyes open, languidly sipping Gatorade.

"Linda got quite hysterical," he said. They were now approaching the Golden Gate Bridge, looming majestically above a low fogbank clinging to the water below. Nagiko took in the stunning view as she listened to the flat tone of Philip's father's voice. Nagiko wondered whether he had developed his gruff demeanor as a balance to his wife's sentimentality. She would be the one to cry uncontrollably; he would stand there like a pillar. Nagiko could almost picture the scene—Philip, between them, weak as a jellyfish, trying to get his bearings. She knew that the last thing that had been on Philip's mind was that meeting with his professor at International House. Now, to wake up nine months later and find yourself, fragile and emaciated, in a hospital bed with your parents standing over you—with no idea of the time gone by—how disorienting that must have been.

Nagiko was wrong, though. Philip had not been thinking of Harvey Chernish at all as he loped across the street up to the I-House entrance. He had been thinking about Tokuda. Now that he had solved this inconvenient problem of getting his thesis on track so that he could continue to stay in Japan, the question of the hidden buddhas had taken over his thoughts. Tokuda was the key; the hidden buddhas were the lock. Maigny had discerned the pattern, and Philip was the one to put them all together. This realization came upon him with an almost physical force, like a wave he felt rise from deep inside his head. And that was the last thing he remembered.

He had been dragged down by that wave. He had a vague sensation of being underwater for a very long time, pulled about, as if by hundreds of tiny hands, tumbled over sand and pebbles. He sensed a woman's arm reaching out. He felt it must be Nagiko's—but when he grasped it, an older woman's face swam into view and he dropped the hand in terror, falling back into the watery dark. Finally, someone hauled him out of the water, up onto the beach. Why was he so thirsty? He could barely move. He opened his mouth, and heard a strange voice rasping a croak for water. The room was so bright he closed his eyes again and forgot everything.

Someone held a glass of water with a straw up to his lips. He sucked it—the rush of water down his throat was a revelation. In fact, everything was a revelation. The doctor prodded his belly and tapped his arms and legs. He tried to move his legs off the bed. Then his mother was standing there, crying, trying to keep him from falling. His father was there too. Then he forgot this.

There was practically no traffic on the bridge. Nagiko had been listening without saying anything. Now she asked, "Could he talk?"

Philip's father cleared his throat. "He sort of laughed and asked us what we were doing there—he was pretty out of it. The doctor said it would take a few days. He was weak, too—lost weight, muscle tone. We talked about getting him some physical therapy."

"And now?" Nagiko persisted. Why was it so hard to get this information out of him, she wondered. It made her uneasy.

Jim Metcalfe was clearly uncomfortable. Nagiko didn't care. "What's wrong with him?" she demanded.

That was the wrong tack. His father retreated to his passive manner.

"We don't know. It's something strange—every time we go in, he recognizes us, but he seems to have forgotten the previous time." They drove past Sausalito. "I suppose I should tell you that Linda asked his old girlfriend from high school—Nora is her name—to come visit. Just to see if he recognized her, you know."

"And did he?" Nagiko ignored what, if anything, he meant to imply by indicating Nora's status as "old girlfriend."

"Yes, but..."

Nagiko waited.

"Look, Nagiko, I don't want to set up your expectations, one way or the other, okay?" he suddenly replied. "We're almost there. You'll be able to see for yourself."

Philip's father turned the radio to Christmas carols, and they were silent for the rest of the trip.

In the lobby of the small San Anselmo hospital Nagiko told Mr. Metcalfe that she wanted to see Linda first, and that she would wait in the lobby for her. And afterward, she said, she would like to see Philip alone.

"If you like…" was all he said, and went off to fetch his wife from Philip's room.

Had she been a good daughter-in-law, Nagiko mused, she would be doing exactly what she was now doing out of selfishness. Properly putting her mother-in-law ahead of even her husband, she would greet her first. She stared at the potted poinsettias. Finally they emerged in the hallway, his arm around her shoulders, saying something comforting probably; she—hunched up, dabbing her eyes with a wadded tissue. At this point Nagiko didn't know what to think. Philip had regained consciousness, but his parents were not acting very happy about it.

"You go on ahead," said Philip's mother. "Jim says you want to see him alone first. I can understand. Take all the time you want."

"Fourth floor, Room 7B," said Mr. Metcalfe, pointing in the direction from which they had come.

Nagiko walked toward the elevator at the end of the hall. She was trembling. Japanese hospitals never had a fourth floor—the number was too unlucky. She stepped out, checking the numbers on the doors. Most of them were open. So was 7B. She looked in. Philip was sitting in a wheelchair facing toward the window. She called out in a soft voice, not wanting to startle him,

"*O-jama shimasu…*"

He wheeled around. "Nagiko!" His wan face broke into a big smile.

Nagiko almost sobbed in relief as she ran over to him. Philip tried to get out of the wheelchair, but he swayed like a reed. Nagiko steadied him and helped him sit down again. He was so thin he looked younger, like a gawky teenager, she thought. But he recognized her! She ran her fingers over his face. She kissed him, "Philip—I had almost given up," she whispered.

Philip had been looking at the live oak trees in the park next to the hospital, when he heard a voice calling "excuse me" in Japanese. He loved the sound of Japanese! He turned his wheelchair toward the door. A familiar woman, very beautiful—his heart suddenly leapt up. He had seen her before. From somewhere her name came to his lips, "Nagiko!" He was holding her, kissing her. It was like a revelation. He was so happy—from the tips of his fingers to the very roots of his hair, he felt blissful.

"I love you Nagiko," he heard himself say. It seemed entirely right.

Then there were noises at the doorway, other people. That was his mother. That one his father. Someone else—the doctor. Each presence registered in Philip's consciousness. And then there was another—Nagiko! He felt so happy. And then he forgot them all and looked at the live oaks in the park next to the hospital.

Bewildered and upset, Nagiko allowed Philip's mother to lead her out of the room down to the doctor's office.

"We thought it best that you see him first, so you would understand," she said.

"I don't understand anything," Nagiko said, pressing her palms into her forehead. "He recognized me…"

"Yes," said the doctor, "it's as if his perceptions touch his deep memories—but they are not anchored to anything. They vanish in minutes, and he doesn't remember having had them. If you walk back in there now, it would be the same thing—he would be delighted to see you—he would 'remember' you, even—but then he would forget."

"Will he get better?" Tears had been coursing down Nagiko's face as she listened to the doctor.

"Nobody knows," broke in Philip's mother.

"There may have been something that happened just before the accident," continued the doctor. He asked Nagiko directly, "Did you ever know him to faint, or partly black out, when you were together?"

Nagiko was about to shake her head when she remembered their visit to Saidaiji. Yes, he had passed out then, and some strangers had helped her drag him outside to the bench.

The doctor took notes. "Anything else?" he asked. She said that Philip had described a similar experience while he was hiking a pilgrimage, but she had not been with him at the time.

"Our current hypothesis," said the doctor after writing that down on his chart, "is that he may be suffering from a variety of Korsakoff's syndrome. But I don't recommend you go airing that diagnosis to all your friends. Usually, Korsakoff's is precipitated by fairly extreme alcoholism coupled with a thiamine deficiency. Obviously, this is not the situation here. There is no polyneuritis that we can detect. It may have been brought on by a concussion, or there is a chance that there is a tumor—although tests so far have not revealed one."

Philip's parents were silent. Nagiko could tell they had heard this from the doctor earlier. This meeting was for her.

"Doctor, could you write this down for me?" she asked.

"Of course," he said. "I will have it typed up for you by tomorrow."

Suddenly Nagiko realized that it was Christmas day, and the doctor had come in specifically for this.

"I'm so sorry to cause you all this trouble…on Christmas…" she whispered.

The doctor smiled. "Don't worry about it. I'm Jewish, anyway."

Nagiko looked at Philip's parents sitting grimly together on the sofa. Her heart sank. She excused herself, to go back to Philip's room one more time. She found him looking at the live oak trees in the park next to the hospital.

Philip heard a voice calling "excuse me" in Japanese. He loved the sound of Japanese! He turned his wheelchair toward the door. A familiar woman, very beautiful—his heart suddenly leapt up. He had seen her before. From somewhere her name came to his lips, "Nagiko!" He was holding her, kissing her. It was like a revelation. He was so happy—from the tips of his fingers to the very roots of his hair, he felt blissful.

"I love you Nagiko," he heard himself say. It seemed entirely right.

Two days before she was to leave, the nurse saw her in the hall. "You seem to have the most luck getting through to him. It's odd—I've never seen a patient quite like this before. When do you go back home?"

"Tomorrow," said Nagiko.

"He's going to miss you…" said the nurse.

"No, I don't think I exist for him when I'm not here," said Nagiko slowly.

"Well, he may not *know* that he's missing you," said the nurse, "but he will."

Nagiko went into his room to say goodbye.

"Nagiko!" He had gotten much stronger over the past few days. Today, he hadn't used the wheelchair at all. He sprang up as soon as she came in the door, taking her in his arms, smothering her with kisses. She laughed, in spite of the spike of sadness that was now lodged firmly somewhere deep in her gut. He was kissing her neck, rubbing his fingers along her spine the way she used to like being massaged. Then he ran his palms over her stomach.

"How's our little *chibi* doing?" he asked. "Any kicking yet?"

Nagiko froze. She hid her sobs by pretending that she was laughing. And then it was time to say goodbye.

For the Fish

IN FEBRUARY NAGIKO DECIDED to go through the boxes of Philip's things that had been sitting in her apartment for almost a year. One box held an assortment of blue jeans, t-shirts, flannel shirts, and a pile of boxer shorts. She saw no reason to send these back to California. The only item she kept was the elegant dark green suit made from her fabric. She wished she had taken a picture of him in it. She sent a small box of memorabilia from his pilgrimage to his parents' house.

She came across the map his French advisor had drawn. It showed the outline of Japan with the hidden buddhas represented by red dots. She had been surprised that there were *hibutsu* in Tokyo—one was near Nihonbashi, only four subway stops away. She set the map aside. In that same folder she also found a handwritten key, listing the dates on which each of the hidden buddhas are put on display. Out of curiosity she looked up the nearby temple. It was the Ōkannonji, and the image was a Guan Yin.

She checked when it would be on view. The seventeenth day of every month. Philip had been so interested in these hidden buddhas—maybe she and Mayumi should try to see some of them. Nagiko retrieved the whole folder, marked "Maigny" from the box and put it aside with the maps.

Jun Muranaka telephoned her at the office the next day. Nagiko felt guilty she hadn't called him. Of course he would want to hear about Philip. Consulting their calendars they arranged to have dinner. As soon as she hung up the phone with him, her secretary rang with a call on the line from someone named Kōji Kon from Maizuru, who said he was a friend of Philip's. Nagiko told her to put it through. She vaguely remembered that Philip had a friend from his days on Mt. Kōya, who he said would come to Tokyo for their wedding. When Nagiko asked about him, Philip had just said, "Kōji's a little hard to describe—but you'll like him when you get to know him…" As it was, they had never met.

He turned out to be very polite, if a little awkward, and he spoke in thick Maizuru dialect. He mentioned his connection to Philip as a student of Shingon, and then he mumbled something that sounded like polite regrets about how things had turned out. Finally he got to the point. "I amu study Engrish…" he said tentatively, as if tiptoeing out on a plank. He got cold feet and stepped back into Japanese. He was going to attend a language program in California for a month in the summer, and he wanted to visit Philip while he was there. What did she think?

The seventeenth of February was one of those bright spring-like days that makes people think of taking their overcoats to the dry cleaners. Everyone was ready to believe that winter was over. Nagiko dressed Mayumi in a pair of red coveralls with pink hearts and a matching pink hooded sweatshirt. Her hands were unmittened. She gave Josefina the morning off to visit a cousin who had just come to work in Tokyo. Although it was three days late, Mayumi looked like a little Valentine.

The "big Guan Yin temple," Ōkannonji, was not very big at all. It was squeezed into a side street in the Ningyōcho district, an area, like Kagurazaka, that still housed one of the city's older geisha districts. They found it easily. The interior of the temple was dark, lit by candles even on this bright spring morning. The *hibutsu* itself was an unusual cast-iron head of Guan Yin. Since the head alone was over five feet tall, the original statue must have been immense. Had it been a standing figure or seated, Nagiko wondered? She tried to imagine the body from which this head had been severed. It was a Guan Yin that not only had seen much suffering, but experienced it as well. Two women were praying in front of the image. One of them was very pregnant. They glanced at Nagiko and nodded. No doubt they assumed that she had come to thank Guan Yin for the fulfillment of a prayer—the safe birth of a beautiful child, from the looks of it.

As Nagiko struggled to light a stick of incense while holding Mayumi in one arm, the pregnant woman offered to hold the baby. Mayumi accepted the handover placidly. Nagiko lit the incense and placed it in the large censer with both hands. She bowed her head and said a little prayer before turning to retrieve Mayumi. She could see that the woman was examining the little webbed fingers. The doctor had said Mayumi could have the operations on her hands and feet any time now. "Best do it before she's old enough to remember anything," he said.

The Metcalfes never called. In March, Nagiko got a letter saying that Philip had moved back home with them. None of the tests had been conclusive, and there was nothing more to be done at the hospital—besides, he kept walking out. They did not ask anything about Nagiko's life. She wrote back, mentioning that a friend of Philip's wanted to visit over the summer. She said nothing at all about Mayumi.

Nagiko took Mayumi to visit more temples in March. Satoko came along.

"So this is what Philip was doing?" marveled Satoko, on the train ride back. "I mean, it's not a bad thing at all, it's just…an unusual sort of interest." She was holding Mayumi who had fallen asleep on her shoulder. "So how many *hibutsu* are there? Are you going to try to see all of them?"

Nagiko shrugged. "Impossible. Some of them are shut away for hundreds of years. And I don't really know how many there are. Philip's teacher made a map, but who knows? We can keep doing it until we get bored, I suppose." She pulled a handkerchief from her bag to spread on Satoko's shoulder where Mayumi was beginning to drool a little on her dress. "Somehow, though, I feel like I'm doing something for Philip—something he would have done himself, if he could."

Mayumi got cranky in June. Not only were baby teeth erupting, but humidity was irritating the fragile skin between her fingers. Again Nagiko thought about scheduling the operation for her hands and feet. Perhaps in the fall, when the weather was cooler.

Few *hibutsu* came on display in June. Maybe they were cranky, too, thought Nagiko. She and Mayumi had curtailed their usual excursions on account of rain. One stir-crazy Saturday, Josefina's day off, Nagiko was reminded of her annual pilgrimage to Fudō-in at this time of year. She never exactly forgot the *mizuko*, but it had receded from her mind, like a senile relative housed away in an institution, visited only on holidays. Nagiko realized that, barring a miracle, Philip was likely to become more like the *mizuko* himself as time went on. Nagiko did not believe in miracles.

Apart from sheer intellectual curiosity Nagiko had no idea what had drawn Philip to study the *hibutsu*. She had never even asked if Philip considered himself a Buddhist. For that matter, she had never asked herself. Was she a Buddhist? In some fundamental way she thought she must be—simply through absorption, if nothing else.

Yet she had gone to Fudō-in in distress long before meeting Philip. It had all started with being awakened by the *mizuko's* cries on a sultry night during rainy season six years ago. Every night of the past week Mayumi's shrieking had reminded her of that. Maybe she should take Mayumi to Kamakura?

"How about it, *palaka*-chan? Shall we go visit Fudō in?" Nagiko babytalked. "Little froggies don't mind the rain..."

Mayumi understood only that they were going out and bounced excitedly in her highchair.

Whom could she call on such short notice? Jun Muranaka had been interested.

"Call me next time you go," he had said. "If you'd like company, that is. That's the kind of thing I wish I had more time for."

Nagiko liked Muranaka. She thought she would like his company at some point, but today was not the day. She and Mayumi would go by themselves.

Fudō-in was crowded. Mayumi was totally fascinated by a skinny little girl who ran back and forth to her stroller, bringing tiny offerings—a pebble, a fallen azalea blossom. Each time the girl ran toward her, Mayumi eagerly reached out.

"What's the matter with her fingers?" the child asked Nagiko.

"They were stuck together when she was born. The doctor is going to fix them."

"Oh," said the little girl. "Will it hurt?"

"No," said Nagiko, "I don't think so."

"Poor baby," said the girl. She kissed Mayumi's hands and ran back to her parents. Mayumi was straining against the belt of the stroller now, so Nagiko wheeled her off in the opposite direction toward the pond, hoping to distract her with the carp. She pulled a cracker from her bag.

"Watch!" she said, tossing a piece in the water. Mayumi's eyes got big. She clung to her mother as a dozen huge fish swam to the surface. Nagiko broke a cracker into Mayumi's hand.

"Here. You throw," she said, moving the child's fist.

One swift white fish with an orange spot on the top of its head moved in and grabbed the cracker. Mayumi squealed. People ambling about the garden glanced at the two of them, the beautiful mother and beautiful child playing with the carp. The tableau caught the eye of Noboru Tokuda, who was coming down the steps from the Jizō cemetery. He almost lost his footing with shock.

It had been over a year since he had waited, day in and day out, for Nagiko to appear. And the child—must be almost one year old, he thought. Then he mentally kicked himself for thinking that an eight-months pregnant woman would have been out visiting temples. What a waste of time that was. He stared at Nagiko now. She didn't look like a mother. She was slim and beautiful, casually but expertly made up. Tokuda noticed these things, and he was astounded. Motherhood always brought frowziness, but he saw none. The child was unearthly. Hair like her mother's, black and shiny as a leopard-lily seed; skin fair, with an undertone of pink; big round eyes—Tokuda didn't think he had ever seen such a lovely baby. He looked around. Where was Metcalfe?

Now the child was taking a bite out of the cracker and laughing before flinging the rest to the fish. Tokuda simply could not restrain his curiosity. He walked toward them. Nagiko saw him out of the corner of her eye, and knew immediately who he was. She straightened part way, still clutching Mayumi's hand.

"Mrs. Metcalfe?" said Tokuda with a bow.

Nagiko brushed the crackers off her fingers and faced him, with Mayumi clinging to the hem of her skirt.

"No," she said simply. "Metcalfe had an accident. We were not able to marry."

Tokuda reeled back, his eyebrows shooting up. Of course! It all made sense. He looked down at the toddler staring up at him curiously. She had deep blue eyes. He noticed her fingers, now sticky with cracker crumbs. She was like a jewel. He bowed deeply, trying to compose his thoughts. Finally Tokuda raised his eyes to look at Nagiko's face. She had picked Mayumi up now.

"Is he...is he..."

"He was hit by a car." Nagiko looked down. "He wasn't killed...it affected his memory though. The doctors aren't completely sure what's wrong. He's back with his family in America."

"But you are not...he is not..." Tokuda felt like he himself had been flattened by a car. He made a huge effort. "Then, he's not coming back to Japan?"

"I don't think it's likely," said Nagiko. Mayumi twisted back toward the fish.

"Crackers all gone," Nagiko told her firmly, cleaning off her fingers.

Tokuda was full of questions, but he felt awkward here in the garden.

"Please," he said, "I need to talk to you about Metcalfe." He stopped. "That is…I'm terribly sorry—it must be quite awful for you…"

Even as Tokuda spoke the usual phrases of condolence, he was struck by how difficult it must be for a single woman to bring up a mixed-race child in Japan. The child didn't look obviously "half." Not until you looked into her strangely deep eyes—yet even then, such a dark blue they did not at all resemble the standard *gaijin* icy blue eye. Something about her utterly captivated him.

"Yes, we should talk," she said. "Excuse me…Mayumi, behave! I can't have you falling into the pond. The fish will eat you up." She put the struggling child down.

Tokuda knelt down and held his hand out to steady her.

"Mayumi, is it? Beautiful name." He touched her arm. "You like the fishies?" he asked. "Shall we go get more food for them?"

Mayumi was calmed by his quiet voice.

"Let's go back to my office," Tokuda said. "I have a supply of gluten puffs for the fish."

"Mayumi-chan! Come on. This kind priest will give us food for the fish. Let's go." Nagiko coaxed Mayumi back into the stroller. Tokuda felt he should offer to push it for Nagiko, but he knew how many stares that would draw. Somewhat embarrassed, he led the way and they followed.

By the time they got to the temple office Mayumi had fallen asleep. Tokuda showed Nagiko in and closed the door. People would think that he was counseling a *mizuko* supplicant and would not bother them. Moving an ashtray off the table, Tokuda apologized for the lingering smell of cigarette smoke.

"It's the boyfriends," he explained. He offered to make tea from a thermos of hot water.

How much does she know, he wondered? The swirling dust storm of surprise at seeing her had momentarily obscured the question, but it now stood out in Tokuda's mind as if lit up in neon.

As she talked, Tokuda realized that Metcalfe must not have said anything to her about their longer meeting. As far as Nagiko knew, Philip had met the priest only twice—once in Nara, once here in Kamakura, with her. She told him about Philip's accident and described his current mental state. He floated permanently in the present moment, she said.

Tentatively, Tokuda asked about Philip's interest in hidden buddhas.

"Oh. He talked to you about that, then?" she asked. "Yes, Philip came to Japan to study Shingon, but one of his professors had interested him in the *hibutsu*. He was trying to see as many of them as he could."

Mayumi gave a little cry and twitched in her stroller. Nagiko leaned over to loosen the strap, and she went back to sleep.

"Philip told me about meeting you in Nara," she said. "He was excited about running into you here. He would have liked to talk further with you— I know he would have."

Nagiko turned her face away and sighed.

"There is so much we never had a chance to talk about," she said quietly. "—so much I don't understand about how these things work…"

"What things?" Tokuda probed gently.

"Well, Buddhist things in general, for example. I'm very ignorant…" Nagiko wove her fingers together to keep them still. "I don't even under-stand, really, about the *mizuko*…or much about reincarnation, for that matter." She unraveled her hands.

"This child here," she extended her palm toward Mayumi. "My child. And his. I've always thought of her as the *mizuko*. I dreamed she was waiting for a second chance, and I could not refuse." She looked directly at Tokuda now.

"Until I came here, I was tormented by that *mizuko*. And you helped me. I was able to get on with my life because I felt that she was somehow under your wing." Nagiko felt this quietly attentive priest would not judge her. Still, the tears welled up.

"I was going to tell Philip about the *mizuko* that winter day we came here. It really was my intention. But…I couldn't. I got scared and changed my mind. While he went up to see the Guan Yin, I ran up to the Jizō cemetery and spoke to the *mizuko*. But at that point, you see, I thought the *mizuko* was no longer there. It had come back to my womb. So I said goodbye to an empty Jizō. And then when I saw him coming back down the steps with you…and when you recognized me, I was so afraid you would say something…"

Tokuda reassured her.

"By the way," he added, "a Jizō is never empty. It may have represented your *mizuko*, but it was still Jizō as well. Jizō is always full—full of compassion."

"So, was the *mizuko* in fact suffering?" Nagiko asked.

She had composed herself and was sitting up straighter now. "I would hear its cries in my dreams. Sometimes I saw it on the riverbank, playing with stones—waiting, it seemed to me. And it aged, too—just like an actual child. The last time I dreamed of it I saw a four-year-old girl fall into the river and turn into a fish. That was when I became pregnant."

It was always difficult for Tokuda to counsel women who wanted to know details about their *mizuko*. The doctrinal basis for the karmic status of aborted children was thin. Luckily, very few wanted such detail.

"Was the *mizuko* suffering, you ask," he finally said. "All of life is suffering…that is the first precept of the Buddha. Suffering is caused by clinging to ephemeral things—we become attached to things, to ideas, and especially to people. But also to fame, to prestige, to wealth—there are endless things we become attached to. Then they change. Inevitably. And we suffer because we can't hold on to them. You felt the suffering of the *mizuko*, and you experienced suffering yourself. That is quite clear. When you came here you made a plea to Jizō for compassion, and it was granted—it always is to those who sincerely seek it."

Tokuda glanced at the sleeping baby.

"Is this child your *mizuko* reborn? To be honest, there is no way of knowing. You cannot tap your stone Jizō to see if it now sounds different. It seems your dreams are telling you she is. But what would you do differently if she were not? Nothing, I suspect."

"I don't understand reincarnation," Nagiko blurted. "It's not only the child…"

"What is it?" Tokuda asked.

Nagiko hesitated. "Do you think it's possible to have had previous existences—to remember thoughts and experiences of different lives?"

This was also difficult. Tokuda knew it was possible. But he also knew that most people who were convinced of knowledge of a former life were fooling themselves. They would read something, or, more commonly now, see one of those historical dramas on television, and identify so strongly with one of the characters they figured they must have been that person in an earlier lifetime. The warlord Hideyoshi, for example, was a favorite of men. It was almost funny if you thought about how many meek office workers Hideyoshi had managed to be reborn into.

"Technically, yes." Tokuda said carefully. "But again, it is very hard to tell what is a karmic connection and what is more likely to be a projection of one's personality and desires.

"What we call karma is really nothing other than cause and effect. What we are at any given time is largely determined by what we did—or thought, or said—at some point in the past. And likewise, what we do at present—and think, and say now—this is what shapes our future. Our past, present, and future lives are connected by karma. It is a natural law—actions yield consequences. We know this is true, even though we are ignorant of the time scale. The consequences may occur in an hour, or they may occur in another lifetime.

"As long as we live in ignorance, succumbing to delusion, greed, and aversion, we accumulate the consequences of karma. And, yes, it can spill over into other lives—like a ripple moving out from a stone tossed in water."

Nagiko had wanted to ask about her unsettling experience of reading *The Pillow Book*, but she felt foolish. There must be many women who felt a kinship to the catty Sei Shōnagon.

"It's normal to feel these connections," he said. "You are not a shallow person. If you feel a strong connection to someone—even someone long dead—then there may well be something there."

"What should I do about it?" Nagiko asked him.

"That's very difficult to know," Tokuda responded. "If the connection helps you, then accept it. If it causes you pain, then you need to try to understand what underlies it in order to break through. Past actions culminate in the present—but you always have choices. You always have the choice to begin dissolving the karmic chain by entering on the path to end craving, delusion, and ignorance. That too, is one of the precepts the Buddha taught."

Nagiko sighed. "Philip was very interested in these things. There was so much I could have learned from him." She saw Tokuda look away.

"He never knew about the *mizuko*," said Nagiko slowly.

"Does he know about this child?" asked Tokuda.

Nagiko shook her head. "According to the nurse, if she asks him about me, he thinks I am pregnant. Perhaps I will remain in that state to him, since he doesn't seem to be able to create new memories."

"This is a terrible tragedy," said Tokuda, appreciating Nagiko's loss while unable to tell her how much this was a loss to him as well. "Isn't there some chance he will recover?"

"That would be wonderful, but I'm not counting on it," said Nagiko with a glance at Mayumi, who had opened her eyes and was looking around. Nagiko figured she was probably wet. She would regret not changing her diaper quickly.

She unbuckled the strap and lifted her out. Very wet.

"So, anyway, I've started visiting hidden buddhas myself. The baby and I. I have a map that his professor drew for a guide. So it's like a hobby, of sorts, but it lets me feel a connection to him." She paused. "Excuse me. This is very rude, but I must change the baby or she will get a terrible rash. Is there somewhere...?"

Tokuda was nonplussed. Change the baby?

"I have everything here, I just need a flat surface," continued Nagiko. "In fact, this sofa here will do just fine. If you'll excuse us..."

Tokuda finally realized that she was asking him to turn his back. Hastily, he did so.

"There. All dry." Nagiko had gotten the baby dressed again, and everything had been tidied and packed away. A whiff of cool antiseptic odor lingered in the air, prickling the back of Tokuda's nose, reminding him of something uncomfortable. But he brushed it aside.

She was standing now, clearly preparing to leave.

"Remember," said Tokuda. "You can still come visit this temple. Raising a child today must be difficult—Jizō can help." He hoped he didn't sound self-serving. The idea of never seeing her again created a hollow sadness inside him. She was now his only link to Metcalfe and his resolution not to let the secret of the hidden buddhas be rendered useless.

"Wait," he said, just as Nagiko got Mayumi resettled in the stroller. He went over to a cupboard and took out a half-full bag of dried wheat gluten puffs. He handed it to her.

"For the fish," he said.

Nagiko thanked him, bowing as she wheeled the stroller out. Talking with this priest had made her feel much better.

Then they were gone. Once again Tokuda was alone.

PART TWO

From Inside Out

PacMan

KŌJI'S FATHER DECIDED HIS SON should learn English. At first, Kōji resisted. He regarded the idea as just another arbitrary paternal decree to thwart. Kōji had been unhappily confronting English grammar since junior high, and had no desire to torture himself further. Take lessons for a year, then you can go to California for a summer, his father offered. Kōji warily agreed. This was his first trip abroad.

On the flight, he tucked his chubby frame into a middle seat of coach without complaint. He would arrive in San Francisco with two other students, and they would make their way to Berkeley, where the language school was located. Now he ran his hand over the top of his head, carpeted in the novelty of inch-long hair. His father had agreed that he could grow it out for the trip. His head was a little tender after last night's farewell party. As it cleared, he began to have second thoughts about his ability to survive in English for three months.

He looked over a map of California in the flight magazine. Berkeley here. San Francisco over here. Where was San Anselmo, he wondered? Anxious as he was to see his friend Philip, Kōji was uneasy because of what Nagiko had said.

By the end of the first week of classes, Kōji's tongue ached from trying to copy the shape of the teacher's mouth.

"Wa-te-e-r," she growled encouragingly.

"uWA-ta-er," Kōji obliged, forcing the sides of his tongue to curl up. He was distracted by the bronze skin and clinging t-shirt of the Spanish girl who sat across the room. Maybe he should be learning Spanish, Kōji fantasized. Damn. He shared a room with Mitsuyasu, a fellow classmate from the English school in Kyoto. Mitsuyasu had immediately gone out and bought issues of *Playboy* and *Penthouse*, secreting them under his mattress when he wasn't looking through them. He teased Kōji.

"You can't look at this stuff—you're supposed to be priest…"

Kōji was furious. Yeah, he was going to be a priest, but he wasn't yet, and why was this guy being such a jerk? He went out and bought his own. The editions of *Penthouse* imported and sold in Japan always had the best bits obliterated with thick black magic marker. The original American version was eye-popping. They would be great souvenirs.

On the Friday before his first free weekend he called Philip.

"I am Kōji Kon," he announced when Linda Metcalfe picked up the phone. "Friend of Philip. I come tomorrow, SatURday. Yes?" He curled his tongue hard.

"That would be lovely," Philip's mother said loudly and slowly. "Where are you now?"

She understood he was taking a bus from Berkeley, and told him she would pick him up at the San Rafael bus station. She was not certain he understood, and thought of bringing Philip to the phone. But they would speak Japanese, and by the time she asked him to translate, he might have forgotten.

"Shee you again," said Kōji cheerfully as he hung up the phone.

Raburi, zat uwudo be raburi…he practiced this new idiom. Once outside of class he did pretty well, he thought.

The bus pulled in and Linda saw a chunky young Japanese sporting an improbable haircut that made his head look rather like a chestnut bur. Peering through thick glasses, his shoulders hunched in trepidation, Kōji looked around for a middle-aged American woman whom he hoped would recognize him. Then he saw Philip, madly waving his arms.

"*Yaa, Kōji-kun!*"

Whew. What a relief. And he looked just the same. Maybe a little thinner. Not much, though. That must be his mother. Kōji noticed a woman with short blonde hair standing beside a car, shading her eyes from the sun, watching them. Hmmm—not much family resemblance. Then Philip was upon him.

"Kōji! What are you doing here!"

"Raburi to see you…" Kōji began, and then he blanked.

"*Chikushō*." Swearing mildly, he reverted to Japanese.

Philip led him across the parking lot where Kōji tried out his English greeting on Philip's mother. This time it lilted off his rolled tongue. She shook his hand, and they got in the car. Kōji was by now a little confused as to what the problem was. Nagiko had tried to explain, knowing that Philip would seem normal the first time Kōji interacted with him. Kōji would just have to experience it himself. Also, Nagiko did not want to scare him off. She hoped Kōji could connect to things Philip cared about—things about which his parents were ignorant and so lay untouched, buried in darkness. Without a key from the outside, that knowledge and those memories were locked away from Philip himself.

Kōji and Philip sat in the back seat of the Volvo sedan, chattering away in Japanese as Linda Metcalfe drove. Her eyes kept being drawn to her son in the rearview mirror. He had been morose lately, and she felt he was slipping away. She had begun to realize that some important part of her only child was closed to her. There were things that she, even with her total acceptance and mother's love, simply could not comprehend. And it was not because of his injury. That was the hard part. She had to admit that Nagiko touched a side of Philip that was shut to her. And now this rather goofy-looking Japanese guy had managed to animate Philip and turn him into a stranger as well. They were joking and nudging each other like a pair of puppies. She focused on the road, blinking away tears.

Philip showed Kōji around the house. Linda could tell by his exclamations that Kōji was impressed by the broad expanse of lawn in back, and by her carefully pruned tree roses. They had been talking continuously since Kōji stepped off the bus, and Philip had managed to carry through in a single unbroken arc of interaction. Then Kōji asked where the bathroom was. Linda knew what would follow.

Sure enough, when he came out, Philip had forgotten. His mother watched the terrible dawning of comprehension on Kōji's face when Philip jumped up in delight, surprised to see him, and asked what he was doing here.

Kōji felt like the rug had been suddenly whipped out from under his feet. The strange story Nagiko had tried to tell him now became clear. Not knowing what to say, he looked over toward Philip's mother and caught the mute suffering in her glance. Never had Kōji felt so put on the spot. This was no joke. What should he do? In desperation he decided to try speaking English.

Philip was surprised. He immediately switched to English, praising Kōji for his efforts. Kōji did not feel embarrassed in front of Philip. He hauled out all the phrases he had learned in class. He asked if Philip would help him practice, and so they did. All afternoon. As long as they kept a session going, Philip was focused. Yet when they were interrupted, it was as if Philip simply let go of the string of that particular balloon, and it went floating off to be replaced by a new one. It occurred to Kōji that it was useful that Philip never got bored. Each time, he seemed to enjoy the novelty of speaking English with him.

In the late afternoon, Linda asked if Kōji would stay for dinner—stay the night too, if he liked. So Kōji said yes. Afterward, he realized that she was grateful. He had rarely been in a situation where something he chose to do totally on his own made such a difference. He met Philip's father at dinner, but Jim Metcalfe spoke quickly, in a low voice that Kōji had trouble understanding, and once again, he became self-conscious. After dinner, tired of English, he switched back to Japanese, probing to see what Philip remembered about Mt. Kōya.

He walked out of the room, turned around, and came back in, enduring the same cheerful greeting and comments about his sprouted-out hair. This would be a test. He mentioned a number of their fellow students, and one by one told him what they were doing now. Philip listened with interest, inter-rupting with questions. Then Kōji left the room and came back in again. He brought up the same names, which Philip knew, but all of the new informa-tion Kōji had just provided had slipped off Philip's memory like eggs off an oiled skillet.

He asked Philip if he ever meditated.

"Oh yes," Philip replied, "all the time."

By now Kōji was in a pair of borrowed pajamas, stretched out on one of the pair of twin beds in Philip's room. He was exhausted. What would it mean for Philip to meditate now, he wondered? Wasn't that the problem—that he was always focused on the present moment? Just before he fell asleep he yawned and asked Philip if he was still interested in hidden buddhas.

There was silence from the other bed. Kōji sleepily figured Philip must have dropped off. Then he heard a choked sob.

"Kōji—I have to tell you something about the hidden buddhas," he said urgently.

"Okay," said Kōji, unnerved, and too tired for heavy conversation. "How about we talk about it in the morning?"

"No," said Philip. "It's really important. I need to talk to you about it now."

"Fine," Kōji replied. "I just need to go to the bathroom. I'll be right back."

Guiltily, he crept out of the room to the bathroom and waited a few minutes. When he came back Philip was asleep.

The next morning promised a repeat of the previous day. Kōji was sick of English. He didn't want to spend the entire day cooped up in San Anselmo either. San Francisco beckoned. Maybe the Metcalfes would let him take Philip into San Francisco? Philip's father lowered the newspaper he had been reading and looked at his wife over the top of his glasses. He declared that a terrible idea—what with Kōji a stranger to the city, and Philip in the state he was. Kōji did not understand every word he said to his wife, but he was utterly attuned to the tone of voice—it reminded him of the way his father gave out decrees at the breakfast table. Just like a Japanese wife, Philip's mother did not oppose him, but when he had left the house she told Kōji she had an idea.

"How about if I call Nora and ask her to go with you?" she said.

"Go where?" asked Philip.

"No-ra is who?" asked Kōji.

Ignoring both of them, she got up from the table and went over to the phone hanging on the kitchen wall. Kōji heard her speaking in a low voice, and then she came back into the kitchen smiling. Nora had agreed not only to accompany them; she had offered to drive. Linda turned to Kōji. Nora, she explained, was a friend of Philip's.

Kōji pricked up his ears. Because of the enduring fame of Ibsen's play, *A Doll's House*, in Japan, Kōji knew that "Nora" was a girl's name.

"Girlfriend?" he asked.

"Well, yes, I suppose you could say that. Old girlfriend."

"She is old?"

"No, no. She went to Philip's high school. Girlfriend from long ago, I meant." Linda chose her words more carefully.

Kōji nodded sagely as if he knew all about previous girlfriends.

Kōji was in the role of big brother now. In Kyoto he had enjoyed introducing Philip to pachinko, to sneaking out, and to Korean barbeque. Few people took Kōji seriously, but in Philip he had found somebody who appreciated his rebellious side, his knowledge of sleazy esoterica. "Appreciate might be too strong—perhaps "tolerate" might be more truthful; and Kōji had missed him when Philip moved to Tokyo. He had never met Nagiko, who looked impossibly glamorous in photographs. He was interested to see what Nora would be like.

"She'll be by in about forty-five minutes," said Linda, wondering what Kōji was saying to Philip that made him grin like that. When Kōji smiled, his mouthful of teeth took over his face and his eyes disappeared into creases behind his glasses. They drank more coffee and made more toast. When a deer wandered up to the back fence behind the tree roses, Kōji spilled his coffee in excitement that was shared by nobody else.

"Pests," Linda Metcalfe told him. "Rose-eating pests. We think of them as big rats."

Kōji was totally confused. He saw an exotic, big-eyed, innocent deer—not a rat. He must have missed something. The deer keep rats from eating the roses? He decided that must be it.

At ten o'clock a battered Volkswagen Rabbit pulled up and Kōji saw a slender woman with long dark-blonde hair pulled back in a low ponytail step out. Nora lived in an apartment in San Francisco now, but often visited her parents on the weekend. Linda had caught her just as she was about to drive back to the city. Nora picked her way over the front lawn, trying to avoid wetting her feet in the dew-sodden grass. She was the image of what Kōji imagined a California girl should look like. She was a few years younger than Philip, he knew, so that would make her about his own age. When introduced, he brought out his now-polished phrases for meeting people, and looked into her clear blue eyes. Really blue—not the stormy dark sea color of Philip's eyes, but brilliant, sapphire at the center deepening at the rim, astonishingly blue eyes.

"Nora!"

"Hello, Philip," she said. She turned and gave Philip a hug.

California people hugged a lot, Kōji noticed. It didn't always mean that they had some special relationship. It was just a way of greeting friends. He hadn't the nerve to try it. Maybe someone would hug him first. Maybe, by the end of the day he would be friends with Nora and he could hug her when they said goodbye. That would be nice.

"So, Kōji, what do you do?" asked Nora as she smoothly merged into the traffic flow of 101 South. "Besides study English, I mean."

From classroom practice, Kōji was prepared for this. He told her he was studying to be a Buddhist priest. His father was a Buddhist priest. He lived in Maizuru, near Kyoto. You know Kyoto? He was twenty-nine years old. His hobby was playing pachinko. You know pachinko?

Nora laughed. Yes she knew about Kyoto. She had a book of the gardens of Kyoto. She didn't know pachinko, though. Kōji had not run into this before. The other foreign students all knew pachinko. He tried to explain, but lacked the vocabulary.

"Korinto game," he said.

Nora shook her head. Kōji was taken aback. He had thought "Corinth game" was English. He turned to Philip.

"Naa—pachinko te Eigo de nan to iu? Korinto geimu wa Eigo ja nai no?"

"Pinball," said Philip.

"Pinball," repeated Kōji. "I am number one pinball."

"Pachinko is a mind-numbing, thumb-bruising, eye-glazing attempt to win a lot of little metal balls in order to support the economy of North Korea," Philip said to Nora. Kōji nodded as if this should be perfectly clear. And, to be polite, "What is your job?"

"Me? I'm an orthodontic assistant," she said. Kōji looked blank.

"Dentist helper," she tried. "Philip—explain what I do."

"What do you do?" Philip asked.

"Philip, I'm an orthodontic assistant," Nora reminded him.

Philip said something in Japanese, and Kōji covered his mouth self-consciously. The first thing Nora had noticed about him was his overlapping incisors. There was an awkward silence.

Just then they came through a tunnel and the Golden Gate Bridge rose up majestically in front of them. San Francisco shimmered like Oz at the other end. Kōji forgot about his teeth and gaped at the scene

"Kōji, is there any place in San Francisco you especially want to see?" Nora asked him.

"Keiburukaa," he said promptly.

"Okay. Cable car. We'll ride the cable car. Anything else?"

"Fuwishamanzu Wofu. Sheefuudo?"

"Fine. We'll end up at Fisherman's Wharf for seafood. That it?"

Kōji desperately wanted to see Carol Doda's famous topless act at the Condor Club, but he couldn't say that to Nora.

"How about we drive down Lombard Street, go through Golden Gate

Park, ditch my car—I mean leave my car at my apartment—and then go back to ride a cable car?"

It all sounded good to Kōji—whatever she said. They caught a bus downtown and joined a queue of tourists waiting to ride the cable car. Nora began to relax a little. She had been avoiding visiting Philip ever since he went back to his parents' house. She had been single for three years since her divorce, and it was just uncomfortable the way Linda Metcalfe still treated her as Philip's girlfriend. Of course she felt very sorry for Philip. She felt sorry for his Japanese fiancée too.

Kōji was not used to the feeling of wind ruffling his hair. Hanging onto the bar of the cable car, he couldn't stop smiling. They poked around Fisherman's Wharf and found a seafood restaurant with tables overlooking the bay. Speaking directly to the waiter, Kōji ordered fish and chips and tea. He felt daring and independent. Life was an adventure, and he was out there, skating on its rim. If language school was far from his thoughts, his father's temple in Maizuru was on a different planet.

After lunch they wandered past the gift shops and arcades. Nora asked Kōji if he needed to buy souvenirs for anybody at home. She knew that Japanese were big on presents.

"What about for your mother?" asked Nora. "A souvenir? Or your girlfriend?"

Kōji was flattered that Nora thought he had a girlfriend. He nodded and was about to step into a shop full of tourist bric-a-brac, when his eye fell on an arcade halfway down the block. Mesmerized he began to walk toward it.

"Kōji?" Nora called. She grabbed Philip by the sleeve and headed after him. "Where is he going?"

They followed him into the dark, noisy arcade.

Kōji was beside himself with excitement. PacMan! The rippled gumdrop shapes of Akabei, Aosuke, Guzuta, and Pinky flitted across a dozen screens. He knew them all. He glimpsed Ms. PacMan with her pink bow and sexy lipstick. Kōji turned his shining face to Philip and Nora.

"Let's eat dots," he said, digging for quarters in his pockets. Pachinko was Kōji's true métier, but he did not sneer at Namco's video games. He had quickly established himself as master player when they had come out four years ago. Yet there was something about the medium of video that left a vaguely unsatisfied feeling, even after consuming all the dots. After two years of whipping through mazes of ever more challenging degree, Kōji had decided that he preferred the physicality of pachinko. Once in a while he enjoyed sweeping into an arcade and stunning a bunch of high school boys, although he hadn't gobbled video dots for at least a year now.

But he had no doubt that he could. And in a style that would be sure to impress. Neither Nora nor Philip had ever played PacMan before, so Kōji realized he would need to show them the rudiments, let them try it themselves, before they could appreciate his skill. He put a quarter in a console

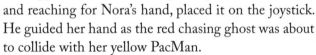 and reaching for Nora's hand, placed it on the joystick. He guided her hand as the red chasing ghost was about to collide with her yellow PacMan.

"Eat dots. Avoid ghosts," said Philip, translating Kōji's instructions. "Oh, and eat the power pellets when you can." Nora laughed as Kōji moved her hand with a quick jerk.

"Here, Philip. You try," said Nora, removing her hand. Kōji winced as her PacMan collided with Akabei, ending the game. Philip found a quarter and started the game again. He made it through the first level and was rewarded with a little melody. Kōji coached him. Pinky is the ambushing ghost. Good, good. Okay, watch out there's Pinky… It was all he could do to stop himself from reaching over and grabbing the joystick. Ahhh—Philip's PacMan got ambushed by Pinky.

"Let's see you do it Kōji," said Nora. "Here, I've got a quarter."

Twenty minutes passed. Kōji had racked up a score of 500,000 points on Nora's quarter. Teenage boys began to drift over to watch. His chomping yellow pie ate every dot, every energizer, every blue ghost, and every fruit that materialized. With fixed concentration he rose level by level. Nora could tell from the murmuring of the gathered crowd that she was witnessing something extraordinary. Then she realized that Philip was no longer standing behind her.

Nora moved away from Kōji. Her place was immediately swallowed by the crowd of boys. Trying not to panic, she pushed her way out, her eyes sweeping the dark room for a sign of Philip. Today she had been lulled into treating him like a normal person. But once his attention was no longer tethered to someone he knew, there was no telling where he might wander. She felt sick.

Then she saw him. In the deserted back corner of the arcade among the old games that customers had lost interest in, there he was, standing in front of a pinball machine, flipping levers and sending cascades of little metal balls shimmering down the face of the console. She exhaled in relief. Leaving Kōji at the center of his crowd, she walked back and put her hand on Philip's shoulder. He was surprised to see her. He told her about pachinko.

"You wouldn't believe it, but this is what keeps the North Korean economy going," he said gravely.

Nora figured that someone in Philip's condition would be prone to attacks of paranoia.

Kōji reached the end of the tenth game. He knew a little musical intermission would pop up here and he could catch his breath. He turned around to reap Nora's praise. She was gone. So was Philip. Instead, a dozen or more teenage boys were cheering and offering him soft drinks and candy. Someone gave him a little twisted tube that looked like a hand-rolled cigarette. Kōji was overwhelmed. But where was Nora? Had they not seen his triumph? The intermission was ending and the game was about to start again. Kōji grabbed a boy standing next to him, and put his hand on the joystick.

"You do," he said, backing out through the crowd. They all gasped. The boy to whom Kōji had given this game went white. Then it started. Desperately he tried to steer through the rain of dots, ghosts, pellets, and fruit. Just as Kōji spotted Nora and Philip, he heard the collective groan as PacMan expired.

"Look, Kōji—pachinko!" said Philip.

Nora had promised to call Linda Metcalfe to let her know how things were going. She put Kōji in charge of Philip while she stepped into a phone booth.

"Stay right here," she said slowly and emphatically to him. She pointed to the phone booth and made the gesture of dialing. She put Kōji's hand on Philip's arm.

"Stay with him—understand?"

"Yes, okay. I understand," Kōji felt guilty that his earlier grandstanding had caused Philip to wander away. "Right here. Me. Philip."

Nora smiled at him. "You're a good friend, Kōji."

She closed the door to the booth and rummaged in her purse for change.

"Hello?" Linda picked up the phone on the first ring. Her husband had been furious when she told him about the expedition. Perhaps she had been dreadfully wrong in facilitating it after all. The scenarios she had fearfully imagined all day now faded at Nora's calm voice.

"Everything's great," she reported. "They're both having a good time—especially Kōji. But Philip's doing fine," she hastened to add, glancing at the two of them standing outside the booth. She waved at Kōji who panto mimed holding onto Philip's sleeve, giving her a thumbs up.

"Well, Jim has said he will come pick Philip up in the city," Linda told her. "There's no reason to make you drive all the back out to Marin. You've done so much today already."

"It's been fun," Nora told her. "Really."

"Still. You know how Jim is when he's decided something."

"What about Kōji?" asked Nora. "He's got school in Berkeley tomorrow morning, right?"

"Could I ask you to put him on a BART train back to Berkeley?"

"Sure. That's fine. Don't worry about it."

Nora hung up and pulled open the heavy louvered door. Kōji and Philip were cackling about something in Japanese. Nora watched them for a minute. He was such a different person in Japanese. So much lighter, she thought. She had long ago gotten over the heartbreak of splitting up with Philip.

"Okay, you guys," she said. She felt like a mother duck. "Let's pick up some chocolate and walk up toward North Beach. Philip, your Dad is going to meet us and take you home. Kōji, I'll show you how to get back to Berkeley."

They cut across to Ghirardelli Square's chocolate shop. Kōji inhaled the aroma. He wanted to buy chocolate for his mother but knew he would eat it all himself if he got it now.

Nora spotted the Volvo and waved.

"Come on, guys," she said, picking up the bag with the chocolate. Philip opened the car door, and Kōji started to get in too.

"Hold on," said Nora, grabbing his arm. "You've got to go back to Berkeley, remember?" With Philip's level of memory and Kōji's level of comprehension, it was amazing the day went as well as it did. Philip seemed surprised that they weren't all coming. Nora put the bag of chocolate in his hand.

"Goodbye Philip. This is for your Mom. Don't forget." Nora gave him a hug.

Jim Metcalfe thanked her for being a good sport, and they drove off.

"Shee you again..." said Kōji, waving as his voice trailed off. His earlier ebullience faded and he felt forlorn and abandoned. Nora put her arm around his shoulder.

"Kōji, do you like Italian food? How about I'll take you to dinner in North Beach. I know an interesting place. Seafood, pasta— lots of garlic...I think you'll like it."

Kōji looked up at her gratefully. He realized he wasn't being abandoned after all. "Sheefudo?" he said hopefully.

Nora tucked her arm in his as they walked up Columbus Avenue. They passed a tattoo museum. It was closed but there was a book of Japanese tattoo art displayed in the window. Nora pointed at it.

"Japanese tattoos are really beautiful," she said. "Do you have any tattoos, Kōji?"

He understood what she asked, and was shocked. How could he possibly explain that tattoos were for yakuza, and he was going to be a priest. A priest with a tattoo? Unthinkable. For all his rebelliousness, Kōji was brought up believing that tattoos were beyond the pale. They were not simply body decoration, they were a social sign—a stigma even. It had never occurred to him to think that they might be beautiful. But because Nora had innocently asked, he looked at the picture of the intricate indigo dragon curling over a man's back, and he suddenly realized that yes—it was beautiful.

These thoughts and revelations tumbled through Kōji's mind in a split second, but all he could say to Nora was "No. No *irezumi*."

"*Irezumi*? Is that 'tattoo' in Japanese? Oh, I see. That's the title of that book," she said. *Irezumi*. Wish I had a dictionary..."

Dictionary? Idiot—he had been carrying a dictionary in the pocket of his jacket all day. With Philip around, he had forgotten about it. He reached into his pocket and pulled out a roll of butterscotch lifesavers, a wrapped piece of saltwater taffy, a Japanese-English/English-Japanese pocket dictionary, and a crumbling joint.

Nora was amused. "Kōji—picking up bad habits already, I see." She plucked the joint out of the jumble in his cupped hands. "Where did you get this?"

"Puckman," he said. "Boizu gibu me candy."

Nora narrowed her eyes. "Do you know what this is?" she said, wagging the object at him.

"Tabako?" he said. "shegaretto?"

"Kōji," Nora said, "this is a joint. Marijuana."

"Mariwana?" Kōji couldn't believe it. He was badder than he knew. Asked if he had a tattoo, discovered carrying mariwana—walking in San Francisco with a beautiful blonde on his arm. If his friends could only see him now…Koji shivered with satisfaction.

"Just be a little discreet with that, okay?" Nora warned.

"Disukurito?"

Nora borrowed the dictionary, found the word, and pointed at it.

"Be careful."

He nodded. "I be careful."

Then Nora said, "Maybe we should have a toke before dinner? What do you say?" she gestured puffing on the joint, pointing to herself and Kōji.

"Now?" he yipped, visibly alarmed.

Nora looked around. She pulled him around the corner of a building. Hands shaking, Kōji searched for his lighter.

"First time?" Nora asked.

"Faasto taimu," he confirmed, too shaken to roll his tongue correctly. He snapped the flame and Nora lit the tip of the joint, taking a quick inhale. Holding her breath, she passed it to him. Kōji looked into her eyes, blue as raw sea slug slices, and drew the heavy sweet smoke down into his lungs. He waited. For what, he didn't know. Nora took one more inhale, offered it to him again, then extinguished it. She smiled at him, took his arm, and propelled him another block up Columbus to the Caffe Sport.

They stepped from the sunny street into a dim grotto hung with fishing nets. Colorful plates, mirrors, dolls, and smoked hams strung like improbable fish adorned the walls and ceilings. A surly waiter led them to a long painted table inlaid with Majolica tiles. The colors swirled before Kōji's eyes, then he found himself holding an oversize laminated menu upon which swam incomprehensible black squiggles. Nora was saying something.

She borrowed his dictionary again. Garlic—she pointed to the word. *Niniku.* He looked down. A basket of garlic-butter infused bread had suddenly appeared. When he moved his arms or turned his head, the air felt as though it were liquid crystal, slowing down his every movement. Nora's blue eyes were steady beacons in the collage of images that languidly swam about his field of vision. He suddenly felt as if he were inside a living mandala centered on Nora's eyes. He smiled and saw that she was laughing.

"Okay, then, why don't I order for us both…"

Nora said something to the waiter, who then plucked the menu from Kōji's hands. She took a piece of garlic bread out of the basket and offered it to him.

Kōji ate garlic bread. He ate salad, salami, and olives. He ate pasta topped with shrimp, scallops, mussels, zucchini, and garlic. It was the best food he had ever eaten, he decided. He was sated—sensually and psychologically replete with a satisfaction that seemed to curl up happily in his belly and radiate throughout his being. When the check came, Kōji insisted on paying. Nora let him.

"*Chippu?*" He asked her.

Finally she realized he wanted to know how much to leave as a tip. She indicated that she would contribute the tip, and Kōji was relieved. He hated this custom that required you to do calculations at the end of a meal. They slipped out into the street, into the nightlife of North Beach. Nora intended to walk Kōji to a BART station.

They made their way past the brilliant neon and garish signs of the strip clubs. Kōji's eyes caromed from one sign to another. "Man Woman Love Act." He was unaware that his mouth was slightly open. As they approached the corner of Columbus and Broadway he couldn't believe his eyes. There, reaching to the sky, was the sign—twice life-size, "Carol Doda topless" it said, nipples blinking invitingly in red neon. Kōji stopped in his tracks.

"Goddess of San Francisco," said Nora sarcastically. "Do you know how old she must be?"

Kōji couldn't move, staring up at the sign, down to the door. A tuxedoed barker caught sight of him and waved extravagantly.

Nora looked at Kōji. "You want to go in, don't you?" she said. "Okay, if you've got the cash, I'll go in with you."

Kōji moved toward the entrance like a paper clip to a magnet. A hostess in a low-cut blouse and miniskirt showed them to a table. His eyes were glued to a piano on a raised dais, a fake leopard skin draped on the lid.

"You know Carol Doda is probably too old to do this any more," Nora said to him. "It will be somebody else—she's a freak anyway…"

Whatever Nora was saying, Kōji didn't care. A saxophone began to play, and lights danced over the piano as a sultry brunette with long hair slid out from behind a curtain. She toyed with a veil for a few minutes, then bored with that, lifted it over her head, wiggling her torso as she did. Kōji was floored. The monstrous melons that jiggled out seemed to have a life of their own. They wobbled and danced. She held them out, spilling over her hands, pale nipples peeking through her fingers. Throwing her shoulders back she waggled her bouncy torpedoes at a man sitting alone at a table near the piano. Leering, he put his hands out rudely, as if lifting sandbags.

Nora rolled her eyes. Why did guys get such a kick out this? She read somewhere that Japanese men were supposed to be turned on by napes, not the boob fetish that reigned in America. She looked at Kōji. His face was suffused with happiness. This was even better than pachinko. He concentrated his attention on those magnificent *oppai*. Circles within orbs, nipples within spheres, Mt. Meru, the breast at the center of the universe—Kōji lost himself in a mandala of tits. The dancer swished around the piano, ending up, back arched, on top of the leopard skin. The stagelights dimmed and Kōji clapped enthusiastically. He had learned new vocabulary from the girlie magazines. Turning to Nora he beamed, "I rabu titsu!"

"Great, Kōji," she replied. "I think its time we got you back to Berkeley."

Nora finally managed to steer him out of The Condor Club onto the street. She waved to a passing cab.

"Dropping one person at Embarcadero BART, then up to Lyon and Fell," she said. She wondered if Kōji was capable of getting to the East Bay on his own. Christ, he's twenty-nine years old, she told herself. He'll be fine. The cab drove to Embarcadero. Nora stepped out with Kōji and pointed him at the station.

"Take the Richmond train to Berkeley, understand? It's a straight shot, but remember to get off. You'll be right in downtown Berkeley. You can find your place from there, right?"

Kōji was nodding. "Bakeri, Bakeri. Hai! No puroburemu."

Nora gave him a hug. "Okay Kōji. Take care. Hope I'll see you again."

"Shee you again!" he repeated as she got back into the cab. He stood on the curb, waving. Then he turned around and practically floated down the steps to the station.

Kōji bought his ticket, then scrutinized the map as he waited for a Richmond train. He realized that he could nip back and forth to San Francisco on this train whenever he wanted. Too bad school took up so much time every day. He counted up the remaining weekends.

When he sauntered into the room he shared with Mitsuyasu, he found his roommate already in bed, heavily engaged with a Penthouse magazine. Startled and trying to cover his embarrassment, Mitsuyasu grumbled at him. Where had Kōji been all weekend? He was getting worried. Kōji ignored him and proceeded to the bathroom to brush his teeth. When he came back in the room he tossed a pack of matches onto Mitsuyasu's bed. Carol Doda's picture from The Condor Club adorned the box. Mitsuyasu looked at Kōji with disbelief.

"You're something else…"

Kōji still didn't say anything. He waited, and sure enough, after a minute had passed, Mitsuyasu was begging to be taken along the next time.

Sakura

IN THE AUTUMN, TOKUDA checked up on his charges at their public showings. Since meeting Philip Metcalfe, he realized that if his life had any meaning at all it must be to actively protect the hidden buddhas, not simply to witness their gradual deactivation. He recalled that moment when everything had become gloriously clear. All the doubts and quiet misapprehensions that over the years had gathered in the corners of his mind were blown away in that gust of absolute certainty. He knew what needed doing. He had discovered a partner to help him accomplish it. This revelation was so complete he'd even gotten over the crushing blow of Philip's disappearance. It simply meant that he would have to do it all himself.

He'd been alone before. He was used to it. Tokuda began to think that the revelation Philip had given him could even solve the nagging problem of his successor. Perhaps he didn't need one. If he could find whatever was snuffing out the powers of the *hibutsu* and prevent it—perhaps for good— then the legacy of Kūkai's system might all realize its ultimate purpose in he himself. After all, Tokuda was the only one to have ever witnessed a dying *hibutsu*—that must surely set him apart.

Yet the revelation was a hard thing to put into practice. In his grandfather's day, over one hundred active hibutsu had shrunk to twenty. Since that big Guan Yin in Tokyo went dark last winter, now there were ten. But ten was a manageable number. He could easily monitor them himself. He was less sure of what, exactly, he would do when he found who was destroying them. It depended on several things. If the person was pursuing the buddhas as prey, then the answer would be easier. Tokuda was fairly sure that he could exterminate him—or her. He practiced imagining himself throttling this incarnate evil with his hands if necessary.

He thought of the fierce guardian deities of Buddhism, their muscled feet clamped firmly on the necks of devils. Destruction in the name of protection. He should take his cue from his own personal deity, Fudō, who used his sword in defense of the faith. What would prevent the malevolent *akunin* from simply continuing to reincarnate? Tokuda had meditated on this question. It was key to his revelation. And then it came to him—the evil could only maintain its mission because it was undetected. Just as the *hibutsu's* power lay in hiddenness, so did the *akunin's* ability to kill them off. If he faced it now, he felt that not only could he contain it, he could very well stop it. And this is how he would preserve the remaining hidden buddhas. The only problem with this plan was the possibility his grandfather had raised that the *akunin* might not be conscious of its destructive power. Could he murder an innocent? Even for a higher cause? In this case, Tokuda was not sure. Perhaps he could enlighten the *akunin* and break this ongoing transmission of evil with compassion. Break ignorance with knowledge. He simply could not tell at this point what he would do, but trusted that when the moment came he would know.

He strained every sense, watching all who came to worship the *hibutsu*, but at no temple did he see, hear, feel, taste, or smell anything at all suspicious. All ten hidden buddhas went back behind doors intact. Tokuda returned to Kamakura and ministered to the mothers of water children.

In October Nagiko received a box of sticky Ghirardelli chocolate in the mail. It had been posted from Maizuru, along with a note saying it was from Kōji Kon. She ate one of the slick dark cubes, wondering how he had fared with Philip. She ought to call him, but it was awkward, and her mind was preoccupied with the upcoming surgery for Mayumi's hands and feet. She ended up putting Kōji's name in her rolodex, and then forgot about him. The following day, two incisions were made on Mayumi's left hand, freeing the ring finger. The right hand required only one cut between ring and middle fingers. The same separations were done on her toes where the webbing mirrored that of her hands. Mayumi was fully bandaged at the extremities, and she howled her outrage. Under that creamy skin and rosy cheeks, behind the long eyelashes and rosebud mouth, the child had a volcanic temper.

"No more *palaka*..." crooned Josefina as she changed the dressings. Mayumi whimpered. She still crawled, quite rapidly, but her attempts to haul herself up to standing were thwarted by the awkward gauze knobs. She lay on her stomach now, alternating between thrashing her limbs in futile protest and going limp. At Nagiko's instructions, Josefina had made a start at toilet training, but all that was forgotten in Mayumi's state of perpetual ire. She was put back in a diaper, which she soiled several times a night, waking Nagiko with her cries.

It was all horribly familiar. Nagiko remembered how the shrieks of the *mizuko* once woke her, jolting her out of fitful sleep. Mayumi's first month home from the hospital had been more of the same. Slowly, mother and child had begun to adapt to each other's rhythms, but now the trauma of the operation shredded those bonds. Mayumi's nighttime wailing resumed, intensified. It seemed as if the child was rebuking her, Nagiko thought.

She had really tried to do the right thing. The abortion was necessary, but hadn't she tried to make things right with the *mizuko*? She could have sent it back a second time, but she didn't. This operation had been another setback. Fixing the one flaw in an otherwise perfect pearl of a child—that was all Nagiko was trying to do. When Nagiko tried to explain the baby's resentment to the doctor, he looked at her queerly. Babies did not resent their mothers—she could tell that's what he was thinking.

Josefina was Nagiko's closest source of maternal experience, and Josefina only shook her head. Poor *palaka*, she repeated, until Nagiko had to ask her once again to stop calling Mayumi that. When Jun Muranaka phoned the office to ask her out to dinner, Nagiko accepted eagerly. She was relieved not to go directly home to a screaming child.

Right before he had last seen Philip, Jun had received a most peculiar offer from Prime Minister Yasuhiro Nakasone. At the behest of someone in a high place—someone not mentioned by name but assumed to connected to the Imperial family, a capable person was sought. This person's job would be to think outside the confines of Japanese politics. Someone not attached to any of the usual bureaucracies; someone who had experience dealing with foreigners, who was clear-headed, knowledgeable, apolitical, and discreet.

"How about it, Muranaka?" the Prime Minister had asked.

It appeared that Jun was not the only one to think that "Japan As Number One" was a snare and a delusion. Some things in Japan worked extremely well. But not everything. The businessmen and politicians who presumed the trend would continue upward in an unending spiral of economic miracles were blinded by Japan's successes. At some point, the rising sun would surely set. And at that point the appointee to this unnamed position would be expected to have a point of view. Jun was assured that his opinions would be taken seriously. The appointment would be open-ended, so as to survive the churning of prime ministers and political factionalism. Jun Muranaka was the unanimous first choice for this position.

He was flattered, dumbfounded, and somewhat overwhelmed. Jun wanted to know what exactly was expected of him. A former prime minister had supported his mission to increase entrepreneurial activity in the country, but this was something much bigger.

"Think about the larger social issues," Nakasone had said. "Consensus is fine, but we need the view of someone who doesn't have to worry about stepping on toes. We'll meet every six months, and we'll chat. All we ask is for you to keep your ears open, and think about things."

Their first chat had been about the two Koreas and the huge resident core of Koreans living in Japan. Pachinko was mentioned, including statistics about how much of its profits were siphoned to Kim Il Sung. No wonder the thundering of pachinko balls had rattled him ever since that conversation. The kidnappings had caused a momentary stir in the news, but if people had known the extent of the disappearances, there would have been an uproar. The more political secrets he was privy to, the more uneasy Jun felt. He was expected to watch, listen, think, and advise. But not to act. Instead he worried. When he heard about Philip's accident, Jun felt like a boxer who had absorbed one too many punches. At least he could try to help Nagiko.

Nagiko had not seen him since Mayumi was born. She presumed he wanted to talk about Philip, although she didn't have anything new to report. Coming up the block, Jun saw her walk up to the restaurant and hesitate at the door. He quickened his steps, reaching her side just as she was about to enter.

"Kiyowara-san…"

As Nagiko turned her head, the loose hood of her coat fell away, and Jun was struck anew by how beautiful she was. He was suddenly abashed. "Good evening," he said.

"Good evening! How have you been?" she asked him. "I'm very sorry I haven't kept in touch."

As they approached the door, she held back, expecting him to walk through first as any Japanese man would do, but he surprised her by holding the door for her. This small reminder of his familiarity with more cosmopolitan modes of behavior told Nagiko that she did not have to play the usual games Japanese men in high position expect of women and underlings. They were shown to a table where a waiter handed Jun the wine menu. He ran his eyes down the list, then passed it to Nagiko.

Asked if she had sampled the Beaujolais Nouveau that had come to market two weeks ago, Nagiko smiled, raising an eyebrow.

Jun laughed.

"Can you name two reasons we Japanese go for Beaujolais Nouveau?"

"One-upmanship—the desire to be first," Nagiko waved her fork, "and…"

"And?"

"I can't think of another reason," she replied.

"The taste," said Jun. "It's very light. It doesn't linger on the tongue. It's the perfect wine for palates used to beer and saké, don't you think?"

"You may be right," she said. "I actually like Beaujolais Nouveau—I just don't like the scramble that goes along with it."

Jun held up his glass. "I propose a toast," he said.

"To?"

"How about to Philip?" he suggested. "How is he?"

Nagiko sighed. She clinked her glass to his. "To Philip," she said. "He's still the same as far as I know."

Muranaka was silent a moment, then raised his glass again. "Well then, to Mayumi-chan. How is she doing?"

Again Nagiko tipped her glass towards his. She told him about Mayumi's operation, and without meaning to ended up spilling the story of the child's rage, the sleepless nights, the guilt she felt. Perhaps it was the wine. She stopped herself, embarrassed, and looked up at Muranaka.

"I'm sorry," she whispered. "I didn't mean to go on like that. It's been a hard month." She produced a smile.

"But the new line is doing well, and Kiji is set to have a good quarter."

"You don't have to force-feed me positive news," said Jun quietly. "I think I understand how difficult it must be."

Nagiko glanced at him, trying to gauge his intent. She could usually tell when middle-aged married men were testing her availability. They thought they were being subtle and indirect when they were utterly obvious. Japanese men were by far the clumsiest at seduction. But she didn't get those warning vibrations from Muranaka.

"Well, difficult, yes," she said slowly, "but not impossible. We'll get through this. Next week all the bandages will be off, and no more antibiotics. There will just be a bit of scar tissue—and she'll have to get used to her fingers all being independent, I guess."

"Are you still visiting hidden buddhas?" Jun asked.

"Not recently. And there aren't a lot on view now until spring. But yes— we might start our trips again." She finished the wine in her glass. "Why? Are you still interested in coming?"

"Yes, actually," said Jun. "Why don't you let me know some places and dates, and I'll see what my schedule looks like. I expect I'll be traveling quite a bit this coming year, but I would very much like to come along—if that's okay," he added.

Jun had no idea how busy he would be come spring. He lived on airplanes. He didn't see Nagiko again for months.

The cherry blossoms that spring were spectacular. A warm beginning of March was followed by cool weather that preserved the bloom. Satoko had a picnic celebration at a private garden with all her ikebana students.

Clippers at the ready, Satoko's students gathered in a semicircle around her. They were not used to creating flower arrangements outdoors. Instead of the defined space of a *tokonoma* alcove serving to frame their creations, here the sky was the backdrop, the trees were their audience. The breeze jiggled their arrangements in dynamic and unfamiliar ways. They all felt quite daring. In class, their materials were always presented to them, chosen by Satoko, already cut. Today they would venture out to bag their own off a living tree.

Dressed in stylish pants and jackets, shod in sensible shoes, the women fanned out over the gentle hills, determined to view each tree before making their choice of branch. Meanwhile, Satoko and Nagiko set up folding tables. Mayumi toddled under the trees, turning in circles until she fell, dizzy, on the grass. She wiggled out of her pink sweater and left it under a tree. Nagiko rescued the sweater and brought it back to the tables. Just then, Mayumi approached with a fallen flower she had picked up.

"*Sakura*," Mayumi chirped, gripping the flower.

Nagiko said bring more, and Mayumi rushed off. She threw herself on top of Satoko's lap with another fistful of fallen cherry blossoms.

"Are you sure you don't want to do an arrangement?" she said to Nagiko. Nagiko shook her head.

"I have to keep track of the little demon here." Mayumi was now tugging at the hem of her jacket. "Keep her out of everyone's hair."

"Well, maybe Mayumi would like to do one?" suggested Satoko. She picked up an oblong container and placed it on the ground at the edge of the mat.

"This will be your first ikebana lesson," said Satoko. Her students watched out of the corners of their eyes, amused. Satoko poured a little puddle of water into the container.

"This is your lake," she said.

She looked around. Spying a rock of the right shape, Satoko called to one of the ladies nearby and asked her to bring it over.

"This is your mountain," she explained, setting the rock in a corner of the container. Mayumi set to work decorating the mossy rock with the twigs and blossoms from her accumulated heap.

Nagiko managed to stuff Mayumi back into her pink sweater, then stretched out and smiled at Satoko who was getting up to attend to her students' creations.

"Thank you," she said.

The women worked four to a table, their voices adding a soft buzz to the spring air. Mayumi had gone off in search of more flowers, so keeping one eye on the small dark head bobbing around the trees, Nagiko watched the students' compositions take shape at the tables. She had not met many of Satoko's students before, but she could tell a great deal about each of them by the way they handled their flowers. Timid, bold, conventional, aggressive—traits you might never suspect by looking at the women's faces were revealed clearly in their arrangements. Could that be why she balked at doing ikebana herself, she wondered? She didn't want others to be able to read her so openly?

Mayumi was now back in front of her blue container, rearranging various parts of it. Satoko came over carrying a cracker and a box of juice. She looked at Mayumi's vase.

"What a good job! Did your mama help you?" she asked, handing the snack to her.

Nagiko had just finished setting out cups and was now coming back to check on Mayumi and praise her first ikebana. The child was squatting on the mat by the container, having neglected to take off her shoes, Nagiko noticed.

"*Kaa-san!*" said Mayumi suddenly looking up at her with a smile. And Nagiko saw that there in the puddle of the container she had piled up stones into a little mound, exactly the way the *mizuko* had done on the riverbank in her dream.

Mayumi snatched the juice from Satoko and plopped down to eat the cracker.

Squeamish about Smell

AS ALWAYS, THE HALL OF DREAMS Guan Yin needed attending, and there were nine others that spring. All these *hibutsu* went on view and were closed up without incident. In spite of his vigilance and his vow to protect the *hibutsu* no matter what it took, Tokuda found himself relaxing slightly. He even allowed himself to notice that the cherry blossoms had been extraordinary this year.

Nagiko's fabrics were now regularly picked up by designers on the international fashion scene. In addition to limited runs of fabric, she created collections of her own clothing, pacing them to debut every two years. They were sold exclusively at one store in five cities worldwide—New York, San Francisco, London, Paris, and, in Tokyo at Kiji's new Roppongi branch. Her instincts told her to resist the temptation to license to a chain. Every two years Nagiko traveled to each of the five cities to meet with the store managers to coordinate the displays.

Satoko brought Mayumi to the new Roppongi store late one afternoon for a small party to launch the new international collection. She called it *Mowa-memu (Moi même)*. It included a felt coat with detachable hood, loose cuffed trousers with a bunched waist meant to suggest a paper bag, a sleeveless vest-jacket with a set of removable interchangeable sleeves, a bias-cut dress, and a heavy brocade bag made of obi fabric that could be worn like a backpack.

People dropped by singly and in small groups. Nagiko stood anchored at the center of the ebb and flow of guests while Mayumi darted about like a small colorful fish, charming everyone with her fearless innocence. Ever since she discovered words, Mayumi delighted in talking to anyone who paid attention. She carefully picked out toast rounds spread with foie gras from the salvers set about the shop, and Satoko found her cheerfully accepting sips of wine from an elderly bearded man.

"Stay with Auntie now," Satoko admonished her, leading her away from the man, who soon left in embarrassment. A woman with frizzed hair made a fuss over Mayumi till the child rebelled, suddenly fatigued and wanting her mother. Satoko located Nagiko standing by a cluster of chairs, talking with Jun Muranaka who had stopped by to offer his congratulations.

Muranaka had tried to ask Nagiko out once each season. He felt that was infrequent enough to be proper. They had now been meeting this way for three and a half years. Jun was different from any of Nagiko's professional contacts. He was smart, funny, widely educated, and a total fashion innocent. Although it was his business now to cultivate people in government, industry, and academia, Jun found he could relax and enjoy himself with Nagiko in a way impossible in any of the other worlds in which he moved. He had always felt shy around women. As an adult he thought he had come up with a workable balance—an amicable if cool arrangement with his wife on the one hand, and expensive hostesses for banter and drinking companionship on the other. Geisha mystified him on the rare occasions when he was invited to teahouses. The only one he felt comfortable with was Umeko in the setting of her club. At one point he had a favorite hostess whom he set up as his exclusive mistress, but she got bored with him and dropped him for a younger patron. Muranaka was secretly relieved. She had been beautiful but dull. He had started avoiding her, it was true.

Had it not been for his connection to Philip, he would never have dreamed of approaching anyone as glamorous as Nagiko. Romance was out of the question, so he relaxed. They still talked about making an excursion to a temple with a hidden buddha, but had yet to actually do it. Nor had he seen Mayumi since he visited the hospital when she was born. But he recognized her immediately at the party. She looked pure Japanese, with a pearly glow to her creamy skin. Her hair was thick and fine with a slight wave, and just as black as Nagiko's. She opened her mouth in a round yawn right at that moment. When her eyes blinked open again, Jun saw they were dark—but in the light reflected from above, he could see they had remained the dark blue of Philip's eyes. She reached for her mother.

"Excuse me," Nagiko said. She sat down in one of the chairs and Mayumi climbed onto her lap. Jun sat down as well. Mayumi promptly fell asleep, one arm draped over her mother's neck. Just then, one of the shop girls nervously approached, leading a customer with a technical question about one of the fabrics.

"Here," said Jun. "You go attend to this. I'll hold Mayumi."

Nagiko looked at him in surprise. "Muranaka-san—I wouldn't dream of burdening you…"

"No, really," he said, and perfectly naturally, as if he carried sleeping toddlers to bed every night, he scooped Mayumi off her lap and settled back in the chair. The child barely stirred.

"I'll be right back," Nagiko assured him.

"Don't worry," Muranaka said.

Nagiko's chair was immediately taken by a flustered Satoko. She had no idea who this man was, but having seen Nagiko give the child over, she didn't dare demand her back. So she perched nearby, hovering like a hen over a purloined egg till Nagiko returned.

"I'm leaving for New York tomorrow afternoon," Nagiko said to him. "My friend Satoko is taking Mayumi home with her while I'm away." They walked out to the curb where a car and driver were waiting. Nagiko ran back into the store to fetch a large shopping bag of toys and clothes.

"These are her new favorites," she told Satoko, placing the bag on the seat next to her. "—and *Uwasan*, of course." Mayumi had a stuffed bear named Oursin who traveled back and forth between Nagiko's apartment and Satoko's house.

She waved as the car drove away. Then Nagiko turned to Muranaka, "Did you give Mayumi a stuffed bear when she was born?" she asked.

He tried to remember. Had he? There were flowers, and something else, perhaps a toy—perhaps even a teddy bear. He couldn't remember.

"Maybe I did," he said. "Why?"

"Oh, Mayumi's had that bear ever since she was born, but we can't remember where it came from.

"A bear named 'sea urchin'?" said Jun. "That's strange…"

"'*Ours*,' French for 'bear.' Mr. Bear—*Ours-san*. Sea urchin, *oursin*." That's how it happened," said Nagiko.

"Are you teaching her French?" he asked.

"A little. Mostly English—that's what she speaks with Josefina."

"And with Philip?"

Nagiko was quiet for a moment. Then she said, "She hasn't met Philip."

"Ah," said Jun. Although Philip was the connection that drew them together, they seldom talked about him any more.

Muranaka gently took her arm. "Come on," he said. "I know you have to travel tomorrow, but let's go have a drink."

He hailed an empty cab, trying to think where he should take her. A nice, quiet club, no hostesses—maybe the bar at the Imperial. It was hard to know where to take a woman who was not, technically, a date.

"Are you hungry?" he asked.

"Not starving…but I could eat something," she replied.

"Ummm… French?"

"No, I had enough foie gras earlier. I could go for a brandy—and maybe a bit of cheese."

"That sounds pretty French to me, but I think I know a place," said Jun. He gave the driver an address just off the Ginza.

The tiny *Club Escargot* was on the third floor of a narrow six-story building. Every floor contained one or two private clubs. *Escargot* was staffed by a single bartender and an elegant middle-aged woman who looked as though she might have had her eyelids surgically altered at some point, although it could just as well have been the extravagant eye make-up.

"We'll have my bottle of Armagnac," said Jun, pointing to the private reserves, "and do you suppose you could find some cheese?"

"I'll see what I can do," she said, gliding discreetly away. Just because a man brought a woman in with him didn't necessarily mean he wanted to be alone with her. The mama-san had a finely developed sense of when customers wanted her to hover at their side, and when they wanted privacy. She whispered something to the bartender who ducked out a back door. She then fetched out the bottle with Muranaka's name inscribed on a tag around its neck, and brought it to their table. When men brought dates, those women made it clear that they would take over from that point. Not this one, though, the proprietress noticed, glancing at Nagiko—she was perfectly content to be treated as a guest herself.

"Cheese is coming," she said, and excused herself to go back to the side of the elderly man.

"Wonder what it will be," said Jun. "Hard to find good cheese in Japan, even in Tokyo."

Nagiko smiled weakly.

Jun cut a wedge of the solid Brie the hostess brought, and offered it to her.

"I suppose we could ponder the mystery of why Japanese have not learned to appreciate cheese."

"That's easy," said Nagiko. "It's the smell. If Japanese see a round of Brie appropriately runny they think it has gone bad."

"Are we that squeamish about smell, I wonder," mused Jun.

"I think we are, yes," Nagiko said. "Especially anything that smells of rot. Natto beans are smelly, but not in a putrid way. Or roasted mackerel—oily, smoky, stinky—but not rank. But I do think Japanese noses are sensitive. For example, when I'm in New York, I am always struck by how over-perfumed the women are."

Jun recalled some elevators he had ridden in American cities where a cloud of perfume had almost made him gag.

"Ah, I know what you mean," he nodded. He became conscious that Nagiko herself had an intriguing scent about her.

"What is that perfume you're wearing?" he asked.

She smiled. "Oh, it's not perfume. It's *zukō*."

Jun looked puzzled. "What's that?"

"Body incense. It's a powder." She reached into her purse and taking out a small stoppered wooden vial, tapped a small amount into her palm. She held it out to him.

"It reminds me of…" he stopped.

"Were you going to say a temple?" Nagiko asked.

Jun turned red. "That would probably not be taken as a compliment," he said. "But, whatever it is, it's very nice. I like it."

She rubbed the powder between her palms and then ran her fingers through her hair. "Hair is a natural fixative, you know. It holds scent."

Muranaka had no idea about such things.

"More brandy?" he asked.

"No, thank you." Nagiko covered the top of her glass with her palm. "It's lovely, but I should probably go home to pack."

At the street, a black limousine awaited.

"Address?" Jun asked. Nagiko told the driver.

Right—Kagurazaka, thought Jun, remembering once having dropped Philip there.

"I hope I'm not taking you out of your way," she murmured.

"Not at all," he insisted—which he would have said in any case although it happened to be true.

The night was balmy. Nagiko rolled the tinted window part way down. She leaned back against Jun with a small sigh, and wordlessly he raised his arm along the back of the seat. Her head rested on his shoulder, and he inhaled the incense fragrance in her hair. He found himself wishing that they would encounter a traffic jam that would delay their arrival in Kagurazaka. But the car flew through the Tokyo streets, meeting all green lights, and in fifteen minutes they arrived at Lion's Head Mansion.

Nagiko gracefully disengaged.

"When will I see you again?" Jun was alarmed at the urgency he heard in his voice.

"I'll call you when I get back next week," she said. Then she softly kissed him on the cheek and stepped out of the car.

"Where to?" the driver asked, after a two-minute silence in which Jun had not told him his destination.

"Oh—sorry…Mejiro…" he gave him the address, then sat back heavily onto the seat, breathing the warm night air mingled with the sandalwood scent Nagiko left behind.

Paris

IT HAD NOW BEEN FIVE YEARS since anything had befallen one of his charges. Tokuda wondered if simply the fact of his fortified resolve was having an effect? Perhaps his years of doubt and indecision had made the *hibutsu* more vulnerable, and now they sensed his determination in the same way he sensed their auras. Unmarried, childless, with no colleagues he could consider close friends, Tokuda's most intimate companions were the hidden buddhas themselves. Every year he visited the two that came out in the summer, one in winter, and the rest evenly divided between spring and fall. A horse head Guan Yin that was shown only once a decade came out one April without any problem. This statue was an unusual avatar of Guan Yin in angry mode—it glowered with furious energy. For Tokuda, seeing this horse head Guan Yin again was like meeting a long-lost brother.

The company Kiji Enterprises was now almost totally identified with Nagiko Kiyowara's work. Then, quite out of the blue, Nagiko's old mentor Atsouko Morikawa asked her to come to Paris to oversee her atelier, *Dessins Morikawa*, for a year while she tested the idea of retiring. The *grande dame* understood that Nagiko had her own line to oversee, but assured her she would get all the assistance she needed. So Nagiko accepted. She saw an opportunity to put Mayumi into a *jardin d'enfants* in Paris, ensuring a perfect French accent for her future.

Once in Paris, though, she realized how indispensable she had become to Kiji. In her absence, the company began to flounder, and she ended up having to fly back to Tokyo every six weeks. She should have listened to Jun Muranaka. He warned her that no matter how many assistants she was given, trying to be the creative head of two companies was impossible. And if the new level of career stress was not enough, Nagiko's plan of immersing Mayumi in French totally backfired. Suddenly plunged into an environment in which she could neither understand nor converse, the child became frantic. Whenever Nagiko went back to Tokyo, Mayumi threw noisy tantrums, frightening the concierge. She missed Josefina. She missed Auntie Satoko. She missed her kindergarten friends in Kagurazaka. French children laughed at her. She had nightmares. Two French housekeepers quit in dismay at the prospect of taking care of this appalling child.

Nagiko was at her wit's end when her old colleague Frédérique Chardonnet rang her up after hearing a rumor that Nagiko was in Paris. They had been close long ago when both were apprentices, but gradually fallen out of touch. Nagiko vaguely remembered that Frédérique had left *Dessins Morikawa* ten years ago, after Madame had diverted her from designing to marketing. Now she learned that Madame's switch had been devastating to Frédérique. It made her rethink her whole career in fashion. She was not cut out to be a designer, fine—she accepted that. But she hated marketing. She decided she'd had enough of the fashion business and went home to Besançon. Family connections got her a job at the city newspaper. And now, she was back in Paris as a *téléjournaliste*. No, she hadn't married. What was a *téléjournaliste*? They must lunch. She would tell Nagiko all about it.

They met that week. Nagiko's somewhat stiff French was overwhelmed by the torrent of Frédérique's confidential chatter. She had brought her miniature long-haired dachshund along in a stylish carrying-case, which she tucked by her feet in the restaurant. Her job was to think up programs to pitch for television specials. Once funded, she would produce them, running off on assignments all over the world for three months or more at a time. In between projects she repossessed the dachshund from her mother and returned to her Paris apartment on the Rue Mouffetard to think about her next project. How marvelous that Nagiko was here now! She so wanted to do a program in Japan! She had no doubt she could resurrect the bit of Japanese she had studied in college.

When she heard Nagiko had brought her daughter, Frédérique was adamant—she must see the child. Nagiko sighed. She had not known what she was getting into when she brought Mayumi to Paris. But childless Frédérique was charmed by her first sight of Mayumi, walking slowly, head down, behind a cavorting crowd of boisterous French children. What a beautiful child! Suddenly she had an idea. She would be Mayumi's *maman* when Nagiko had to go to Tokyo! This rush of yearning was exactly how she felt when she knew she had a winning project. Her half-buried regret at never having had a child, her love of things Japanese—it would be perfect.

"*Konnichi wa, Mayumi-chan*," she said when the child warily raised her eyes to appraise this flamboyant red-headed stranger accompanying her mother. Frédérique pulled back the flap on the bag tucked under her arm. A petite and pointy black nose emerged. Mayumi's eyes widened.

"*Comment s'appelle t'il?*" she asked shyly. It was the first time Nagiko had heard Mayumi use her French without prodding.

"*Il s'appelle Genji*," Frédérique replied, stooping down so that the dog's bright eyes were level with Mayumi's. His name is Genji.

She took Mayumi for long strolls along the boulevards, where Frédérique basked in the attention they attracted from passersby. She called herself Mayumi's French mother, and when they sat in a café drinking *citron pressé*, that's what she would say to people who asked. Genji often accompanied them. Mayumi adored the dog, proudly holding his leash as he trotted along on their walks, kissing him on the nose when it was time for him to jump into his carrying bag.

"*Dans le sac, Genji! Sautez!*" Mayumi commanded.

"Are you really my French mother?" she asked Frédérique one day. One of her classmates had teased her about being Japanese and Mayumi had responded hotly that she had a French mother too. Her tormenter accused her of lying. When the child saw Frédérique pick her up from the kindergarten, he was silenced, but only briefly.

"Why don't you look like her, then?" he taunted, and Mayumi was at a loss.

Not expecting to fly back to Tokyo so often, Nagiko had let Josefina go and sublet the Kagurazaka apartment. This meant that she had to stay in a hotel on her trips back. Satoko offered the extra room in her house, strongly hinting that Mayumi was welcome to stay behind with her as well, but Nagiko declined.

"Thanks, but it's too far away from downtown. I have to be efficient on these short trips." Regarding Mayumi, she reminded Satoko that giving her a year of exposure to French at age six was a fabulous opportunity. She still believed it, even if the first three months had been hell. What she didn't tell Satoko was that staying in a hotel also made it easier to see Jun.

The prospect of Nagiko's going overseas for a year had made them face up to the change in their relationship. Jun visited Paris once a season, following their habitual dinner schedule, but he also took a room at the Okura Hotel every time Nagiko came back to Tokyo. In this way they ended up spending twice as much time together the year Nagiko lived in Paris than they ever had when they both lived in Tokyo.

By the time Satoko came to visit Paris in October, Mayumi had become effectively fluent in French. They had been there eight months. And now Mayumi loved having visitors. She was eager to show them around the neighborhood where all the shopkeepers knew *la petite fille Japonaise* and made a fuss over her. When Jun visited, she slipped her hand into his and skipped along the broad sidewalks of the Parc Du Champ de Mars. They were both amused that her childish French was so much more comprehensible than his. If their errand was to buy bread, Mayumi spoke to the *boulanger* and Jun pulled out his wallet. When asked *"C'est ton Papa?"* Mayumi shook her head vigorously. *"Non! C'est mon Oncle Jun!"*

Just at the time of Satoko's visit, the sudden resignation of a temperamental key designer required Nagiko to spend even more hours at the atelier, so Frédérique ended up taking Satoko around to see the sights of Paris. At one point Frédérique felt familiar enough to ask Satoko who, she wondered, Mayumi's father could be? But all Satoko would say was that it was a terribly sad story, and change the subject. If Nagiko had not revealed Mayumi's paternity, she was not about to. When Frédérique had casually asked Mayumi, the child replied *"Je n'ai pas de papa,"* as matter-of-factly as she would have said she didn't have a dog.

Every evening Nagiko went through the packet of messages her secretary in Tokyo airmailed to Paris. Among the layouts for ad copy that spilled out of the envelope was a letter from someone named Nora Lohan in California. Nagiko opened it, trying to place the name. Nora—Philip's old girlfriend—she remembered his father mentioning her. What did she want? Nagiko quickly read through the letter. Nora was studying a little Japanese, and now thinking of going to Japan to look at gardens. She wanted to contact Philip's friend Kōji Kon. Did Nagiko by any chance have an address for him? Nagiko scribbled a note in her fat daybook to call Kon the next time she was back in Japan.

A few weeks later, checking off things to do in the Tokyo office, she came to the note. In her rolodex under Kon was a number for a Shingon temple in Maizuru. She dialed it. Kōji was now the head priest, since his father had retired. She introduced herself, thanked him for the chocolate sent so long ago, and mentioned that a friend of Philip's wanted to correspond with him.

"What friend of Philip?" stuttered the flustered Kōji.

Nagiko was amused. "Nora Lohan. She's thinking of coming to Japan next year. She's been studying Japanese...it seems Philip has been coaching her."

"Really?" Kōji said, switching to English. "Um...I have study English long time now."

"Wonderful!" Nagiko told him. "You can show her around Kyoto. I'll send her your address."

As she copied out the address of the Kashiwadera temple in Maizuru, something rang a faint bell. His temple, didn't it have a *hibutsu*? That must be it, she thought. Why else would she have heard of it? She would check Professor Maigny's old list. She should have asked Priest Kon while she was on the phone.

After hanging up with Nagiko, Kōji's mind was in a daze. How many times had he thought about his California adventure since returning to Maizuru? He had thought about Nora, too—he hadn't even known her last name. He would have liked to write to her, but somehow asking Philip's parents for her address was too embarrassing. He doubted he could write something coherent anyway. Better just forget it. But when he was introduced to an American college graduate assigned to Maizuru by the JET program for the purpose of teaching local people proper conversational English, on an impulse, Kōji signed up for evening lessons. This let him fantasize about going back to San Francisco some day. He had imaginary witty conversations in his head—mostly with a phantom Nora.

Why didn't he ask Nagiko for her address while she was on the phone? Kōji kicked himself. He should write Nora first. Just then the phone rang. It was Nagiko, effusively apologetic about bothering him again, but wanting to ask about the temple's *hibutsu*, of all things. Yes, Kōji told her, the temple had a thousand-arm Guan Yin hidden buddha. The surrogate image was believed to be an exact copy. The last time the hidden one had been shown? Let's see... Philip had asked him that, too. It was in 1932, when his father had been a young man. Kōji had asked him at Philip's urging. And the next time, well, it was supposed to be shown once every fifty years, but it was not taken out in 1982, a fact that disappointed Philip greatly as he remembered. He didn't know when it would be on display next. Who made that decision? she asked. He didn't know. The head priest, probably. Yes, he was the head priest. Well, all right, he would investigate to see what was involved. Yes, he would let her know. (What was the deal with her interest in hidden buddhas, he wondered. Some leftover legacy of Philip's?) They said goodbye and hung up. Damn! Once again he had forgotten to ask her for Nora's address.

The Moss Temple

NORA WROTE TO KŌJI AS SHE WAS PLANNING her trip to see the gardens of Kyoto. He wrote back advising her not to come in the summer. How bad could it be, she thought? She arrived in late June. The heat was a shock. Luckily, the interiors of the temples she visited for their famous gardens were usually fairly cool. She was told so often that such-and-such a garden was better viewed in the spring or the fall that she finally began asking if there were *any* gardens that favored summer. She would only be able to catch the first hint of autumn before she had to go back to California. In general, however, the gardens of Kyoto—Zen gardens, tea gardens, Imperial gardens, and even courtyard gardens—were such masterpieces that she didn't mind at all not seeing them when the connoisseurs said she ought. Someday, I can come back, she thought, and it will be even better.

She had been told that the Temple of the Golden Pavilion, Kinkakuji, was gaudy and crass. Someone advised her to instead go to the Silver Pavilion, Ginkakuji. So she did. And there she found an example of a dry landscape style of garden with a wide expanse of raked white pebbles that made her squint. She learned that a shogun had built this as a villa, and that upon his death it was turned into a temple—nicknamed the Temple of the Silver Pavilion precisely because its design was based on the famous Golden Pavilion on the opposite side of the city. Well, just because it's so famous, that's no reason not to see it, she decided—no matter what people said.

And so Ginkakuji led her to its forebear, Kinkakuji. And she found the garden there wondrous. The pavilion itself, she knew, had been torched by a crazed young monk some time ago. A famous Japanese writer whose name she couldn't remember had written a novel about it. The building, set at the edge of a large mirror-calm pond, glimmered in the morning light on the day she visited. Cicadas droned in the background. Yes, it *was* very golden, hovering by the water, the slightly upturned tips of the roof corners giving it a bird-like sense of having just alighted. But the garden—compared to most of the temple gardens she had seen so far—was huge. She rambled slowly along its artful paths. And then she read that this one too had been based on an earlier garden—that of the Moss Temple. The Moss Temple was on her list of must-see gardens. Nora felt like she was following a thread—from silver to gold to moss.

She could easily imagine Philip in Kyoto. His dark hair would have allowed him to blend in of course, but even more than that, she had noticed that he morphed into different body language when he spoke Japanese. That's what really allowed him to function here. Nora had always been a little intimidated by Philip, even when they went out in high school. There was something about him she couldn't quite grasp. Nora was suddenly reminded of the famous Zen rock garden at Ryōanji—the first garden on her list. Ryōanji's garden consisted of fifteen rocks placed in a flat bed of raked sand about the size of a tennis court. A dry landscape Zen garden.

Nora had arrived at Ryōanji mid-day, among throngs of tourists. She had knelt on the verandah facing the composition of sand, stone, and moss, trying to understand why this was the most famous garden in Japan. The sand looked hot, and the moss looked thirsty. She didn't see a mother tiger fording a stream with cubs, as one book suggested. People came and went. The cicadas pounded in the background like a high-pitched jackhammer.

And then the sky clouded up and a summer thunderstorm burst over the city. After about twenty minutes the sun came out, and the puddles that had rumpled the crisp lines of raked sand evaporated in little clouds of steam. As they dried, the rocks revealed shadows and crags that had not been there before. The moss glowed. During this whole interlude, as people rushed about behind her, Nora had stayed in one place on the verandah, watching the garden's transformation. She changed her position twice more before leaving. And then she realized that nowhere was there a vantage point from which all fifteen rocks were visible at the same time. This is what reminded her now of Philip.

Nora alighted from the bus and walked past the curiously named Bell Cricket Temple thinking it might be worth a visit someday as well, but continued up the hill toward the Moss Temple. At the entrance was a sign in Japanese and English. The English half said, "Closed. Quota Full." She had not run across anything like this at the other temples. Finally she noticed a set of brochures at the entrance. Because of the damage thousands of tourist feet had inflicted on the delicate mosses, the priests had closed the garden to the public. One could, however, send a postcard to make a reservation. Nora folded the brochure and put it in her purse. She walked back down the hill past the Bell Cricket Temple. No quota system here, she noticed, so she went in—what was a bell cricket she wondered? She liked the name. Presumably it sounded nothing like a screaming cicada.

Tomorrow Kōji was coming into Kyoto to meet her for lunch. She could ask him to help her fill out the postcard. She was sure it would be better to have it addressed in Japanese. She knew that Kōji was now a full-fledged priest—the head priest of the temple where he grew up—but it was hard to imagine. She hadn't seen him in the five years since they had met in California. She recalled leading him through North Beach, both of them slightly high, his eyes popping out of his head—a head that would probably be shaved now…would she even recognize him? They had spoken on the phone after she arrived in Kyoto, and she was impressed at how much his English had improved. She said a few things in Japanese, which made him laugh.

Nora had not brought a lot of clothes with her. She constantly felt underdressed in Kyoto where the women she saw on the streets always looked very put-together. She had only one decent dress, a light blue sundress with narrow straps that crossed in back. She put that on now, along with the only pair of sandals she had brought. She might be able to find clothes here, but shoes, no. She wore a size 9, which seemed to be just above the upper limit of Japanese women's footwear. She picked up the wide-brimmed white straw hat she had begun wearing for sun protection, and headed out of her tiny room. Passing her outside on the sidewalk, one of the students she knew from the neighborhood complimented her dress.

"Berry naisu," the girl said. "*O-deito desu ka?*"

"*Hai*," said Nora. Yes, she supposed it was a date. She wondered what the Japanese called a social engagement between a man and a woman before they had the English loanword, "date."

Nora walked slowly, searching for the restaurant Kōji had picked. She looked up just as a polished wood door slid open and a man stuck his head out. Even though the head was shaved bald as a grapefruit Nora would have recognized that grin anywhere.

"Kōji!"

He was wearing his priest-black robes, the lightweight hemp version for summer. Nora looked at him from head to foot.

"*Suteki,*" she said. Kōji burst out laughing.

"You think priest looks 'cool'?"

"Very cool," said Nora. "Am I allowed to hug you?"

Kōji hesitated.

"Ah, maybe not good idea. This not California."

"Of course—sorry," Nora said.

"No, *I* sorry—very sorry," replied Kōji, leading her toward the cool cave of the air-conditioned entrance.

Nora had never been inside such an elegantly understated or expensive Japanese restaurant. She tended to eat at places that had window displays of wax models of things on the menu. That way she always knew what she was getting. The prices at those kinds of places were reasonable as well. She would never have dared enter a place like this on her own. In fact, she probably would not have guessed from its sleek exterior and discreet sign that it was a restaurant at all. The kimono-clad waitress led them to their table. Kōji had already ordered for them both.

"In Japan, we like to eat tradition," said Kōji. He picked a white morsel of something out of a bowl of clear soup.

"This one called *hamo.* I think you don't have." He pulled a well-thumbed dictionary out of the fold of his robes.

"Wait, is here—'pike conger'! You like pike conger?"

"Pike conger?" said Nora blankly.

"Very delicious. Full of little bones. Too many bones, so cook chops very much…" Kōji made cleaver chopping motions with his hand. "So we eat bones too."

Nora plucked the curled bit of fish from the lacquered bowl. She would not have known the texture was due to the tiny soft bones chopped into the flesh.

"Kyoto people are like little bones of *hamo,*" said Kōji.

"You mean Kyoto people like to eat *hamo?*" said Nora.

"No, I mean yes, they like to eat…pike conger…but they also (he riffled through his dictionary again) *resemble* hamo."

"How so?" Nora asked, puzzled.

"Because, Kyoto people very *ki-muzukashii*…what you call…

Nora now pulled out her own dictionary.

"*Chotto matte kudasai,*" she said. She found the word. "Hard to please, fastidious, picky," she read.

"Too much trouble. Like little bones in *hamo*," he nodded.

Nora laughed. "But Kōji—aren't you a Kyoto person? You're not like that."

"No. I not Kyoto. I Maizuru," Kōji replied. "Different. When I at school with Philip, Kyoto people think I country boy."

In this comment, Nora understood something about Kōji. His goofiness, the joking around with Philip. He had been the class clown she now realized, the country boy from Maizuru.

"I'd like to visit Maizuru sometime," she said.

"OK. You come Maizuru," Kōji beamed.

More exquisite dishes of various sorts of seafood were brought to their table.

"Kōji, this must be costing a fortune," said Nora, taking in the beautiful way each dish was presented—sea urchin on ice, one perfect scallop on a cool bamboo leaf.

He blushed. "Seafood…" he said. "Maizuru better, but sometimes expensive in Kyoto OK." He asked Nora about what she had seen in Kyoto so far. She talked about the various gardens, and then remembered that she wanted his help filling out the request for the Moss Temple. "But I couldn't get in," she said.

"Not get in?" Kōji was surprised. He had been to the Moss Temple—it must have been in junior high school—and he didn't remember any restrictions.

"They put in a new system," Nora said. "To protect the moss—probably from junior high school students like you."

Kōji was indignant.

"Just joking," Nora said.

"No, I understand joke," Kōji said. "But they not let you in? Very rude."

"It's okay," Nora put down her chopsticks. "It's for the good of the moss. And anyway, I have time."

Kōji drew himself up. "I get you in," he said.

"You can do that?"

"Of course! I am priest now. I can go any temple."

"Wow," said Nora. "That would be great."

Kōji's mind was already working out a plan.

He told Nora he would arrange it after O-bon. Mid-August in Kyoto was a busy time for the temples, with everyone making pilgrimages to the family graves.

"People come to temples, so priests very busy. Priest's wife especially busy taking care of visitors."

Nora was surprised. Kōji had not mentioned his wife.

"When did you get married, Kōji?" she asked.

"Oh," he reddened. "I not married. My mother, father push me very much, but I not like girls they find for me."

They were walking past the Zen temple Myōshinji. A pale gray-striped wall enclosed the compound. Inside was a village of many smaller sub-temples. One of the first, on the west side as they entered, was the Taizō-in. Kōji looked at a small sign posted at the entrance gate.

"There is garden here," he said. "Maybe famous. Have you seen?"

Nora hadn't.

"They all have such poetic names," she said. "Ryōanji—'peaceful dragon'; the temple of the golden pavilion; the moss temple. What does 'taizō-in' mean?"

"'-in' means temple," Kōji began, "taizō means..." he struggled to explain. "Like...you have some special thing you don't want other people to knowing. You hide. Make secret place for it. That means 'taizō'..."

"So, maybe the garden here is the hidden treasure," said Nora.

And it was. Even Kōji was amazed. He had seen temple gardens his whole life. He took them for granted. Ponds, paths, azaleas, maples, moss— it was a landscape vocabulary with which he was utterly familiar. But despite the fact that they lay practically at his feet, Kōji had never in his adult life made a trip to a temple specifically in order to see a garden. He was sheepishly reminded of how Philip had tried to get him to go along to the Hall of Dreams in Nara. He had done something stupid, he recalled now, and blown it off.

And here was Nora—she had come thousands of miles to look at these gardens that he could have visited, had he chosen to do so, any time he wanted. They walked onto a pebbled path that meandered around to a pond fed by a brook.

"I suppose this is another garden that I should see in the spring," Nora said with a sigh. "That's what everybody is always telling me—or the fall."

Kōji raised his hand to shade his eyes, looking toward the pond.

"No—this is good time," he said. "I show you."

They approached the still water of the pond and Nora could see that it was full of lotuses. Not water lilies, but actual lotuses, in all stages—teardrop shaped buds, dark pink partially opened flowers, and full blooms that had whitened as they opened, the pink tinge having retreated to the tips of the petals. A few green pods stood up on strong stems, their petals and stamens having fallen onto the round umbrella like leaves floating on the surface. Water drops puddled into cabochons in the center of some of the leaves.

"Oh, this is beautiful," breathed Nora.

"Summer," Kōji said. "Best time."

Nodding as he listened to Nora's words punctuated by smiles and hand gestures, Kōji understood her enthusiasm, and even, sort of, the gist of what she was saying. He became slightly mesmerized watching her mouth move, and had to shake himself. Had she asked him a question just now? She had stopped talking and was looking at him expectantly.

"Kōji, did you hear what I said?"

"Yes?"

Nora laughed and punched him playfully on the arm. She then drew back, contrite.

"Oops. Sorry, I probably shouldn't do that. Bad for your image."

Kōji didn't smile.

"Really, I'm sorry," Nora said. She thought she had offended him. She became quiet and took her fan out of her purse.

Kōji looked at her. How could he say what was in his mind? Being with Nora reminded him of that brief period when he had been free of the expectations of his father and mother, of the priesthood he was destined to make his career. By studying English he was able to hang on to that taste of freedom. He had practiced in his head largely by imaginary conversations with a phantom Nora. He had not expected to see her again. His nervousness when he got her letter was the fear that she couldn't possibly live up to his fabrication. He was not prepared for the possibility that she would be even more appealing in person than she was in fantasy.

"My mother has fan like that," he said. "Very nice smell..."

Nora brightened and wafted a sandalwood breeze in his direction.

Kōji called the priest at the Moss Temple to arrange their visit. He told his mother that an American acquaintance of his unfortunate friend Philip was visiting Kyoto, and since this person had been extremely kind to him when he was in California, there was simply no way of getting out of showing this person around. This person wanted more than anything else to see the garden of the Moss Temple.

"Remember those chocolates I brought you? Philip's friend showed me the place where they're made," he told her, emphasizing the necessity of paying back the favor.

"Why don't you bring him to Maizuru?" said his mother, assuming that the friend of whom he spoke was male. "You can take him to the fish sausage factory."

Kōji did not clarify. "If there's time," he said, "maybe I will."

Kōji met Nora at the Bell Cricket Temple and they walked up the slope to the Moss Temple together from there. The abbot had arranged for them to come in before the day's quota of visitors. Kōji was very deferential to the old priest, and Nora could tell that they had been granted an extraordinary favor. Then the priest said something to Kōji who responded in a way that made Nora think there was some sort of problem.

"What is it?" she asked.

"All visitors must draw copy of *Heart Sutra* before go into garden," Kōji said. "I tell him you not learn Chinese characters, but he says even foreigners must do."

"That's fine," Nora said. "You could help me."

They knelt on thin square cushions placed in front of a narrow low table.

"You okay, sit like this?" Kōji asked Nora.

"Sure," she said. "No problem." Nora had been to a tea ceremony and knew that she could hold out on folded knees for at least half an hour.

A young priest came into the room with two pieces of paper. He gave Nora a sheet with several hundred very complicated looking Chinese characters. The writing was pale. Then she realized that she was meant to copy by tracing directly on top of the shadowy lines. Kōji's sheet of paper was blank.

Beside each cushion lay an inkstone, a stick of ink, and a brush. Kōji showed her how to drip a tiny puddle of water onto the stone and rub the smooth dark stick of compressed ink into it until the puddle had turned velvety black and thick. Hesitantly, Nora dipped her brush in the ink. When she touched the paper the ink seeped over the pale line, obliterating the character. She pulled back in dismay.

"Oh no—I've ruined it already!" She looked at Kōji, her hand trembling.

"Here," he said. "I help you." He moved next to her, his body pressing into her side as he took her right hand in his. The brush was in her hand, but her hand was now under his control.

"Too much ink," he said, moving her hand back to the stone and pressing some of the liquid out. "Now, let's go…"

He poised her hand next to the unfortunate blot over the first character. Nora felt her wrist being lifted, as if on the upbeat to a piece of music. She relaxed her hand, giving it over to Kōji's mastery. She imagined what it would be like to be able to write like this, with total assurance.

As he finished each character, Kōji paused to pronounce it. Nora was able to match it to the phonetic syllables on the side. He wrote a particularly complicated character and when he finished she called out *"RA"* along with him. She felt him shudder with surprise. After that Kōji waited for her to read out the sound when he finished the strokes. In this way, they made their way, character by character, through the sutra. About halfway through, they ran out of ink, and had to stop to make more. Nora rubbed the inkstick on the stone, Kōji added drops of water. Neither of them said anything. Nora picked up the brush again and waited for Kōji to take her hand.

By the time they finished, Nora's legs had gone to sleep. Kōji let go of her hand and moved back, his face wet with perspiration. The entire left side of his body where he had pressed against Nora was damp. She slumped to the side and moved her legs.

"Ow," she said. *"Itai…"*

"One more thing," Kōji told her, indicating a blank portion of the paper. "Over here you write your wish. Then you take sutra up and offer to Buddha."

"My wish? Can I write in English?"

"Is OK," said Kōji.

Nora took up the brush on her own now. She felt like a bird trying to fly with clipped wings, but she wrote "I wish to come back to Japan."

Kōji surreptitiously read what she wrote as Nora flexed the kinks out of her legs. Then she stood, wobbling for a few seconds before taking the paper to the priest at the altar. Kōji stood up abruptly.

Nora marveled. "Don't your legs go to sleep?" she asked.

"No, I used to it," Kōji said. "This my job."

Kōji and Nora followed the young priest into the garden where morning sun filtering through the branches bathed everything in greenish light. Ferns, shrubs, and trees glowed like jade. So, too did the lichen-etched rocks. Everything was softly smothered in moss. Nora was entranced. Tree roots were snuggled in green velour. Up close, some of the mosses resembled miniature forests of tiny cedars.

To have the moss garden totally to themselves was a rare privilege. Nora understood this immediately. It was beginning to dawn on Kōji as well. He had vaguely remembered from his school trip here long ago that the garden was designed by the famous Zen monk Musō Soseki—although the subject of Musō was something of a sore point inside the Shingon sect, because before studying with Chinese masters and turning to Zen, Musō had been raised in the Shingon tradition. Still, Kōji had to admit, when it came to gardens, Shingon didn't have much to offer. Shingon had mantras and mandalas as spiritual discipline; Zen had gardens.

But Musō had brought one thing from Shingon when he made this garden, Kōji noticed. To the enlightened mind, the pure world of paradise and the profane world of the present are not fundamentally different things. Musō demonstrated his enlightened wisdom by combining them in a garden. The human mind has a tendency to create a dichotomy between purity and defilement—but this too, is delusion. Both are artificial distinctions springing from imperfect understanding. The great teacher Musō did not learn that from his Zen masters. No doubt he felt it in his very bones from his Shingon upbringing.

As they stepped slowly along the path, Nora now and then stooped over to examine a clump of furry moss, stroking it like a small animal.

"I wish I could be a plant here," she said to Kōji. "My skin is so happy— it is just drinking this air."

Kōji took a deep inhale. There were worse things to be than a tree growing in a moss garden, he thought.

"This is really different from all the other gardens I've seen," Nora remarked. "In some ways, it doesn't seem like a garden at all—it's like walking in the woods. Everything is so natural. But then, you know it's not—it was all planned this way."

"Moss not planned," Kōji said. "Moss come later, by itself."

"*Honma ni?*" said Nora, expressing her surprise in local dialect to tease him.

Kōji shook his head. "Be careful," he said, "you turning into Kyoto girl…"

Kōji pulled out a map of the landscape that the young priest had given him. "Famous stone," he said indicating a huge flat-topped boulder. "Called *zazen* stone."

Nora picked her way toward it. "Meditation stone?" Up here the paths were barely discernible. "Can we sit on it?"

Though no one was around, Kōji looked over his shoulder.

"Ah, OK—why not?" He felt very daring. He realized that even without ropes or barriers of any kind, there were certain things that a Japanese would simply not think to do. The constraints were internalized after a while. He climbed up after her. Then, just like a Japanese girl, Nora took out her handkerchief and spread it on the rock before sitting down.

"White pants," she said. "That was dumb."

Kōji crossed his legs and sat down next to her. He felt Nora relax against him like a backrest. They sat there, back to back, balanced. Kōji felt such a combination of pure and impure impulses that he had to make himself breathe slowly to maintain his composure.

"When did the moss come?" Nora wanted to know.

Kōji pulled out the brochure. "This temple burn down in 1467. Later rebuild, but then flood. Rebuild again, more fire. Then temple forgotten. Moss takes over."

"Usually," he continued, "gardener try to clean up—keep moss out. In Kyoto, very easy for moss to grow."

Kōji had never spoken this much continuous English in his life. It was exhausting—yet it seemed to be working. He had never felt more confident about his ability to communicate.

"I love moss," said Nora.

"I love moss, too," Kōji answered. And after that there was not much to say.

Guan Yin of Royal Ease

SPRING HAD ALWAYS BEEN Tokuda's favorite season. He looked forward to the moist balmy weather, and the soft green and pink creeping up the mountain slopes of Kamakura. Over these past few springs he had relaxed in the confidence that his own positive attitude was radiating protection around the hidden buddhas. And then, in a single vicious swipe, one was snuffed out. Tokuda was devastated. It was a rarely opened Guan Yin he hadn't seen since he was a child, but remembered as evoking the sweetest taste on his tongue. In overconfidence and for convenience he had arranged his itinerary such that he didn't reach that temple until the second day. The *hibutsu* was dead when he arrived. An ominous tremor struck just southwest of Tokyo. Seismologists deemed it a possible warning of an impending major quake. There was no doubt in Tokuda's mind that these events were connected.

The sting of this failure now pierced him at every temple. He came to dread the spring. The soft bloom of flowering cherry in April made him nervous. The only positive emotion he allowed himself was the feeling of relief every time a hidden buddha was tucked back into its cabinet unharmed. The other priests of Fudō-in noticed that their colleague Tokuda, who had become quite cheerful over the past few years, suddenly withdrew into distracted silence.

In the middle of April Nagiko had to go to Osaka to approve the final details for a new Kiji retail store. She decided to combine the trip with a visit to the famous *hibutsu* of Kanshinji, a temple tucked in the mountains south of Osaka. Taking little excursions to view temples with hidden buddhas was now Nagiko's main way of freeing her mind from the constant irritations that arose in the running of Kiji. Since *hibutsu* tended to be sequestered in out-of-the-way temples on varied timetables, viewing them was mildly challenging—yet that too suited her. She disliked being a regular tourist. At the same time, she was not inclined to rough it on a lengthy pilgrimage. A day's sortie to see something only viewable at that designated time appealed to her. And though she didn't consider herself particularly religious, Nagiko found these buddha images very moving, even the not-so-beautiful ones.

The Kanshinji statue came on view once a year, for two days in April. It was an exquisite example of early Shingon sculpture, dated to the ninth century, and beautifully pre-served—partly, no doubt, because it was closed up most of the time. It was the darling of art historians as well as devout believers. Roughly the size of a small person, this Guan Yin sat in the pose known as "royal ease." Nagiko had been curious to see it ever since Philip showed her a photograph of the languidly sensual bodhi-sattva sitting on a lotus flower, foot on foot, one leg crooked in front, the other bent with raised knee. Even with six hands, one of which rested thoughtfully on its right cheek, the figure looked totally natural. The Kanshinji Guan Yin had been first on their list to visit after their honeymoon. This was a *hibutsu* remarkable enough that she had invited Jun Muranaka to come along.

They were sitting in reserved seats on the Green Car of the bullet train whooshing across the Kantō plain toward Osaka. Mayumi, head bent over a comic book for young girls, was sullenly jiggling one free foot with the other, shoeless, tucked under her. It was almost the same posture as the Kanshinji Guan Yin, although Mayumi managed to imbue it with an impatient irritation completely the opposite of royal ease. Nagiko knew she was unhappy because, at the last minute, Jun had been unable to come.

Mayumi was bored with hidden buddhas. She had been eager to take this trip only because her *Oncle* Jun was coming. She had barely gotten to see him since their return to Tokyo. He went out with her mother, but she was left at home. He never stayed with them now either. She didn't understand this new stiffness. In Paris, they had been almost like a family. Nagiko had not informed her that they would be by themselves until they got to Tokyo Station. She feared Mayumi would make a scene. But the child had just shrugged and buried her face in her thick comic book as soon as they found their seats. Nagiko reached over to stroke her hair out of her eyes. Mayumi pulled away.

Last summer, they had been back from France just two months when Nagiko found out that a rare *hibutsu* would be put on public display for the first time in thirty-three years at a temple called Manshōji, in the hills near Kobe. This temple was famous for its peony gardens. Nagiko easily convinced Satoko to come along to see it. Mayumi had entered second grade in April, smoothly reconnecting with old friends and classmates. She was glad to see Auntie Satoko. Yet the trip to the peony temple had been a disaster.

They had waited in line to glimpse the image, but having seen it, the two women lingered in the dark interior, examining the ceiling carvings. Mayumi disliked the chill prickle of the temple so she had slipped outside, drawn back to the warm sun.

What had gotten into her, her mother demanded later when they found Mayumi sitting beside a peony bush. She had broken off dozens of fully opened blossoms and rotund buds, arranging them around herself in a frilly display of red, white, and deep pink. Dark-haired Mayumi seated in the center of a mandala of petals looked like a delicate bodhisattva herself. Other tourists pointed, whispering, yet hesitant to interfere. The child was so methodical in her rampage—perhaps it was some sort of ceremony? People didn't know what to think. Satoko saw her first. She was shocked at the destruction of the carefully pruned peony bushes. Nagiko was furious. She yanked Mayumi up off the ground and apologized to the priests, offering to pay for the damage. They refused politely, saying there was no permanent harm done to the plants—but they were not smiling. Nagiko left an envelope with 20,000 yen in the offertory. She was humiliated.

She punished Mayumi by leaving her behind on subsequent trips through the fall. Mayumi didn't care. She preferred staying home with Josefina to being dragged to musty old temples. Then, in November, Nagiko and Jun decided to go together to see the famous Hall of Dreams Guan Yin in Nara. This time, Mayumi very much wanted to come. She promised perfect behavior. Nagiko relented and invited Satoko along as well, reserving separate rooms at the Nara Grand Hotel—one for her and Jun, one for Mayumi and Satoko.

They all agreed that this statue was eerie. The adults laughed when Mayumi hid behind Jun rather than face it. Afterward, they went to see the huge bronze Buddha at Tōdaiji, where Mayumi was excited by all the tame deer that wandered up and nuzzled her pockets. Jun bought her a handful of deer food from a dispenser. Mayumi turned around with her back resting against Jun's legs, holding out the pellets in her cupped hands. At that moment, a current of attention rippled through all the deer in the vicinity. They turned their heads toward the child at the center of this knot of three people. Nagiko reached for Jun's arm. Satoko looked around in alarm. For about six seconds, all the deer in the park appeared to be converging upon them. Mayumi laughed in glee, then in one motion threw her handfuls of kibble up in the air and the deer scattered.

"Are you hungry?" Nagiko asked Mayumi as the snack trolley lumbered down the aisle toward them.

Mayumi looked up. "Ice cream," she said dully.

"Don't you want a sandwich?" Nagiko unwrapped a neat crustless rectangle. Mayumi shook her head. She pulled the lid off her cup of ice cream. Nagiko sighed.

"Look, I know you're disappointed he couldn't come. I am too. Really. But you know who's most disappointed?"

Mayumi looked warily at her mother.

"Yes. *He* is. He looks forward to spending time with us…"

Spending time with you, Mayumi thought to herself, scraping the top of the ice cream with its little white plastic shovel.

Nagiko reached into her handbag. "*Oncle* Jun gave me something to give to you," she said, pulling out a small box wrapped in silver paper. "It was to be for your birthday but he asked me to give it to you now—so you would forgive him for missing this trip."

Mayumi brightened. She fingered the ribbons on the box.

"Aren't you going to open it?" her mother asked.

Mayumi carefully untied the knot and pulled off the sticker. Before lifting the lid, she shook the box lightly. It rattled. She lifted the square of white cotton under the lid, glimpsing a silver dachshund, then a bear. It was a charm bracelet.

"Let's see," said Nagiko.

Mayumi drew the chain out, link by link.

"Oh, that's so cute!" said her mother. "Look at all the charms on it. There's the Eiffel tower, a dog who looks just like Frédérique's Genji, a teddybear—do you suppose that's Uwa-san?"

"Yes, Uwa-san," said Mayumi slowly. "And a deer, and a frog, and what's this supposed to be, Mama?"

Nagiko fingered the charm in question. "Hmmm. A baguette, maybe? Remember how you and *Oncle* Jun used to go out to the bakery in Paris?"

"When we were in France," Mayumi said softly, "People used to think *Oncle* Jun was my papa..."

"What did you say to them?" Nagiko asked carefully.

"I said he was my *Oncle* Jun," Mayumi said, "but..." she turned to her mother with a glaze of tears. "Mama, who *is* my papa?" she asked.

Nagiko was prepared for this. She knew Mayumi would eventually ask. But it had not occurred to her that what Mayumi wanted to hear was that Jun Muranaka was her father. And she wanted to hear a reason why he didn't live with them and why it was a secret. And she was also afraid that it had something to do with her—with her strange eyes, with the scars on her fingers. And now, dangling the silver charm bracelet from him between her fingers, she had finally asked that question.

"Your papa..." said Nagiko (by now Mayumi had crawled over to her lap, leaving her ice cream to turn to soup on the window ledge). "Your papa...died before you were born."

Mayumi started. She had not expected this. "He's dead?"

So it was not Jun after all. For so long, what she had hoped (that Jun was her father) and feared (that he rejected her) were equally sideswiped by this revelation.

"But, but..." She started to sob. Nagiko stroked her head as Mayumi's tears plopped messily onto her crisp linen blouse.

"He was a good friend of *Oncle* Jun's."

"What happened to him?" Mayumi managed to choke between sobs.

"He had an accident," Nagiko said. "A car accident. Right before we were to get married."

By now, Nagiko was quietly crying as well. The conductor who came by to punch tickets just then, averted his eyes. Skipping the mother and child, he hoped they would have composed themselves by the time he made his way back through the car.

Mayumi clutched the silver charm bracelet so hard the chain made dents in the flesh of her palms. Nagiko peeled her fingers back and shook the bracelet out. She wrapped it twice around Mayumi's narrow wrist, fastening the clasp.

"*Oncle* Jun was, in a way, how we met," Nagiko told her. "And he cares for us very much." She touched another of the charms. "Look, this one is Guan Yin. That's how *Oncle* Jun met your father—they were on a pilgrimage to many temples."

"To see hidden buddhas?" Mayumi asked.

"Ah, yes, I suppose so. Your father was very interested in hidden buddhas."

Mayumi drew her face back from Nagiko's damp chest. "Is that why we always go visiting hidden buddhas now?" she demanded.

Nagiko drew a handkerchief out of her purse, and dabbed Mayumi's tear-stained face.

"Yes," she said.

"To pray for my papa?" Mayumi continued. She took the handkerchief and rubbed her eyes.

"Could I have some tea, please?" she asked. She hiccupped once and disengaged herself from her mother's lap. Then she climbed back to her seat. This changed everything. She picked up the cup of puddled ice cream and carried it gingerly to the washroom where she dumped it in the sink. Then she washed her face and looked closely in the mirror at the deep pools of her dark cyan eyes.

From Osaka they changed to a local train that headed toward the mountains. About twenty people were waiting at the station for the bus to the temple. Mayumi clung to Nagiko's hand. Old women smiled at them.

"Going to Kanshinji are you?" an elderly man leaned over to ask Mayumi.

"Yes sir. To see the Guan Yin *hibutsu*," she responded in a clear childish voice. The old man nodded approvingly to Nagiko.

"Such a well brought-up daughter you have…speaks right up…"

Nagiko bowed slightly. She squeezed Mayumi's hand.

A nearly-empty bus came and everyone piled in. The road soon became steep. They could see whole mountainsides turned fluffy pale pink with the bloom of Yoshino cherries. Though the landscape was almost deserted, the temple grounds were crowded. Nagiko and Mayumi followed the throng heading toward the main building. While they waited, Nagiko gave Mayumi coins to buy cold drinks from a vending machine near the temple office.

A priest with thick glasses sat on a bench near the vending machine, sipping a can of cola. He watched as a beautiful little girl looked over the proffered array and carefully fed her coins in. She pushed her selection and checked the can that was produced—an ice coffee, he saw. Then she went through the procedure again, and this time a brightly colored can of lemon squash came out. He couldn't help appreciating the solemn intensity she devoted to her mission. But there was something else that drew his eye to her as well. The shape of her mouth, her eyes, reminded him of someone. He couldn't place it though, so he just smiled when she looked his way. She smiled back shyly. His eyes followed as she returned to the line snaking its way into the main hall. She gave the cans to a woman who opened them. She looked vaguely familiar, too. She was very elegant. Not someone Kōji knew personally, but he was sure he had seen her somewhere. Or perhaps her picture. Maybe she was famous? He watched the two of them as he lazily finished his cola. He wanted to go back inside to view the *hibutsu* again himself. But he could have the priest let him in through the back. He didn't have to wait in this line.

Kōji dropped his empty can into the recycling bin, then sauntered past the line of tourists and worshippers. Suddenly he stopped. It hit him who the woman was—Philip's fiancée, Nagiko Kiyowara. Of course. He had never met her but Philip had showed him pictures. On the train just yesterday her name had caught his eye in an advertisement for her shop opening in Osaka. And the child—those eyes, that mouth—they were Philip's eyes, his expressions. The ineffable resemblance that had arrested him earlier—it was Philip. Kōji shivered as if he had seen a ghost. He swerved back toward the front of the temple so he would walk by them again. A child—Philip had a child! Kōji stationed himself at the entrance and engaged the priest there in conversation. Finally Nagiko and Mayumi came through and handed their tickets over. He took a close look. He was sure.

Kōji followed unobtrusively a few paces behind as the two of them came in view of the statue. The mother pointed out the round golden jewel the figure held in one of its six hands. "The wish-granting jewel," she said to the child. The statue was skillfully lit so that it emerged from the surrounding dark in a soft pool of light that almost appeared as if it were coming from within the image itself. Worshippers had lit candles and sticks of incense in the front of the hall.

"Mama, can I light a candle for Papa?" he heard the child ask. Kōji was shocked. What? Had Philip died? He was sure Nora would have told him. They had written one another regularly since she returned to California. She always mentioned Philip. Koji had been thinking of introducing himself to Nagiko and the child, but now something made him hold back.

"Yes, you can light a candle," the mother said. "Mayumi-chan, over here."

The child skipped over to the rack of candles, her white anklets flashing in the dim light. "You can make a wish on the magic jewel too."

Kōji watched Mayumi tip the candle into the flame of one already lit, then place it on the crowded flickering rack. She bent her head and put her palms together, fingertips touching her chin.

"Can I tell what I wished?" she asked her mother.

"What did you wish?"

"I wished my Papa was still alive," she said loudly enough that several people glanced over at them in sympathy.

Kōji was horrified. A gust of breeze from somewhere roiled the candle flame and eddied the gray smoke curling up from the many sticks of incense. He looked over at the serene Guan Yin. Now the expression on its face struck him as slightly weary. The cheek resting on the hand—lost in thought, or just bored? The middle left hand holding up an icon of the karmic wheel. Now it reminded him of a spinning top, casually balanced on the middle finger like a toy. The lotus bud proffered by yet another left hand…as if, here—it's the last one—take it…

Maybe his eyes were playing tricks. He closed them. Before dawn this morning, as a Shingon priest himself, Kōji had come into the hall with the Kanshinji priests to participate in the mystic rituals for this Guan Yin. He had been moved as never before through a state of almost sexual arousal to a deep meditative realization of union with the deity. The feeling had left him emotionally drained. He had been waiting to view the image once again, less intensely, while it was surrounded by worshippers. He had been just about to go back in when he happened to see the child at the vending machine.

Kōji opened his eyes. The Guan Yin that had transported him beyond his desires, flooding him with an overwhelming sense of completeness—he no longer recognized it. Now he forgot about Nagiko and Mayumi as he stumbled outside to gather his wits. Perhaps it was the shock of seeing the ghost of Philip in the child's smile that skewed his perceptions? Kōji walked away from the crowds of chattering worshippers toward a deserted imperial mausoleum on the other side of the temple grounds. He had a sudden urge for a cigarette, even though he had promised Nora he would quit.

As he stood there, unnerved, another priest walked by from the direction of the mountain. Kōji recognized him from the morning's ceremonies, for this priest was, like himself, a visitor. They had been seated together at breakfast and exchanged a few words. Kōji had mentioned this was his first time to view the Kanshinji *hibutsu*. The other priest apparently had been here many times. The man looked at Kōji's face as he stopped to greet him with joined palms.

"Everything all right?" he asked mildly. "Kon-san from Maizuru, isn't it?"

Kōji grunted, and fished a large handkerchief out of his sleeve to mop his forehead. The other man showed no sign of moving on. Instead, he sat down on the stone steps leading up to the raised enclosure of Emperor Go-Murakami's tomb. The day was quite warm, and he too used a handkerchief to wipe the sheen of perspiration off his face.

"So, what did you think of the famous *hibutsu*?" the seated priest inquired.

Kōji was not feeling particularly talkative, but he didn't wish to be rude. After a moment he sat down as well.

"Ah, well…this morning was…" Kōji stuttered, "it was…kind of hard to put in words," he ended lamely.

"I know," the other man said calmly. "I know exactly what you mean. That is a very powerful *hibutsu*. One of the most powerful, probably." He spoke with such authority that Kōji's reluctance to speak of the experience softened slightly. He realized that the other man had probably felt much the same things he had. Perhaps that's what drew him back to Kanshinji year after year. Kōji picked up a twig of cedar that lay near his foot. It's feathery needles were not as soft as they looked.

"That *hibutsu* has really led an exciting life," the priest remarked.

Kōji thought this an odd way to talk about a statue. "What do you mean?" he asked.

"How old are you?"

"Um, thirty-five," said Kōji, puzzled.

The other man counted backward. "Well, the year before you were born this poor Guan Yin was mugged," he said.

"What?"

"Raped, almost, you could say."

Kōji stared at the other priest.

"Yes. Nowadays nobody talks about it. You certainly won't find any mention of it at the temple."

"What happened?" Kōji was curious now.

"It was in December. Very cold. There was a man who had studied to be a priest for a while, but dropped out. Mentally disturbed, most likely. In fact he died a few years ago in a mental hospital. Anyway, he was obsessed with this beautiful Guan Yin. He wandered in these mountains, staying at temples, studying art books, and gradually he became convinced that this statue held miraculous power."

"The wish-granting jewel?" Kōji asked.

"Exactly. He wanted to steal that power for himself."

Kōji pursed his lips. He found it perfectly believable that someone could lust after this lushly beautiful bodhisattva holding the jewel that granted all wishes—but *steal* the jewel? Indeed, someone would have to be crazy.

"He had carefully plotted how he would hide in the temple one night and break into the altar. But three nights before he was going to carry out his plan he had a dream."

"How do you know this?" Kōji suddenly asked.

The other man shifted his position. "I went to visit him in the asylum when he was an old man. I was interested in this kind of vandalism—why someone would do what he did."

"So, what did he dream?" Kōji asked.

"He told me that in his dream he was crouched behind a pillar, keeping out of sight. Finally he heard the head priest bolt the main door. He could see a glow coming from the cabinet. He flung open the doors. Right then he saw the statue's source of power. He said it was a glowing sphere—like a red moon. It rose up out of the body of the image and flew away. He woke up then. But he realized that the statue had been left powerless."

Kōji was a little confused. "But you said that was his dream, right? If he thought it was powerless, why did he continue? What was left to steal?"

"Indeed. He told me he gave up his plan after that dream. But he couldn't get the statue out of his mind. It haunted him. Finally he realized he had to destroy it."

"What!?"

"As I say, the man was deranged. It's happened before, you know. The Temple of the Golden Pavilion? People remember that because Yukio Mishima wrote a novel about the crazy priest who burned it. Someone could just as well write a novel about the Kanshinji Guan Yin…anyway, one night in December, he crept into the temple, waited till everyone was gone, and then smashed open the cabinet and embraced the statue. He tried to pull it down from its lotus pedestal but it was too heavy. He ended up breaking off two of its hands."

Kōji was shocked. He took off his glasses and rubbed the bridge of his nose. "Which hands did he break?" he finally asked.

"The right hand holding the *mala*-beads, and the left hand with the lotus bud. He took them to a rice field about a quarter mile from here. Scraped together a fire, and then he burned them."

"He *burned* the statue's hands??" Kōji was dumbstruck. Now he was anxious to go back again and take another look at the Guan Yin. Would knowing the suffering it had endured change his perception yet again?

"But the amazing thing is," mused the other priest, "the statue had not lost any of its power at all. The man truly was crazy."

"How did the police find him?" Kōji asked.

"After a couple of days, he felt remorse and he turned himself in. He showed them where he had burned the hands and they were able to retrieve part of the lotus bud. That little bit of the original lotus is inside the replica that was carved to replace it."

Kōji shook his head. "That statue is even more remarkable than I thought. You know, I had a strange experience with it this afternoon…"

The other man looked up.

Kōji somehow felt a need to compensate this other priest for his story. "Yes," he continued, "this morning during the ceremonies I felt like I had never experienced such a, such a *melding* of my self with the universe…" he felt the priest's eyes watching him.

"…but then, this afternoon, when all the people were there, I went back in, and when I looked at the statue, I don't know…it seemed different." He faltered. It would sound awful to describe the look of ennui he had felt on the bodhisattva's face.

"How different?"

"Like it was...world-weary somehow," Kōji managed. "It's just kind of strange, you know, how your perceptions can shift like that..."

The other man stood up and brushed the fallen cedar needles off his robes. "Well, perhaps we should head back," he said. "Are you staying for the closing ceremonies tonight?"

"Unfortunately, no," Kōji said. " I have to get back to my temple tonight."

They walked silently back toward the main courtyard, still full of worshippers. Out of the corner of his eye Tokuda imagined he saw Nagiko Kiyowara in the river of visitors flowing down the long stone steps away from the main building, but he wasn't sure. A beautiful woman and a beautiful child. He hadn't seen her in years. But he couldn't follow her, even with his eyes, because he had other things more important to tend to now. He strode purposefully back into the main hall where the Guan Yin of Royal Ease held court for her many admirers. Even with all the noise and the smoke and crowds, Tokuda should have been able to feel a twinge of the powerful presence of this *hibutsu* as soon as he glimpsed the figure, glowing within its cocoon of museum-quality back lighting. He drew closer with a feeling of panic. Straining all his senses, he detected no hum, no glow, no fragrance. Nothing. He looked at the figure. Indeed, its hand resting on its cheek conveyed nothing so much as a world-weary sigh. It was dead.

A Wake

TOKUDA HAD FELT SPARKS of suspicion before, but all had fizzled out. This was different. The myopic priest from Maizuru ignited a firestorm of distrust in his heart. Where had he gone? Tokuda had lost sight of Kōji in his single-minded rush back to the main hall.

There, he saw him standing off to the side of the thinning crowd of worshippers. His head was bowed and it seemed he was doing some sort of mudra with his hands, although Tokuda couldn't tell from the angle of his turned back. Suddenly Kōji lifted his head, stared intently at the *hibutsu*, and smiled. He turned around and catching sight of Tokuda, came ambling over in his direction. Tokuda stiffened.

"Ah," said Kōji. "Thanks for telling me the story of this statue. I'm much obliged to you." He seemed relaxed now. "I don't know what came over me earlier. Maybe it was all the people. But now when I look at this Guan Yin, I feel the pity, the compassion, just as strongly as I did this morning. I feel like my understanding has been deepened—thanks to you."

"It was nothing," said Tokuda guardedly. Was this young priest trying to throw him off, he wondered. Pretending now that he didn't feel anything wrong?

There was no longer any need for Tokuda to participate in the rituals for closing up this dead statue. He couldn't bear the thought of staring directly at yet another failure. Last fall he had suffered his biggest defeat when the powerful Hall of Dreams Guan Yin had been deactivated. When he had returned to the Hall of Dreams on the last day, he was too late. The glow of that strange long-hidden *hibutsu* his grandfather had been particularly concerned about was now dark as a cinder. It wasn't even creepy any more.

Tokuda walked out of the main hall with Kōji, straining to tamp down the feverish certainty that was growing in his mind. He had to think of a way to draw him out, find out where he had been, what he knew.

Kōji, meanwhile, just thought the other priest was being polite.

"No need to see me off," he said when they reached the main gate. "You're staying for the closing ceremonies, isn't that right?"

"Actually," said Tokuda, "I've decided to head back myself. I guess I can skip the ceremony for once. There's someone I need to drop in on in Kyoto."

"In Kyoto?" Kōji said. "Well, we're heading the same direction then."

They were caught up in the last crowd to leave the temple before it shut its doors to the public. The bus was packed. When they got to the station, they had forty-five minutes before the Kyoto train.

"How about a beer while we wait?" Tokuda suggested, indicating a restaurant.

"Sure. Sounds good," Kōji agreed. They slid open the grimy glass door and found a table. It was rare for priests to enter this low-class eatery. The surprised waitress scurried over to their table and wiped it with a rag.

"Beer, one large," said Tokuda.

"Coming right up," she chirped and bowed, setting down a dish of dried squid and peanuts.

Tokuda asked the sort of questions any casual friend would as he worked his way toward the subject of hidden buddhas. He discovered they both loved raw sardines, although neither of them was tempted to order them at this restaurant so far from the sea.

"So, you felt the Kanshinji *hibutsu* was fine after all?" Tokuda inquired after the beer arrived and the waitress had poured their glasses.

"Yes," said Kōji. "I came back and looked at it thinking about all it had been through. Because of what you told me." He refilled both their glasses. "Somehow it seemed both stronger and more vulnerable at the same time. I really can't say what rattled me earlier."

Tokuda didn't say anything.

"These hidden buddhas are pretty interesting," Kōji continued. "I never used to pay much attention to them until recently. I had a friend who was really interested, but I just ignored him at the time. I was kind of obnoxious about it, I think. My own temple has one, you know—the Kashiwadera."

"Yes, it's a thousand-arm Guan Yin, if I'm not mistaken," said Tokuda. He knew that it had been deactivated three centuries ago, and had never bothered to visit.

"Yes. It hasn't been opened in decades," Kōji said. "I've never even seen it myself."

"There's no need to always go poking into these things," Tokuda said quietly. "Some things are better left hidden. Like the Hall of Dreams Guan Yin, for example. That one was forced open a hundred years ago. It would have been better left closed."

"I know what you mean," said Kōji, chewing on a piece of squid. "That one certainly gives one an odd sensation."

"You've seen it then?" inquired Tokuda casually.

"As a matter of fact, I saw it for the first time last fall," Kōji said. "It was one of those things I just never got around to before. A friend of mine convinced me that it was important, so I decided to finally make the trip." He had gone with Nora. It was their last excursion before she returned to California.

"Last fall?"

"Yes, why? Were you there too?"

"No, unfortunately I missed it," said Tokuda. "We'd better finish up here. No, please, let me get this."

Kōji tried to pay for the beer, but Tokuda insisted. Another piece of the puzzle had fallen into place. He would keep a lookout for this priest from Maizuru from now on.

It was a little past eleven when Kōji got back to Kashiwadera. The night was still balmy. The crescent moon had now disappeared, leaving a sky full of stars. Kōji recalled how much brighter those same stars had looked at four o'clock this morning, deep in the mountains at the Kanshinji temple. He hoped his mother had saved him some dinner. He was starving.

His mother had left the outer door of the head priest's residence unlatched. Kōji slid it open quietly so as not to wake them. Down at the end of the dark hallway a small light shone like a beacon in the kitchen. It was the "keep warm" orange indicator of the automatic rice cooker. Near it was a plate covered in plastic wrap. Kōji peeked. Mackerel. He put it in the microwave as he scooped out a ladleful of rice. Just then he heard a noise from the far hall. He turned around to see his mother, wrapped in a cotton yukata, old felt slippers on her feet, shuffle into the kitchen.

"There's soup on the stove," she said.

"Thanks," Kōji mumbled. "You don't need to get up."

The microwave bleated.

His mother didn't move.

"You had a phone call about an hour ago," she said, watching Kōji pick at the plastic wrap which had stuck to the fish. She held her arms across her chest, her hands tucked into the yukata sleeves.

Kōji looked up.

"From America."

"What?" He frowned. "Who was it?"

"Who else would call you from America?"

Kōji's chopsticks stopped halfway to his mouth. "Nora?"

"Why, yes. Nora-san. That nice young woman from California you brought by to visit last summer." She took in her son's reaction.

"Her Japanese has improved," she said.

Kōji set his chopsticks down and looked at his mother. "Why was she calling?" he asked. Nora had never called him from the U.S. before. "Must be something important."

"Maybe she's calling to tell you she's getting married," said his mother.

"What!"

"Just guessing," the older woman smiled to herself as she turned on the burner under the pot of *miso-shiru*.

"Mother!" Kōji narrowed his eyes. "That's enough, okay?"

"I don't know why she called," she said calmly, stirring the cloud of bean paste that had separated from the stock, "but she left a number and asked that you call. All in Japanese, she said every number, very clearly. My, it takes a lot of numbers to call America…"

"Could I have it, please?"

"Here, eat your dinner first," said his mother, serving up a bowl of the soup. She placed it in front of him. Kōji made no move.

She sighed. "Here." She pulled a folded piece of paper out of her sleeve and smoothed it open. "This is called the 'country code'…"

He snatched it out of her hand.

"I know. I've been to a foreign country before, remember."

"Well. Give her my best," said his mother. Without further comment, she went back to bed.

As soon as she left, Kōji shoveled the rice into his mouth along with bites of oily mackerel, then washed it down with the soup. It was hard to think on an empty stomach. Why would Nora call? He had a letter from her just last week. Nothing much was going on. She always included a few sentences in Japanese. His mother had rattled him with her comment, and Kōji was annoyed at himself for falling for it. She always figured out ways to remind him he was not yet married.

Glancing at his watch, he calculated the time difference between California and Japan. Kōji became more apprehensive as he did the subtraction. There could only be one reason for Nora to call like this. He suddenly recalled the child he had seen at Kanshinji earlier today (was it just today?) in her face, the ghost of Philip's features that had struck him so queerly at the time. Kōji suddenly knew, even before he made the call, that Nora was going to tell him that Philip had died.

The number was that of her parents' house, but Nora herself answered. She was calm and matter-of-fact. Yes, it happened yesterday. Quietly, in his sleep. He was at home. His mother went in to wake him when he didn't appear for breakfast. There would be an autopsy today. A vigil at his parents' house tomorrow, and the church funeral the day after that. Kōji listened closely. He just said "ah—" after each of Nora's statements. He couldn't tell what she was feeling. Then there was a silence on the line before she spoke again.

"Kōji, I don't suppose there's any way you could come for the funeral, is there?"

Kōji had already thought about this before he telephoned.

"Yes. I come," he said. "Call you back later today." He would book his flight as soon as the airline office opened. He figured he would be able to take the train to Tokyo and fly out from Narita tomorrow evening—that is, this evening. It was now midnight.

"Really?" her voice caught. "Kōji…*arigatō*…this really means a lot…and maybe, could you do some Buddhist ceremony? At the wake, maybe?"

"Wake?" Kōji didn't understand, but Nora foresaw this odd word and had looked up the vocabulary in advance.

"*Tsuya*," she said.

"Ah. Of course, I can do," Kōji replied. "Specialist."

Before he went to bed Kōji unpacked and repacked his small suitcase. He turned off the light and noticed a light in his parents' room switch off afterward. He would tell them at breakfast, he thought before falling asleep.

Kōji woke early to the sounds of his father opening up the temple. Yawning, he turned over, then remembered he was going to California and sat up. By noon he was on his way to Tokyo. He called Nora with his flight number and she said she'd be waiting for him at the San Francisco International Terminal.

"Oh—I almost forgot—I've been trying to call Nagiko Kiyowara, but there's no answer," Nora said. "Could you maybe leave a message at her office?"

Kōji promised he would.

He knew that Nagiko wasn't home—he'd seen her in Osaka. From a phone book at the airport he found the number for Kiji's main office. He called and eventually got connected to Nagiko's assistant. Kōji identified himself as the head priest of Kashiwadera in Maizuru and gave her Nora's number. He asked that it be conveyed to Kiyowara-san as soon as possible. Without mentioning any detail he merely said that the matter was serious. He knew that, coming from a priest, his message would sound dire. In breathlessly polite tones, the young woman promised to convey it immediately. Satisfied that he had done what he could, Kōji bought a newspaper and settled down in one of the uncomfortable molded seats to await boarding. On the plane he slept fitfully. He dozed off and woke up from vivid dream visions of Philip and the elfin child who looked like him. And then that serious priest he had met at Kanshinji would appear, frowning, full of questions. The six-armed *hibutsu* seemed to smile at him, then lose interest. He woke with a start several times, to the annoyance of the businessman in the seat next to him. Kōji was embarrassed. Had he called out? He couldn't tell. He tried to think about Nora instead, and eventually fell into a long deep sleep.

And then he was walking through the same international arrivals gate he remembered from almost five years ago. What an adventure that had been—he smiled indulgently at his younger self, all the while searching the crowd standing behind the barrier. Today was different. He was being met. And then he saw her. Nora was standing apart from the all the chattering families straining and pointing as the doors opened. She was dressed in dark blue, hair pulled back in the familiar ponytail. She smiled and raised her arm in greeting.

Kōji waved back. And then he was standing in front of her. She put her arms around him and he hugged her back.

"Welcome to California," she said. "It's wonderful to see you."

They got in her car. "I think it's important that you're here. It just wouldn't be right for Philip to get completely sucked back into the Catholic church now. His parents have agreed to let you do a Buddhist ceremony at the vigil at the house tonight. The *tsuya*…"

Kōji nodded. He had brought the ritual implements he would need. He performed Shingon funeral rites for parishioners so often that it was second nature. They pulled up in front of Philip's parents' house. Linda Metcalfe's rose bushes along the front walkway were full of fat buds. She had seen Nora's car and now came walking toward them. Her watery eyes darted from Kōji's shaved head to his Buddhist robes before she pulled herself together.

"Thank you for coming, Kōji," she said.

He bowed deeply. "I very happy to come for Philip," he said.

"You look so, so…" she seemed slightly dazed.

"Dignified?" Nora tried to help her out.

"Yes. Dignified…I hardly recognized you…" Linda Metcalfe recalled the goofy fuzzy-headed young man who had stayed with them five years ago. She felt dizzy now. Five years of taking care of Philip, having her son, but not having him. Nora gently took her arm and led her back into the house.

"People are coming at six o'clock," she said to Kōji. "Nora says you're going to do some sort of ceremony?"

The dining room table was piled with food. Kōji began to wonder how the Shingon rituals would appear to these people, in this American living room. Nora exclaimed at an elaborate flower arrangement that had not been there earlier.

"Those came while you were gone. From Nagiko," Linda told her. "I feel terrible…I should have called her. You must have done it?"

Nora nodded. "Kōji did," she said.

Kōji turned toward the hall where he remembered the living room to be. He dropped his suitcase with a short gasp. There was Philip stretched out in a polished upholstered casket. Somehow he hadn't expected that. Jim Metcalfe was sitting next to it in an armchair. He slowly raised his head at the sight of Kōji, but it was clear he didn't recognize him. Kōji looked around for Nora. He was going to need her help.

Hesitantly Kōji took a worn-out folded garment from his suitcase. He opened it out.

"What's that?" Nora asked.

It was the pilgrim's jacket Philip had worn on his journey around Shikoku. Kōji had found it discarded in his room after Philip left for Tokyo, and had picked it up, suddenly feeling ashamed. Philip had made the pilgrimage and come back changed. Kōji had sensed the transformation and wondered why he himself couldn't summon up that kind of resolve. He had tucked the tattered jacket away and kept it, like a talisman. Amazingly enough, he still had it. Even more amazing, he was able to find it. Once, they had joked about it handily serving as a shroud for pilgrims who died en route. It seemed fitting for it to come back to Philip now. All these things Kōji told Nora. She went to talk to Linda Metcalfe, and when she came back, she said, yes, he should put it in the casket.

Kōji was intrigued that this Catholic custom of the wake was so similar to the Buddhist. Even the words pointed at the same idea—*tsuya*, "all night long." People were staying up, a-wake, exactly.

Nora looked at Philip and then dropped her gaze. "What else do you put in the coffin?" she asked Kōji.

"Pilgrim's robe, straw sandals. Special head towel. Philip did journey of temples, so he had these. Other people not do journey until die. Still, they prepared. Also knife."

"A knife?"

"To keep evil spirits away…" Kōji noticed the look on Nora's face. "But not necessary," he added hastily.

"You know…maybe I can find his other things," Nora said, suddenly remembering something. "Hold on a sec…" She went to the kitchen to talk to Linda Metcalfe, and the two of them went into Philip's room to look through boxes in the closet. Ten minutes later Nora came back triumphantly, holding a narrow folded headband and a pair of old straw sandals. They had been packed away in a box Nagiko had sent. Philip had opened the boxes and showed them to Nora several times.

"Are these what you need?" Nora asked.

Kōji was surprised, but he nodded and placed them in the coffin with the old jacket. People came quietly into the living room to pay their respects, then wandered to the dining room, whispering questions about the Japanese priest sitting on floor with Nora. More and more people came in. The whispers grew louder.

"Nora, when I should start?" Kōji asked nervously. People were eating in the other room.

"After the Catholic priest arrives," she said. "Come on, let's get something to eat. You must be hungry."

Kōji wasn't hungry, but he shyly followed Nora into the other room. People suddenly became very quiet. Nora cleared her throat and introduced him. She made a little speech, which Kōji was surprised to find that he understood most of. She talked about Philip's time in Japan, how he studied Buddhism, and that he, Kōji was an old friend from those days who went on to become a priest himself. And furthermore, that right after Father Sebastian from St. Aloysius arrived and said the rosary, Priest Kon was going to perform a Buddhist mass that all were invited to stay for.

Then she put together a plate of food and handed it to Kōji.

"You had better eat something," she said. He realized he was hungry after all. Someone gave him a beer.

Father Sebastian arrived, and everyone trooped into the living room. The Catholic priest glanced at the low altar with the incense burner, but he didn't say anything. Everyone bowed their heads as he recited the Apostle's Creed, the Our Father, three Hail Marys, Glory Be to the Father, announced the first Mystery, repeated the our Father, said ten Hail Marys, and worked his way through the rosary. Kōji could pick out a word here and there, yet he could tell that everyone else in the room was totally at home with this prayer. Kōji knew that it was a mantra of sorts.

Nora gave him a nudge. People cleared a path as he made his way to the makeshift altar. He had decided what he would do. First he purified the space, then, rather than the full set of sutras his own parishioners would have expected him to chant, Kōji recited just one, the *Heart Sutra*, the one that he had heard Philip himself sing out so many times. At the closing phrases, he was astonished as Nora's voice softly joined in, but his voice did not betray his surprise. Then, in a burner where he had started a coal earlier, he took a pinch of powdered incense, raised it to his forehead, and sprinkled it in the censer. He did this three times, ending with a bow, his hands folded in front of his chest. He looked at Nora, her cue to perform the same action, as he had instructed her earlier. Nora held out her hand to Linda and helped her. One by one, most of the guests came up and sprinkled a pinch of incense over the coal.

And when they had finished, they headed back toward the dining room. Linda's friends took away the empty casserole dishes and platters to replenish them in the kitchen. The table was as full as it had been in the beginning.

Now Kōji filled a plate himself and took another beer. People asked him questions about the rituals, the sutra, the incense. He answered as best he could. No one ever asked these kinds of questions in Japan. Still, he felt he managed pretty well. He had a Scotch and water. He met Nora's mother and father. Everyone was eating, drinking, talking loudly. By eleven-thirty Kōji's head was spinning. He closed his eyes for just a moment.

When he opened them, Nora was leading him to Philip's bedroom. It was a little quieter now. Some people had left, but Philip's father was still sitting in the living room. Other people moved in and out.

"Kōji…" he heard Nora speaking softly. "You must be terribly jetlagged. You sleep here tonight." It was the same twin bed he had slept in on his previous visit. He tried to protest, but then he felt Nora's hand on his arm, and he suddenly was too weak to resist.

"*Oyasumi nasai…*" she whispered. And then he fell asleep.

Four hours later his eyes flew open. He looked at the luminous numbers of the alarm clock by the bed. Four-fifteen. He raised his head. A light seeped in under the closed door. Kōji made his way toward it, seeking to locate the bathroom. As his head cleared, he saw that the low light was coming from the living room. He groped his way back to the bedroom for his glasses, and smoothing out the creases in his robes, tiptoed toward the light. The air-conditioner had been left on full-blast. Philip was still there of course, and his father and mother, sitting next to one another sharing a blanket across their shoulders, asleep on the couch. Nora was there too, wrapped in a sweater, her chin drooping toward her chest. Kōji quietly sat down on the floor next to the casket and began to chant sutras softly under his breath.

Nora awoke as the soft pink light of dawn filtered into the room between the cracks of the blinds. She blinked and stretched. Then she saw Kōji, eyes closed, his *mala*-bead rosary draped over his hands. She thought at first he was asleep, but then she saw his mouth moving and realized he was praying for Philip. She slid off the chair and moved next to him, sitting properly, Japanese-style. Her skirt fanned out next to Kōji's robes, and he felt her warmth next to his shoulder.

For a few moments more the room was suspended in this quiet knot surrounding Philip, and then the knot unraveled as life started up its relentless forward push. The Metcalfes woke up, disoriented at first but gradually, painfully, picking up their bearings. They shivered and stood up. Linda took her husband's arm and led him off to shower and change clothes. Alone in the room except for Philip, Nora squeezed Kōji's hand.

Nagiko and Mayumi were at the new Kiji store in Osaka when her assistant called with Kōji's message. And like Kōji, Nagiko was under no illusion about the probable reason for Nora's call. She prepared herself before picking up the phone. She made sure that Mayumi was occupied with her coloring books, and beckoning the manager aside, she told the woman she was not to be interrupted.

From Nora she found out that the priest from Maizuru was going to California. That struck her as a little odd, but she was relieved that someone from Japan would be there. She really must make an effort to meet this priest when he came back. She told Nora it was impossible to go to California now, but she would try to come in a few months. She told her how grateful she was, keenly aware of how these platitudes rang all the more hollow when you really meant them.

Nagiko's hand shook as she hung up the phone. It really was over now. The expedient reality that she had made up to live by and even told to Mayumi, had been rendered true. There was one person she needed to call. Today was Friday. She tried to remember when Jun had said he would be back from his trip to China. Was it today? Slowly she pulled her address book from her purse. His home number. She had never called it. Now she dialed. His wife picked up the phone. Smoothly Nagiko identified herself, and the reason for her call.

Kiyowara from Kiji, yes, the woman wrote it down. Her husband's American friend (Nagiko spelled out the name M-e-t-c-a-l-f-e) yes…has died? Oh, how terribly sad. Yes, she would give him the message. He would be getting home tonight.

Nagiko gave her Nora's address in California in case Jun wanted to send flowers. Her number? Of course. Nagiko gave her the office number for Kiji. The woman seemed quite unaware of anything between Nagiko and Jun. Whether she was or not, Nagiko could not tell. It was the sort of thing a Japanese wife would never reveal.

"Thank you very much for taking the trouble to call. I'm sure Muranaka will be grateful," the wife said politely.

"Not at all," responded Nagiko. She hung up before the lump in her throat choked off her voice.

Kōji showered and changed into the other set of black formal robes he had packed at his mother's suggestion. He shaved his face, but did not bother with the fast-growing stubble now covering his head. Meanwhile Nora had gone back to her parents' house to change to a black dress. At St. Aloysius, he sat next to her and her parents for the service. Kōji had never been inside a Catholic church before. He was fascinated by the stained glass, the hushed murmurs, the organ music rolling over their heads from somewhere on high. Afterward, they drove in procession to Mt. Olivet cemetery where Kōji couldn't help being reminded of graveside scenes in numerous foreign movies he had seen. It was both familiar and odd. He felt like a miscast actor—as if someone should yell out "Cut! What's that Buddhist priest doing in this scene?" Jetlag must be creeping up on him again.

After the funeral, Kōji had five more days in California. He had justified taking a week when he bought his ticket because it made the plane fare a third cheaper than if he had turned around and gone directly home. So, as they were leaving the cemetery, when Nora asked him when his return flight was scheduled, he coughed and squirmed. He had his excuses ready—that he was staying to economize on airfare, and maybe he might travel around California a little, now that he was here, it would be a shame to waste the opportunity to go to Yosemite, perhaps...Nora beamed at him and said that was great. She would take some time off work to accompany him—that is, if he wanted company.

And then Kōji allowed himself to become aware of why he had wanted to stay on—even, much as he respected and missed Philip, why he came in the first place.

It was late evening, precisely ten days after Nora first called, when Kōji got back to Maizuru. Even in this short time his hair had grown into a reasonable version of a crew cut. He was wearing khaki pants and a polo shirt Nora had bought for him in Calistoga.

On the bullet train from Tokyo he drowsed off into a pleasant reverie of the past week. They had not made it to Yosemite, but that didn't matter. After the post-service luncheon they went back to pick up Kōji's suitcase at Philip's house where he said his farewell to the Metcalfes, and then Nora had driven them back to her apartment in San Francisco. Wordlessly, she changed out of her black dress as Kōji watched, and then they tumbled onto her platform futon bed where they spent the remainder of the day making love, falling asleep, and waking up again only to repeat the sequence.

Kōji smiled, remembering the feel of Nora's sleek flank pressing against his back. They drove up the coast to Mendocino one day, staying the night in a bed-and-breakfast on a sandy bluff in sight of the sea. They drove to Calistoga where they took mud baths. Kōji had balked at the idea—"Bath? In mud?"—but Nora convinced him to try. It was like sinking into a vat of warm bean paste. Then you showered and soaked in a tub of cucumber-scented water. It was in fact pretty nice, Kōji decided, although he kept finding bits of grit in various creases, both his own and Nora's.

They made plans. Yesterday, Nora took him to the airport. Kōji woke up now as the train approached Kyoto station. Last time he had been here was when he had said goodbye to that piercing-eyed priest he had met at Kanshinji. Now the moon was in that awkward stage between half and full. It looked unstable, like it was about to tip over. The cherry blossoms were starting to scatter. He wondered if his parents would be waiting up for him.

They were. His mother took in the un-priestly fuzz of hair and his sporty clothing, and then something else about her son as well. She couldn't tell exactly what, but she knew from the way he greeted them that something had changed.

"I'm back," he said.

"How was it?" his mother asked, moving his suitcase from the entrance. "Did you actually do a Shingon service?"

"Yes. I shortened it a little, but it went fine."

"His poor parents," said his mother. "I feel so bad for them—losing their only son like that." She continued, "Did you see Nora-san?"

"I did."

"Is she well?"

"Yes," Kōji responded. "As you suspected, she's getting married…"

"Really!" his mother sounded surprised.

"Yes." Now Kōji dropped to the floor and bowed to both his parents. "To me. With your permission."

Bees of Brittany

BERTRAND MAIGNY HAD SET HIS BUDDHIST studies aside after receiving the news of Philip Metcalfe's accident. He knew that without this idiosyncratic student's help, the chances of furthering his theory about the meaning of the hidden buddhas was doomed. He might as well just give it up. Philip's fiancée had written to him in almost flawless French, hopeful at first of his full recovery. But time passed, and he heard nothing until he received a letter ten years ago—in Japanese this time—saying that Philip had "entered Nirvana" as the euphemism put it.

After years of not publishing anything, Maigny felt a deep and simple urge to see a product emerge from his efforts. His neighbor Michel convinced him to cultivate bees. Unfortunately, as soon as he set up his apiary boxes, almost every hive in France became infected with the Asian bee mite, *Varroa destructor*. This little arthropod, like a tiny crab, attached itself to the bee, hiding between its abdominal segments like a tiny vampire, sucking the bee's blood, weakening it, and transmitting viruses. An infected hive would die out after just a few generations.

Bertrand Maigny was uncomfortably reminded, yet again, of *mappō*. Soon the wild bees began to die out too. No bees meant not only no honey, but no pollination. The farmers became worried. No pollination, no crops. This invading mite fully lived up to its name, *destructor*. Maigny could not face struggling with another sign of *mappō*. He gave up trying to keep bees.

When Annette had a stroke and could no longer keep house for him, her granddaughter Gabrielle stepped in. She had known Grandpère Bertrand ever since her grandmother had brought her along to play with the professor's funny dog. Gabrielle was the one who discovered poor Kookai at the side of the road where he had wandered in his near-sighted old age and been struck by a speeding Renault. No bees, no career, no dog. Maigny no longer cared if the world went to hell. For him, everything he once loved was gone.

And then one summer day when he was hiking in the mountains, Maigny noticed a bee working its way through a patch of clover. There were several bees. His eyes wandered across the flowers—there were bees all over. Curious, he shaded his eyes and tried to follow where they went when they rose up, legs heavy with pollen, but he soon lost the small zigzagging shapes against the glare. He happened to tell Michel about his discovery at the end of summer. Michel got excited. Could Bertrand remember where he saw them? Perhaps they could find the nest.

"What for?" Maigny asked.

"To capture it of course!"

"It's impossible to see where the bees go," scoffed Maigny.

Michel raised his eyebrows. "There are ways," was all he said.

The next day the two of them set out to retrace Maigny's early summer hike. He found the meadow easily enough, but the clover was mostly gone. Bertrand threw up his hands. Michel, however, made his way over to a clump of blue globe thistles he spotted growing near a rocky outcropping. There, busily combing the flowers, were the bees. Michel slipped the pack off his back and removed a glass tumbler and an insulated wine cooler. As Maigny watched, he slowly crept up to a low thistle and in one quick motion clapped the glass over the flower, trapping the bee. It buzzed angrily.

"Now what?" asked Maigny.

"She will tell us where the nest is," said Michel.

Maigny looked doubtful. "Are you planning to torture her for the information?"

"She won't feel a thing."

Michel snipped the thistle stem and carefully slid a piece of cardboard under the glass. Then he removed a bottle of chilled Vouvray from the cooler and lowered the tumbler, bee, and flower into the pocket where the wine had nestled. He uncorked the wine, took out two glasses, wiped them on his shirt, and poured for himself and Bertrand.

"Are you going to get the bee drunk, too?" Bertrand joked.

"Now we wait a few minutes," said Michel. "*A votre santé.*" He took a long sip of the wine and passed Maigny a jar of olives. They waited, Maigny did not know for what, in the warm late summer sun.

Finally Michel said, "that should be enough," and he took the tumbler out of the cooler. The chilled bee was quiet. Moving quickly, Michel pulled a red silk thread from his pocket and tied a slipknot at the end. He lifted up the hindquarters of the recumbent bee with the stem of his pipe, and slid the thread under its abdomen. Then he gave a gentle tug to tighten it.

"There," he said. "Time to pack up, and be ready to run."

By the time the sun had warmed the bee into action, Michel had recorked the wine, put away the olives, and shouldered the pack. With a lurch, the bee rose in the air, circled twice, then headed for the trees.

"Follow!" shouted Michel.

And now, thanks to the red silken banner trailing behind, they were able to track it with their eyes. They bounded, like two old goats, over the uneven terrain, striving to keep the delicate fluttering thread in sight.

The nest was in an old oak stump not far from the edge of a clearing. Michel rubbed his hands.

"Now what?" asked Maigny.

"Now we go home," said Michel.

Maigny sighed. The way of the beekeeper was mysterious.

Michel made a mental note of the place, then decided he needed a stronger reminder, so he built a little cairn of rocks. That winter they went back, this time carrying a small axe and a Styrofoam box. Michel broke open the stump, revealing a mass of huddled bees.

"The queen is in the middle," he said. "We get her, and the rest will follow."

He put on gloves and reaching into the groggy mass scooped out a living ball of bees. Maigny stood back in amazement. It was just as Michel had said—with the queen removed, the remaining bees straggled about confused. But as soon as they caught her scent they traipsed along with purpose, right into the box.

Michel was happy to help Bertrand get back to keeping bees. The more hives in the village, the better. Carefully, they transported the nest back to Maigny's empty hive box. Perhaps these wild bees were resistant to the *Varroa* mite, he told Maigny. Though the population of wild honeybees had taken a big dip, some had survived without benefit of human help. They had their own resistance. Michel was becoming disillusioned with insecticides.

"All it does is make these devil mites stronger," he confided. "Poison the weak ones, the strong ones are left to reproduce. I knew there had to be wild bee strains that are naturally able to resist, and *alors*—you go and find one. *Aïe —merde…*" He was stung again.

"And that's another thing," he continued. "The scientists all say the foreign strains are stronger. But I think we should stick to our local bees. The ones that evolved here. I'm through playing sorcerer's apprentice—it's upset the natural balance of things. *Abeilles de Bretagne en Bretagne!*"

In place of commercial apistan strips, Michel experimented with pungent wintergreen oil and patchouli. Maigny smiled to himself. He didn't know how much to believe of Michel's ranting. "Bees of Brittany" sounded good, but he would wait and see. Now his bees were thriving. When the hive got too full, the old queen led half the bees off in a swarm to look for a new nest, while those left behind hatched out a new queen to take her place. With Michel's help he coaxed the swarm to a new box, and so his colonies grew.

On this particular spring day, Bertrand Maigny was driving his old Citroen back from Quimper. He passed small orchards of white-flowering apricot trees. They reminded him of Japanese cherry blossoms. The Japanese didn't go apricot viewing though—he had always wondered why not. Beautiful flower followed by luscious apricot fruit. Japanese *sakura* had no fruit. Perhaps that was the point—ethereal beauty leaving nothing to sink your teeth into. He noticed yellow dots between the rows of trees. Dandelions. They too would contribute flavor to his spring honey.

The apricots in bloom then reminded him of the chanterelles he collected in the fall, because, in Japanese, these were called "apricot mushrooms"—from their color, he supposed. Which was no odder than calling them "chanterelles" because they squeaked when you sautéed them. Singing apricot mushrooms…one image drifted into the next in his mind, like the clouds that bumped and dissolved into one another in the spring sky above.

Maigny had just met with the editor of the highly acclaimed magazine series *Que sais-je?* over lunch. They wanted him to write a volume on some aspect of Buddhism. He should choose something that could be both specific and detailed, yet shed light on larger issues. They did not want a bland general survey. Maigny was flattered. He had given a great deal of thought to what he would write about, and today he had presented his theme—the mandala. The subject of hidden buddhas was too painful for him now, and too arcane, in any case. Even Shingon was too narrow. But with mandalas he could cover a lot of ground. The editors were enthusiastic. *Bon.* He began to plan his outline. He would be as busy as one of his *abeilles* for the next nine months. A year later Professor Bertrand Maigny's short book called simply *Le Mandala Bouddhique* came out from Presses Universitaires de France. He had never written for a non-specialist audience before. Maigny was surprised to discover he had a knack for it. The text had come together quickly, tripping so lightly off the keys of his typewriter that he was sure it would be sent back with demands for major changes. Nothing that easy could be any good. But the editors were delighted to receive the manuscript ahead of schedule. In their experience, academics dithered endlessly. Instead of a list of requested changes, they sent him a check. He had opened this letter at his desk, in his study overflowing with notes and plans for his grand theoretical treatise on esoteric Buddhism, none of which had been published. Maigny looked down at the check. Perhaps he had been going about his career the wrong way all these years?

In Paris, Frédérique Chardonnet had just returned from a hellish trip to Africa. Her idea had been to revisit the areas Leni Riefenstahl photographed in the early 1970s—three decades of civil war later. The documentary was to be called *The Lost Generation of the Sudan.* Frédérique was not prepared for the malnutrition, the starvation, the bugs, the dirt, the hopelessness. Especially the bugs. Yet she had stuck it out for four months. She still had little white scars from fleabites below her knees.

No more filming in Africa, she resolved. No more war documentaries for a while either. She had brought back a lot of footage, which she then spent two months editing. And after all that, the station decided not to run it. Too depressing, they said. Her dachshund Genji had died of old age at her mother's house while she was away. Frédérique was beyond tired.

Usually she had a stack of projects clamoring to move to the center of attention even as she was winding one documentary down. But now, nothing jumped out to pique her interest. She liked Paris best when she was rushing around making plans to leave it. Was it time to sit back and take stock? She felt old and stale. She was fifty-two. Today she had a long overdue appointment at her favorite hair salon. Even her hair was looking tired, its once carefully-maintained strawberry blonde fading at the temples.

Frédérique passed a bookstore on her way to the salon. She needed something to read while the colorist worked his magic.

The bestsellers all looked boring. She noticed a table with a display of the newest volumes from the series *Que sais-je?* She picked up *The Buddhist Mandala*. Maybe it was time to get serious about a project in Japan…she bought the book. It was such a pity that she had not been able to do a documentary there, Frédérique thought to herself. It had not been for lack of trying. Right before going to the Sudan, she had proposed a documentary on *Les Vies des Geishas* to La Cinquième. To her great surprise, they had turned it down. She had thought with the popularity of that novel written by an American man that this would be an easy sell. Two years before that, she proposed a biography of Madame Morikawa, and prior to that one on the martial art of *kendo*. The outfits and face-protecting cages of *kendo* were so dramatic, the crash and clash of bamboo swords was so exhilarating, Frédérique had been tempted to take it up herself. Yet there was no funding available for either of those things she was told. People were not so interested in Japan any more. It was a pity. Well, maybe she could get them interested in a program about Buddhism. If only she came up with the right hook…

After the air kiss for Monsieur Emile, after the clucking and sympathy (she showed him her fleabites), Frédérique plucked *The Buddhist Mandala* out of her bag and settled into the stylist's chair. She noted that the author was a retired professor living in Brest. He kept bees? Fabulous. She could interview him. If he was articulate, she could even take a crew to film him. Already, her mind began to plan.

Mandalas, she read, *are maps of the universe. They are used as an aide to meditation—especially in esoteric Buddhism, which has many secret mystical rituals.* She liked the sound of that. *Truth cannot be expressed in words alone, but it can be indicated by images—pictures linked to a deep understanding of reality. A mandala can be considered such a link.* That was very interesting, she thought. In fact, it resonated with the reason she was in filmmaking. What you could show with the camera was infinitely more persuasive than what you could write. With a picture, you could create a reality. This made a lot of sense.

*A graphic rendition of the spiritual universe, realm upon realm, infinite buddhas…*Frédérique's eyes began to water from the ammoniac pong of the hair colorant. The diamond mandala. The womb mandala. Circles within squares, within more circles within yet more squares. Buddhas swam in her vision. One, the static crystal diamond-hard unchanging world of transcendent truth. The other, the soft and squishy world of physical phenomena. The cosmic buddha linking them together. Her mind started to plot out a story—The Diamond and the Womb—the visual possibilities were enticing.

In Japan, the esoteric Buddhist sect Shingon takes the view that the two aspects of reality—the unchanging cosmic aspect and the mutable physical aspect, the sacred aspect and the profane—are not different. But, this truth of the cosmic order is not something that can be understood verbally. It can only be grasped visually and symbolically.

Monsieur Emile wrapped her head in plastic. Frédérique peered at the color reproduction of the two mandalas in the center of the book. Each tiny buddha held its hands in a different gesture. Frédérique supposed they must be something like the medieval Christian saints and their icons. Saint Sebastian with his arrows, Saint—Simon, was it? with the saw? She read that a Shingon monk in training would learn the mudras, the hand gestures associated with each image, and meditate on them one by one, working his way first through the womb mandala, then the diamond. Eventually he would reach a visual and symbolic comprehension of all the buddhas and all their relationships across and through both worlds, uniting himself with cosmic buddhahood.

Maybe she could hire someone to draw an animation of this—to illustrate the mental process. It could be great. Maybe too expensive, though. They always put her on such tight budgets. How she would love to go to Japan. Frédérique hadn't seen Mayumi since she came to Paris for a quick visit with her mother five years ago when she was twelve. Now she was almost seventeen. *Mon Dieu*, she would be a totally different person. Perhaps Japanese girls retained their innocence longer—but French girls changed shape, look, and attitude when they hit their teens. Their gestalt suddenly flipped from child to young woman. Boys lagged. To see a mixed group of teenagers was funny—girl-women and boy-children. What would Mayumi be like now? It was difficult to tell anything from the pictures Nagiko sent. There was a coolness between those two, Frédérique felt. She knew that Japanese were not naturally demonstrative, but even taking that into account…

Emile took the final snip of her bangs, and offered her the mirror to check the back.

Frédérique gave him a big smile. He relaxed. His client had had such a funny succession of expressions all afternoon. He didn't think she was angry about her hair, but one never knew. Now she looked animated—five years younger than when she had walked in. He had done his job well. Africa had taken a toll on her freckled skin, he noticed. She should use more sunscreen.

It had not been difficult to locate Professor Bertrand Maigny. Frédérique called to ask if she could come chat about his book. Maigny hung up the phone in disbelief. A television producer was interested in *Le Mandala Bouddhique*! She was driving from Paris the day after tomorrow to meet him and talk about a possible program. He told Gabrielle there would be a guest for lunch and could not resist mentioning that she was a filmmaker.

"*C'est vrai?*" Gabrielle was impressed.

Frédérique had been reassured by Maigny's telephone voice. She could judge whether or not someone would be a good interview after talking with them on the phone for two minutes. Maigny would be good. She told him she would love to see his bees too. Frédérique was also skilled at figuring out what people liked to talk about. By warming them up with things close to their hearts she managed to get them to reveal things they would never have dreamed they would tell someone they just met. Before she even broached the idea of a documentary on *Le Bouddhisme Ésotérique* to her bosses, she needed to find out from Maigny whether or not there would be a suitable hook for this story. Maigny was looking out the window of his tidied-up study when Frédérique's turquoise-blue Renault Floride drove up. The top was down. He saw a woman get out, unwind a white scarf, and shake out her wavy red-blonde hair. She removed her sunglasses and took a compact from her purse. Checking her lipstick, she snapped it closed again, and bent over the side of the car to reach for a fat notebook in the back seat. Maigny was mesmerized. The filmmaker! She perfectly fulfilled Maigny's idea of what such a creature should look like. He glanced around his study, trying to imagine how it would appear from her point of view. He took a deep breath and went to answer the door.

"Professeur Maigny?" she extended her hand. "Frédérique Chardonnet."

"*Enchanté, mademoiselle.*" Maigny kissed her fingertips.

Frédérique knew exactly how to handle him.

Maigny led her into his study where she ran her eyes over the volumes of texts in many languages. She began.

"*Kore*," she said, indicating a bookshelf with her salmon-colored manicure, "*minna yomimashita ka?*"

Maigny had not expected this. He chuckled.

"Yes, I have read them all," he said. "You speak Japanese, then?"

Now Frédérique lowered her eyes modestly.

"Not at all," she demurred. "But I shall study hard if it turns out I can go to Japan to film." She knew it was always better to disclaim any ability, and then pop out a surprising phrase. Sitting down in the armchair he indicated, she crossed her legs, opened her notebook, and gazed up at Bertrand Maigny with her large sea-green eyes.

"I learned so much from your book on mandalas," she said, not untruthfully. "It's what inspired me to want to do a documentary on esoteric Buddhism in Japan." She smiled. Flattered, Maigny began to tell her all the reasons he chose the subject of the mandala.

Nodding, writing, she let him go on, then,

"Do you mind if I record you?" she asked.

She might as well record it, as she couldn't possibly write it all down. Besides, she needed to concentrate on encouraging this flow of knowledge in certain directions.

As she set up the tiny tape recorder, she noticed a map of Japan on the wall by his desk. It was marked with red dots, radiating out more or less from the center of the country. She would have to ask about that. Below it, a filing cabinet was labeled "*bouddhas cachés*. Frédérique brushed a loose curl from her eyes and pointed to it.

"You have buddhas hidden in your filing cabinet?" she joked.

Maigny laughed. "Hidden buddhas, yes. But not perhaps what you think."

"What, then?" she asked, curious.

"Ah, that. I suppose you could say that was my life's work," said Maigny. "The hidden buddhas of Japan. *Hibutsu*, they are called…" and encouraged by Frédérique's questions, Maigny found himself telling her about the images secreted away in certain temples, believed to have special powers, only viewable on certain days. He told her about Kūkai, the founder of Shingon, and if she were going to do a program on esoteric Buddhism, she should start with him.

"This is fascinating," Frédérique breathed. "I don't suppose there is a tomb or something, that we could film?"

"Indeed there is." Maigny told her about Kūkai's entombment on Mt. Kōya. A strange sort of tomb—since followers did not believe he was dead.

"They think he remains there waiting to awake and usher in the new age after this world has self-destructed."

Frédérique blinked. "Self-destructed?"

Maigny explained *mappō*.

"In Buddhist cosmology, it is believed there are three different ages. The 'age of the Law' was the period when Sakyamuni Buddha lived and attained enlightenment in India. When he left the world by entering Nirvana, the 'era of appearances' began. During this time span, without a living buddha on earth, the Buddhist law became distorted. The third age is called *mappō*—the 'end of the Law.' *Mappō* is an accelerating process. It degenerates into total chaos and the end of the world. In medieval Japan, it was widely thought that *mappō* began in the year 1052."

"How long does *mappō* last?"

"Some guessed a thousand years, some ten thousand. It's hard to predict the apocalypse precisely."

"So, counting from the year 1052…well, then it could be pretty soon, *n'est-ce-pas?*"

"The year 2052 by some calculations."

"Then what?" asked Frédérique.

"After *mappō?*" Maigny raised his eyebrows. "Scripture says that Miroku, the Buddha of the future will appear then."

"And then? When Miroku comes?"

Maigny had not been asked so many questions since he retired from teaching.

"Well, that is all speculation of course. But a buddha living in the world would end the chaos of *mappō*."

"How would people know Miroku?" Frédérique was now genuinely curious.

"A very good question," Maigny conceded. "The sutras talk about some heralds—the oceans rising is a sign—some kind of rare flower called 'the dragon blossom' coming into bloom—but there is no standard vision of what Miroku will look like, if that's what you mean."

"But Kūkai will presumably know?" Frédérique said archly.

She was very happy. The more Maigny talked the more sure she was that "the hidden buddhas of Japan" would be the hook she could use to get the funding this project would need.

"So, do you think Kūkai is still there? In his tomb?" She asked.

Maigny chuckled. "He could very well be. Mummified perhaps. He even spawned a heretical group of monks who tried to copy him by doing their own mummification."

Frédérique turned those luminous green headlamps on him again.

"What do you mean, doing their own mummification?"

"They are called *sokushinbutsu*. You might call them self-made mummies. It's quite interesting, actually. They began the process while they were still alive…"

Just then Gabrielle appeared bashfully at the door to announce lunch.

Frédérique could hardly believe it. Self-mummifying priests—she had hit the jackpot.

"You must tell me more over lunch," she smiled, closing her notebook. "May I bring the tape recorder?"

The dining room was simple with dark oak furniture. Frédérique much preferred these old country houses to sleek Parisian apartments. When she gently steered him back to the topic of the self-mummified monks, Frédérique was taken aback when Maigny said,

"Ah yes—they are quite something to see. All dressed in their fancy robes and whatnot."

"You mean they still exist?" This was even better than she realized.

"There are maybe half a dozen or so," said the professor, buttering a piece of bread. "About two hundred years old. Mostly in the north—you've been to Japan, yes?—you know Yamagata? In the mountains there."

"And you've seen them?" Frédérique set her fork down. "They are not hidden buddhas, are they?"

"Oh no. They are worshipped as having attained buddhahood, but they are not hidden. Anyone can see them."

—and film them, Frédérique hoped.

"I would have thought," she said, "that Japan was too humid for mummification. How did they manage it?"

"Not all of them succeeded," replied Maigny. "And you are right, Japan is so humid that it was an even greater challenge. Technically, they are not mummies exactly, because their internal organs were not removed."

"Then it's even more amazing," said Frédérique.

"They slowly and methodically shriveled themselves to nothing. During the first thousand days they only ate nuts and seeds. And they meditated, of course, and did other austerities. By the end of this period they would have lost most of their body fat."

Gabrielle brought out a baguette, some cheeses, and honey.

"From your hives?" Frédérique asked.

"Of course," Maigny smiled proudly. "Spring honey. This year's crop." He continued, "For the second period, also a thousand days, they restricted their diet even further."

"From nuts and seeds?"

"Yes, now they only ate tree bark and scrapings from pine roots. *Moku-jiki*—'wood eating' it was called. By the end of this stage, they looked like living skeletons."

"But why?" asked Frédérique.

"Why?" repeated Maigny, arching an eyebrow. "Why did they do it? Well, on the practical level, they were trying to reduce the moisture in their bodies as much as possible. On the spiritual level, they were trying 'to become buddhas in this life.'"

"Which you said was heretical?"

"Their way was eventually considered to be a perversion of esoteric beliefs. One of the basic tenets of Shingon is that it is possible for a person to attain buddhahood during his lifetime. Not after you die, not after a million turns of the wheel of karma, but body, soul, and language in this immediate life can become one with the buddha nature."

Trying not to interrupt, Gabrielle came quietly in from the kitchen bearing a beautifully browned *clafoutis aux abricots*. She set it in the middle of the table with a pitcher of cream.

"That is what sets esoteric Buddhism apart," said Maigny. "Shingon teaches its adepts the means and the practices to live a life of enlightenment."

"But why were the mummy monks heretical?"

"In a way they were demonstrating ultimate hubris. If they succeeded, they knew they would be enshrined and worshipped. Also, as I'm sure you know, in Japan, asceticism is sometimes admired simply for the self control it demonstrates. The almost superhuman will to deny physical sensation. I don't know what Kūkai would have said about them. They were copying him, after all. But the practice came to be regarded as a freakish misreading of Kūkai's intent. And it was eventually outlawed."

"I see," said Frédérique. "And was there a third stage?"

"In the third stage, they denied themselves apricot clafoutis," said Maigny, serving Frédérique a rather too-large helping. She laughed.

"Then I shall never become a buddha."

"As they neared the end of the period of wood-eating, they began to drink a special tea containing sap from the lacquer tree."

"But isn't that poisonous?" Frédérique's eyes widened.

"Exactly. Poisonous and preservative. Diuretic and emetic. Not only would the priests lose even more moisture, the lacquer built up in their bodies—internal insecticide. Now they were ready for the fourth stage. The priest would enter a stone chamber, just large enough to sit in lotus posture, and he would meditate. This was his tomb, and he was walled in…"

"Still alive?" Frédérique exclaimed.

"…with a hole for a breathing tube. He had a bell, which he was to ring every day. When the bell ceased, the tube was removed and the tomb closed up for a year. Then it was opened to see if the priest had succeeded in becoming a buddha."

"Would it be obvious?"

"Probably. Most of them in fact rotted, and were simply sealed back up. But a few were preserved and taken out and enshrined in temples. Scientists now think that one of the reasons there were more of these self-made mummies in Yamagata is because there is a high arsenic content in the groundwater in those mountains."

"This is simply fascinating," said Frédérique dreamily. "Who ever thought there were self-mummified buddhas in the mountains of Yamagata? Now, Sensei, you must show me your bees."

She had everything she needed.

PART THREE

Outside Does Not Exist
Inside Does Not Exist

i-mode

IT WAS FRIDAY NIGHT. Mayumi was hanging out with three friends in Shibuya. They ordered specialty pizzas at Napori, then shopped for a while, then went for ice cream. It was just ten o'clock. Mayumi was not interested in *para para* dancing at a club, but she didn't want to go home yet. If her mother was there, they would get into an argument. Then again, she might not be home—Nagiko didn't go out with Jun much these days, but she often worked late. Either way, the apartment was boring. These girls were boring. They all wore glittery eye shadow and pale lipstick, except for Kiko who wore a plummy red. Mayumi was the only one who hadn't bleached her hair henna. Their eyes were tan, blue, and gray. Mayumi sometimes wore contact lenses too—to make her eyes dark brown. But tonight her deep blue irises were naked, accented by thick kohl eyeliner. In the constant morphing of hair and eye fashion, Mayumi appeared no more foreign than her fully Japanese friends.

They all spent a great deal of time and money maintaining their signature looks—their outfits were studies in fashion outrage. Kaori only wore Takuya Angel. Erin liked anything with ruffles, and Kiko of the pale skin and ruby mouth wore the black crinolines of Lolita Goth. For Kaori, Erin, and Kiko, changing looks implied a psychological crisis. But Mayumi was a chameleon, always trying out different mixes. Her friends would have been shocked if she ever wore the same combination twice. She was five foot seven, and as close as a living person could come to approximating the unrealistic proportions of an animé cartoon character—slender but busty, with long legs, and those wide-set extraordinary eyes. It was not only geeky teenage boys who panted after Mayumi.

Her *keitai* sang the ringtone melody she'd just downloaded—Gackt's *Marmalade* from the *Rebirth* album. She took the tiny phone out of her purse and read the e-mail. "U R the *daiyamondo*," it read. Who was this guy? It was not a Tokyo number. Cryptic—but nice. He didn't message very often. Mayumi had never met him in real space. She had a number of these intimate strangers with whom she shared a disembodied familiarity.

She idly tapped out an answering message, ignoring her companions.

"(>_<) **Bored**," she typed.

Mayumi had even more virtual friends than bodily ones. If their messages were interesting, she might go on to meet them in the flesh, but usually those encounters were disappointing. It was better to keep e-friends in cyberspace. Every now and then, however, she allowed herself to be talked into a physical meeting that provided her with a nice chunk of cash.

She had on a skimpy flippy miniskirt in the Burberry plaid her mother hated, even if it was worn ironically. Her panties—which flashed when she sat down—were matching Burberry plaid. In screaming contrast, her low-cut blouse was purple Lurex with a shivery long black fringe at the bottom edge. She had rubber-soled tabi on her feet. Originally they had been solid black, but she had decorated them with gold thread. Her hair was gathered into ponytails, one over each ear, and she wore a pair of glistening earrings that looked like costume jewelry but were in fact real diamonds. She put her *keitai* away.

"I'm going home. See you guys later."

"Hey—wait!…" It was Erin. Her pink Lovegety had started to blink and sing a little melody of bleeps.

"Where is he? What does it say?" Kiko ducked her head down to look at the device in Erin's palm.

"Is it a guy?" Kaori asked, "or somebody you know?"

"Omigod, it's a guy!"

"Where? Where?" The four girls scanned the milling crowd, trying to spot a boy who would be anxiously peering into his hand at his own Lovegety.

"What level?"

"Just chat? Or go out?"

Erin blushed. "He's looking for a girlfriend."

The others squealed.

"Wait a minute…I think I see him…just to the left of the door to Quattro. Ew. Turn yours off. See what he does."

Erin looked in the direction Mayumi had pointed. A short teenage boy in a school uniform was indeed standing by the door, peering anxiously at an electronic device. A look of disappointment crossed his pimply face. He raised his eyes to search the swirling crowd. He had just been rejected. Who was it? His eyes fell on Mayumi and his mouth dropped open. She turned quickly on her heel, giving him a peek of her panties.

The others protested that it was too early, but Mayumi claimed a headache. She sidestepped a group of young men leaning against the barrier set up around a recently planted ginkgo tree. They pretended not to watch as she strode away, each step flashing a glimpse of Burberry cheek. Out of sight of her friends, she took out her *keitai* again. She wasn't going home yet. She scrolled to a number she had never called before, and pressed send.

Jun Muranaka was still in the office. His head hurt. Yesterday he had had his first meeting with the new Prime Minister, Junichiro Koizumi. Jun was sure he had convinced him that making a visit to the Yasukuni Shrine on August 15 was a bad idea. He reminded him that the last time a prime minister made an official visit to this Shinto shrine, other Asian countries made a huge fuss. To them, Yasukuni symbolized everything they had suffered under Japanese imperial aggression. This sort of thing damaged Japanese business abroad. It was Jun's responsibility to be completely frank with these politicians, and he had to say this—it simply wasn't worth it.

"But Mori visited last year," the prime minister protested.

"'Heart of a flea, brain of a shark'—or maybe the reverse," Jun reminded him of his predecessor's reputation.

"Fine. I won't make an official visit…Hashimoto made a mistake."

Jun was mollified. He assured Koizumi that this was the right decision.

Earlier today Jun listened to the news as the Prime Minister announced that he would not make an "official obeisance visit" to Yasukuni Jinja. But then he couldn't help adding that he would reserve for later the decision about whether to go as a private citizen.

Jun's heart sank. Why couldn't he make him understand that these hairsplitting maneuvers just perpetuated the problem. It was precisely an *official* visit that the conservatives wanted—they didn't care about Koizumi's personal opinion on the spirits of the war dead. He would not please them by this half-assed "going as a private citizen." And did he think the Chinese would quibble about what hat he wore? Headlines in Chinese newspapers would read 'Japanese Prime Minister Honors War Criminals.' Great. He would alienate everyone.

Jun had now seen a dozen prime ministers sweep in and out of office. With any luck, this one's tenure would be as short as most of his predecessors. Why is Japan always trying to hide things, he mused to himself. A civil society needs to come to terms with its history. Look at Germany. Look at France. Holocaust denial is illegal in Europe. Japan doesn't even have the guts to deny. We simply hide things we'd prefer not to see. Ignore them, and eventually people forget. But the trouble is, not everyone is willing to forget. Especially not outsiders. It infuriates them. As far as they are concerned, Japanese have not expiated our guilt, we've only hidden it.

Over the years Jun had gotten to know his counterparts—other governments cultivated people like him too. Why does Japan keep doing these things, they always asked. They couldn't understand something like Yasukuni. Didn't the Japanese realize that by glossing over the behavior of Japanese soldiers in China, by dropping these issues out of the textbooks, by insisting on praying at the repository of Class-A war criminals, that they were simply feeding a desire for revenge?

His *keitai* burbled Bizet's *Toreador Song*. Jun jumped. These new portable webphones were not a technology he felt at home with. He preferred his land line office phone, because he could leave it to his secretary to cull the messages he needed to deal with. His *keitai* number was only known to a few people, including the Prime Minister, who could call him at any time. He spoke curtly, hiding his trepidation.

"Muranaka," he answered.

For a moment there was no response, then a whisper,

"*Oncle* Jun?"

"Mayumi?" he was taken aback. She had never called him before. He didn't know she had this number. She must have gotten it from Nagiko. Suddenly Jun was worried.

"Is everything all right?" There must be some emergency—that was the only thing he could imagine.

"Mayumi—what is it?"

A pause. "Are you busy?"

"What a strange thing to ask—eleven p.m. on Friday night, in my office…"

"Are you at your office?"

Jun realized that since she had called his *keitai*, she wouldn't necessarily know where he was.

"Mayumi, where are you?"

"I'm in Shibuya," came the whispery voice. "Can I come see you?"

"What? It's late…"

"Please?"

What could he say? He hadn't seen Mayumi for a year, but he knew from Nagiko that she was difficult, and that they fought. It was awkward. But something in her voice convinced him not to turn her away.

"Of course. I'll be here for another hour. I'll tell the guard in the lobby to let you in."

"Thank you…" She hung up.

And that was another thing. He had never been comfortable with the way Nagiko hid things from Mayumi. It was not his place to say, so he kept quiet, but why should Mayumi have been kept in the dark about her father? Nagiko, of all people, should not have succumbed to this disabling Japanese urge to hide things. What was she afraid of? She was an artist who saw pattern, understood pattern, and created it. But as a woman, she lived outside the pattern. And somehow that had ended up crippling her.

He knew it was hard being a Japanese single mother—and he felt guilty that he had not done more. They had been together fourteen years—could it be that long? Together yet not really together. She had never hinted that she wanted him to divorce his wife. Would he have? Jun asked himself. Almost certainly, in the beginning, he would have—if she had asked. But she hadn't. Perhaps she didn't want that. Did he love her? Another thing he hadn't directly thought about in a long time. People didn't ask themselves that question in Japan. Japanese were amused but mostly embarrassed by the way Western women demanded demonstrations of love from their men all the time. And the way the men obliged.

Yet, weren't Japanese men secretly a little envious as well? To be able to hold hands with your wife in public. Such a simple thing—he had seen people do it all the time in America and Europe. He had held Nagiko's hand when they walked through the parks of Paris. It was so natural. Yet it was impossible in Japan. Teenagers got away with it, but he'd predict that once they married, even the flamboyant creatures of this modern generation would revert to their cramped Japanese roots.

Nagiko. Yes. Yes he did love her. It hit him squarely now—they should have married. And they should have done it while Mayumi was small. His wife would have been embarrassed, but she would have gotten over it. Divorce was not such a shameful thing any more. Her life would barely have changed. He would have given her the house, the dog, all the stuff they had accumulated. He and Nagiko had somehow settled into this pattern of independence. They understood that about each other. They understood one another very well. It was a rare thing. He had taken it for granted.

It was a twist of fate that Mayumi had called him at this moment. They really should have a talk—after all, he was probably the closest thing she had to a father figure. It would have been awkward to bypass Nagiko to reach her, but she had contacted him herself. She was the one who wanted to talk. That was encouraging.

The guard in the lobby of Jun's office was nodding off. He jerked awake at the swish of the revolving doors. His eyes popped open. Had Mr. Muranaka not instructed him that he was expecting a visit by a young lady, he would have marched this young slut right back outside again. He never imagined that Mr. Muranaka was the sort to go in for teenage prostitutes. Just went to show, you could never tell about people. But still, this was a shock. In his office! The man had no shame.

His kept his face expressionless as Mayumi walked up and told him the name of her "client."

"Muranaka-san is expecting you," he said tightly. "25th floor."

Mayumi knew exactly what the man was thinking. Her *keitai* buzzed. Message from Kiko. She tapped in a reply on her way to the elevator.

"Going to sleep now <(~,~)>"

She switched off the phone.

She had been to this office only once, with her mother, years ago. Still, the corridor was vaguely familiar, as was the set-up of the receptionist's desk. Jun's office would be tucked away in a private room behind that. He came out now. She noted his reaction, the way his eyebrows lifted for a split second before he controlled them.

"Mayumi-chan…you've… grown up a lot," he managed to say.

"Hi, *Oncle* Jun. Long time no see," she tilted her head and smiled at him.

"Whew. I was afraid you'd try to speak French with me," he joked.

"I've forgotten all my French," Mayumi said.

"Oh, that can't be true. I'm sure it would all come rushing back the minute you went to Paris," Jun said. "When was the last time you were there?"

"Um, six years ago," Mayumi replied, looking around the office. There were no pictures, just a lot of boring books and magazines. A computer screensaver of a snowscape glowed pale blue on the desk.

"That looks refreshing," Mayumi remarked.

Jun didn't quite know what to say to her, so he offered her a drink. Then he had to rummage in the refrigerator in the other room to find something. Luckily there were two cans of orange soda. He brought them back and gave one to Mayumi.

"Please," he said, "have a seat."

She sat down and Jun couldn't help noticing her Burberry patterned underpants. Whoa—he imagined Nagiko was not too happy about that. The lurid purple shirt, the textured fringe, the incongruous Burberry miniskirt were the antithesis of the artfully coordinated colors and textures that characterized Nagiko's creations. And then those day-laborer's split-toed shoe-socks. Good lord. Could this really be considered fashionable? Yet there was no denying that Mayumi managed to carry it off. Jun suddenly felt out of his depth. He tried to remember the little girl he had doted on in Paris. The one he used to take to buy bread.

Mayumi took a long gulp of the sweet orange drink. Jun thought the artless way she drank indicated that perhaps a certain childish innocence still remained underneath the studied façade.

"So..." she said. "My mom's probably told you what a bad girl I am."

Jun denied it.

"It's true," said Mayumi composedly. "We fight a lot. But the other day she finally told me about my father..."

"Really?" Jun was relieved. "I'm very glad to hear that, Mayumi. I've always felt it was a mistake not to tell you."

"Yeah, she finally admitted that. So...that was good...but..."

Jun looked at her, waiting.

"She said you were his friend. That you introduced them..."

"Well, in a way, yes, I suppose I did..."

"So, I was wondering if maybe...you could tell me something more about him..."

He was a little surprised Nagiko had not let him know that she was going to tell Mayumi the truth, but Jun was thankful he did not have to risk contravening her. This would make it so much easier now to bond with Mayumi. He suddenly remembered the Polaroid that had been sitting in the back of his desk drawer. Umeko, had snapped it the night he took Philip out for drinks in Akasaka, and mailed it to him months later, after she heard about Philip's accident. Jun had meant to pass it on to Nagiko, but then he misplaced it in a suit jacket he rarely wore.

"Here," he said. "I have something for you to give your mother. I suppose she's shown you pictures already, but she's never seen this one."

Mayumi's dark blue eyes gleamed. This was even better than she hoped. A photograph! Now, the only question was how to get him to reveal the name.

Jun handed her a slightly out-of-focus picture of four people sitting on a sofa—an elegant woman with upswept hair, wearing kimono. A young woman with a mass of '80s-style curly hair, in a low-cut evening dress, bracketed the group on the other side. Between them, there was *Oncle* Jun, his face somewhat shiny, a rather silly smile on his face. And next to him—a tall young man with dark hair falling in his eyes, a dark suit, also a goofy smile...it was him, her father. Hey...he was a good-looking guy. Mayumi drank in the image.

Meanwhile Jun was scrabbling in the desk drawer again.

"Something else. I have one of his cards here somewhere. He had them made to show he was a student at Columbia University. He was a smart guy, your Dad—but I'm sure your Mom's told you that..."

Mayumi couldn't believe it. She lowered her head politely and held out her hand for the business card Jun now pulled out.

Philip Metcalfe
Researcher
Institute for Japanese Religion
Columbia University

Philip Metcalfe...Mayumi Metcalfe...this was almost too easy. She now had his name *and* his picture. And she had found out on her own. Her mother didn't know she knew. Until the explosion that would inevitably come when Muranaka would unwittingly reveal to her mother what he had done, Mayumi was in possession of her own secret. Her hands began to tremble. Then her shoulders shook. Jun became alarmed. Mayumi was crying. He had no experience whatsoever of teenage girls, and didn't know what to do. Suddenly she stood up, both hands to her face, quivering with sobs. Hesitantly, Jun stepped over and folded his arms around her. She was taller than him by about an inch.

Jun didn't know what to say, so he made comforting noises as he patted her back. He didn't even understand why she was crying. She had completely lost control. Emotional overload, probably. She'd had a tough time. But maybe this would clear the air for reconciliation. She smelled like orange soda.

As they stood there, gradually her sobs diminished into occasional hiccups. Her face was buried in his shirt, smearing it with mascara. Now she wiped her eyes with the backs of her hands and put her arms around him. She ran her long fingernails down his back, then brought her hands tenderly to his face. Her lips brushed across his cheek and then, before Jun realized it, her mouth fastened on his and she was kissing him. He tried to disengage, but now her tongue was in his mouth and she was pressing against him. He pulled away in consternation.

"Mayumi! Stop it!"

She crumpled forward as Jun took her forcefully by the shoulders. Her head hung, face turned to the side. She didn't look at him.

Jun was rattled now. This was much worse than he thought. No wonder Nagiko was upset.

"Mayumi…"

She was limp. Gently he tugged the ponytail over her left ear, and pulled her face around. He smoothed the hair back, and gravely kissed her on the forehead. She did not resist.

"You are like a daughter to me," he said. "Surely you know that? If I haven't made you feel that over the years, then it is my fault, and I humbly apologize to you." He handed her a box of tissues. "Come on, it's time to get you home."

Mayumi slipped Philip's card and the picture into her purse, and then plucked out a wad of tissues.

"Okay," she said. "I'm sorry…"

Jun waited for her to go into the bathroom to wash her face and fix her hair. He looked down at his shirt. It was smeared with lipstick and mascara. He wiped a tissue over his own perspiring face. Traces of lipstick and makeup came off. He moistened a handful of tissues with the only liquid at hand, orange soda, and swabbed his face. He could wash later. Now, it was important to get Mayumi home.

She came back into the room, composed and quiet now. Jun led her to the elevator and down to the lobby. Walking past, he greeted the guard. The man answered with averted eyes in a monosyllable, and Jun suddenly realized what he must think, looking at them. He was mortified. He'd have to explain. Catching a glimpse of his own shirt, he realized nothing he could say was believable. Grimly, he walked Mayumi out to the curb in front of the building. Even at this hour, tired businessmen stood on the corners, waiting for cabs. Taxi drivers knew this, and were relatively plentiful.

The evening was warm, but Mayumi was shivering now. Jun was angry, no denying it. But at who? Mayumi? She was to be pitied. Nagiko? She was certainly partly to blame for Mayumi's reaching this state. But he was mostly angry at himself. He held his arms stiffly at his side, and then he caught sight of himself in the reflective glass window. Stupid stiff Japanese businessman—that's what he looked like. Like a dumb stick, standing next to, but aloof from, the wilting, knock-kneed shivering teenager. He felt like howling.

Instead, he put one arm around Mayumi's shoulders and raised the other to a taxi hurtling along the street toward them. Its automatic door swung open and Mayumi slid her long legs in. Jun reached in his pocket and pulled out a 5000 yen note. He put it in Mayumi's hand. It was double the amount the taxi fare would be, he knew. He gave the driver the address of the apartment in Kagurazaka.

"Give my best to your Mom, okay."

"*Hai.*"

"I'm not going to say anything to her about tonight, you understand…"

"*Hai.*"

"Goodnight, Mayumi."

"Goodnight."

The cab pulled away. Jun turned back to the office building with a shudder. In the elevator he almost retched at the sickly sweet smell of the orange soda on his skin. Mayumi's eyes reminded him so much of Philip. He thought of how they had met on the pilgrimage, and then he suddenly recalled the story of the Holy Man of Mt. Kōya. Right now he felt like nothing so much as that monk who had been swept off his feet. Jun felt a keen urge to leave Tokyo and tramp the route of the 88 temples.

In the cab, Mayumi switched her *keitai* back on. It was past midnight. She scrolled through five messages that had collected since she turned the phone off. Nothing interesting. She looked out the window. A man stood on the next corner, obviously hoping to snag a cab. Middle-aged. Not bad looking. Had a bit to drink, probably, but not wasted.

"Stop there," Mayumi ordered the driver. "I see a friend of mine."

The cabbie seemed doubtful but he pulled up to the corner.

"Open the door," Mayumi said.

"Want a ride?" she called out.

The man looked surprised, but he got in.

"Shibuya," Mayumi told the driver. "Tōkyū Plaza."

Mayumi leaned back against the door, letting one knee fall onto the seat. The man's eyes were riveted on her thighs. She moved slightly, exposing the Burberry triangle of her crotch.

The man started to sweat.

"How much do you have?" asked Mayumi. She abruptly brought her knees together.

The man looked up at her face. She was younger than he first thought. Then he noticed her low-cut blouse. But extremely well developed. Maybe not that young after all…you couldn't really tell by faces. He fumbled in his pants pocket.

"Twenty-thousand yen…"

"Okay," she said.

"Okay?" He reached over to touch her inner thigh. "Where?"

"Here," she said.

"What?"

"Now." She folded the bills and tucked them in her purse.

"Shhh," she giggled as she moved one leg on top of him, reaching to unzip his pants. "Pretend we're not doing it, so the cabbie won't get mad."

He came almost immediately. By the time they reached Shibuya, he was wiggling his fingers deep into the slippery juices of Mayumi's crotch and trying to get his tongue inside her bra. The cabbie was disgusted.

"Tōkyū Plaza," he said, pulling to a stop.

Mayumi pulled herself away from the man's groping hands and jumped out of the cab.

"I get off here," she said. "Bye." She disappeared into one of the subway station entrances.

"Where to?" asked the cab driver.

The man groaned. "*Chikushō…* "

What did you expect? The driver felt like asking him. He just hoped he'd saved some cash for the fare.

Mayumi skipped down the steps to the station and sauntered through the brightly lit underground maze. She emerged at a different exit and came out to the street. There she got into a another cab and headed home.

By now her mother ought to have gone to bed, she figured. She inserted her key quietly in the lock. Good. The apartment was dark. She undid the tabs on her footwear and pulled them off her hot feet. Then she noticed her mother with her feet tucked up, curled on the sofa. Maybe she had fallen asleep there. Mayumi tiptoed toward her room.

"*O-kaeri nasai.*" Nagiko's voice was low but sharp.

Mayumi jumped.

"*Tadaima,*" she squeaked.

The mundane call-and-response of homecoming held foreboding.

"Where have you been?"

"With friends…in Shibuya…"

"Erin called here two hours ago to see how your headache was."

"Oh…"

"So, don't lie. Who were you with?"

Mayumi was used to this. It was annoying. Tonight, however, she felt quite calm—even a little sorry for her mother.

"Okay. I was with *Oncle* Jun."

"Liar!"

"If you don't believe me, you can call him," said Mayumi, yawning.

"All right, I will." Nagiko was fuming. "But before I do, I hope you remember that we are meeting Frédérique tomorrow afternoon—this afternoon. She arrived yesterday, and wants to tell us about her new documentary. She said she thought we could help."

"Yeah, okay." It had totally slipped Mayumi's mind. She breezed past Nagiko, heading to her room, and Nagiko caught the unmistakable whiff of sex as she passed. Suddenly a disquieting thought crossed her mind. She took her *keitai* from her purse and hesitated before dialing. Then she pressed send.

"Muranaka." The voice sounded very tired.

"It's me. I'm sorry to call you this late," Nagiko whispered. "Was Mayumi with you tonight? Just yes or no. I know you probably can't talk now. That's all I need to know now."

She was sure that Mayumi had invented the story as a cover up. Why did she let herself bother Jun at this hour?

"Mayumi?" Jun hesitated, "No, I haven't seen Mayumi. Is she missing?"

"No, she's home."

"I'm glad she got home all right."

Jun had hesitated just enough for Nagiko's dark suspicions to erupt again.

Mayumi's room was quiet, as if she had simply dropped into bed like a fallen leaf. Nagiko picked her way barefoot to her own bedroom and lay down but did not fall asleep. Her mind raced in a spiral that kept leading to the same terrible place. She knew Mayumi was out of control. But Jun? Not Jun. Impossible. Yet…everything Mayumi did these days seemed calculated to wound. The way she dressed, the way she acted. The people she associated with. She confided nothing. Nagiko suspected her of meeting men by arrangement through i-mode sites. "Compensated dating" the news-magazines called it. Teenaged girls earning money for Gucci handbags by casual prostitution. Mayumi had access to all the Gucci handbags she could possibly want through Nagiko's network. But Mayumi wasn't interested in name-brand luxuries. What was it then? She had become totally opaque. But Mayumi with Jun? Once again Nagiko found her thoughts leading along the same spiral to this dark center. No.

They both avoided coming home these days. Mayumi had been doing "petit runaways" for the past year—staying at a friend's house for a night or two, calling just often enough to deflect Nagiko's impulse to report a missing person. She went to stay with Satoko for a week, and whatever she had said and done there was enough to cause a rift between her mother and her oldest friend.

There was always enough going on at Kiji to absorb Nagiko's attention, so she turned to her work for solace and distraction. Jun seemed to be doing the same thing. His mysterious political job that he was not at liberty to talk about took more and more of his time. He was in China, or South Korea, or someplace he couldn't mention, more than he was in Tokyo. They saw one another infrequently. When they did, Nagiko could not avoid revealing her anguish about Mayumi. Who else could she turn to?

But tonight was just too blatant. Nagiko knew she had been with a man. Curled up alone on her futon, the sounds of nighttime Tokyo insistently nattering through the closed windows, Nagiko wondered what Mayumi was capable of. She shuddered. Surely not that. Jun would never. He said he hadn't seen her. Mayumi was lying again. She had some boyfriend and they had gone to a love hotel. The last thing Nagiko wanted to do tomorrow was help Frédérique with her documentary on hidden buddhas.

When Mayumi was little, she had looked up at her with Philip's eyes. The memories those eyes evoked brought Nagiko to tears. At the point when Mayumi stopped looking her straight in the eye, Nagiko's tears dried up. The *mizuko* crept into her thoughts. Once banished from Nagiko's womb, she had been determined to reclaim her place. And now she resisted everything Nagiko represented. It was like living with a negative of yourself—as if Mayumi were trying to blot out all of Nagiko's achievements, her artistic sensibilities, her friends, even her claim on Jun. There was a pattern. Much as she didn't want to, Nagiko couldn't help but see it.

During the day she squelched these thoughts firmly under a rock. The school counselor called her to meetings. Satoko had once offered to help. They all saw her as a single mother dealing with a wayward child. That was the rock. But the maggots underneath stayed hidden—the feeling that Mayumi was somehow slowly chewing away at her life energy—those thoughts only crept out at night, when Nagiko was alone. This was not the way a mother should feel. But this child—surely anyone would be provoked beyond endurance by such behavior. Even as a *mizuko* Mayumi had pushed mercilessly. Nagiko concentrated on the monotonous flashing of a billboard that seeped through the closed blinds, and finally drifted off.

Mayumi always slept as late as possible. Her windowless room was a dark cave. Nagiko didn't even try to wake her. She figured if they left by twelve-thirty they would have plenty of time to get to Frédérique's hotel. She dreaded a confrontation with Mayumi over the lie about Jun. She had to put it off. She needed her to be in a good humor and be polite to Frédérique. Nagiko showered and dressed. They were out of bread and coffee. She decided to go out and pick up a few things at the grocery while Mayumi slept. From her closet she pulled out a simple shift made of *Akashi chijimi*, navy blue with tiny crosshatches in white. She was using a lot of traditional kimono fabrics in her collection this year.

She needed coffee. The café next to the convenience store was open, already frigidly air-conditioned even at this early hour. Shivering, she ordered coffee, toast, and a boiled egg, and glanced through the newspaper as she ate. Stupid Prime Minister. She flipped to the fashion section.

Back at the apartment, all was quiet. How much time would Mayumi need to get ready Nagiko wondered? She slid the door to her room open a crack.

"Mayumi-chan. Time to get up. We're leaving in an hour."

A muffled croak.

Nagiko slid the door further, sending a beam of light into the dim shambles.

"Don't. I'm up..."

Nagiko slid the door closed.

"There's coffee. And croissants," she said.

She heard the rustling of bedclothes and went back to the kitchen. She heard Mayumi go into the bathroom and turn on the shower. Twenty minutes later she came out and went back to her room with a towel on her head.

Nagiko poured Mayumi's coffee and set out the pastry.

Half an hour passed. Mayumi still had not emerged from her room.

"We'll be late..."

"Coming...five minutes..."

Mayumi had figured there was no point giving her mother a chance to tell her to change. She emerged, giving her hair a final brush.

"Let's go," she said.

Nagiko bit her tongue. Mayumi had on a pair of pale green wide-leg silk trousers that almost brushed the floor. Over that, a pink embroidered tunic reached the top of her knees. That was layered with a gauzy blue scoop-necked blouse worn over a striped t-shirt. She pushed her hair back as she reached for a pair of platform sandals from the shoe shelf in the entry.

"When did you get another piercing?" Nagiko asked.

"That? Two months ago," Mayumi answered. "It's totally healed now."

She had silver hoops in her lobes and a small titanium ring further up in the cartilage of one ear. This is what Nagiko had just noticed.

"Well, no face piercing, okay? Eyebrows or nose."

"How about tongue?" Mayumi said, sticking hers out. They were on the elevator now. Mayumi was taller than Nagiko.

"You must be joking..."

"Of course. That's disgusting," Mayumi laughed.

The subway was not crowded. Body language even more than their faces revealed the generation gap between mother and daughter. Legs sprawled, Mayumi was a bird of paradise in fantastic plumage hunched over her *keitai*, working her thumbs furiously over the tiny keypad. Next to her Nagiko was a compact, exquisite dove. As they approached Roppongi, more and more people got on the train. Surreptitiously their eyes were drawn to Mayumi. Only if they stayed on for more than two stops did they notice the elegant woman sitting next to her, gazing straight ahead, her hands in her lap.

They walked into the lobby of the Grand Hyatt in Roppongi Hills fifteen minutes late. Frédérique did not see them right away but they spotted her easily. She was standing with her scruffy-looking French cameraman, talking with a clean-cut Japanese cameraman whom Frédérique was meeting for the first time. With them were an interpreter and a liaison person from Fuji Television which was co-sponsoring the filming of the documentary—now called *The Secret Buddhas of Japan*. Frédérique's hair and laugh were unmistakable.

For a moment she did not recognize Mayumi, then she caught sight of Nagiko and her eyes lit up. She rushed to them. First Mayumi—she took her hands and kissed her on both cheeks. She stepped back and regarded her, head to foot.

"*Bienvenue à Tokyo*," Mayumi said in a perfect accent.

Delighted, Frédérique turned to Nagiko.

"*Naturellement, elle se souvient de son français*," she said.

Nagiko just smiled. Mayumi had refused to speak French with her at all, so she had no idea how much she remembered. Now Frédérique turned to her and enfolded her in a perfumed hug.

"I am *so* excited to be here," she burbled. "I have been trying to get a project in Japan for years—years!"

Frédérique made introductions. The Japanese all exchanged business cards. The French cameraman struck up a conversation with Mayumi. Finally Frédérique waved the schedule that Mrs. Watanabe from Fuji Television had typed up.

"Okay, we head to Yamagata tomorrow, to film the mummy monks. Two days. Then back to Tokyo for film check, one day. Then Kyoto for a week. Then back here. Subject to change, of course, but that's the idea. Now—

I need to spend some time with my friends." She indicated Nagiko and Mayumi.

The cameraman said something to her.

"With Mayumi? Well, all right. She would be a fantastic guide to Tokyo I'm sure—if it's okay with her mother. Nagiko? Can René scoop Mayumi up and have her show him around a little? This is his first time to Tokyo."

Nagiko glanced at Mayumi who was looking demurely in her direction. It was obvious that her assent was expected.

"But wait—first, I have a present for you," cried Frédérique, wheeling back to Mayumi. She took a small package from her bag.

It was a flacon of Chloé perfume. Mayumi immediately undid the stopper and dabbed some behind her ears. Frédérique noticed her piercing.

"All the young people in Paris are piercing themselves as well," she remarked to Nagiko, as the heavy scent of tuberose and ylang-ylang wafted from Mayumi's direction. "In all sorts of places…"

Mayumi giggled.

"All right, then," Frédérique turned to René and Mayumi. "But be back here by six-thirty. We have a dinner with the head of Fuji Television. Now—"she tucked her arm in Nagiko's and steered her toward the café in the lobby. Everyone scattered. Nagiko noticed René's arm already casually draped over Mayumi's striped shoulders as they disappeared down the escalator.

Frédérique admired the fabric of Nagiko's dress as they walked. She had not lost her eye for textiles.

"She is a handful, yes?" she remarked, raising an eyebrow.

Nagiko did not know anything about the mummy monks of Yamagata, so Frédérique filled her in on what she had learned from Bertrand Maigny. She took a well-worn copy of Maigny's mandala book from her bag, and Nagiko recognized the name of Philip's professor. How odd! But then again, perhaps it wasn't odd at all. How many experts on Buddhism could there be in France? She tried to focus on what Frédérique was saying. Why start out with these freakish mummies Nagiko wondered?

Frédérique sensed her repulsion.

"This is television," she said. "You have to get the viewers hooked—no, even before that, from my point of view, you have to get the producers hooked. Otherwise they won't give you the money to do anything. That's why we start here. We have already gotten permission to film."

"And the hidden buddhas?" Nagiko asked. "Have you permission to film them as well?"

Frédérique exhaled sharply. "Some yes, some no. I really need someone in the Buddhist establishment to be an advocate." She looked keenly at Nagiko. "I thought perhaps you might know of someone—from your travels perhaps…" Her voice trailed off as the waitress brought them iced coffees.

Nagiko was about to shake her head when she remembered Kōji and Nora. She had not had much contact with them since the wedding. How many children did they have now? More than one, but she couldn't remember exactly.

Frédérique stirred the crystal syrup into her glass of coffee.

"Yes," Nagiko said. "I think I know someone who can help you."

Frédérique put her hand on Nagiko's arm and gave it a squeeze.

"Fabulous!" she said. "You must join us for dinner."

But Nagiko declined. She was exhausted, and Frédérique's strong perfume was beginning to give her a headache. It was the same scent she had given Mayumi.

"I should go home and call Priest Kon," she said. "I don't have the number in my cellphone but I know it's somewhere in my files."

Frédérique did not object. "Well then, at least you must let Mayumi join us?"

"Of course."

Leaning back in the air-conditioned taxi, Nagiko shuddered a deep sigh. She felt obliged to help Frédérique, but she couldn't help feeling uneasy about her plan to "unmask" the hidden buddhas, as she put it. What would Philip have thought? Yet she seemed to have the blessing of Philip's old professor, so how bad could it be? Putting her in touch with Kōji and Nora could be a positive influence. More than anything, Nagiko felt an urge to talk to Jun. It was Saturday. Should she call his private cellphone again? She would have to—she couldn't bear having his wife pick up the phone at home. His was the last number she had called. She took her *keitai* out of her purse and pressed send. It rang once:

"This is Jun Muranaka. I will be unavailable for the next three weeks. If this is an emergency, please call my secretary." The office number followed.

Nagiko was taken aback at the recorded message. Usually Jun told her when he was going away for more than a week. She knew she needed to be discreet about calling his *keitai* because he would drop whatever he was doing to answer. It could be the Prime Minister, or the Head of the Imperial Household Agency, or some other frightfully important person. She had respected that and usually called his office line. Obviously he was not carrying it now. Where could he have gone? Nagiko knew his secretary Hiroko. Should she call her? Was this an emergency? She didn't know. Her self-assurance melted. She had spoken with him just last night. Perhaps he would call her. Nagiko felt sure he would. She should wait. She put the phone away.

Back in her apartment, the message light on her desk phone was blinking. Three messages. Two were from people at the Osaka branch of Kiji. The third was from Jun. Nagiko listened to it once, then replayed it. It was very short.

"It's me. I've decided to get away for a while, so I'm doing the Shikoku pilgrimage. I'll be on this trek for three weeks. Sorry. I know this is out of the blue. It was a sudden decision. I love you."

That was it. She played it again.

"*Ai shiteru yo*—I love you."

Nagiko trembled. Jun was a typical man of his generation in that he seldom voiced any sort of endearment. It would have embarrassed both of them. But what could have made him suddenly drop everything to go off on this pilgrimage? At one time they had joked about doing it together when they were old. She listened to it one more time.

"It was a sudden decision."

It must have been. He hadn't said a word earlier. How sudden? Since last night? Once again Nagiko's train of thought twisted down a dark tunnel.

"*Ai shiteru yo*—I love you."

He had never said that before. Nagiko tried to resist the queasy feeling that her life was unraveling at its edges. She erased the messages. Okay. She had a job to do for Frédérique. She would focus on that. She was pretty sure Kōji's number was in that old address book in the bottom drawer. Yes.

A woman's voice answered in Japanese. Nagiko asked to speak to Nora.

"This is Nora."

Nagiko identified herself and Nora switched to English.

Nagiko asked about the children, about Kōji, and about Nora herself before coming to the reason for her call. Putting the most positive spin she could on the project, she told Nora about Frédérique and her documentary, and how she needed a priest willing to help her get access to some *hibutsu*, and possibly be interviewed on film. Nora said she thought Kōji would be able to help. He had taken the twins to a baseball game in Osaka, but would be back later that evening. She would have him call.

Nagiko hung up the phone. The croissant and cup of coffee she had made for Mayumi that morning still sat on the kitchen table. Nagiko poured the cold coffee down the sink. When Josefina had lived with them, the apartment was always neat, but Josefina had gone back to the Philippines when Mayumi entered junior high school. Nagiko gathered up discarded food containers, old magazines, and garbage, sorting it into separate bags for the trash. She continued picking up and straightening, working her way into the living room, the bathroom, finally coming to the sliding door closing off Mayumi's room. Hesitating briefly, she pushed it open.

She knew the room contained a wardrobe, a single bed, a desk, and a desk chair but the wardrobe was the only object visible above the heaps of cast-off clothing, magazines, and stuffed animals. A tidal wave of clothing cascaded from its wide-open doors. The back of the chair was draped with a damp towel. The room smelled of Mayumi. It was hopeless. Nagiko couldn't even begin to straighten this room. A small space had been cleared on the desk where one of Mayumi's purses lay open, rummaged-through for wallet and subway pass. It was the varnished leather Vuitton she had carried last night. A mirror and lipstick had rolled out. Nagiko stepped over the piles of worn-once shirts. She stared at the bag, then reached out and picked it up.

What could it tell her about this child she no longer knew? Anything? She turned on the desk lamp and peered inside. A half-empty pack of cigarettes. A wad of tissues. A mirror. A business card. A photograph. Nagiko gingerly removed the photograph and flipped it over. She gasped. Philip. Jun. Though she had never seen it, she immediately knew when it had been taken. She looked at the card. Philip Metcalfe. Where did Mayumi get these? Then, she knew. The card fell from her hand. Mayumi hadn't lied. Jun had.

With trembling fingers, Nagiko re-arranged Mayumi's things just as they had been. She backed out of the room. Philip. Jun. Those silly grins. Mayumi knew everything. Jun had told her. She now understood why he left Tokyo so suddenly, why he felt the need to purify himself on this pilgrimage. He must have regretted it immediately. She suddenly felt a wave of nausea and stumbled into the bathroom.

If she'd had the uneasy sense earlier that her life was unraveling, she now felt it had been ripped into shreds. She threw up until she was hollow. Still her shoulders heaved. The phone rang. She ignored it as the answering machine came on. It was Kōji Kon. Nagiko let the message go on. She didn't want to talk to anyone. She found an old bottle of Scotch in the back of a kitchen cupboard and poured six ounces into a cup of the milk she had bought for coffee this morning. Then she took a tablet of the zolpidem her doctor had prescribed for anxiety and insomnia.

The phone rang again. She did not pick up. It was Mayumi. They were at dinner. She said Frédérique wanted to know if she had made contact with Priest Kon? There was a lot of noise in the background. Then Frédérique came on. Mayumi was so terrific, they were having a fabulous time. So sorry Nagiko was not there. She had had a fabulous idea—could Mayumi come along for the filming? She could be such a help. She and René had really hit it off. She could be of great assistance as an interpreter. Please call. Late was fine. Nagiko listened in a haze. Then she walked unsteadily to her bedroom and collapsed on the futon.

Mayumi came home late. She saw the message light flashing on the phone. That was odd. Frédérique said her mother had gone home. She peeked into Nagiko's room. Yes, she was there, asleep. Mayumi listened to the messages. Priest Kon. He would be happy to help the documentary team. She wrote down the number of the mobile phone he gave. The next message was hers. She cut it off. Where had her mother been? Why hadn't she listened to the messages? She was acting weird. Mayumi was determined to accompany Frédérique and her crew to film this documentary, no matter what Nagiko might say. She called Frédérique with the news.

"I will call Priest Kon in the morning and explain everything to him," she said.

Frédérique was ecstatic.

"Did you tell your mother that I insist you come along?"

"She said it's fine," Mayumi replied without hesitation.

"Great. Our train is at ten-oh-five. I've asked Ms. Watanabe to get you a ticket. Come to the hotel at nine-thirty."

Mayumi said goodnight and clicked off her phone. She went into her room and packed a small suitcase for the trip to Yamagata. She spied her purse on the desk and removed the picture and the business card Jun had given her. Should she take them? No, she would hide them here. She tucked them into an old comic book on her shelf. Then she set her *keitai* to bleat a wake-up alarm, and set it down as far away from her bed as she could so that she wouldn't turn it off and go back to sleep.

Mayumi bounded up when her cellphone woke her. Yawning, she opened her door. The apartment was quiet. No smell of coffee. She peeked into Nagiko's room. Still sleeping. She showered and dressed. Purposely making noise, she made her own coffee and scrounged around for yesterday's croissant. It was nine o'clock. She had to leave.

"*Okaasan...*" she called in to Nagiko. Her mother didn't stir.

Mayumi became impatient.

"I'm leaving, okay? I'm going with Frédérique. I'll be gone till Wednesday. Did you hear me?"

Strange. She wrote a note and propped it up on the saltshaker on the kitchen table. Then she left.

Blowfish

TEN YEARS HAD GONE BY since he had seen the priest from Maizuru, and during this time nothing had happened to any hidden buddha. In March, though, Tokuda saw the news reports of the destruction of the buddhas of Bamiyan. There were no more Buddhists in Afghanistan, but the Taliban had seen fit to smash any remnants of a non-Islamic past. The dynamite reverberated ominously throughout the world. Suddenly everyone was concerned about the destruction of buddhas.

In July, Tokuda had two summer *hibutsu* to look after. First he went to Shidōji to watch over the lone hidden buddha on the Shikoku pilgrimage circuit. Then, he went to Nara for the "naked Jizō" of Denkōji Temple. On the twenty-third of July a monk and a nun would strip this three-foot high, sweet-faced, anatomically ambiguous wooden image of Jizō of its silk robes and dress it in new ones. The old garments would be cut into strips and given to believers, who regarded these scraps of fabric as powerful talismans. Of course no one beside Tokuda knew that this naked Jizō was one of the ten still-powerful *hibutsu*.

Only ten. Still, as long as even one remained, Kūkai's safety net would hold. Tokuda's predecessor Zuichō had rescued this naked Jizō from a cloistered sanctuary at Kōfukuji that had been vandalized in the late nineteenth century under the Meiji government's policy of bashing Buddhism. He had brought it to Denkōji for safekeeping. In the thirteenth century, another predecessor had rescued this same Jizō from a fire at the Chisoku-in, a branch temple of Tōdaiji. Because of this connection, Tokuda felt especially protective toward this *hibutsu*.

Every hidden buddha had its own signature effect on his senses. Some glowed with different colored auras, some vibrated a more musical hum than others. This naked Jizō was the most fragrant. His grandfather had had the same reaction. To Tokuda, the odor was so enticing, so enveloping, that when he approached the altar he had trouble believing it was not smelled by everyone. How could he describe it? It smelled of spikenard and amber. Of cassia, clove, labdanum, and sandalwood. During the ceremonial dressing of the statue, Tokuda would stand back behind the crowd and give himself over to the wonderful scent. It was like listening to music with the nose. He was thinking about his grandfather when he became aware that the priest sitting opposite him at the communal dining hall had said something.

"Did you hear about tomorrow?" the priest repeated. They had just finished the evening meal.

"What about tomorrow?" Tokuda asked, with an involuntary twitch of one eyebrow.

"It's being filmed—the ceremony of dressing the Jizō." This priest was short and scrawny. His skinny neck stuck out from the collar of his black kimono like a tortoise's head extending from its shell. He had a prominent Adam's apple that bobbed up and down when he talked.

"Really? By whom?" Tokuda frowned. Any extra attention turned on the remaining hidden buddhas made him uneasy. He had no idea whether an active image could be deactivated by being viewed on film. He didn't think so, but he would prefer that it not be put to the test.

"Fuji Television. And some French program..."

"French?"

"That's what I heard. Some French filmmaker doing a documentary. And Fuji TV filming them filming—or something like that." The other man laughed. "Who will film the filmmakers filming the filmmakers?" he guffawed, his Adam's apple bouncing disconcertingly.

Tokuda didn't smile.

"Well," harrumphed the first priest, swallowing his smile, "I heard they are looking for priests to interview, too. If you're interested there's a call to audition tonight at seven over by the main hall. Here's our chance to be on television." He waved a flyer he had picked up.

"Wonderful," muttered Tokuda.

The other man decided Tokuda was a sourpuss. He excused himself. What was wrong with being on TV? He was certainly going to offer his services. Tokuda walked out of the refectory into the warm early evening. He picked up a flyer as he left the building.

Fuji Television in collaboration with Chardonnet Films is producing a documentary on 'The Secret Buddhas of Japan.' The July 23 ceremony of the clothing of the naked Jizō of Denkōji is to be featured. If you would like to be interviewed for possible inclusion in the film, please come to the main hall at 7:00 p.m. on the evening of July 22. Be prepared to sign a release.

Tokuda crumpled the paper in his fist and tossed it in a trash basket. He could see a knot of people gathered in the courtyard in front of the hall already. He walked in the opposite direction, grumbling to himself. Then he turned around and walked back.

A table had been set up. Behind it were seated a golden-haired foreign woman who waved her hands a great deal, a sober middle-aged Japanese woman, and a strikingly tall Japanese girl. Two young men shouldering huge cameras stood several paces away. The tortoise-necked priest was among the crowd waiting to give their names. Then Tokuda did a double take. Standing behind the table was another priest, wearing glasses, looking over a list. Tokuda approached nearer to make sure.

There was no mistake. It was Kon. And he seemed to be with the filmmakers rather than the supplicants. Now Tokuda was truly alarmed. He had spent the past eleven years thinking about what he would do if he actually caught Kon at a *hibutsu* temple. Now all those thoughts came back to him in an onrushing wave. Tokuda walked toward the group, feigning nonchalance.

Kōji caught sight of him and raised his hand in greeting.

"Oi—Tokuda-san, if I'm not mistaken..." His eyes disappeared in the crinkle of his smile. "How are you? What a coincidence! Are you here to participate?"

"No, I usually come to this ceremony," Tokuda replied.

"Really! This is my first time. Another case of the base of the lighthouse being dark, I suppose."

Tokuda looked from Kōji to the women seated at the table. "Are you part of this?" he asked him.

"Well, I sort of got roped in," Kōji admitted with a sheepish smile. "Favor to a friend. And then my father knows the head priest here, and the timing all worked out, so that's how we ended up at Denkōji. Not so many *hibutsu* come on display in the summer. They're on a tight deadline." He pointed toward the film crew. Tokuda at first thought he was speaking of the *hibutsu*. He quickly realized his mistake. Of course, it was the filmmakers who were on a deadline, not the buddhas. Kōji was looking at Tokuda appraisingly.

"Say, you ought to audition. You have a good look about you—dignified—like a Buddhist priest ought to look. Unlike me…" Kōji grinned behind his thick glasses and rubbed his hand over his shaved head.

Tokuda said nothing. He was thinking about what his next move should be. It wouldn't do to make Kon think he was on to him, he decided. The best course would be to act casually interested.

"So, what's this documentary about, anyway?" he asked.

"*Hibutsu*, basically," Kōji replied. "How they only exist in Japan, and believers think they have special powers." He looked around to see who might be listening, and lowered his voice. "It's a little embarrassing, frankly. They decided to start out with those mummy monks in Yamagata. I'm afraid, from what I've seen, it ends up rather garbled. Although they got some great footage of those mummies…Have you ever seen them? I haven't. But now I'm tempted…which, I suppose, when you think about it, is the way these things are supposed to work…"

"What do you mean?" Tokuda was genuinely confused.

"Well, the way she explained it," Kōji indicated Frédérique with a tilt of his head, "in order to educate people, first you have to get their attention. Makes sense—if you don't grab their interest, nobody will even bother about what you want to say. And even somebody like me now, seeing what they filmed—makes me want to go see for myself. It contributes to international understanding, too."

"Ah." Tokuda nodded. He thought Kōji was naïve. "So, after filming here tomorrow, where are they going next?"

"Let's see," Kōji pulled a folded schedule from his sleeve. These are not all one hundred per cent certain yet, but here's the list of places I am trying to get permissions for. She's agreed to make donations to the temples—I'm counting on that to get us special showings."

He showed Tokuda the list. Seven of the temples listed held what Tokuda knew to be still-active *hibutsu* images. He breathed deeply. This could not be coincidence.

"Why are you doing this?" he asked simply, looking directly at Kōji.

Kōji was taken aback.

"Why?" He stuttered for a moment. "I'm…I've been hired as their Buddhist consultant…for authenticity…to catch mistakes. I'm going to talk about Kūkai in an interview…"

Suddenly Kōji felt uncomfortable under Tokuda's unwavering gaze. Why was he doing this? He was flattered, okay, he'd admit that. People looked at him with new respect as he toured about with this international entourage. And the fee they were paying him was welcome extra cash. He had three children to support. Nora approved. And then he felt a small resentment welling up. Who was Tokuda to question him? Hadn't he just complimented him and offered him a part in the project? Kōji folded up the schedule and tucked it back in his sleeve.

"If you'll excuse me," he said. "They need me now." He bowed to Tokuda and walked toward the cameramen.

Tokuda bowed wordlessly. As he passed by the table where people were jostling to sign releases he overheard an elderly priest talking about the famous camellias of Denkōji and how the crew really ought to come back in the early spring to see the marvelous falling of the camellia blossoms. Tokuda was embarrassed for the man. Couldn't he see these people were not interested in Denkōji? Still less, its camellias? All they cared about was getting their shots of the naked Jizō. The young Japanese girl was listening and translating into French for her companion who nodded, bored. That must be Chardonnet, the French producer, Tokuda figured. Foreign women attracted him not at all. But the young girl—what a fascinating face. She was an unusual beauty. He watched her for a while, standing at the edge of the crowd. He had to tear himself away.

The next morning Tokuda was up early. Silently he ate rice and miso soup with the monks, including the tortoise-necked one who left abruptly as soon as they had finished breakfast. The ceremony of opening the inner shrine to re-clothe the Jizō image would start at nine. By eight o'clock the hall was full of worshippers. He slipped into the back, senses quivering, to wait. He could smell the unearthly fragrance of the *hibutsu* and sense the faint hum from behind the closed doors of the unopened inner tabernacle.

At eight-thirty he heard a babble of voices outside. The head priest came in with the two cameramen to do their lighting check. The Japanese crew-member asked politely whether it was possible to see the image before the actual ceremony. To Tokuda's disgust, the head priest obliged by opening the wooden doors. A burst of fragrance assailed his mental nose. The Japanese cameraman held his light meter by the Jizō and read off numbers in English for his French colleague. Soon, Frédérique, Mayumi, Kōji, and Ms. Watanabe from Fuji Television entered. More worshippers, barred from entering because the hall was now full, stood outside, grumbling.

Frédérique went straight up to the altar to examine the image. Mayumi followed. Kōji engaged the head priest in conversation. No one noticed Tokuda. What Tokuda noticed was that the glow surrounding the image had begun to fade. The celestial hum was growing fainter. And the fragrance was slowly slipping away as if a censer had been extinguished. He glared at Kōji, looking for a reaction. Priest Kon seemed totally oblivious.

Late that afternoon, Frédérique was very happy with the rushes. They had captured a lot of interesting footage. She was already in an expansive mood at dinner when she suddenly remembered that today was Mayumi's eighteenth birthday. She ordered bottles of champagne at the hotel's French restaurant. Frédérique had faxed their itinerary to Nagiko and tried calling several times to tell her how well things were going and how helpful Mayumi was, but Nagiko's *keitai* phone appeared to be turned off. Finally Frédérique called the Kiji office. Nagiko's secretary told her yes, Kiyowara-san had come in and received the fax, but she was on a business trip at the moment. Frédérique asked Mayumi if she had spoken to her mother.

"Sometimes she likes being unreachable," Mayumi said. "When she's out gathering inspiration for a new collection. That's probably what she's doing now. Don't worry about it."

Having Mayumi to herself over the course of the week reminded Frédérique of years ago in Paris when she had been Mayumi's "French mother."

"Do you remember Genji?" she asked.

"Jump in your bag, Genji," Mayumi recalled. "That's what I used to say. He was so cute—I loved that dog!"

How different Mayumi was when Nagiko was not around. Perhaps she ought to intervene somehow, Frédérique thought. But how? She decided to simply treat Mayumi as she would any bright young colleague. Encourage her. She lavished praise on her sense of design. She loved the outfits she put together. Had Mayumi ever thought about opening her own studio? Mayumi tilted her head and looked at Frédérique. It had never occurred to her. How would she do that? Frédérique suggested a business plan. With the Kiyowara name, she was sure Mayumi could get financing. They talked about marketing.

"Or maybe you should open a shop," Frédérique suggested. "You're a trend-setter, Mayumi. You could gather clothes and accessories and help girls create a look. No one else would think of putting that crazy little sweater with those pants—but you see the possibilities. You have a real talent for fashion."

Mayumi felt as though a box had been opened, and she was allowed climb out. Suddenly everything looked different. She had never been interested in going to college. Conversations with Nagiko about her future always stumbled on this fact and never went anywhere. But here was a different path. Maybe she really could start her own fashion line, her own shop. Not in Tokyo, but somewhere else, away from her mother. This was why she had never considered fashion design. But fashion was in her blood. She lived fashion design.

There was something, too, about finally knowing who her father was, that gave her an anchor. She used to feel like she was floating. Nothing ultimately mattered as she drifted from one interest to another, from one boyfriend to another, from one sexual encounter to another. None of it affected her deeply. She was not sure how she would act on the knowledge of her father's identity, but simply having it filled a hole in her life. Maybe someday she would trace family in America. At least she now knew where to look. It was not Paris as she had long suspected. Her father was not French—he was American. He studied Buddhism. She had been amazed when Priest Kon told her he had known her father—even more amazed when she realized his wife Nora had known her father too. She promised Kōji she would visit them in Maizuru soon.

Mayumi now translated for Frédérique, made phone calls, and did errands. The cameraman René was totally infatuated. She flirted but held him off. Her focus had changed. She messaged her friends in Tokyo that she was unavailable, and kept her *keitai* tucked out of sight. Priest Kon got them permission to film *hibutsu* in several more places, including Seiryōji, which housed a famous statue of the historical Buddha Sakyamuni.

Kōji had earned Frédérique's deep and often-expressed gratitude. This *hibutsu* had been designated a National Treasure—getting permission to film it had been a real coup. The image had a hollow interior in which were found internal organs made of silk. Frédérique was already thinking of how she would edit the footage—cutting from the human mummies of the introduction to this wooden buddha with silk organs would work really well.

At the previous two temples Mayumi had noticed a priest whose face seemed familiar. She caught him staring at her and then turning away. She asked Kōji about him.

"Oh, him. His name is Tokuda. He's interested in *hibutsu*. That's really all I know about him. A strange man."

"He's rather good-looking," Mayumi opined. "If he didn't always frown so."

"Well, I did ask him if he wanted to be interviewed once, but he wasn't interested. He keeps to himself," Kōji said.

"Frédérique noticed him too," Mayumi added. "She said if only he would consent to be in the documentary—I just love the way he looks..."

She lowered her voice. "Has he been following us? I'm sure I've seen him before. This is our last *hibutsu*. Maybe you could ask him one more time?"

Tokuda now had all the proof he needed that Kōji was the agent that was killing off the remaining hidden buddhas. He followed along helplessly, as yet again Kōji entered a temple with a displayed *hibutsu* and its aura faded. He was quite sure, also, that Kōji was unconscious of what he was doing. That made it harder. How could he convince someone to stop doing what he wasn't aware of? But could he stand to see the Seiryōji image deactivated? He knew it would happen unless he acted soon. How could he lure Kon away from the others? He always seemed to be in the thick of things, speaking English with the Frenchwoman, making phone calls, joking with the beautiful teenager. Tokuda was desperate. Then he had an idea.

He remembered that Kōji was a connoisseur of seafood. They had talked about fishing when they were on the train from Kanshinji back to Kyoto, arguing about the best way to prepare sashimi from freshly-caught sardines. The plan came to him suddenly. To make it work he had a lot to do before dinnertime. He would have to find a fish. But it was the wrong season for the fish he needed—if only he'd thought of this sooner! Tokuda found a phone book and looked up specialty restaurants.

In the morning, as expected, Tokuda found the filmmakers wandering about the extensive temple grounds at Seiryōji, planning their shots for tomorrow. He spotted Kōji and strode over to him, a friendly smile on his face.

"Kon-san!" he called out. "Could we talk? I've been thinking over what you said about improving international understanding with this documentary. I'd like to be part of it—if it's not too late..."

Mayumi was standing nearby and overheard his remarks. She glanced at Kōji, who returned the look with a smile, as if to say "what do you know…"

Kōji and Tokuda went off to confer for several minutes. Then Kōji came back alone.

"What did he say?"

"He said he knows the secret of why the hidden buddhas were established in the first place—by Kūkai," said Kōji, shaking his head. "It's kind of off-the-wall, but he told me some stuff that only a very highly placed Shingon priest could possibly know. Maybe he's on to something. Anyway, he wants to have dinner tonight to discuss it."

"What did you tell him? We're supposed to have a technical meeting at dinner tonight."

"I don't need to be part of that," said Kōji. "I told him yes. Who knows? This could be great for the documentary."

"Well, you'd better tell Frédérique," Mayumi said.

"Of course."

"So where are you going for dinner?" Mayumi asked. She stretched an arm over her head in a yoga pose.

"Place called Mokugyo. It's near the river."

"So what kind of place is it?"

"Mokugyo? It's a fugu restaurant," said Kōji.

Tokuda was worried that Kōji would turn up his nose at the idea of eating blowfish in August. Connoisseurs considered fugu a winter delicacy.

"That used to be true," Tokuda had nodded when Kōji made precisely this objection. "But now, they farm them. Raise them in big cages in the ocean. There's no reason not to eat fugu in any season now. And," he added, "this place Mokugyo is unusual. The chef is a former priest…"

"Ah—that explains the name," exclaimed Kōji.

"Yes." Tokuda smiled. "He offers a special service if you know him well."

"What's that?" Kōji asked, although he immediately guessed.

"He will serve fugu testicles."

"*Honma ni?*" Kōji lapsed into dialect. It was illegal to serve the toxic livers or testicles of fugu. The organs would have been carefully excised by a licensed chef as soon as the fish was killed. But everyone knew that the most exciting way to eat fugu was with just a touch of the poison. It gave a buzz and tingle of narcotic euphoria that one turn-of-the-century writer likened to drinking absinthe.

"It's probably awfully expensive to eat there…" Kōji said apologetically. Tokuda knew then that he had him.

"Don't worry about that, "he replied smoothly. "I get special consideration."

Kōji had no reason to doubt him.

They agreed to meet at Mokugyo at seven.

As soon as he left the grounds of Seiryōji, Tokuda began to perspire. This was not going to be easy. He had chosen this restaurant only because of the name. He could make a plausible connection to having a special "in" there—which was lucky for him, although it would be disastrous for the restaurant.

First he would need a disguise. No, first he would need to locate his fish. Fidgeting on the train back to central Kyoto he went back and forth in his mind. He chided himself for losing focus. He needed to be calm and methodical about this. All right—find the fish first. Think. It was almost eleven. He realized right away that the fish markets would not sell live fugu and risk amateurs bungling their sashimi. Fugu sold for food would already be de-toxed by a specialist. He needed a live fish. He'd once spotted a blowfish in a huge decorative aquarium in a fancy restaurant. Someplace must sell them as pets. He would go to a fish fanciers' emporium. All species of fugu carried neurotoxin in their eyes and organs. He just needed to locate a specialty shop. Then he changed his mind. Disguise first, he realized, then fish. It wouldn't do to have a Buddhist priest wandering around asking about procuring a live fugu. Especially not after what would be in the news tomorrow.

Back at the inn where he often stayed in Kyoto, he looked at an out-of-date tattered copy of the Yellow Pages. Most people would look up information like this on the internet now, he realized. He had never used a computer, but this was not the sort of quest he could ask someone to help him with. He figured that an aquarium store listed in a three-year-old phone book would probably still be in business, so called the first likely number he came across.

"Your pet fugu died and you're looking for a replacement? Sorry, we don't carry puffers. Too aggressive in the tank. Who might? Around here? Saaaa…I don't know. There's Yokuwa Tanku in Tokyo, but you'd do just as well to order from a breeder online. That's probably your best bet."

Tokuda tried another. And another. Finally, someone gave him the number of a specialty breeder in Kobe. He glanced at his watch. He could just make it to Kobe and back if this worked. He called the shop and told the man who answered that he was looking to replace his pet fugu.

"What kind was it?" the man asked.

Tokuda had no idea. He said the first thing that came to mind.

"A *tora fugu*."

"A tiger fugu? You must have a pretty big tank…"

"Oh yes, a huge tank," Tokuda replied, feeling his face start to sweat again.

"Have you ever kept a grass puffer?" the man asked. "Or how about an eyespot puffer?"

"Uhh…"

"They are lovely fish," the man went on. "Much prettier than the tiger fugu. Nicer personalities, too."

"Do you have some?" Tokuda asked.

"Sure do. Purple puffers too."

Tokuda decided to probe.

"Aren't purple puffers highly toxic?" he asked.

"Ain't no puffers that ain't," the man replied. "How long did you say you've been keeping fugu?"

"I had my tiger for five years," Tokuda said, grabbing wildly for a number he hoped was in the ballpark of the blowfish lifespan.

"Well, you must be doing something right then," said the shop owner. "That's a long time for a fugu. Died of old age?"

"Yes…"

"Sorry to hear that. What was his name?"

"His name?"

"What was your fugu's name?" the man repeated.

"Oh. His name was…Stripe."

"Poor old Stripe," the man commiserated.

Tokuda sighed, as if overcome by the memory. "Could I come see your fish today?"

"Come ahead. I'm open till five. What did you say your name was?"

"Suzuki."

"See you this afternoon then, Suzuki-san."

There was no time to lose. Tokuda changed into a pair of slacks and a knit sports shirt. If only he'd had time to find a hairpiece or something to disguise his shaved head. He had bought a baseball cap on his way back from the Seiryōji Temple. It would have to do. He was athletic enough that the outfit looked plausible. Middle-aged guy who did weekend golf, stayed in shape. He glanced in the mirror. The image that looked back at him was that of a murderer. He was shaken for just a moment. He bought a pair of reading glasses with thick black frames at a kiosk in the train station. They hid his distinctive eyebrows.

Luckily he found the tiny store without having to ask anyone for directions. Hida's Ornamental Fish, by appointment only. He rang the bell.

"Who is it?" It was the voice of the man who had answered the phone.

"Uh, it's Suzuki...Stripe's owner..."

He was buzzed in.

The store was on the third floor. Tokuda walked up. Mr. Hida was waiting at the door. He was a wiry, sharp-faced man with bad teeth and a hooked nose that reminded Tokuda of an eel.

"Welcome." He displayed his crooked teeth in a smile.

"Thanks," Tokuda said uncertainly. He stepped inside the small dark room with floor-to-ceiling fish tanks. He hoped he could conclude this transaction quickly. Once his eyes adjusted to the low light he saw unusual fish everywhere. Besides several species of fugu, Hida pointed out cichlids and African catfish, even a huge eerie silver coelacanth. Tokuda's eye was caught by a squarish spotted fish with big eyes and a rounded snout.

"Cute, huh? That's a *kokuten fugu*. In English they call it 'dogface puffer'," said Hida.

"Really looks like a dog, doesn't it?" Tokuda was amused in spite of himself.

"So..." Hida rubbed his hands together. "We need to find you a replacement for Stripe..."

Tokuda debated on whether to say he was in a hurry, but decided against it. A man looking to replace a beloved fish would not be in a rush. He did say that he needed to be back in Kyoto by six or his wife would be angry.

Mr. Hida held up his hand.

"Say no more," he said. "I understand. I've got one too."

Tokuda presumed he meant a wife.

There were two *tora fugu* in a large tank with no other fish.

"Where'd you get Stripe?" Hida asked him.

"Caught him myself," Tokuda answered. "In Karatsu."

Hida chuckled. "Kyūshū, eh? Lucky fish—lucky that somebody didn't try to eat him, that is. Can you believe I've had people come here trying to buy fugu to eat?"

Tokuda winced. "That's terrible…" he managed.

Hida continued hotly. "I screen my customers carefully. My fish only go to good homes." He looked at Tokuda who was scrutinizing the pair of tiger fugu. "Which one do you like?"

Tokuda shifted his weight. "It's so hard to know," he said. "And I really hate to break them up. I used to get the sense that Stripe was lonely sometimes—all by himself…" Tokuda surprised himself at how natural it felt to say that.

"Why don't you get them both?" suggested Hida.

"That's just what I was thinking," Tokuda replied. "My tank's big. I'll get the pair." He hesitated. "What are their names?" he asked.

Hida revealed his snaggleteeth again. "Oh, I don't name them," he said. "I'd get too attached."

Tokuda said he would like to buy the dogface puffer as well.

"It's so cute…I've really fallen for it."

"You'll need a separate tank," warned Hida. "You can't put him in with the tigers. And you know that if a fugu dies in a tank with other fish, it's likely to poison them all."

"Of course. I'll be very careful," Tokuda said.

"Need anything else? Snails for keeping their teeth in condition?"

Tokuda shook his head as if he had plenty of snails.

"Just the fish."

Hida went about slowly removing each fish into a heavy reinforced plastic bag. "You don't want to alarm them, or they'll puff up," he said. "And you never want to take them out of water. If they inflate, you'll have a hell of a time getting them deflated again. If that should ever happen," he knitted his brows, "here's what you do. Hold them under water tail down, and jiggle them till they burp up the air."

"Right."

"—but it's better not to take them out of water in the first place. There." He tied a tight knot in the third plastic bag and carefully put the three fish in a cardboard box. He tied it with heavy twine and added plastic handles.

"It's heavy—can you manage it?"

"It'll be fine," Tokuda replied, sneaking a glance at his watch. "I'm very obliged to you." He paid Hida in cash.

"Come back again if you need anything else," Hida walked him to the door. "Nice talking with you."

On the express back to Kyoto, Tokuda started to get nervous again. How was he going to cut out the livers? He would need to stop at a stationery store to buy an Exacto knife. And then how was he going to transport the livers to the restaurant? He really should keep them cold. Perhaps a bag of frozen vegetables would to do the trick. He'd put the livers in a plastic bag and tape them to the frozen peas. Need to buy tape, bags, peas at the Seven Eleven. He had an hour and a half before meeting Kōji at Mokugyo.

At five minutes before seven Tokuda was seated in a small private tatami-matted dining room in the restaurant. Tucked in the voluminous folds of his Buddhist robes was a rapidly defrosting package of frozen corn with a plastic baggie taped to it. They had been out of peas. Tokuda closed his eyes and breathed slowly. As he pursued his mission during the day it gradually dawned on him that it would look suspicious if two people ate the same dinner of fugu and only one of them got sick. He would have to eat enough of the liver to become convincingly ill himself. He probably had enough fugu liver to kill four people. How much was enough to send a person to Nirvana? He would try to make sure that Kōji got somewhat more than enough and that he himself got somewhat less. But there were no rules here. Tokuda decided he was prepared to die if he miscalculated.

Once he had made that decision, he felt much better. He had nothing against Kon personally. He felt sorry for him. This was a terrible thing to do. But it was the only way now. The entire line of secret transmission from Kūkai culminated in this mission. Tokuda was sure of it. And if he had to lose his life in the process, so be it. It was a small price to protect the world. The corn lay coldly next to his thigh. A few minutes after seven, the waitress slid open the door and Kōji followed her into the room, apologizing for keeping Tokuda waiting.

They began with the traditional first course of paper-thin slices of fugu arranged like chrysanthemum petals overlaying a Chinese blue and white plate. The pattern of the plate gleamed faintly through the translucent pieces of fish. Kōji was in heaven.

"It just never occurred to me to eat fugu in the summer," he said, happily spearing another slice of fish and dipping it in the pungent sauce. "But it's perfect. Cold, refreshing to the eye…I could compose a haiku on summer fugu…You know—this is something I talk about with my wife sometimes— she's American—how in Japan we get stuck in these ruts of association. Like fugu is for winter. I mean, I can see how originally that might have made sense, in the days before refrigeration and all, but we get so used to the association fugu=winter that we just don't even think about eating fugu in August. What a pity! Your friend here at Mokugyo ought to do an advertising campaign for summer fugu. I'm a convert, now, that's for sure…"

Tokuda smiled and poured him another glass of beer. He wanted to make sure Kōji drank a lot before the last course of fugu stew. When the waitress came back in, Kōji said, "You told the chef we ordered fugu testicles, right?"

The woman was used to this sort of banter. As they ate, Tokuda told Kōji the story of the secret line of transmission Kūkai had set up to monitor the network of hidden buddhas all over Japan. Kōji was fascinated.

"I had a friend once," he said between bites of fugu, "who was convinced there was something very important about the *hibutsu*. And now you're telling me that in fact the hidden buddhas were set up to protect the world from *mappō*?" He took another long swig of beer. "By Kūkai himself?" He looked at Tokuda through somewhat hazy eyes.

"How come we never learned about any of this in our studies on Mt. Kōya?"

"It's a secret transmission," repeated Tokuda. "And what I'm telling you is that I am the current holder of this line—my own grandfather was my predecessor." He refilled Kōji's glass.

"But Kūkai had a reason for making it secret," he continued. "Something is out to destroy the protective power of the hidden buddhas."

Now Kōji looked up at him through his thick glasses. He found Tokuda staring directly at him.

"There is a destructive force that kills the *hibutsu* when they come on display. Many have been deactivated in this century. It seems that the process has been accelerated recently."

Now Kōji put his chopsticks down. He looked a little uncomfortable. Tokuda noted this. The waitress came in to clear their plates and bring in the ingredients for the *fugu-chiri*.

"Thank you. That will be fine. We'll cook it ourselves," Tokuda told her.

"Are you sure?" she asked. Carrying out the used plates, she left them alone. She was not about to argue with a priest.

"If you need to unload some of that beer, this would be a good time," Tokuda prompted.

"Good point," said Kōji. His face was quite red from the alcohol. "I think I will." He excused himself.

As soon as he left the room, Tokuda untaped the plastic bag hidden under his robes. He turned the fire up under the portable burner and slipped the eyes and livers of Mr. Hida's late fish into the broth. Each had puffed up in alarm when he took it out of water, then deflated like a punctured balloon at the first cut of the Exacto knife. Tokuda disposed of their remains in a public trashcan on his way to the restaurant. Quickly he added the scallions, pale mushrooms, white cabbage, carrots, and fugu chunks. By the time Kōji came back, the mixture was bubbling away.

Standing at the urinal, Kōji mulled Tokuda's revelations. This was far stranger than he expected. He had no idea how he was going to approach Frédérique with this. Was Tokuda going to say he wanted to reveal what he had just told Kōji on film? Did the man actually believe it? Or did he regard it as some weird superstition that he thought would be of interest to the filmmakers? Maybe Tokuda was trying to grandstand now. Maybe he wanted to upstage Kōji and everyone else who had been working on this from the beginning? Although he could feel his sense of indignation starting to swell, Kōji decided he would just listen now, and decide afterward what to tell Frédérique. It was in his hands, after all. If he thought Tokuda was a crank, then he would simply say they shouldn't bother with him.

By the time he came back to the room, he felt confident about what he would do. He sat back down, ready to continue the fugu feast.

"Say—when do the testicles appear?" he asked.

"You're sure you want to try testicles?" Tokuda asked, expertly dividing the fugu stew into two bowls. "You're a family man, after all."

"Bring 'em on…"

"They come at the end," Tokuda said. "We'll see how we feel after the rice and the burnt-fin saké—that stuff can give some people quite enough buzz. Even the raw fugu we ate could have an effect. That's the way they do it here."

Kōji dipped into the bowl of stew. "So can you tell me," he said, "which of the *hibutsu* have this special power you were talking about?"

Tokuda took a bite of carrot, and put his bowl down. He did not have much appetite. "Well, among those that lost their power in the last ten years, there are the Hall of Dreams Guan Yin at Hōryūji, the reclining 6-armed Guan Yin of Kanshinji…"

"Isn't that where we met?" Kōji asked, slurping the last of the soup from his bowl.

Tokuda refilled it, making sure to scoop up the innocuous-looking bits that had collected on the bottom of the pot. He then forced himself to eat more from his own bowl.

"The naked Jizō of Denkōji…"

"Say, I think I'm feeling a bit of fugu," Kōji said. "Kind of a tingle, isn't it?"

"I suppose…could be…" Tokuda replied. He wondered when he would start to feel it as well. Numbness was reported to start about fifteen minutes to half an hour after the poison was ingested. He noticed that beads of sweat were forming on Kon's forehead.

"Whew, I'm feeling pretty full," Kōji said, pulling out a handkerchief to swab the top of his head. He pushed his bowl away. "Maybe that's enough…"

"I agree. Why don't we walk outside—perhaps down along the riverbank. Clear our heads a bit?"

Kōji excused himself and went to the bathroom again. When he emerged he looked pale. Tokuda took care of the bill. Before he left the room he picked through the remaining soup and removed anything that looked like a bit of liver or eyeball. He put these bits back in the baggie. He would toss them along with the soggy corn when they got outside. He was starting to feel a creeping numbness on the roof of his mouth. They left the restaurant and walked toward the Kamo River.

The riverbank was full of young people, especially couples walking hand in hand in the shadows. Kyoto is a city full of Buddhist priests. No one noticed the two men dressed in black robes, talking earnestly as they threaded their way through the crowds. They had walked as far as the Nijō Street bridge when Kōji gasped he needed to rest for a while. To be honest, he wasn't feeling at all well. Tokuda was rather lightheaded himself. He waited as Kōji stumbled to the edge of the water and threw up. Tokuda took his arm and helped him over to the slanted embankment where Kōji slid limply to the ground.

"That's okay, we'll rest here a while till you feel better," said Tokuda. He was fighting to control his own dizziness. Kōji's cellphone rang and he fumbled to answer it.

"Never mind," said Tokuda. "You can call back in a little while."

"Nora..." croaked Kōji. His chest was heavy. His veins felt like they contained lead, not blood. He could barely move. Thoughts arose in his mind, but he couldn't speak.

Tokuda was overcome by a wave of dread. This, too, was one of the symptoms of fugu poisoning he had read about. He couldn't stand up now if he tried. The muscles in his legs were twitching, and his mouth filled with saliva. He tried to spit, but felt the wetness simply roll down his chin. He crumpled down next to Kōji. Neither of them spoke. Their throats were paralyzed.

Time passed, and it was now quite late. Kōji's nausea had abated but he had lost control of his limbs. He realized it was the fugu—that the chef had made a terrible mistake. And he could feel someone sprawled next to him. Of course, Tokuda had been poisoned as well. How bad was it? Would he lose consciousness? Would somebody find them? One after another these thoughts arose in his mind. He panicked. They could actually die, he thought. What a joke—no it wasn't a joke! Nora! People passed by, he could hear voices. Help! He tried to cry out—but no sound emerged. His mind raced like an engine unable to engage its gears. His cellphone rang again, the William Tell overture. It was dark by this bridge and in their black robes the two priests were almost invisible. Passersby averted their eyes from the sprawled figures and left them alone.

Now his heart rate had slowed considerably and breathing was becoming difficult. Kōji willed his mind into the familiar mode of meditation. The triple poisons of anger, jealousy and greed, which had coursed through his veins so recently were transformed by this other poison now. The teachings of Shingon seemed to dissolve into his very blood. Images of the Womb Mandala—deities representing body, thought, and word—appeared to him in brilliant clarity. Or, more precisely, it seemed that he had entered that mandala, and that he came face to face with all four-hundred fourteen divinities pictured therein. Amazingly, he knew them all and they knew him. He recognized faces—there were parishioners, childhood friends, students from the monastery, his fishmonger, the grocer, people who looked vaguely familiar, including some Westerners. He had seen them all before. He recognized the passions that motivated them all, and felt them as his own. He saw a scowling Fudō and realized it was Tokuda. As he circled toward the center of the mandala, drawn in with gathering energy as if to the center of a vortex, there were his mother and father, his teachers, his children, Kūkai. There was Philip! Nora!

As dawn began to lighten the sky over the eastern mountains, Kōji's mind reached the cosmic Buddha in the center of the Womb Mandala. And then all went dark before suddenly exploding in the illumination of the Diamond Mandala. Earth, water, fire, air, void—the five elements of existence, now charged through with the sixth element, the white light of understanding and consciousness brought him to the top center plane. The cosmic Buddha in the middle of the Womb Mandala was the wormhole to the nine planes of existence represented in the Diamond Mandala. They shimmered as different levels of reality. He understood then with his entire being that he belonged to all of them, that all were reflected through him, and that the cosmic Buddha was no different from he himself, and their essence was the universe and all beings.

Fear Not

FRÉDÉRIQUE AND MAYUMI TOOK an early train out to the western suburbs where Seiryōji temple was located. The morning air was pleasantly cool and moist. All in all, the filming was going better than she had any right to expect. The camera guys and Ms. Watanabe would come along with their equipment in a taxi after they'd had their coffee. Kōji would meet them at the temple at ten. Yesterday, René was able to film the statue's silk entrails, on display in a case on the upper floor of the main hall. Daintily stitched by nuns a millennium ago, there were lungs, kidneys, heart, liver, gall bladder, and intestines—even a blue silk spleen. The quasi-realistic body organs were not discovered until 1954 when the figure underwent minor repairs. Frédérique planned to use this in the script in talking about the secrets held by the hidden buddhas. She was wondering if she could get Juliette Binoche to narrate.

"Frédérique-san?" Mayumi asked tentatively. She had lain awake in the middle of the night thinking about plans for the future. Next week the filmmakers would be gone. The thought of returning to Tokyo depressed her—what was there to do but go back to her aimless routines of avoiding her mother. Frédérique had put ideas in her head. Maybe she really could start her own business. Not in Tokyo—but here, in Kyoto. Young people in this city were keenly interested in fashion. This could be exactly the right place for a shop that carried unusual items. A little store in the Teramachi district perhaps, where waves of young people and international tourists whooshed through the arcaded streets every day.

Frédérique had dropped off, her head nodding.

"Frédérique-san..." Mayumi spoke a little louder.

Frédérique opened her eyes and ran her fingers through her tousled curls. What beautiful skin this girl has, she thought to herself as she looked at Mayumi. She had been toying with the idea of bringing Mayumi to Paris.

Get her started in a modeling career. She would be fantastic. She had shown such independence and been so helpful during the filming, Frédérique was becoming charmed with the idea of keeping her around. She'd have to convince Nagiko, though.

"If I had my own shop, then could I go to Paris and it would be a business expense?"

"If you were buying items for your shop, then yes, it would…"

"Would you help me find things?"

"Of course." Frédérique rolled her shoulder blades a couple of times and stretched. Then she put her hands on Mayumi's shoulders. "I would adore helping you with your shop."

Mayumi smiled. "I want to do it," she said. "I really do. In Kyoto. I've been thinking about what to call it…what do you think of *Monde Palaka?*"

"It's fabulous!" Frédérique figured there was plenty of time to fiddle with the name. What Mayumi needed now was encouragement. She also realized that Mayumi lived at the leading edge of youth fashion. Japan and Japanese designers were exploring this frontier in more interesting ways than anyone. Mayumi's mother had been a pioneer—no, Madame Morikawa had been the pioneer—but she had been a Japanese woman designing in the French mode. Nagiko was an original. And Mayumi? What was Mayumi? Frédérique wasn't sure—she was talented, that was certain, but unpredictable.

Mayumi stretched her legs like a young gazelle.

"What's *Monde Palaka?*" Frédérique asked, "Palaka's world? Who's palaka?"

"That's what my Filipina nanny Josefina used to call me. Palaka is frog."

"Your nanny called you 'frog'? Why?"

Mayumi held up her hands in front of Frédérique's face.

"See the scars?"

Frédérique squinted.

"No…"

"Here." Mayumi ran her index fingers along the insides of each hand.

Frédérique saw that they looked slightly uneven, that was all. She dimly remembered Nagiko saying something about it a long time ago.

"When I was born, I had webbed fingers and toes. I had an operation when I was one year old to separate them. That's what the scars are from."

"You can't be serious," exclaimed Frédérique. "No one could possibly notice."

Mayumi examined her hands, then crossed her arms and enfolded them in her armpits. "I notice," she said.

"Then why in heaven would you want to call your shop 'Frog's World'?" Frédérique asked, genuinely puzzled.

"Because I'm perverse..." Mayumi started to laugh. Frédérique was nipped with an insight into Nagiko's difficulties.

Then she stopped laughing. "Josefina loved me even when I looked like a frog," she said.

"Well, frogs are definitely cute...how about *Monde Kaeru*? I'm afraid nobody except you and the Filipina housekeepers will know what a palaka is," said Frédérique, trying to push the conversation back to practical matters. "I like the half-French, half-Japanese flavor of it."

Mayumi was quiet.

"Don't worry about it. The name can come later," Frédérique said. "First you need to think about what kinds of things you'll be selling—a vision for your store." It occurred to her that this was an opportunity to plant a seed. "You know, maybe it would be a good idea to spend some time in Paris before you open your shop..."

Mayumi looked up.

"For example, have you ever thought of modeling? Professionally, I mean."

"I'm too tall," Mayumi said. "I went to see an agency in Tokyo last year and that's what they said."

"Not for Paris," said Frédérique. "You would just knock them dead in Europe."

"Really?"

Frédérique noticed Mayumi was rubbing her fingers. She suddenly recalled something she had read in one of the books Professor Maigny had recommended. "You know, I read that webbed fingers and toes are one of the marks of the Buddha..."

Mayumi laughed.

"It's true—there were a whole bunch of things," Frédérique said. "I can't even remember them all. Let's see, long fingers and toes—that was one. Round heels that stick out, that was another. Straight limbs, webbed fingers, arched feet...his...male thing...fully retractable."

Mayumi giggled.

"Hold on, I've got a list in my notes somewhere..." She took out her laptop. "Yes, thirty-two marks of the Great Man, exhibited by the Buddha. This gives me an idea..."

Mayumi was looking over her shoulder at the list.

"The thing about this *hibutsu* we're filming today is that it's supposed to be a copy of a likeness some Indian king had made of the Buddha when he was alive. So, it might be interesting," Frédérique continued, "to see how many of these 'marks' we can see on this statue.

"Forty teeth, deep blue eyes, eyelashes long like those of an ox, a lump on the top of his head..."

"I've never seen a statue or picture of the Buddha where you could see his teeth," said Mayumi doubtfully. "Or eyelashes, or—his male thing..."

"What about the naked Jizō?" Frédérique reminded her.

"Yes, but...that was the bodhisattva Jizō—not the Buddha..."

"Good point. Still. This could work very nicely. Viewers are interested in this kind of personal stuff—even about the Buddha."

"Do you really think I could be a model?" Mayumi asked suddenly.

"Absolutely no doubt in my mind," Frédérique responded. "Let's talk to your mother." She folded her laptop closed.

Nagiko had discovered Mayumi's note when she got up at noon. The drugged sleep had left her groggy. The table was littered with flaky crumbs surrounding Mayumi's empty coffee cup. On the back of a torn envelope, "Have gone with Frédérique." That's all.

Just as well, Nagiko thought. She could not face Mayumi right now. Her stomach rebelled at the thought of coffee. She made a small pot of green tea and ate a handful of grapes. A wave of sheer desolation rose up and engulfed her. She put her head down on her arms and waited for it to pass. Later she got dressed and went out. Were people staring? It was surprising that they weren't. Surely the pain must show? But even the flower lady she'd seen for the past twenty years chatted cheerfully as she sold Nagiko a bouquet of yellow lilies and white campanula.

Back at her apartment, Nagiko took out her ikebana shears. She picked out a low, bowl-shaped dark brown vase, and sat down at the kitchen table to make an arrangement. She thought about Satoko, and tears prickled at the back of her eyes. She hadn't spoken with her in over a year. Some argument they'd had after Mayumi had run off to stay with her for a week. Nagiko made an effort to concentrate on the flowers. She snipped and arranged. When she placed the vase on the low table in the other room however, she realized the proportions were all wrong. She pulled the flowers out, re-snipped the stems, and re-arranged them. Then she lay down on the couch. The wave of despair rose up again.

Tomorrow she could go back to the office. Tomorrow she would feel normal again. She should eat something. These thoughts arose one by one. Where were they coming from? Herself, of course. She was used to taking care of herself. But who was this "she"? Who was this "herself"? Her mind was becoming unmoored. Probably it was hunger. So eat. All right, I will. Inner voices arguing. "She" was trying to take care of "herself." Instant ramen in the cupboard. Primordial soup. It had enough salt to preserve a mummy. Nagiko broke an egg into the bowl of noodles and stirred it with chopsticks. Protein.

She felt better after eating the ramen. The warmth in her belly seemed to pull the rest of her disembodied self together. She noticed the yellow lilies—how lovely they were paired with the delicate white bells of cam-panula. Her mind came back into focus. The sliding door to Mayumi's room was closed. Nagiko pulled it open with a jerk. Not much different from the chaos she had seen Friday. There was Mayumi's Vuitton bag on her desk, but closed now, clasp neatly fastened. Nagiko wanted to see the picture again. She opened the bag, but it was gone. So was Philip's card. She looked around the desk. Maybe she had imagined it? The sudden thought crossed her mind like a firework exploding in the sky. But it faded as quickly. She hadn't imagined it.

The next day she went to her office earlier than usual. She had several meetings in the morning, a client lunch, a quick trip to the Roppongi store, then drinks with visiting Americans. They went out to dinner later, where Nagiko charmed them. She got home late. No messages. That wasn't so bad. She felt almost normal. Similar day on Tuesday, except there were phone messages at home from Frédérique. On Wednesday, there was a fax at the office. It, too, was from Frédérique, detailing their filming itinerary. Mayumi was going to tag along the entire time. She hoped Nagiko could hook up with them at some point.

Nagiko was sitting at her desk when the back of her throat clenched up again, and the urge to sigh overtook her with physical urgency. She had to leave. She told Miss Kōda to cancel her meetings for the rest of the day. No, for the rest of the week. Maybe next week too. She had to make an urgent business trip. She would be in touch, of course. Then she had her call a car, and she went home.

The pretense of normality crumbled. It took great effort to do ordinary things. She wasn't strong enough to continue pretending things were ordinary. The urge to dive deeply into a new project, to give herself up to thinking about new fabrics, new designs, beckoned like a beacon of sanity. Never a wife, yet quickly a widow, a betrayed mistress, a failed mother—a failed daughter too, for that matter. Philip, the ghost of his memory, hidden away like something precious, had been dragged into the light. Jun Muranaka— she had come to think of him over the years as her quiet soul mate—had done the unforgivable. Did he think that simply saying "I love you" in a phone message would make everything fine again? She had no doubt that Mayumi had seduced him, and she thought that he had probably resisted. But in the end he had succumbed. Mayumi, her daughter, the *mizuko*, had poisoned everything. Nagiko forced herself to open the door to Mayumi's room again. Hateful. How could she live like this? A butterfly emerging from this squalor. A beautiful, poisonous butterfly.

Nagiko shuddered at the memory of her long-ago dream of the *mizuko*. She had not forgotten the stony riverbank, the child in a pink sweater piling up stones in the rain, turning to look at her. "*Kaasan*", she had said. Mommy. And she had been ready to risk everything at that point, to let this *mizuko* stay in her womb, to be born.

And now the tears came. A horrible mother. She was a horrible mother. She would never be a wife, and she would never see Jun again. But how could she escape Mayumi? This child was devouring her, but these were bonds she couldn't walk away from. The taste of ash filled her mouth, her tears became gummy as glue. You can't escape the bond of motherhood, said her voice of reason, the same voice that made her eat, made her go to the office, made her arrange flowers—the voice of self preservation. No, you can't escape, so you might as well face Mayumi and have it out. Go find her. You haven't lost everything—yet. But if you lose Mayumi, you will. Be a mother. There's no other way.

Nagiko looked at the fax from Frédérique. She knew where they were and where they would be. The day after tomorrow was Mayumi's eighteenth birthday. They would be in Nara, at the temple called Denkōji. Nagiko pulled out a box at the back of the storage closet where she kept a few things from her grandmother, then she took out her suitcase.

In the early morning hours of the twenty-third of July, a small crowd of worshippers waited outside the main hall of Denkōji, murmuring amongst themselves. Just before eight, the door was opened and they rushed in, pushing to get as close as possible to the front for a better view of the dressing of the Jizō. Most of them were elderly—women with gold teeth, backs bent like lobsters, several leathery old men. A few younger people stood out because they were taller. They hung back as the single-minded old people surged forward like a herd of goats. Nagiko too, held back, then slipped into the hall. She wore a gauzy dark blue silk summer kimono that had belonged to her grandmother, pairing it with a plain beige striped obi. Her hair was pulled away from her face into a severe chignon. She wore only a touch of make-up. Mayumi had never seen her in kimono.

Nagiko sat off to the side in the shadows. Out of the corner of her eye she saw that a priest was standing not too far from her, his eyes closed, inhaling deeply. She thought it a little odd, but since his eyes were closed she felt comfortable casting a longer glance in his direction. Why was she drawn to look? Suddenly she realized—it was him! Priest Tokuda from Kamakura. A little cry escaped her throat, which she covered by coughing. He opened his eyes and looked around the hall. He appeared not to recognize her. She would approach him after the ceremony. He was just the one she could talk to, she knew it. Her heart pounded in her chest.

At eight-thirty she heard a babble of voices outside. The head priest came in with the two cameramen to do a lighting check. The young Japanese cameraman asked politely whether it was possible to see the image before the actual ceremony, and the head priest obliged. He held his light meter by the Jizō and read off numbers to his colleague. After about ten minutes Frédérique and Mayumi came in. More worshippers, barred from entering because the hall was now full, stood outside, grumbling.

Frédérique went right to the altar to examine the image. Mayumi followed and stood behind her, looking straight ahead. Neither of them noticed Nagiko. Her eyes were fixed on her daughter. Mayumi seemed different. Deferential to Frédérique, quietly serious, she appeared much older than the girl who Nagiko had last seen disappearing down an escalator with the French cameraman's arm around her shoulder. Not just older—Mayumi seemed an entirely different person. Now she was walking over to him, translating some instructions from the priest. There was nothing flirtatious about her manner at all. She was wearing a short crocheted sweater and loose cut sky blue pants. Her long hair was gathered back in a clip. Off to the side, the priest Tokuda had moved from his spot. Nagiko was taken aback to see his face contorted with dismay. He seemed to be looking for something. Then, abruptly, he left before the ceremony even got started.

Nagiko was torn between leaving to follow him or staying to watch Mayumi. She stayed. When the ceremony ended, however, she rushed out to look for the priest. He was nowhere to be found. She walked as quickly as she could with the kimono skirt constricting her steps, out to the main gate, but he was gone. She hesitated, not ready to confront Mayumi—at least not here.

She took a tissue from her sleeve and dabbed her nose. How convenient kimono sleeves were. The ultimate pockets! How many years since she'd worn kimono? She could hardly remember. Pre-Mayumi. Pre-Philip even. Had it been high school? Funny, how the body memory remained. She couldn't tie the obi—she had to have an old woman at the inn help her this morning, but here now she'd been wearing it all day, and felt quite comfortable. She appreciated how the obi held her together. It was like soft armor. Sitting on the tatami at Denkōji was made easier by the support of this brace of fabric. She liked the way the crossed-over front of the kimono made her feel safe, properly packaged, presentable. She had needed a different persona to pull herself into this journey, and the kimono had been exactly right.

Nagiko unfolded Frédérique's fax and looked at their schedule. She hardly recognized the Mayumi she had seen today. Maybe she should wait a few days to talk to her. Yes, she would wait until their last film site, Seiryōji. She needed more time to think about what she would to say. She went back to her inn and took a very long bath.

Frédérique and Mayumi had coffee at a little café near the Arashiyama terminus of the train line before walking to the temple. Mayumi had begun to imagine the possibility of going to Paris with Frédérique. Like a caged bird that had unexpectedly been released, the freedom made her slightly giddy—which way to fly? Frédérique was trying to concentrate on the physical attributes of the Buddha on her checklist, while Mayumi kept interrupting with questions about modeling. The cameramen and Ms. Watanabe arrived. Kōji ought to be here. At ten-thirty there was still no sign of him so Frédérique asked Mayumi to call. The head priest came to say they were about to open the doors of the inner shrine.

"We have to start without him," said Frédérique when Mayumi told her there was no answer. "He'll probably come rushing in. Okay, cellphones off, everyone. René, I want a slow pan from the top of the head down the entire statue. Just look at those clingy folds! Must have been some sort of knit…"

Worshippers had clustered to the front of the hall for the showing of this National Treasure. They were even more curious about the filmmakers, and many of them stuck their faces into the camera.

"So much for being an objective eye," exclaimed René to his counterpart from Fuji Television who seemed to be enjoying filming the worshippers overrunning René.

Mayumi tried to glimpse a hint of webbing on the hands and feet of the statue, but the fingers were held together in the mudra of fearlessness—right arm bent up at the elbow, palm out, fingers up; left hand, also palm out but extended, fingers down. If they were webbed you couldn't tell. She felt her *keitai* buzz in her pocket. Odd— she was sure she'd turned it completely off. "Convert jealousy and envy into wisdom," read the message. Mayumi checked the number. It was from a virtual buddy she hadn't heard from in a while. Just then the cameras both trained on the priest who was explaining the pose of the statue.

"It's called the 'fear-not mudra,'" he said into René's camera, while pointing at the statue's hands. "It is the pose of the Buddha immediately after attaining enlightenment. This mudra has the effect of converting jealousy and envy into wisdom."

Mayumi was fiddling with her *keitai*, not paying attention. The priest was going on about the statue—how it was supposed to be an actual likeness of the Buddha, how this species of rare tropical wood was not found in

Japan, how the silken entrails came to be discovered… Frédérique encouraged him to talk, knowing that in the end she would cut most of it. They finished filming around noon. A large part of the crowd of worshippers left the hall when the crew did. A slender woman wearing a pale ash-gray hemp *Ojiya chijimi* kimono with a black and white checkered obi lingered behind. Frédérique's eye was caught by the delicate fabric. It took a full minute before she realized the woman was Nagiko.

Mayumi now came bounding out of the dark interior through the main door into the bright sun. She saw Frédérique talking to an elegant woman in kimono, and headed toward them, skipping, until she got close. It was—her mother! She skidded to a stop, her mouth hanging open.

"*Okaasan?*"

Nagiko turned around.

"Doesn't she look fabulous in kimono?" Frédérique gushed. "I wish I could wear kimono. These hips, though…"

"What are you doing here?" asked Mayumi.

"I just wanted to see how things were going," Nagiko said mildly. "Frédérique invited me to join up with all of you at some point. I know today is your last day of filming."

Frédérique felt the tension, like a barometric low pressure zone between them.

"We were going to pack up here and then go have lunch," she said to Nagiko. "Why don't you join us? Tonight too—it's our farewell dinner with everybody. Speaking of which," Frédérique turned to Mayumi. "Has anybody seen Kōji?"

Mayumi switched her *keitai* on and auto-dialed his number. Still no answer.

"I'll call Nora," said Nagiko. She turned and walked a few steps away in order to hear.

"Nora left for Kyoto," said the older man who picked up the phone. "This is Kōji's father. Who is calling?"

Nagiko identified herself and then listened, occasionally responding,

"Yes…yes, I understand…of course. Please call me if there's anything I can do."

She turned back to Mayumi and Frédérique who were sensitized by her body language that something was terribly wrong.

"?"

"There has been some sort of awful accident, it seems," Nagiko said. Her face had gone white.

"Kōji?"

She nodded.

Early that morning, as dawn lightened the Kyoto sky, a bearded man emerged from his blue-tarped living space under the Nijō Bridge. He stretched and scratched. He would collect aluminum cans for an hour and then go scrounge some breakfast. The young people who caroused on the riverbank at night always left plenty of good pickings—food and aluminum cans both. Occasionally he came across a rumpled drunk, sleeping off the previous night's excess. He walked slowly, scanning the ground a few paces ahead. He stood up straight after bending over for a beer can, and noticed, about 100 yards ahead, a curious mound of black. He made his way toward it, poking through the tall weeds at the glint of a can. As he got closer, he felt uneasy. There were two of them. They were priests—this didn't look good. One was curled in fetal position. The other lay stiff and straight, his glazed eyes open, reflecting the newly risen sun.

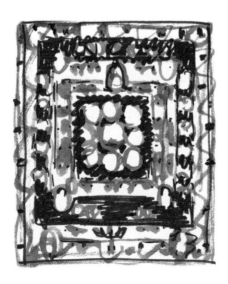

Hannya

FRÉDÉRIQUE AND MAYUMI ARRIVED BACK in Paris the first week of September. So did most of the city's population—Parisians who had spent an indolent August being seen on the Riviera or tucked away in Provence. The dense sunlight of late summer subtly shifted to the transparent light of early fall, energizing the mass reflux into the city. Cherries and peaches disappeared from the market at the lower end of the Rue Mouffetard.

Frédérique had her hands full. The last week in Japan had been a disaster. They had just wrapped up the final filming session when the news broke: Shingon Priest Dies from Fugu Poisoning! The Japanese reporters had cranked up a media frenzy. They didn't care so much about the French filmmakers—no, they turned their relentless spotlights on Nora Kon, the American wife of the Buddhist priest who had died. The fugu restaurant, Mokugyo, was shut down, the chef stripped of his license. People were reminded of the famous case of Mitsugoro Bandō VIII, the Kabuki actor who died after dining at a fugu restaurant. Might it, possibly, have been suicide? Kabuki fans still argued about the incident. What about the priest? The reporters wanted to know—had he been suicidal? The fact that the distraught chef committed suicide two days later solidified his guilt in the public mind at the same time that it expiated it.

The media also came sniffing around the other priest, the one who had survived. Before allowing the reporters to interview him, the doctor gave him the grim news that his friend and dining companion had not made it. Tokuda closed his eyes and said a prayer of thanks. To all of them he gave the same story—he and Kōji Kon had been no more than casual acquaintances. They both loved seafood. During dinner they had been discussing the documentary for which Kon had been serving as an advisor. All true. Tokuda did not like to lie. Yes, they had asked for fugu testicles. It was a tragedy. If only it had been him instead of the younger man with a family.

He regretted it deeply. As it was, the doctors told him he had barely escaped with his life. Yes, he prayed for Kon's soul every day. And this was true, too. He also prayed for the innocent chef who had felt compelled to take his own life—also by fugu poisoning, quite deliberate.

Tokuda did not tell them about the vision he had as he lay there on the bank of the Kamo River next to Kōji, the paralysis spreading through his limbs and torso, each breath heavy as a lungful of sand. Like Kōji, Tokuda's mind sank into the familiar grooves of deep meditation. Also, like Kōji, he began to visualize the Womb Mandala. His personal deity, the mystic immovable guardian king Fudō was, as usual, his entrance portal to the mandala. But as Tokuda wandered amidst the myriad deities, he saw no familiar faces. With a sickening sense of acceleration, he felt himself swept into the central vortex converging on the cosmic Buddha. In the crack of an instant, he was spit out into the realm of the Diamond Mandala.

Nine levels of reality shivered and popped around him. He could tell through fleeting shards of perception that some were beautiful and others were hellish. But all was confusion. He had lost sight of the cosmic Buddha as he was yanked about with no clarity or purpose. His paralyzed body may have been immovable like Fudō, but his mind was tumbled in a dizzying succession of perceptions. Roaring filled his ears, lights and colors blinded him. It was horrible. Finally he lost consciousness altogether, grateful that death was bringing this torture to an end. When he woke in the hospital two days later he was afraid to let himself sleep lest he fall into the fractured facets of the Diamond Mandala again. At his bedside stood a bouquet of roses and gaillardia that had been sent by that Frenchwoman.

Frédérique did not want to linger in Japan, but she had to cement relationships she might need later. She sent flowers to Nora and to the other priest, the handsome one she had hoped to film. She needed to figure out what to do about Mayumi. Mayumi was now determined to come to Paris, and Nagiko had not reacted well at all. One would have thought she would have been relieved at Frédérique's offer. Mayumi needed supervision, clearly, but with a light touch. At first, when Nagiko refused to let her go, Mayumi had exploded in a cold rage. She would never go back to Tokyo, she said. Her mother would never see her again. Finally, Nagiko relented, but not gracefully, and not with her blessing. Frédérique was in an awkward spot.

But now, in Frédérique's second-story three-room flat on the Rue

Mouffetard, Mayumi had settled down. She played at being the shopper and the cook. Housekeeping was a novel experience. In the mornings she went to modeling auditions, and in the afternoons she attempted to cook. Within two weeks Mayumi was called back at three agencies and given modeling assignments. Frédérique turned her attention to editing the footage she had brought back from Japan.

Mayumi had stood in front of a display of frozen escargots one day, dazzled by the variety of sizes and configurations of flash-frozen snails in cubes of parsleyed butter. Finally she chose a half dozen of the *extra gros*. That night at dinner, Frédérique complimented her as usual, but seemed distracted.

"How is the editing going?" Mayumi ventured.

Frédérique cushioned the last buttery snail on a chunk of bread and chewed it thoughtfully.

"It's coming along..." She had some great sequences, in fact, but somehow it wasn't jelling. She needed something to tie it together. Maybe someone to guide the audience? That was it—a talking head. Of course! She laughed out loud as she mopped up the last of the garlic butter.

"What's so funny?" Mayumi looked at her.

Frédérique called Bertrand Maigny the following morning.

The last time she had driven to Brest, almost a year and a half ago, the apricots had been in season. Now the air held a slight nip. Professeur Maigny had seemed happy enough to hear from her again, but did she detect a note of misgiving in his voice when she told him the focus of the documentary had been switched? Instead of looking at mandalas, the film was now about the hidden buddhas. After a pause, Maigny said maybe he could help her out, but he wanted to see what Frédérique had filmed before making a commitment. That was fair enough. On the back seat of her Floride were three videotapes of roughly patched-together sequences. Mayumi came along, too. Frédérique counted on her to help charm the old man into participating.

The rebuilt farmhouse was just as Frédérique remembered. Bertrand Maigny seemed to have aged, though. Perhaps it was the shock of September 11. He was in his eighties, after all. Politely, Frédérique inquired after his bees.

"Half my colonies died," Maigny informed her.

Frédérique was taken aback. Gently, she steered the conversation to the documentary. She told Maigny she hoped he realized that he himself was the reason she had decided to change the focus of the film. She had found their original meeting so inspiring, and the topic of hidden buddhas so rich, she felt that people would respond to the inherent interest of the subject. Surely she had mentioned earlier that she had always hoped to film an interview with him? He was so articulate—such gravitas, yet such an engaging way of explaining things...

Maigny allowed himself to be softened. Well, why don't we just take a look at what you've filmed, he suggested. Frédérique had remembered to ask on the phone whether or not he owned a videocassette player.

"We are not as provincial as you may think, here in Bretagne," he had said. "Not to worry—I have a *magnétoscope*."

Now she pulled the videotapes out of her bag. Mayumi sat next to Maigny, keeping up a running commentary in Japanese and French about the locations of the various temples and statues as they appeared in the as-yet unnarrated film. He found her delightful. He had forgotten how *agréable* Japanese women could be.

There was the famous wooden statue of Sakyamuni at Seiryōji. Maigny knew it well. Eh! The naked Jizō of Denkōji! That one he had never actually seen before. Maigny was amazed at the places Frédérique had managed to get access to.

"How in the world..." he began.

Frédérique smiled modestly. She told him about priest Kon who had been so helpful, and who had died so tragically on the last day of filming.

"We're dedicating the documentary to him," she added.

"It was very creepy," Mayumi said quietly.

"What was, *ma chère*?" Maigny turned to her.

"Priest Kon—dying like that. But the hidden buddhas, too. I think they're scary."

Frédérique was surprised. Mayumi had never said anything like this before.

"My mother used to drag me to temples to see them," Mayumi explained. "Ever since I was little. She was sort of fixated on them. And she never cared that I hated those trips." Mayumi had directed the last remark to Frédérique.

"I remember one time when we visited some temple where the gardens were full of peonies. It was chilly inside, and I was pulling her hand, trying to make her come out. But she kept talking with Auntie Satoko, and wouldn't come. Finally, I went outside by myself." Mayumi looked down at her hands. "I was so angry at her..."

Frédérique knew it was good that Mayumi was finally examining these feelings, but it was unfortunate that it had to happen here, now, in front of Professeur Maigny. Yet he seemed interested, sympathetic even.

"And what did you do?" he asked her.

"I think I started breaking off the flower stems," Mayumi said, touching her forehead with her fingertips. "I haven't thought about this for a long time." She closed her eyes, trying to remember.

"Yes. And then she and Auntie Satoko came out, and she was furious. She punished me by leaving me at home for the longest time. But that was what I wanted..." Now she looked up at Frédérique again. "I didn't want to go to these stupid temples any more..."

Mayumi—shut up now, Frédérique tried to signal with a look.

Mayumi's mouth dropped open, as if she suddenly realized how that sounded.

"Oh! I'm sorry—I didn't mean...I meant, when I was little, I thought..." she stopped in confusion, blushing furiously.

But Maigny did not seem put off. He simply looked at Mayumi thoughtfully, nodding his head.

Frédérique's shots of the hidden buddhas, the temples, the surrounding streets of Kyoto and Nara, evoked a swell of nostalgia. Ah—how Japan had changed. Yet, how much it was still as he remembered. And the hidden buddhas—years ago he had come to a dead end in his study, sequestering them away in the papers of his filing cabinet—the *bouddhas cachés* that Frédérique had noticed and inquired about. He had tried to forget about them. It suited an old man better to spend time cultivating his skeps—at least there would be honey. But this past summer had been so odd. The bees died so there would be no honey. The newspapers editorialized about global warming and predicted ever more deadly heat waves. But was it possible that global warming itself was an indication of something even grimmer? Maigny tried not to be pessimistic, but were there not signs of *mappō* everywhere one looked? The appalling destruction in New York overwhelmed the world news, but perhaps that was just the beginning of more terrible things to come.

He glanced into the distressed deep pools of Mayumi's eyes. Extraordinary, Maigny thought to himself. They almost look blue in this light. And it suddenly hit him—of course the *hibutsu* would seem frightening to a small child—they were charged with supernatural power. Children could easily be more attuned to those emotional wavelengths. He had spent many years looking for evidence in the texts of esoteric Buddhism that would explain the hidden buddhas. He had never found it. But perhaps he had been going about it the wrong way.

"May I see the videos again?" he asked Frédérique.

"Of course. I'll leave them with you if you like," she responded.

"And what about those mummy monks?" Maigny inquired. "Did you film them as well?"

Frédérique picked up the third videocassette and slid it into the *magnétoscope.*

Bertrand Maigny agreed that Frédérique could bring her photographer to film an interview. Perhaps she could come up with a list of questions before they met so that he could think about how to respond.

"That's a fabulous idea," Frédérique agreed. "Can I fax them to you? Via the University perhaps?"

"We are not so primitive as you think, here in Bretagne," he repeated his earlier remark with a slight twitch of his upper lip. "Why don't you send them *courrier électronique?*"

"You do e-mail?" Frédérique reddened.

"It's B *point* Maigny *escargot* univ-brest *point* fr," he rattled off.

Mayumi, having regained her composure, suppressed a smile.

That week Maigny watched the raw videocassettes several more times, all the while thinking about Mayumi's outburst. Frédérique e-mailed him a list of questions about Buddhism in general and hidden buddhas in particular. Her queries were completely predictable. He watched the tapes again. How different things might have been if Metcalfe had lived. Maigny could easily imagine that Philippe would be the one Mme. Chardonnet would be interviewing now, not him. Long ago Maigny had theorized that Kūkai had created a network of powerful buddha images. He had postulated a secret transmission of this knowledge in the mode typical of Shingon. Logically, it made perfect sense. But maybe this wasn't a puzzle to be solved by logic, or scholarly documentation of texts. Bertrand Maigny's outlook at age eighty-six had changed from the time when he had been in the academy. He had set his research aside. And what had he been doing instead? Keeping bees.

But his bees were dying. Not only his. Beekeepers all over France estimated that 90 billion of their bees had died over the past decade. That was it! He closed his eyes and rubbed his unruly white eyebrows. Of course! How could he have missed it? It was happening right before his eyes. His theory of Kukai's system of hidden buddhas was not only correct, it was real—and it was in danger of failing. The protection of the hidden buddhas was weakening, with disastrous effect for the world. Maigny sat down heavily on his comfortable sofa in front of the video. The *hibutsu* must be losing their power.

Throughout his professional life Bertrand Maigny had relied on his scholarly abilities and theoretical skills as his tools to carve out knowledge. On Mt. Kōya he had discovered another kind of knowledge—religious esoteric wisdom—and he had turned that wisdom itself into an object of erudition.

When had he stopped feeling comfortable with his instincts? It had been so long he couldn't remember. Then look what had happened when he followed his nose and suggested "the mandala" as a book topic—the text had practically floated onto the page. He'd made a tidy little sum as well. It had led, truth be told, to this documentary movie, bringing him full circle back to the hidden buddhas. And they were losing their power.

Isn't that what you ought to say in the interview? This thought struck Maigny almost more forcefully than the revelation itself. Imagine—renowned Buddhist scholar Bertrand Maigny gets up and expounds his theory of the hidden buddhas. And then he says the world is in danger of coming to an end. He knew how such a statement would appear in the eyes of his colleagues. Any residual academic credibility he had would go down the drain. He could imagine the sniggers.

But this is what you should do, said that voice, the one he had rarely listened to before. Because somebody who is in a position to do something about it will understand the message. The rational Maigny resisted. It would destroy his legacy as a scholar. He lumbered up off the sofa and went out to look at his beehives.

When Mme. Chardonnet returned the following week with her cameras, tape recorder, and make-up specialist, Maigny had decided what he would say. The lovely young Japanese girl didn't come this time. She had a modeling job. Frédérique chose his study as the backdrop, cutting tight to Maigny's face and torso sitting at his desk.

"Now, just relax," Frédérique said. "I'll ask questions, and you respond as if we were talking. It doesn't matter if you stumble—I'll fix it all later. Don't worry, it will be very smooth in the film." She didn't expect him to stumble, but sometimes people seized up when they knew a camera was trained on them. She lobbed the first question by asking him to explain how Buddhism first came to Japan. Maigny smiled his pedagogue's smile and began.

After half an hour, Frédérique stopped the camera to set up a different angle. He was fabulous, she told him. How did he do it? Another thirty minutes passed. They broke for coffee.

"I think we are close to wrapping up," Frédérique said, stopping René again to check the angle.

Maigny cleared his throat.

"I have a few more thoughts on the hidden buddhas I'd like to record," he said.

"Of course," said Frédérique. "René, one more take, please. Claire, can you fix that shine on the professor's nose?"

Looking straight into René's lens, Maigny began. Frédérique adjusted the microphone. Then she listened to what Maigny was saying. She glanced at René. He usually concentrated on the lighting, how things looked in the camera viewfinder, paying no attention to content. But he returned Frédérique's glance. René had spent the past three months chasing after Mayumi and after these hidden buddhas. Mayumi had eluded him. But he'd gotten interested in the *hibutsu*. What Professor Maigny was saying now was news to him. The end of the world?

This is fabulous, Frédérique was thinking to herself. She smiled encouragingly at Maigny. The producers were going to love this.

Nagiko stayed in Kyoto another two days after the film crew dispersed and Mayumi had taken off for Paris with Frédérique. She sought the quiet of a luxurious *ryokan*. Yet the humid envelope of Kyoto summer heat only exacerbated the cold fury growing in her heart. The child was a viper. Even after Mayumi had done the unforgivable, Nagiko had come seeking her, prepared to forgive. But Mayumi had rejected her—embarrassed her in front of Frédérique. Then she had cut all ties and left.

Her work was the only thing in her life now that gave her any measure of comfort. By the time Nagiko ventured back to Tokyo, Mayumi's room was empty. Bed, wardrobe, desk, and chair remained, but everything else was gone. She had even gotten rid of her books. Clearly she was never coming back. Nagiko plunged into plans for a new collection.

At the end of September Jun Muranaka called. Back from his pilgrimage, he had immediately been swept into a round of secret meetings in China and Korea. Sorry he hadn't contacted her. But he had done some hard thinking during this time, and they really needed to talk. Nagiko turned him down. She told him Mayumi had gone to France to pursue a career in modeling, and she was trying to adjust to the change in her life. Sorry, but she needed to be alone now. She said she'd call him, but weeks passed and she never did. He left messages which she did not return. One night Nagiko found him waiting for her outside Lion's Head Mansion. She was forced to tell him directly she didn't want to see him again.

Jun had hoped to explain everything. He wanted to help her cope with Mayumi, yes, but Mayumi was secondary. Jun was prepared to leave his wife and start over with Nagiko. The cloudy swirl of his life had settled into clarity over the past few months. He knew what he really wanted. But she did not let him talk. It never occurred to him that Nagiko could think he had allowed himself to be seduced by Mayumi, but he was stung by the chilly glitter in her eye. The words froze before they could leave his mouth. Jun got back in the car where he had been sitting, watching for her. He told his driver to take him home.

Nagiko's new line would debut the following autumn. It was a study in shades of black. From examining her grandmother's formalwear black kimonos, Nagiko had long ago realized that what was called "black" was usually a very dark licorice-brown. From natural dyes you could produce not one, but many blacks. Once, watching an artist at his easel, she had asked why, among the tubes of crimson, yellow, viridian, and white, there were no tubes of black paint.

"Black from a tube is dead," he had said. "I make my own blacks." He had demonstrated by dabbing various colors in a circle then pulling them into the center. Mixed together in differing amounts, they produced a range of quiet dark hues, any one of which could be called black. The image of that palette had stayed with Nagiko. She thought of it as the artist's mandala.

The Buddhist theme was obvious. Besides the inky colors, there were evening gowns that resembled priests' robes, and dense cloaks based on the patchwork technique of traditional vestments. One design, a fine-gauge knit, hung in rippled drapery from the right shoulder, where it was clasped by an ornamental ring. It might have seemed Greek unless you were familiar with Chinese Buddhist statues of the Northern Qi dynasty. The cutting of the cast-off robe of Denkōji temple's naked Jizō had inspired Nagiko to design a frock made of shredded strips. This one was bone white.

Usually Nagiko shared her insights with the other Kiji designers, gathering reactions and making adjustments as ideas coalesced into fabric, and eventually into pieces of clothing. But not this time. It was clear to her colleagues that this single-minded vision brooked no collaboration. Nagiko interpreted any voicing of misgiving, no matter how diplomatically phrased, as betrayal.

She decided Hannya would be a good name for the new collection. *Hannya* means "wisdom," but thanks to a famous Noh play, people think Hannya is a demon. The oxymoron appealed to Nagiko, and she designed a batch of t-shirts with the collection's logo to promote it.

The only breaks Nagiko had taken this year were visits to temples. She was drawn more than ever to view obscure *hibutsu*. She could go online to check the calendars of viewing dates. She made her way to a remote mountain monastery and an old village temple. There was a *hibutsu* conveniently located in the heart of Kyoto that she had not seen before. These temples were the only places she felt a sensation of inexplicable quiet happiness. The rest of her life shriveled.

Frédérique's film, *Les Bouddhas Cachés du Japon*, was scheduled to be shown on French television in June. The producers were surprised at the level of interest the topic of hidden buddhas had generated. They were prepared to give Chardonnet Films carte blanche funding for any future project. Frédérique urged Mayumi to call her mother. Mayumi said she would, but Frédérique knew she hadn't. She took it upon herself to put together a portfolio of photographs from Mayumi's modeling assignments to send to Nagiko.

Bertrand Maigny steeled himself for the airing of the show. Few of his colleagues were aware of his involvement in the filming, but after June 16, they would all know. As he expected, he was treated to an embarrassed silence. No one accosted him directly, although a few, including Professor Harvey Chernish, now at the University of British Columbia, felt compelled to write a sarcastic review asking why they never bothered to engage a fact checker? Frédérique was solicitous of Maigny, calling to make sure he wasn't taking it too hard. Privately, she was a little surprised. As she said to the station executive, everyone recognized Maigny as an expert on the hidden buddhas. How was she to know he had never published any of these views before? Of course they both knew that the controversy did nothing but provide more publicity for the film, and it was immediately scheduled to run again at the end of summer. She sent a copy of the program on DVD to Nagiko.

In Japan, Fuji Television ran the program in July. Noboru Tokuda had been on the lookout for it ever since returning to his quarters in Kamakura. He was grateful that the fugu scandal had finally died down. Thanks to a spate of irreverent cartoons in the weekly news magazines, everyone in Japan had heard of the priest who died from eating fugu testicles, but few of the supplicants who came to Fudō-in for *mizuko* rites were aware that Tokuda was the surviving priest. He slipped back into routine. The only thing to mar his deep relief at having removed Priest Kon was this annoying film.

Yet, what difference could it possibly make now? Tokuda convinced himself that it would have no effect on anything. His uneasiness came from force of habit. He had spent so much of his life in a frame of mind in which the hidden buddhas were hidden. Bringing them out in the public eye had always been inherently dangerous. Yet Tokuda knew that pictures of the *hibutsu* were of no consequence. Photographs of the Hall of Dreams Guan Yin, an Important National Treasure, for example, had been displayed on postcards for years. Film was even less substantial than a picture. What was film but a thin piece of celluloid? It wasn't even 'film' any more. It was vibrating particles of light, streaming through the ether to dance on a television screen in a kaleidoscope of red, green, and blue dots.

Still, he felt a twinge of trepidation when he saw an ad in the Yomiuri Evening Newspaper about the French-made program on hidden buddhas scheduled to air that week. Tokuda had found a small portable television set among a jumble of old appliances set out on the curbside for pickup. He asked the housewife who was tidying up the piles of garbage whether it was broken.

"Oh, no. It works," she replied. "But we got a new one that matches the living room decor better..."

"May I?" Tokuda asked.

The woman was embarrassed. She insisted on running back to the house for a cloth to clean it up before letting the priest take it. Back in his room, Tokuda tested the set. He would be ready.

Jun saw the newspaper ad for the program while he was flying back to Tokyo from Seoul, tired and depressed. His wife wasn't home. She had gone to her hometown, Matsuyama, for the mid-summer O-bon festival. She did not expect Jun to accompany her. The dog was at Prins-Prins, the pet hotel, so the house felt even emptier than usual. Jun had by now pretty much managed to squelch the thought of calling Nagiko even before it arose. He poured himself a Scotch and water and sat down in front of the new high-definition television set. Philip had been keen to study these hidden buddhas, he recalled.

The program was narrated in Japanese with subtitles for the remarks of Bertrand Maigny, Professor Emeritus of Buddhist Studies, Université de Bretagne. Jun thought the whole thing rather over the top. He didn't know quite what to make of the Professor's remarks about *mappō* and Kūkai's master plan for the salvation of the world. He'd never heard anything like that before. Maybe this was some new scholarly discovery? He yawned and turned off the TV. He didn't need to hear the panel discussion of eminent Japanese priests who had been taped discussing the film.

Noboru Tokuda watched the program with fascination and horror. He recognized the name of Metcalfe's professor. Before he had a chance to think about what this film would mean, an announcement cheerily reminded viewers to stay tuned for the following panel discussion by four distinguished priests representing the Zen, Shingon, Tendai, and Jōdo sects. Tokuda waited impatiently for the commercials to end. One by one, the priests were introduced. Each was asked to state his impression of the film. One by one, politely, they indicated they thought Bertrand Maigny was a crackpot. The program segued into the evening news showing O-bon dancing at various locations throughout Japan. Tokuda switched off the set. He unplugged it and wrapped up the cord. It had served its purpose. But he didn't return it to the curbside. As long as he had it, there was no reason he shouldn't watch the Sunday evening historical dramas now.

Nagiko had still not gotten around to looking at the DVD Frédérique had sent, and she was at dinner with a client when *The Secret Buddhas of Japan* aired. She happened to catch the last bit of the panel discussion when she got home. A Zen priest was saying how the whole idea of secreting statues away from view was misguided and not orthodox Buddhist tradition anywhere else. She wondered briefly what Philip would have said about that, but then her thoughts were pulled back to her Hannya collection. It was scheduled to debut in six weeks and there was still so much to do.

This concept hadn't quite taken off as Nagiko had hoped. Parco had pulled back from staging an event, and Kodansha had turned down the idea of a Hannya-themed art book. Weeks ago she had written the head priest of the Hannya-ji temple in Nara proposing a large donation from Kiji in exchange for staging a fashion show on the temple grounds. Hannya at Hannya-ji…Finally today she received his polite rebuff. Well, one less thing to manage, Nagiko thought, trying not to be discouraged.

Mayumi had been modeling in France for over a year. Frédérique had been right—she had the look. After her first modeling job, which featured only her right ear bearing an emerald pendeloque, Mayumi got assignments for hair, makeup, and lingerie ads. Then there was a runway show, then a mail-order catalog, then a TV spot. In the spring she modeled one outfit on the catwalk for Eymeric Francois's *Fleurs du Mal* collection. After that, she had more offers than she could handle. She was known professionally simply as MAYUMI, no last name necessary. The Japanese fashion magazine *Non-no* wanted her for the October special wedding issue.

Mayumi burrowed into Paris life. She walked everywhere in the city, honing her observations of people, of fashion, of style. She was a genius of the eclectic mode. She treated the shops of Paris as her palette and the outfits she created from them were her masterpieces. Fairly quickly Mayumi discovered that modeling was not so interesting, because then she simply became the canvas for someone else's concept. Her thoughts kept returning to the idea of having her own shop. She had been desperate to get away from Japan, but now she was beginning to feel she could go back.

Despite the fact that she reveled in being a bad girl in Tokyo, Mayumi never failed to be surprised at the relentless brusqueness of Parisians. She missed being able to stand at a bookstore for as long as she liked, browsing through a bestseller. You couldn't do that in Paris. Or, as in Japan, sit in a café for hours on end, nursing a single espresso without a waitress giving you a dirty look. Then, too, you always had to be on your guard for pickpockets. Mayumi had enough experience not to be taken in, but she had seen the way the little gypsy children flocked to Japanese tourists like pigeons to crumbs.

Another thing she noticed about shopping in Paris was the paper bags. Even the nicest boutique would stuff your purchase in a nondescript shopping bag. She thought of her mother's signature bags for Kiji. Maybe she should open a Japanese-themed boutique in Paris…no, that would bring her into her mother's orbit, inevitably. Forget that. A year ago, she might have had to use the Kiyowara name to get financial backing, but now her own image as MAYUMI would do the trick. She had her finger on the pulse of international fashion. With a foot in both worlds, she knew how to present it to the Japanese market. The French Mayumi shook her head at the herd mentality of Japanese teens. The Japanese Mayumi was surprised at how French girls, otherwise dressed to the teeth, often ignored their shoes.

Mayumi knew that young Japanese girls aspired to cutting edge fashion, but they lacked confidence. She recalled her high school friends. Each one had chosen a look, painstakingly re-creating it every time she got dressed. But not one of them could come up with something original. That's what her shop would be—a kaleidoscope of originals. Mayumi sketched out ideas in her imagination. She would pull the elements together, give them the imprimatur of MAYUMI taste, and offer them for sale. She discussed her plan with Frédérique, who reminded her of a conversation they once had.

"Don't you remember? You wanted to call the shop Piggy—or Froggy, or something?" Frédérique teased her.

Mayumi blinked her heavily mascara'd eyelids.

"You're right! I had totally forgotten…"

"You should call it MayumiMode," said Frédérique.

In September, Mayumi was walking down the Rue de Rivoli, when she glanced at the window display in Mouchou Monde, the only store in Paris that carried her mother's collections. Hannya? This was the new Kiji line? She couldn't bring herself to go in, but she examined the dark outfits in the window. Her mother really had gone off the deep end with this Buddhist stuff. Who would wear these things? But later that afternoon, in the Old Marais district, she saw a girl wearing one of the Hannya t-shirts.

By October, it was clear to Nagiko that Hannya had been a mistake. Even her core clientele had, for the most part, taken a pass on adding to their wardrobes from the Hannya line. The only item that was in demand was the promotional t-shirt. Nagiko was bewildered. She had never suffered such artistic rejection. People at the Kiji office tiptoed around her. Conversations trailed off when she approached. Alone at her desk, she found herself browsing the bookmarked website that listed *hibutsu* all over the country, before she caught herself. Wasn't this obsession precisely what had led to the disastrous Hannya collection? Nagiko closed the *hibutsu* window and opened her e-mail program. Ten messages, one from Frédérique. Nagiko's only news of Mayumi was through Frédérique. It seemed she was doing quite all right for herself with this modeling. Occasionally it was embarrassing to have a client congratulate her on Mayumi's behalf.

Just today the young woman who managed Kiji's Roppongi branch had said something about Mayumi and the current issue of *Non-no*. Nagiko had to pretend to know about it, but it made her angry that she had been totally in the dark. She stopped at a kiosk in the subway station to look for the issue. It took a moment to sink in. *Non-no*. The special wedding edition. There on the cover was Mayumi, radiant in a strapless white wedding gown, a bouquet of orchids and stephanotis trailing from her hand. Nagiko's hand shook as she paid for the magazine. From deep inside she felt an upwelling of rage.

The New Year

TOKUDA STAYED UP ALL New Year's eve. There was the ceremony, starting at midnight, of striking the temple bell 108 times. Fudō-in remained open till dawn for those who wished to watch the first sunrise of the new year. Tokuda had joined the crowd slurping up "year spanning" noodles for good luck, as they gathered to view the glowing red orb through the wreaths of mist over Sagami Bay. In the past, this auspicious and sacred time made him edgy. Would he be able to continue his mission for yet another year? How many *hibutsu* might he lose? But this morning his heart was at peace. It swelled with the beauty of the first sunrise that looked exactly like those paintings on the hanging scrolls people put in their alcoves for New Year's Day.

Tokuda felt expansive, hopeful, and quietly satisfied. Looking around at the crowd bundled in their mittens and scarves, he saw families with sleepy children, old people, and teenagers. He smiled to himself knowing that they were ignorant of what he had done for their sakes. The sun peeked over the horizon, rose in the sky, and the yawning crowd dispersed. Tokuda yawned himself. Some people would come to visit ancestral graves or *mizuko* today, but not many. He had his first hot bath of the year, then took a little nap. As far as he was concerned, it was going to be a peaceful year, maybe even with a little bit of happiness for all.

There were five hidden buddhas left. During the filming of the documentary, Priest Kon had managed to deactivate half of the last ten that Tokuda had been monitoring. But these remaining five were now safe.

Nagiko Kiyowara did not watch the sun rise on New Year's Day. She'd been up late New Year's Eve, pretending social cheerfulness. Kiji's last few seasons had been terrible. Nagiko knew she was to blame. Far from rubbing her nose in the failure of Hannya, her clients tried to tell her she was ahead of her time—that people didn't understand her vision. Nagiko smiled wanly, appreciating their intentions, but never for a moment believing them. The honorable thing would be to resign. Mr. Satō, director of Kiji Enterprises, refused to countenance it. He told her that if she needed a break from Kiji, she should take it. Go visit her daughter in Paris for a year, or New York. Do something completely different. Come back refreshed, with new creative insights. She had been working too hard.

Nagiko felt that was what Hannya had been all about—a new creative insight. It had failed spectacularly. Publicly she had put a positive spin on Mayumi's leaving. But maybe a leave of absence from Kiji would be a good thing. Nagiko was doubtful, but she said she'd consider it. She also considered throwing herself under a subway train.

She missed Jun. But when she thought about him, eventually those thoughts led to Mayumi. Mayumi was the dark center, like a live coal covered in ash, at the core of her being. The more Nagiko tried to force herself not to dwell on Mayumi, the hotter the coal glowed. She had dreams of an amorphous watery embryo growing and changing into a child, into a snake, into a beautiful woman, into a demon. Nagiko wanted more than anything else to be free of it. She had enough presence of mind to realize that she might be having a mental breakdown. Perhaps she needed a psychiatrist? Certainly a Western-trained analyst would scorn the notion of a *mizuko* being the root of her problems. A psychiatrist would assume the *mizuko* represented a symbolic accretion of neuroses. She knew that Parisians popped anti-depressants with the equanimity of nibbling *pommes frites*. Maybe she should try to cadge some black market Prozac?

Nagiko sighed. Maybe she should just go away for a while. But where? She recalled how Jun kept returning to the Shikoku pilgrimage when the pressures on him became too intense. Perhaps this was the key to his sanity? He had certainly beat a hasty retreat to the pilgrimage after his seduction by Mayumi—and it seemed to make him able to live with himself, Nagiko thought, not without bitterness. But maybe she should try it, on her own. Philip had done it. He'd talked about what a great psychological change the journey had wrought in him as well. At least she could use the opportunity to sort out her thoughts.

She told Mr. Satō and her colleagues that she planned to take a leave of absence beginning in May. She was vague as to what precisely she planned to do while she was away. "Travel, probably…" she had said.

Priest Tokuda had cut back his travel schedule since the fugu incident. There was no longer any need to run uneasily from temple to temple like a nervous hen. Except for Seiryōji, which reminded him too much of Priest Kon, he visited the other temples at his leisure, knowing there was no longer any need to scrutinize visitors on the days the hidden buddhas were shown. Now, just for his own pleasure, he stopped to enjoy the Yoshino cherries blooming in the hills of Nara, and he took time to appreciate the rhododendrons at Murōji. In July, instead of running off to Shikoku, he stayed in Kamakura, quietly helping celebrate O-bon at Fudō-in. And when the documentary aired, and nothing happened, he exhaled the dregs of his remaining trepidation.

Nagiko had not set foot inside Kiji for six months. If anything, she felt worse now than when she left. Time, that precious fourth dimension that usually was stretched so thin, now threatened to suffocate her. She had clicked through the websites of the 88 temples on Shikoku, trying to decide what to do. She considered a bus tour for pilgrims, but decided against it. Who knew what sort of people she would be thrown in with? Finally she picked a taxi service that drove between temples and included inn reservations. She dressed the part, in white pants, white jacket and headband. She bought the staff, *mala*-beads, and straw hat online. Also a pair of white running shoes. Doing the circuit this way, she seldom ran into the same group of pilgrims twice. It was a lonely trek. Most of the others on the pilgrimage were in groups. But she pushed on, getting her booklet stamped at each temple along the way. She returned to Tokyo exhausted and disillusioned.

While she was away, Nagiko's team at Kiji had pulled together a collection of favorites from various past lines. Kiji Classic it was called, and was doing quite well. It even contained two items from Hannya. The off-white dress of shredded strips, which had belatedly proved popular, was one. The other was the demon-logo t-shirt, which had become something of a cult among teenagers. Nagiko dropped by the office. People seemed glad to see her. Their concern was gratifying, but Nagiko was painfully conscious of the fact that she had no new ideas. She also noted how the company ran perfectly well in her absence. That was not so gratifying.

"By the way, congratulations on Mayumi's new shop in Kyoto." Nagiko's assistant came up to her. She naturally assumed Nagiko had been there for the opening. She gushed about her website, www.MayumiMode.com.

"Oh," said Nagiko. "No…unfortunately…I was abroad then…" she lied.

She felt like she had been punched in the stomach. So Mayumi was back in Japan. Under the ashes of Nagiko's heart the hot coal of resentment stirred to life again. The pilgrimage had not extinguished it at all.

Could it be coincidence that her own descent into failure, depression, and loneliness exactly paralleled Mayumi's rise in the world? Now more than ever it seemed to Nagiko that the *mizuko* had grown into a beautiful demon at her expense, by stealing her creativity and success. She was a husk, sucked dry. People asked when she would be coming back to the office. She worked hard to appear noncommittal. Soon, probably. Maybe. She had a few more things she wanted to do before coming back. She excused herself and fled.

Back at her apartment she looked at Mayumi's website. There was a blog where she talked about her favorite cafés in Paris, her pet dachshund named Freddo, her modeling career. There were clothes and accessories one could acquire at her shop or online. Or, you could buy a whole Mayumi-coordinated outfit, top to bottom. There was even a Mayumi *eau de cologne*. She had totally branded herself. Grudgingly, Nagiko marveled at the display of business acumen. Who was behind her? It must be Frédérique. Again, she felt betrayed.

Tokuda took a trip to visit Shikoku's eleven-faced Guan Yin at Shidōji in September. A display of hand-cultivated chrysanthemums in pots was set up in the temple courtyard, tended by elderly men wielding bonsai clippers. Spider mums rested on metal collars. All lateral buds pruned away, the energy of each plant had been trained into a single magnificent bloom. Tokuda especially liked the plants with smaller blossoms that had been clipped and shaped since spring to bloom all at once in a graceful, draping train.

The old men acknowledged Tokuda's interest as he strolled past them on his way to the central building. Tokuda was thankful that Priest Kon had never done the 88-temple pilgrimage—he said he regretted not having done it, he planned to do it, but he hadn't. Tokuda's plan was to just go sit quietly in the main hall, listen for the *hibutsu's* peaceful hum, then come back and talk to the old men about their special chrysanthemums. For some reason, this was a hobby that appealed more to men than women. Tokuda could even see himself raising chrysanthemums someday.

He bowed deeply before entering the hall. Even here he should have been able to sense a faint vibration as he approached. Perhaps his mind was distracted by the flowers. He took a deep breath and focused. The chrysanthemums receded, as did the murmur of people in the courtyard. Tokuda's eyes adjusted to the dim light. He felt the drop in temperature as he stepped in from the sun-warmed steps to the cool interior. He smelled the familiar temple smell of years of incense smoke permeating the wood and tatami.

But he felt nothing.

Then, a sickening sense of dread rose up through his gut, engulfing him. This was not possible! He didn't move. People wandered in and out, glancing briefly at the priest who seemed lost in meditation, head bowed. It looked like he had fallen asleep. They smiled.

Inside his unmoving body, awareness strained to breaking, Tokuda's mind raced. Maybe it was an aftereffect of the fugu poison on his nervous system? Had he noticed any difficulty with the other *hibutsu*? He was grasping at straws now. He drew on his long-honed powers of concentration to quell the panic clawing at the edges of his mind. This *hibutsu couldn't* be dead! Kon was dead. Kon hadn't been here.

Suddenly he re-experienced the same nauseating feeling of his mind shattering into the cracked shards of the Diamond Mandala as he had while lying next to the dying priest Kon. Had he saved the world or simply murdered an innocent man? His patron icon, Fudō the immovable, with whom he had always identified as the defender of the faith, rose up before him. The fierce blue face, the fangs, the club raised against enemies of true understanding—was this he himself, or was he now the object of his wrath?

Tokuda had been so sure. He was the bearer of the secret tradition. His revelation had been that he must preserve the hidden buddhas at all costs. He had made a terrible mistake. He felt the fury of Fudō shaking and stamping him, and he could do nothing but succumb. Yet, through another shard, he saw himself standing firm. He still held the responsibility...*he* was Fudō. The evil force relentlessly snuffing out the *hibutsu* was still out there. He could not lose sight of that. His mission had been set back, but he must not be deterred.

A pair of casual visitors saw the quivering priest off to the side of the main altar, and, exchanging furtive glances, did not linger.

In October, Mr. Satō, the chairman of Kiji Enterprises, and his wife invited

Nagiko to an outdoor performance of bonfire Noh at the Kamakura Shrine. The chairman knew about Nagiko's interest in Noh, and was hoping to use this occasion to convince her to come back to work. The program was the play *Miidera*, a famous example of the "person-gone-mad" genre. Nagiko let herself be talked into it. She had never seen this play performed. In any case, it would be rude to decline Mr. Satō's invitation

Nagiko hadn't been back to Kamakura in years. She was reminded of the priest, Tokuda, whom she'd seen during the filming at Denkōji. She'd run outside wearing kimono, trying to catch him that day, but he had disappeared. Her memory was clouded by the catastrophic events that came after. Yet, when she now thought about going to Kamakura, it was Tokuda's face that floated into her mind, and she realized she still wanted to see him.

From the train window she saw persimmon trees at the edges of embankments, bare black branches hung with deep orange orbs. The maples had just begun to turn. Clumps of pampas grass waved silver fronds in the breeze. As soon as you got outside of Tokyo, autumn was beautiful. Nagiko felt her spirits lifting a little.

She hadn't known there was a temple fair at Fudō-in today. Booths full of knickknacks lined the street up to the main gate, and the odor of charcoal-grilled squid wafted through the air. Nagiko slipped through the crowds. Perhaps this had not been a great idea. But once inside the temple grounds she was glad she had come. A hedge of golden osmanthus filled the air with a sweet gardenia-like scent, and the lower garden was resplendent with purple lespedeza. Toad lilies and lycoris clustered at the side of the pond.

Where would she find Tokuda, she wondered? She probably ought to have called first. Slowly she crunched through the graveled courtyard and into the office adjacent to the hall housing the giant Guan Yin. Three young priests were on duty. Nagiko asked one of them if Priest Tokuda was available.

"Tokuda? He's in seclusion. Has been for a while."

Nagiko looked stricken.

The young priest hesitated. "Does he expect you?"

"Ah…yes. Yes he does…" It slipped out before she could stop herself.

"Well, then. I'll see if I can find him," he said, standing up. "Please wait here. Excuse me—who shall I say…?"

Nagiko told him her name. While she was waiting she looked at the information posted on a bulletin board for those who came seeking requiems for their *mizuko*. The temple continued to do a good business in water children, it seemed. Now there was a limit to the time your Jizō would be allowed to stand in the cemetery. After two years, the effigy would be ceremonially "disposed of" the pamphlet stated. Nagiko was lost in thought when she heard a voice behind her.

"Kiyowara-san?"

She turned. It was Tokuda, although she hardly recognized him. He was gaunt. The lines of his face were deeply etched, and his striking eyebrows contained some white hairs. Nagiko was keenly aware of how she must appear to him as well. She had thrown a patchwork cloak from the Hannya collection over a rather severe tailored gray dress. Had she remembered to put on makeup? She rubbed her finger furtively along her cheek to make sure.

"I was told you asked for me," he said.

Nagiko lowered her eyes, aware of the curious looks from the young priests behind the counter. "I know it's terribly presumptuous, but I wonder if there's someplace we could talk..." she said in a low tone.

"Of course..." Tokuda bowed slightly and indicated that she should follow. He led the way past the bell platform, down the stone steps. Neither of them spoke until, passing the Jizō section, Tokuda slowed his steps and turned his head,

"How many years has it been?" he asked softly.

"She's twenty now," Nagiko replied.

"An adult. Hard to imagine, isn't it?"

"Strange indeed."

"Is she well?"

"She seems to have made a success of things."

Under the conventional parental modesty, Tokuda heard a weary diffidence. Nagiko mentioned that she was going to see that evening's Noh performance at the Kamakura Shrine. Tokuda was familiar with the Noh repertoire so asked the name of the play. *Miidera*—she told him. The story of a woman deranged by the loss of her child.

They continued all the way down to the foot of the mountain, where Tokuda turned down a narrow path alongside the main worship hall. The path opened onto a small private building with a little garden. He slid the wooden door aside and Nagiko followed him in. Tokuda sat down opposite her, hands stiffly resting on his knees. Three weeks earlier, on Shikoku, he had discovered with horror that the hidden buddhas were continuing to lose their power. One by one. After rushing to check the other four, he had wearily returned to Kamakura.

That was last week. Whatever was draining them had worked fast. There was now but a single remaining *hibutsu* left untouched. It was displayed annually, for one day in January. Technically, he didn't have to worry about it until then, but Tokuda's nerves were taut. He had been fasting and meditating in an attempt to see his way from this point. Kiyowara-san's visit pulled him back to the world of human concerns.

He looked closely at her now. He saw a tight-lipped, once-beautiful woman, whose eyes radiated suffering. Tokuda winced. He remembered the first time they had met. She had been in a fragile state then, but nothing compared to the psychological pain that confronted him now. For this moment, at least, he was distracted from his obsessive concentration on the hidden buddhas.

"Do you remember," Nagiko asked him slowly, "that once I asked you about the theology of the *mizuko*?"

Tokuda did. Kiyowara-san was unusual in asking. Most people didn't want to know. He nodded, "Yes," he said. "And didn't we talk about reincarnation?"

"Yes, but...the *mizuko*..." Nagiko was determined to put this in front of him.

Tokuda recalled his own counsel—even if karma was the fate we were born with, we still had to create our own reality by our own moral choices.

"I probably told you that there is much we don't know about the *mizuko*. And as to whether your—now grown-up—child was that *mizuko* you solaced here...that was impossible to say. But you said she has made a successful life for herself..."

Nagiko laughed bitterly. "Successful. Yes. But..." She had never before given voice to her true thoughts about this resentment that was eating away at her sanity. "Do you believe in possessing spirits, Priest Tokuda?"

"Spirit possession?" He wondered where Nagiko was leading.

"Like an incubus—a force that can suck the life out of another..."

This was precisely what Tokuda had been fixating on. "I think that can happen, yes..." he responded warily.

"Well, my daughter—the *mizuko*—is such a force."

But Tokuda, of course, had been only thinking about the *hibutsu*, so he was taken aback.

"The *mizuko?*" he asked.

Nagiko's carefully constructed façade crumbled.

"What is happening to me?" she gasped. "I feel like my life energy is sucked away by her. It's always been like this. Even when she was a *mizuko*. That's when it all started." She clenched her hands. "I don't understand…my life is in shambles. There was a time when visiting temples made me feel better—you know, I started going to temples to see *hibutsu* a long time ago—because I was thinking of Philip. But now, I don't know. It doesn't do any good. Nothing does. I went on the Shikoku pilgrimage this year, and it didn't help at all…"

Of this jumbled confession, what Tokuda heard was "*hibutsu*" and "Shikoku pilgrimage."

"You went on the 88-temple pilgrimage?" he repeated. "When?"

"This past summer. June and July."

"The entire circuit?"

"Yes…"

"Did you get to temple 86—Shidōji?"

"As luck would have it," Nagiko said, "the day I happened to be there was the morning of the day their *hibutsu* was on display…"

Tokuda felt a vast chasm opening up before him.

"And before that…you had visited other temples with hidden buddhas?"

"Yes. Since Philip's…accident. It became something of a hobby." Nagiko stopped twisting the handles of her purse. "I think it actually turned into an obsession," she said. "I don't suppose you pay much attention to fashion, or things like that, but my last collection was inspired by my visits to these temples…it was called Hannya…" She lifted the edge of her cape.

Tokuda indeed was unaware.

"Did you visit…Kanshinji?" he managed. "Seiryōji? Denkōji?"

Nagiko was slightly taken aback. "Yes," she said. "All of those."

"Ōkannonji in Tokyo? Hōryūji—The Hall of Dreams?" He was not conscious of the fact that his voice had grown louder.

"Ah. Um…yes…" Nagiko said, bewildered at the look that had come into the priest's eye. "I've been to those, too…"

Tokuda felt like shrieking. Again, it was as if the world had splintered into different realities. His mistake…his terrible, terrible mistake. It wasn't Kon. He knew that now. A new shard glimmered into his awareness. Could it instead have been this woman who had hovered at the edge of his life for twenty-five years? Where had she been, which *hibutsu* had she seen? Her connection to Metcalfe was vibrating in his mind.

And, if this suspicion was correct, then what should he do? He recalled, too, that long ago she had asked him about reincarnation. She had wanted to know how it worked. Was it possible? And she had wanted to know because she had had intimations, echoes of former lives…

It all clicked. Suddenly Tokuda remembered. He *had* seen her at Kanshinji, hurrying down the stone steps right at the time when his eye had been set on Kon. What an idiot he was! Idiot! Idiot! Blundering singlemindedly down a trail, assuming he had the answer. And making such a terrible mess of it. His head was in his hands now. He looked up to see her, drawn back, eyeing him with concern. But then,

"Are you all right?" she asked. She put her hand out and touched his arm.

A human touch. Tokuda had not experienced that in he couldn't remember how long.

"Why am I so drawn to these hidden buddhas?" Nagiko suddenly asked him, a note of desperation in her voice.

Tokuda now thought he knew.

Ever since his visit to Shidōji, Tokuda had been living in a revolving kaleidoscope in which terror, sense of duty, and self-doubt churned in contorted patterns. He was exhausted from the mental effort of keeping his bearings among the shifting mirrors. But at this moment, the perception of Nagiko's hand on his arm was warm. This simple expression of human concern melted through the deep shame that had gripped Tokuda's heart in icy humiliation. He had murdered in order to prevent even greater, terrible destruction. His motive was only that—to save the world. He had gone against all his principles for the sake of a greater act of mercy.

He had been a fool, but he was not evil. The sickening proliferation of different realities shifting in and out of his awareness now came into focus. He felt suddenly stabilized, as if recovering from an attack of vertigo. His sense of reason and intuition started functioning again as he regarded the woman sitting across the narrow table. She was the one. Nagiko Kiyowara—albeit unconsciously—held the power to destroy the hidden buddhas. Indeed, had been unwittingly asphyxiating their protective auras for years—centuries, even.

It was his duty to prevent her from coming in contact with a *hibutsu* again. But he would not use violence to stop her. That had been his mistake last time. He would use the truth. And perhaps that would alleviate her distress as well. Life entailed pain, there was no escaping that fact. Suffering, however, was optional. That was the heart of what the Buddha taught. By understanding the truth, suffering could be overcome.

Tokuda lifted Nagiko's hand and held it in both his own, tenderly, as if it were a bird with a broken wing. He looked into her tea-colored eyes. "You are drawn to the hidden buddhas for a dreadful reason," he said simply.

"Dreadful…?"

He saw the micro-movement of her eyes. She would not expect this, of course. She was consumed with the problem of a wayward daughter, and then, Tokuda assumed, her age was probably a factor as well. Beautiful women must find it difficult when their looks begin to go. She would not be aware of the deeper karmic energy that had been pushing her to seek out the hidden buddhas.

"Long ago," he began, "Kūkai saw that the world was rapidly falling into decline, and that it was even in danger of collapsing. But he did not believe the time was ripe. He fought ignorance by preaching the Buddhist law and performing ritual ceremonies for the emperor. He engineered irrigation ponds and public works for the common people. He instructed disciples in the secret teachings. But he did something else as well. He set up a number of hidden buddhas in various temples across the land. These images contained the power to slow the pace of *mappō*."

Confused, Nagiko withdrew her hand. "I don't understand what this has to do with me…"

"No. I'm sure you don't," Tokuda looked at her with pity. "I'm quite sure you don't. But please listen."

Nagiko was trembling now. She had revealed the unsavory secret of her misery—her bitter revulsion against her own daughter—and now felt as if her innermost being was exposed like a raw wound. She half expected that the priest would be repulsed, tell her she should pray for compassion to enter her dark heart. But she held onto the slip of a possibility that he just might comprehend and finger the real culprit, the *mizuko*. Give her a special prayer or something to dispel its grip on her life energy. Or, at least, help her understand it. If anyone would be able to recognize the reality of this succubus, it would not be a psychiatrist, it would be a priest—this priest. This is why she had come. She tried to concentrate on what he was saying. Perhaps all this talk of Kūkai was leading up to something—a solution for her.

Tokuda, meanwhile, wanted to make sure what he was going to say would be comprehensible. "Do you know what *mappō* is?" He had better start with the basics.

"*Mappō?*" Nagiko blinked. "The chaos the world endures before it ends? The last age of the Buddha's law?"

"You are quite educated in these things…" Tokuda smiled sadly.

Nagiko smiled back uncertainly.

"There have been many times throughout history when people have thought we were in the age of *mappō*. But so far, human beings have managed somehow to muddle along. The reason is…that we have been protected by the power of Kūkai's hidden buddhas."

"I'm really very ignorant," Nagiko responded. "I had no idea about that."

"No, of course not. No one does. Well, that's not completely true—your fiancé Metcalfe knew about it."

Nagiko's head jerked to the side. "Philip?"

"Yes. He and his professor. It was quite amazing, really, how they figured it out. It's a secret tradition, after all—the most deeply kept secret. And it goes straight back to Kōbō Daishi himself."

Nagiko was trying to digest this information. But she *had* heard it before—"You mean, what he said in that documentary?" She bit her lip. "That was Philip's professor, wasn't it? But how do you…?"

"How do I know this is true? I am the current holder of the line."

He said it so simply and straightforwardly that Nagiko was unsure whether she understood. If there was a centuries-old secret transmission, one wouldn't just reveal it over a cup of tea.

"Why are you telling me this?" Nagiko felt a sudden chill, and wrapped her cloak closer.

"Because I need your help."

She didn't know how to respond. Tokuda pushed on.

"Over the years, something has been sucking the power away from these hidden buddhas. As long as even one of them retains its protective aura, the world will not slide into the final throes of *mappō*. But matters have become quite worrisome recently."

"How many hidden buddhas are there…with this power?" Nagiko asked cautiously.

Tokuda gulped and took the plunge.

"There is only one now," he said.

"Nagiko's eyebrows went up. "But there are hundreds of *hibutsu*," she protested. "I've looked them up online."

Tokuda winced. The World Wide Web had done the hidden buddhas no favor.

"The temple priests have no idea," he said. "As far as they are concerned, it's just hoary tradition. Say a temple has a *hibutsu*—the head priest of that temple has the right to uphold the practice or change it as he sees fit. Some of them even permit their *hibutsu* to leave the temple, to be put under lights at museum exhibits. Others have decided to open them permanently to public view—maybe they forbid the taking of pictures as a nod to tradition, but that doesn't mean anything. Many *hibutsu* were rendered powerless centuries ago. The priests have no idea what they are really about. No one has any idea. The secret was so well kept, and so few have the ability to sense it. Your Metcalfe, had it, by the way—the ability."

Nagiko was listening closely now. She wanted to hear more about Philip.

"We were planning to join forces," Tokuda continued. "Metcalfe and I. Maybe his professor too. We were going to protect the remaining *hibutsu* from this force (he almost said evil force, but stopped himself) that has been extinguishing them." Now he looked directly up at Nagiko. "I can't tell you how devastated I was. I waited months for him to contact me. Of course, I hadn't known—until I saw you and the child that day—what had happened…"

Nagiko felt tears welling up, spilling over her lower eyelids.

Tokuda looked around for tissues, but there were none. She was digging, fruitlessly, in her purse. He took a large white handkerchief out of the sleeve of his robes, and held it out.

Wiping her blurry eyes with one wrist, Nagiko reached out and grasped

Tokuda's hand. "Does this have something to do with his accident?" she asked.

How could he answer that? This was a distraction, in any case. He wanted to get past Metcalfe to what he needed to tell her.

Tokuda began to have second thoughts about his plan. He could see that Kiyowara-san was entirely focused on her personal pain and loss. What would she do if he gave her the knowledge of the power she unknowingly held? He felt a flutter of doubt whether she would be able to deal with the truth. But there were different levels of truth. Even the Buddha preached "expedient truth" according to the ability of his listeners to comprehend… He must persist. She appeared frozen now, gripping his handkerchief and his hand in it.

Tokuda moved the handkerchief to her face. She relaxed her grip as he drew it slowly across her cheeks, over her closed eyes. Then he took both her hands in his.

"I'm going to tell you something important," he said. "You must listen to me. When the last remaining *hibutsu* has been stripped of its aura, then there will be nothing to prevent the process of *mappō* from reaching its conclusion."

"What is the conclusion of *mappō*?" Nagiko whispered.

"The world ends. Or, I should say, 'this' world ends. There are to be more worlds—better ones, perhaps. Miroku, the Buddha of the future, is supposed to be waiting."

"The world ends…" Nagiko repeated.

"The signs of *mappō* have been getting stronger," Tokuda continued. "The carnage of war, the degradation of the environment…in the twentieth century more *hibutsu* have lost their power than in any time before. The connection is obvious when you look." He paused. "But I think I know the instigator—the immediate cause, you could say."

He held her hands firmly now. "I have reason to think whatever is destroying the hidden buddhas is incarnated in you yourself…"

Nagiko's eyes flew open, and she tried to pull away.

Tokuda attempted to calm her. "This is not something conscious on your part. I'm not saying that you are an evil force." He let go of her wrists. "There has always been a kind of tension in the world, a pulling away from the law of the buddha—a pull away from order to chaos. Whether we should call it 'evil' or not, I can't even say."

She had turned away from him, but now twisted her head back.

"But this force exists," Tokuda said quietly, "and at this moment in time, it appears that it lives in you."

She went slack. "And it has nothing to do with the *mizuko*?"

"I don't think so, no. Unless, perhaps, indirectly. But I'm quite sure the hidden buddhas lie at the heart of your suffering."

"If this is true," Nagiko said, breathing deeply, "then what can I do about it?"

Gingerly, Tokuda put his hands on the table to keep them from quivering.

"You can stop viewing hidden buddhas," he said quietly.

"And will that give me my life back?" Nagiko asked.

Tokuda didn't know, but "Yes," he said. "You will begin to feel better, I'm sure."

Nagiko turned her face away from him now and took a small mirror out her purse. She dabbed at the muddy traces of mascara under her eyes. "Excuse me," she said. "Is there a bathroom here?"

Tokuda stood up, somewhat unsteadily, and showed her where it was. He had taken no solid food for forty-eight hours. He would need to eat something soon. While she was out of the room he made a small pot of *hōjicha* from a thermos of hot water, and poured two cups. He sat back on the low sofa, and gazed at the featherfan maple in the corner of the garden. Its wide paw-like leaves were fading from orange to yellow. Nothing had changed, but things appeared different in the late afternoon light. Nagiko came back in the room, composed now, face smooth, faintly fragrant with perfume, and a light gloss of lipstick. She accepted the teacup he offered.

"So," she said, pinching her fingers to swab the pale smear of color from its rim, "what is this last *hibutsu* that I must never see?"

Tokuda was afraid she would ask him this, but he had made his decision.

"It's at Miidera, in Ōmi."

"Really? Miidera? Well then," said Nagiko, putting down the teacup. "I've already been to Miidera, so you must be mistaken about me..." With her hair combed, make-up fresh, the conversation they had just had seemed surreal.

And her comment threw Tokuda as well.

"But what did you see? When were you there?" he asked.

"Let me think. I was there in…must have been five or six years ago in the spring. I remember the cherry blossoms. And I saw…" Nagiko tried to remember, "…a thousand-arm Guan Yin statue. Yes, and I think also a Fudō guardian—and an Aizen guardian, might it have been?"

Tokuda was, if not exactly relieved, at least confirmed.

"Those images are all in the main buildings," he said. "But in the Hall of the Virtuous Guardians? Did you see the Kariteimo image?"

"Kariteimo? I've never even heard of that one," Nagiko said.

"That's it."

"That statue is the last hidden buddha?"

Tokuda nodded. "It's a lovely statue of a mother holding an infant."

"Who is Kariteimo?" Nagiko asked.

"Now she's a protector of mothers and children, but originally she was a demon," Tokuda said. "Many Hindu deities were absorbed into Buddhism early on. According to legend she bore a thousand babies and killed them all—except for the last one. The last one, she loved more than anything. But then she started hunting human children, stealing them away at night to eat their flesh and drink their blood. Finally Sakyamuni Buddha hid her beloved one away under an iron bowl. The demon, crazed with grief, wandered the world searching for him. She came to the Buddha to ask the child's whereabouts. And the Buddha used her grief to open her understanding to the righteous path."

"And she stopped killing children, presumably?"

"She became enlightened. Her love for her last child opened her heart into compassion for all mothers, all children. So that's how she is worshipped now."

"Why have I never heard of her?" Nagiko asked.

"She's not well-known. If they've heard of her at all, people think of

Kariteimo as simply another avatar of Guan Yin. It's only the older sects like Shingon and Tendai that preserve her identity."

"And when is this Kariteimo on display?" Nagiko asked. "So I'll be sure not to go?"

Tokuda took a deep breath. "The first week of May," he said.

Nagiko felt lightheaded as she left Fudō-in. She wondered if she could sit through a Noh performance, even one by firelight. The knowledge Tokuda had thrust upon her was like a torch inside her chest. It completely subsumed the bitter coal of Mayumi. She hardly knew what to think. She, Nagiko Kiyowara, had been undoing Kūkai's protective mantras over the course of many reincarnations. What would chairman Satō think? Or his wife? They would be chatting before the play and Nagiko could casually mention that, oh, by the way, she had the power to bring the world to an end. She smiled, in spite of herself. It was so preposterous.

She looked around now at the people who passed her on the street. What would that businessman think? Or that housewife? Or that college student wearing a fashionably scrunched knit cap? The priest had told her to call if she needed to see him for whatever reason, but now that she was out of his presence, Nagiko felt she had awoken from a bizarre dream. Priest Tokuda was more than a little bit around the bend, she concluded. He was obsessed. And that wild glint that came into his eye…this meeting had been emotionally unsettling, to say the least. No, she didn't imagine she would be calling him again.

But maybe he had a point—whether or not she had some unconscious supernatural power, maybe it *was* time to stop going to temples, visiting hidden buddhas. These short pilgrimages had started as a way to stay in touch with Philip and then metamorphosed into a hobby, and—face it—her own fixation. The *hibutsu* had not helped her shake the miasma of Mayumi, nor had their inspiration done her design work any good. Maybe it was just time to forget about them. Nagiko felt the cool October breeze on her face. She had left her patchwork cloak back at the temple, and now she was a little chilly.

Maybe she should do a spring collection to shake off the pall of Hannya? She mentioned this to Chairman Satō during the intermission. He encouraged her enthusiastically. She couldn't concentrate on the play as colors sifted through her mind. The new green of an onion sprout. The unfurling leaf of the coral maple, brilliantly chartreuse against red bark. Filmy fabrics. A crimson weft with a navy warp—shot with an occasional gold thread. Ruffles…ruffles? Why not? Or perhaps she should be thinking about designing for the fashion-conscious young men she noticed on the streets. They were all wearing hats this year. How had she not picked up on this before? It was as if the crisp evening breeze was blowing away gray veils, and the world was newly clear upon her sharpened senses.

The Miidera Bell

NAGIKO RETURNED TO KIJI. The rest of that fall and winter she plunged into plans for the spring line to be called *Haru Hanibii*. Her colleagues joked that the queen had come back to the hive. Mr. Satō liked what he saw in the "Spring Honeybee" collection. There was a velvet of cut-warp silk pile on silk weft that slipped through your fingers like liquid. It was so slippery it had to be hand sewn, but it was like wearing water. And there were items with ruffles. One of the dresses fluttered like a fritillary with every step, another was as layered as a full-blown rose. The collection was small, exquisite, and Nagiko's clients came flooding back.

Mr. Satō decided to launch a flurry of publicity for the line in March. He had an idea. He would ask Kiyowara-san's daughter Mayumi who'd been making such a name for herself modeling abroad, to do a photo session with the new collection. He looked at her website, www.MayumiMode.com. Her sensibility was edgier, more hip than Kiji, but it wasn't as if there was no connection. And it might be good to inject a little bit of sting into the honey-eyed ruffles of *Haru Hanibii*. He would arrange it as a surprise for Nagiko. Satō appreciated how she had been so modest about Mayumi over the years. One would have expected a bit of bragging, or nepotistic pushing—but, on the contrary, Kiyowara-san hardly ever mentioned her daughter. Well, now they could share the spotlight and that in itself would be a great publicity angle. A mother-daughter fashion dynasty.

Mayumi was floored to get a call from the head of Kiji Enterprises. She was even more shocked when she found out what he wanted.

"Is this my mother's idea?" she asked cautiously.

"Oh, no," replied Satō. "She doesn't know about it. I was thinking of surprising her."

Mayumi felt an unanticipated pinch of disappointment. Nothing had changed. Her mother would never collaborate with her on anything.

"Well, she'd be surprised all right," she said. "I suggest you talk it over with her first." She knew Nagiko would nix the idea out of hand.

"But…you'll do it, then?" Satō seemed to be oblivious to the tone of Mayumi's voice.

Could she do it anyway? Mayumi considered this. It would be great to get a cash infusion for her business. Getting started had cost more than she had expected. She would have to be clever about it though.

"Sure, I'll do it. You're the one who's hiring, right? The deal is between you and me, yes?"

Satō thought her very businesslike. She asked for more money than he expected, but he figured that he was dealing with an international model now. Trying to do this on the cheap would give the wrong impression.

Suddenly she knew how to make it work.

"Let's really make it a surprise," Mayumi suggested. "Let's do the whole photo shoot in secret and then amaze her with it."

Satō fell for it completely. The following week Mayumi came up to Tokyo. With the complicit help of Nagiko's assistant who smuggled samples out of the Kiji studio, Satō made arrangements for a full day photo shoot. Mayumi brought along her own makeup artist, an androgynous young man wearing silver drop earrings. She also had definite ideas about the poses she would strike. Sometimes she didn't even put the clothing on, but instead draped it provocatively over her body. Satō had not planned to stay the entire day, but he now rationalized being there to supervise. He could not take his eyes off Mayumi. In between poses, she seemed not to care that her nudity was carelessly on display. He imagined that this was how international models behaved. The photographer didn't bat an eyelash, nor did the makeup artist, who ducked in, between shots, to brush powder blush on Mayumi's naked breast. Satō had to keep wiping the droplets of sweat that kept appearing on his balding brow.

He offered to take Mayumi to dinner when they were finished filming, but she said she had to get straight back to Kyoto that evening. She gave him a disappointed face. Some other time. Then she kissed the air near both his cheeks in the French fashion, leaving him jelly-kneed in a *yuzu*-scented cloud of *Eau de Mayumi*.

The poster that was to go up on the subway billboards the following month showed a profile of Mayumi's face, eyes closed, tongue reaching out toward a ruffled riot of fabric petals. The title was brushed in grass-script style down her cheek. The Kiji logo looked as if it were a tattoo on her shoulder. Satō was pleased. He couldn't have explained the look he wanted, but as soon as he saw the poster he knew the vision had been captured. It was a perfect balance of sweetness, sophistication, and cool. He couldn't wait to see Nagiko's reaction.

MayumiMode was on Sanjō Avenue in Kyoto, two blocks south of the walls enclosing the imperial palace grounds. Fully a quarter of the narrow 400-square-foot store was taken up with a deep window display. Upstairs was a six-mat room, plus a 6-by-4 linoleum floored kitchen area. Mayumi had investigated renting in the Teramachi arcade, but the price of space there was simply prohibitive—plus she would have had to find living quarters separately. She decided that she didn't need the high traffic exposure to tourists in any case. Most of her business, she suspected, would be done online.

When she lived with Frédérique, Mayumi noticed how the French were comfortable living parsimoniously in private if that meant they could make a more lavish display in public. They knew their priorities on this score. Growing up, Mayumi had always been embarrassed by her mother's apartment in Kagurazaka. She considered private stinginess an unattractive Japanese trait, born of necessity perhaps, in a land where space itself was the biggest luxury. Yet, the French were the same way.

With Frédérique's encouragement Mayumi had come back to Japan not quite a year ago. MayumiMode Ltd. opened for business in June. Her best seller so far was the French costume jewelry she had brought back from Paris. In addition, she offered two different coordinated looks that she changed monthly. Thinking of the body like a paper doll, she mapped its regions into five parts—head, neck, torso, hips, and legs. With these five units, plus accessories, she made a grid of items to mix and match. Mayumi tried to include six items with each outfit, aiming to charge on average 80,000 yen for the ensemble. People could also buy individual elements, and she kept track of what was most popular.

A pair of mannequins named Mayu and Yumi wore the outfits of the month. They posed in the shop window, sitting or standing in a still-life tableau of Mayumi's devising. One month they appeared to be watching a tank of live angelfish. Another scene had them at a table drinking espressos. Attentive passersby would notice that the pastries on their plates changed daily, and that sometimes one or the other mannequin had crumbs on her face. When Mayumi obtained a long-haired miniature dachshund, she let him live in the window display, strewn with puppy toys, for a month.

Mayumi discovered she had a knack for running a business. She preferred creating the outfits and putting together the window displays to fiddling with finances, but she got a thrill out of making the numbers work too. The biggest ongoing headaches were finding suppliers and storing inventory. She hired a professional accountant and business manager, and ran through a series of fashionably bored young women to mind the store. If a lucrative modeling job came along, she took it—even if it meant flying to Paris for three days. She would use the opportunity to refresh her stock. She spent nothing on herself, and plowed everything back into MayumiMode Ltd.

Of course it helped that she was frequently taken out to fine restaurants by men with expensive taste who liked being seen in her company. Her own wardrobe was minimal—she mostly wore her stock, always trying out new combinations. Mayumi kept her private room above the shop spare. There was a bed, a table, a reading lamp. No one visited her there. It was her space, and then her and Freddo's space. Luckily the accountant was crazy about dachshunds and took care of Freddo when Mayumi was away. She kept one bookshelf of notebooks for her design ideas and ran her website off a Macintosh laptop. Tucked away in a tattered Dr. Slump comic book was the old Polaroid of her father, carefully wrapped in tissue paper along with his academic business card. Next to it was a leather envelope with the packet of her father's letters Bertrand Maigny had given her before she left France.

Frédérique had not pushed Nagiko about Mayumi's paternity. When her first inquiry was met evasively, she didn't pursue it. Not that Frédérique cared particularly, although she was curious. She assumed it had been a married man, probably French, probably high-placed, who had paid Nagiko off for the secrecy. She wondered if Mayumi herself knew. Frédérique had watched Mayumi blossom since coming to Paris. Although the poisonous maternal connection still lay buried and unresolved, Frédérique knew that she had done the right thing.

Even after a year together, Mayumi still managed to surprise Frédérique with her odd combination of French and Japanese sensibilities. The Japanese were very keen on official rules, Frédérique knew, unlike the French who tended to ignore the kinds of regulations posted to ensure orderly social conduct. Yet both French and Japanese clung like leeches to tradition—those unspoken but binding rules regarded as the nature of the universe. Yesterday afternoon Frédérique had seen Mayumi blithely park the Floride in an illegal space—"just for one minute…"—and then click her tongue after a woman walked by wearing Capri pants and stilettos. "That's so *wrong*," she had remarked to Frédérique.

"Mayumi, *ma chère*," Frédérique said, "I don't know whether you are French or Japanese sometimes." She suddenly realized this might be a casual opening wedge into the subject she had not broached. "Perhaps you are both?" she suggested. "Your father must be French, no?"

"French? My father?" Mayumi laughed. "No, he wasn't French. He was American."

"You know him then?" Frédérique tilted her head, amazed. "He is American?"

"Was. He's dead."

"Oh." Frédérique waited to see if she would volunteer anything else.

Mayumi had emptied a bouquet of mascara wands out of her purse, and was sorting through them.

"For some reason, my mother kept it all a secret—she's big on secrets, in case you hadn't noticed…" Mayumi tossed a stray hair over her shoulder. "But I managed to find out a little about him. His name—Philip Metcalfe. What he did—studied Buddhism at Columbia University."

She chose one mascara and dumped the rest back in her bag.

Now Frédérique looked over the tops of her reading glasses.

"Studied Buddhism? Did your father know Bertrand Maigny, then?"

"I don't know," said Mayumi looking up. "I never thought to ask the professor."

Frédérique put down the newspaper she had been reading. "I think I remember him mentioning something about a graduate student from Columbia he had been working with on the hidden buddhas thing. But he met with some sort of freak accident…Did your father die in an accident?"

Mayumi had squirreled the knowledge of her father's identity away, intending to investigate further. But then she had gotten swept up in Frédérique's documentary, and then left precipitously for France, and then her modeling career took off. The photograph and business card were among the few personal items she brought with her to Paris, happy enough just to have them as talismans. With those keys she could look for clues later, at her leisure. How did he die? When she had been around eight, she remembered her mother telling her, a) that her father was not Jun Muranaka and, b) that he was dead. Had she said how he died? Mayumi couldn't remember.

"I don't know that either," Mayumi said, furrowing her brow. "In fact I don't know much about him at all."

"Well, why don't you call Professeur Maigny before you go back to Japan?" Frédérique suggested. "At least find out if he knew him."

"B *point* Maigny *escargot* univ-brest *point* fr?" Mayumi needled Frédérique. "*Escargot*—that was so cute."

"Call him, silly, don't e-mail," said Frédérique.

Mayumi drove to Brest two days before she left France. Bertrand Maigny was overwhelmed with memories. He saw that Mayumi's eyes were Philip's eyes. An entire generation had gone by, he realized sadly. He told her what he remembered about Philip, and when she left, he gave her the folder of aerograms and letters young Metcalfe had sent him.

The ads for *Haru Hanibii* blossomed on Tokyo billboards the second week of March. Satō waited impatiently in his office for Nagiko to rush in, bursting with excitement. She would have seen something in that morning's paper, or possibly even on the subway. He could hardly contain himself. She called just before noon. He could tell from a slight quaver in her voice that she could barely contain her emotion. He was also called by several reporters who sensed a story behind this collaboration and wanted to interview the Kiyowaras, mother and daughter. *Synergy*, that's what it was, Sâto told himself. An editor from *Vogue Nippon* called to congratulate him on the superb photo layouts. They also loved Mayumi's website and were thinking of featuring it in May, along with her shop. What were her influences from her mother? How did they collaborate on "Spring Honeybee"? Were there plans for a joint collection? The publicity bubble glistened in Satō's mind. He wondered what Nagiko would think about formalizing some sort of relationship between Kiji and MayumiMode.

That morning Nagiko strolled into the Ogawa coffee shop where she usually had breakfast before heading to the office. She picked up a copy of the *Mainichi News* on her way in. Her eye caught the Kiji ad right as toast hovered halfway between plate and mouth. Something was profoundly wrong.

The piece of toast floated there, suspended in the moment of disbelief. She thought she saw her collection, the Kiji logo, and Mayumi's face. In what world would these things co-exist? Nagiko took a deep breath, closed her eyes, then resolutely opened the paper again. *Haru Hanibii*. Kiji logo. Mayumi's face. There was no mistake.

Her fabrics, in a riotous bouquet. How had they been obtained? Who had photographed them without her knowledge? Mayumi's tongue reaching toward the silken petals—Nagiko could see that it was meant to suggest a honeybee drawn to nectar, but it reminded her of a snake. A snake about to devour its prey. A snake with the Kiji logo tattooed on her shoulder. Was she losing her mind? She would get to the bottom of this. Leaving the newspaper at the table with 800 yen for her check, she stood up and flipped her sweater around her shoulders, the crystal-sewn sleeves falling like a scarf over her chest. She marched out to the subway.

There, on the wall opposite the tracks, the same image mocked her, in full color, larger than life. Nagiko gasped. She now suspected what she would find at the office. Indeed, the poster was prominently featured in the lobby, and the tongue pursued her even in the elevator. It took a supreme effort to smile at her assistant, whom (she now realized) must have sneaked the fabric out of the studio.

"Isn't it great?" people burbled. "Mr. Satō is so proud of this."

Nagiko was not about to make a scene. She did not need to feign surprise, for the surprise was real enough, but she had to work hard to pretend delight as she wormed the story out of the other designers. So, this had been Chairman Satō's idea, and Mayumi had played right along. He no doubt thought he had done her a great favor, and was waiting for her to come rushing in with thanks. Nagiko couldn't face that, so she called him. Then she left the office.

She didn't answer her phone, though it rang all afternoon with reporters and editors wanting interviews or photo opportunities with her and Mayumi. Satō called at the end of the day to say that he had witnessed an amazing energy between Kiji and Mayumi, and he was prepared to offer Mayumi a position of some sort, perhaps as Kiji's house model. Could they discuss this?

Nagiko absorbed each interview request like a blow. She put everyone off and avoided Mr. Satō. The snake was most certainly trying to devour her. A position at Kiji? Nagiko could hardly breathe. Satō couldn't understand.

He was accustomed to Nagiko's moods, but Mayumi, too, was behaving strangely. Publicity was the lifeblood of this business. Why weren't these two jumping at these offers? To be fair, Nagiko had a trip to London, Paris, and New York that had been planned months ago. But Satō had the inescapable feeling that she was using the trip as an excuse. He decided to have it out with her when she got back.

Nagiko was in agony. Last fall she had been driven to seek out the priest who might understand the sullen cloud that had lodged in her heart. The encounter had been strange beyond belief, but oddly enough, in its aftermath she felt restored. Perhaps this result was not what Tokuda had meant, but as it turned out, letting go of the hidden buddhas had been the solution. She was able to forget Mayumi, to seal her life off from her daughter, and finally stamp out that smoldering resentment. Things were going fine, she had begun to feel normal and sane again—and now this. The Noh mask of the demon Hannya haunted her dreams.

She returned to Tokyo from her business trips on April 30. Hadn't Priest Tokuda said that the last *hibutsu* would be on display at Miidera the first week of May? Nagiko felt a perverse and irresistible urge to go see it. Why shouldn't she? If she had the power to bring the world to an end merely by viewing an image, then she must be meant to exercise it. She almost wished it were true. She allowed herself to contemplate the world coming to an end. At first it was shocking, but the more she thought about it, the more it began to give her a rebellious thrill.

She couldn't help scanning the news for signs of *mappō*. War, of course, there was always a war going on somewhere. That was not so unusual. But other things were going wrong. Frogs were dying out, stinging jellyfish were taking over the beaches of the Mediterranean, bacteria were gaining the upper hand over antibiotics. The glaciers were melting, butterflies disappearing, and hurricanes getting stronger. If you wanted to see signs of *mappō*, you could find them everywhere. It was not just human greed, folly, and cruelty, although you saw enough of that, but the patterns of nature itself were yawing wildly out of kilter.

All her life Nagiko saw patterns. Not only did her greatest delight come from creating pattern, but her foothold in reality depended on it. The only view of karma that made sense to her was as a pattern that repeated itself with variations throughout numberless reincarnations. But when patterns unraveled into chaos, she became disoriented. When a thread became so tangled you couldn't possibly undo it, you cut it off. That's what she felt like doing. Cutting everything, one snip. If Tokuda were right, this would be the last *hibutsu* she would ever see.

It took her till mid-afternoon to get to Miidera. She hadn't bothered to book a hotel for that evening, which in a rational moment she realized was simply stupid. Did she think everything would suddenly go dark and disappear? She had no conception at all of what was supposed to happen—aside from nothing. She could hardly call up Priest Tokuda and ask him. All she knew was that in her confused jumble of emotions, only one thing was consistent—an inner voice urging her to see this *hibutsu*.

Miidera was an extensive compound of buildings. She had to look at a map of the grounds to get her bearings. Where was the hall Tokuda spoke of? The Hall of Virtuous Guardians? She located it on the map just past the pavilion sheltering the famous bell of Miidera, reputedly the most beautiful-sounding temple bell in all Japan. She recalled the Noh play, *Miidera*. A deranged mother had a dream that told her to journey to this temple to find her heart's desire, her lost child. When she arrived, she managed not only to flout the medieval prohibition against women entering temple grounds, but even, once inside, to strike the bell.

Nagiko smiled grimly to herself. She might indeed be considered a deranged mother, but she was not searching for a lost child. On the contrary. In the play, the clear tone of the bell, ringing forth in the pure light of the moon, brought the grieving mother enlightenment. Just at that moment, Nagiko heard the deep gong of the bell. She looked back toward the pavilion. A young couple had just swung the heavy pole into the bell, and now were standing there, the woman with her hand to her mouth, giggling in embarrassment. They walked away, hand in hand. Nagiko approached and read the sign.

STRIKE THE BELL 300 YEN

A bargain for enlightenment, she thought. All right. She'd do it. The only question was whether to wait till after she'd viewed the hidden buddha. But perhaps it would not be possible then. Right. If Tokuda's theory about her was correct, there would be no more bells either. She had no hundred-yen coins, only a thousand-yen note. Fully conscious of the ridiculous contradition, she folded the money and inserted it into the slot of the payment box. Fine, she'd ring it three times.

Her hands smarting from gripping the rough rope attached to the pole, Nagiko waited for the last wave of sound to ebb away. Then, as if her resolve was fortified by the reverberation, she headed back toward the Hall of Virtuous Guardians. A cloth banner hung in front of the building, announcing the special showing of the temple's rare Kariteimo image, a nationally designated Important Cultural Property. In the picture, it looked like an Italian Renaissance *pietà*. She stepped over the raised lintel into the interior of the hall. Like all temples, this one was dimly lit. The statue was set far back behind a row of pillars. Curtains had been drawn aside, absorbing the flickering candlelight in their dark creases.

The demon-turned-goddess Kariteimo was in a seated position, left leg crossed on her lap, upon which she held a clinging infant. Her right hand held, not a wishing jewel, but a pomegranate. Probably brightly painted at one time, the deep folds of her robe were shadowed dark with candle soot. The statue's full round face and loops of hair resembled a seventh-century Chinese beauty, but the robes and pose would have been at home on a Madonna and child in the Uffizi Gallery.

Nagiko thought the statue beautiful and unusual. But did anything change? She stood still, staring at it as people passed behind her, taking perfunctory glances and shuffling on. The expression on the statue's face was more human than goddess. Nagiko stepped outside into the clear, spring-scented air. Did she feel anything different? Of course not. She gazed out at the view of Lake Biwa, feeling nothing but foolish. Might as well find someplace to stay in Kyoto tonight. She pulled out her *keitai* and selected the number for the Hotel Fujita by the river. It was an old standby where the manager knew her and would find a room even during this first week of May, when everyone was traveling. She joined the crowds making their way back to Kyoto, had a late dinner at the hotel, and went straight to bed. It had been an arduous and disappointing day.

The display window at MayumiMode had just been transformed into a garden of potted peonies for May. The mannequin named Mayu wore overalls, a loose red shirt, a silver chain-link belt, chunky split-toe socks and lacquered wooden *geta* sandals. She held a hat under her arm, but had draped on her head a traditional thin cotton *tenugui*, its ends fastened up. There was a smudge of dirt on her face. The other mannequin, Yumi, looked like a peony herself in a pink and white dress of many layers. She had beige leggings, deep maroon high heels, and a matching maroon shrug. Mayumi was fond of silver these days, so she had given her a multi-strand silver necklace threaded randomly with garnet beads. Yumi's hair was platinum this month, held back in a dark green knit hat that accordion-folded into a headband. She sat on garden bench, a sequined purse dangling from her hand.

The shop opened at eleven. This morning Mayumi had been up early. She took Freddo for a quick walk when she went to fetch coffee and rolls. She needed to update her website. At noon, she showered and dressed, and was just about to go out when the phone rang. It was her mother.

Mayumi was speechless. Nagiko wanted to visit her shop.

"Where, ah…where are you?" Mayumi stuttered.

"The Hotel Fujita," Nagiko answered smoothly. "I could walk over in ten minutes. Have you had lunch?"

Nagiko had woken up in her river-view room on this second day of May, pulled open the curtains, and watched the sun rise over the eastern mountains. In the shadows retreating under the pink glow of dawn she felt her own personal *mappō* dissolve. It hadn't occurred to her until this moment that one world ending and another taking its place might be a totally seamless event. Is this what Tokuda had meant? Nothing had changed. Everything was different. The tightness that had clutched Nagiko's ribs, constricted her lungs, and clenched her jaw, had melted away during the night. Hannya was gone from her dreams. She probed her heart for traces of the resentment that had poisoned her life. Gone. Her upper lip quivered and relaxed into a smile.

She must call Tokuda. How had he known that telling her *not* to visit this hidden buddha would assure precisely that she did? He was a very astute counselor. She had to push her obsession through to the end in order to recover. But even before that, she must call Jun Muranaka. She had resolutely shoved him from her thoughts, but now the effort of the struggle to forget him had melted also, and memories came flooding back. She had been so unfair—not listened, not let him explain. She took her *keitai* phone from her purse. Ah—she had deleted his private number. No matter. She would find it tonight. And Satō—she must call Chairman Satō. He had left annoyed-sounding messages since she got back to Japan two days ago. But first, before anything else, she must call Mayumi. She connected her laptop to the internet and found the address and phone number for MayumiMode. It was too early to call, so Nagiko ordered breakfast from room service, then walked out to the long paved stretch along the Kamo riverbank. A stanza from the Noh play *Semimaru* ran through her head—

> *the karmic bonds run deep,*
> *though the world ends deranged,*
> *sun and moon serenely stay their*
> *course unchanged.*

Her deranged world had ended. The dark doubts and secret fears she had attached to Mayumi over the years dissolved. Pure white egrets waded the shallow waters then flapped up to preen in the trees on the bank. Her suspicions of Jun—she let them all go. Housewives walked their Akitas, students rode bicycles. She had built up her own vicious *mappō* and stewed in its toxic miasma, unable to step beyond it. A young man sat on the slanted embankment practicing his saxophone. But the world ending was not catastrophe, it was a rebirth. A bearded homeless man picked up stray aluminum cans. Nagiko noticed everything. Back at the Fujita, she showered and changed her clothes, and at noon she called Mayumi.

They hadn't spoken for years, although each had surreptitiously followed the career of the other. How had she reacted to the poster, Mayumi wondered. She expected Nagiko would be furious, yet she didn't sound angry on the phone just now. Mayumi waited nervously on the sidewalk in front of her shop, Freddo's leash looping her hand. She drew in a long slow breath. Yet even before she saw her approaching up Teramachi Street, Mayumi realized that there was a reason she had provoked her mother by doing the poster. And she realized she had forgiven her for all the secrets, and there was no longer any need to run away.

Nagiko hesitated then quickened her pace until she was standing in front of her. Mayumi smiled.

"*Okaasan…*"

"Mayumi-chan…" Nagiko looked at her daughter, then over her shoulder to the storefront of MayumiMode. The dachshund barked, then stretched his paws up to her knee.

"Freddo, down!" Mayumi commanded.

Nagiko stooped and ruffled the wavy black fur of his long ears. "That's okay...why 'freddo'?"

"*Naso freddo*. His cold nose is my alarm clock."

Freddo's plumed tail waved in a frenzied wag.

"He likes you," said Mayumi.

Nagiko reached down and picked him up.

Mayumi pushed open the door to her shop, and still holding the leash, led her mother inside. Nagiko's eyes took in the clothing, the jewelry and the elaborate window scene Mayumi had arranged.

"Maroon and silver..." she said. "Very nice."

Mayumi smiled.

"And I see you are still fond of peonies..." Nagiko arched one eyebrow, then dropped her gaze, hiding her tears. She had missed so much.

Miroku

THE YEAR OF THE TIGER started off bitterly cold. Mayumi had brought Freddo to Tokyo for the New Year holiday. She stayed with Nagiko and Jun in Azabu, in the house they had moved into when they married six years ago. Jun was always the first one up, so he offered to take the dog out for his morning walk. He felt ridiculous putting Freddo's stylish little coat on him, so he just clicked the leash into the collar ring. "You've got your own fur coat," he said, opening the door. Damn, it was cold. Freddo lifted a paw, and looked up at Jun without moving. Just then Mayumi came scuffing out to the foyer in pajamas and slippers. Kneeling down, she inserted the dog's feet through the sleeves of his woolly winter walking coat.

"Have a nice walk, guys," she said, yawning as she shuffled back to the kitchen.

Jun had five days in which he didn't have to go anywhere; Kiji was closed till January fifth; and Mayumi shut her shop for the first week of January. The three of them holed up in Tokyo, no plans, enjoying the luxury of sheer idleness. Nagiko would turn sixty this year, and Mayumi teased her about creating a collection all in red to celebrate. This would also be Jun's last year as special government consultant. He tried to imagine what it would be like when it ended. Early on he had thought he could make a difference. Later he despaired. Finally, he decided he must try to do his small part and hope for the best. Thus he diligently kept his eyes open, meeting with similar roving consultants-without-portfolio in South Korea, China, and Taiwan as well as the United States and several European countries. He even had an acquaintance in North Korea whom he had met in 1994 at Kim Jong Il's installation as Dear Leader.

When the Dear Leader's eldest son was arrested at Narita International Airport in 2001 for traveling on a fake passport with the excuse that he only wanted to visit Tokyo Disneyland, Jun had been the one dispatched to debrief him and escort him out of the country. (He had, in fact, only wanted to go to Disneyland.) Jun was appalled. He spent two days with the heir apparent to the Dear Leader, a man thirty years old, traveling on a forged Dominican Republic passport with a Chinese alias translating as "fat bear."

"Everyone in Asia is jealous of Japan," the fat bear had told him matter-of-factly. "Someday we'll get revenge."

"Revenge for what?" Jun had asked him, genuinely puzzled.

"All the secrets," he had said. "All the denials." He wouldn't be more specific.

Since then, fat bear had been mostly spotted in the saunas and casinos of Macao. And then he was passed over. Yet who could know how it would come out in the end? Jun read the reports, noting the youth of the Dear Leader's last son and newly designated successor—why, the boy was the same age as Mayumi. Jun winced every time he thought about the navy's scramble to send warships into the Sea of Japan when North Korea launched that stupid missile last April. Tokyo had been put on high alert, and Jun felt his nerves had still not recovered. Time to retire. The World Expo was scheduled for Shanghai this year. Vietnam was gearing up for a bid for the Olympics. Japan would host an APEC summit. No question that the world's focus would be on Asia. If he could just get through this last year. . . .

Freddo sniffed his way down the street. He lifted his leg at three different spots and then hunched, shivering. Jun picked up the steaming result with the plastic bag he'd stuffed in his pocket, dangling it fastidiously until he passed a trashcan. Freddo now started to whine so Jun picked him up and carried him back.

"Cold paws?" he murmured. The dachshund leaped into his arms.

He pushed the gate, setting the dog down while he found his keys. Freddo shot inside, galloping toward the kitchen where Mayumi had made coffee for herself and Nagiko, milky tea for Jun with his incipient ulcer. Satoko was coming over later that morning to discuss a joint flower/fashion show to kick off the new year. Mayumi was trying to decide what to add to her new perfume, Cocolavande, a blend of chocolate and lavender that still needed something to take off the rough edges.

Noboru Tokuda greeted the new year from his usual perch on the platform facing Sagami Bay at Fudō-in. The year's first sunrise had been disappointing. Smothered in a frigid fog, the rising sun remained hidden, manifesting only as a gradual weak lightening of the sky. Tokuda yawned, shivered, and trudged back to his room. This would be a slow week. He didn't have to go anywhere until the third week of January, when he would stay one day and night at Gyōganji Temple in central Kyoto. Their hidden buddha, a thousand-arm Guan Yin that had never been photographed, would be opened on the seventeenth and closed back up the next day. It was the last *hibutsu*. He wasn't seriously worried about it since Nagiko Kiyowara had stopped visiting hidden buddhas, but he regarded it as his sacred duty to keep vigil. Besides, this was the best time to enjoy the statue's effect on his senses as he kept guard. Because the temple was located on a busy street, right in the heart of Kyoto, it was remotely possible that she could simply stumble upon it if she were in the area. He would not permit that to happen.

He had been astounded when Kiyowara-san had come back to see him in early summer seven years ago. She appeared a decade younger than when he had seen her before. He had not expected she would actually seek out the one *hibutsu* he had told her was the last. Yet he must have considered the possibility that she would be desperate enough—otherwise he would not have had the foresight to give her a false one, inspired by her mention of the Noh play *Miidera*. And yet, by some mysterious process he didn't understand, that "expedient truth" as he had justified his action, had ended up being her salvation. She gave him more credit than he deserved, appearing to think he had engineered the whole thing.

At least he hadn't bungled things this time. He could only feel grateful that his chosen course of action had led to such an unexpectedly satisfactory outcome. He concluded that the destructive karmic energy that had been pushing this unhappy woman along a path not of her conscious choosing, was now defused. He had averted tragedy by compassion rather than violence, and this thought humbled him. Every day he continued to chant a prayer for Priest Kon.

She brought her daughter with her once, and he met with them despite the signs he was coming down with his usual rainy season cold. The *mizuko*—that's how she introduced her, joking. The young woman smiled. Tokuda was dazzled, even as he sneezed.

"Haven't we met before?" Mayumi asked, trying to place his face. He looked familiar.

Tokuda thought he'd seen Mayumi as well, but couldn't think of where.

Suddenly Mayumi exclaimed, "The documentary! You were at some of the temples we filmed—yes, Mme. Chardonnet wanted to film you!" She stopped. "And, weren't you the one who had the fugu dinner with Priest Kon...when he..."

Tokuda blanched and fell into a coughing fit.

"Oh, you poor man!" Mayumi's sympathy ran through him like a knife.

Bertrand Maigny was turning ninety-five. On the occasion of his birthday, Tokyo Buddhist University was putting together a festschrift in his honor. In addition, the president invited him to come give a lecture on a topic of his choosing. The embarrassment over Maigny's participation in the documentary on hidden buddhas had been forgotten, and the careful precise scholarship of his earlier work was now receiving long overdue attention. While that was gratifying, Maigny had no desire to talk about some arcane theological point he had written about in detail decades ago. He decided to talk about recent developments in theoretical physics. The theory of loop quantum gravity, defining space-time as a network of braided links, implied that space itself was just a web of information. Space, in other words, did not exist. To Maigny, this sounded a lot like the text of the *Heart Sutra*—form is emptiness, emptiness is form. The original nature of all things is neither born, nor is it extinguished. There is no purity, likewise no defilement. There is no gain, likewise no loss. The physics of the *Heart Sutra* would be the subject of his talk.

Tokyo would be cold, he remembered, taking out an old suitcase and packing a cashmere vest, gloves, and a wool beret for his bald head.

Tokuda arrived in Kyoto on January 16 in order to be at Gyōganji early the next morning. He was a spectator rather than an officiant, but the priests here were accustomed to seeing him every year. Tokuda breathed in the spicy fragrance and faint warm glow seeping from the wooden cabinet. He was at peace. He had brought a thermos of tea and a boxed lunch of rice and condiments, so he didn't have to leave the compound. That evening he had been invited to share the Gyōganji priests' meal. All morning and afternoon, he sat in a state of heightened awareness, observing the visitors streaming in and out of the temple.

Just after he had tweezed the last bit of cold rice with his chopsticks and wrapped up his empty lunch box, Tokuda noticed a beautiful tall young woman in a striking red wool coat with attached capelet. The shape was that of an old-fashioned Inverness overcoat. She had on elbow-length yellow leather gloves, which she removed to buy her ticket. It was Mayumi Kiyowara. He stretched his legs and walked over to the booth.

Her head turned when he called her name.

"Oh—Priest Tokuda! What are you doing here?"

"I come every year for the opening. What are you doing here?"

"My shop is just up the street. I'm on a lunch break. Have you eaten?"

He held up his empty lunch box as he accompanied her toward the open front bay of the hall. "Yes, just finished."

"Oh, too bad," she said. "I'd invite you. You know I've never been in this temple before. It's, like, a block away, but, well, 'base of the lighthouse...' as they say."

"Yes, dark. The base of the lighthouse is always dark..." Tokuda's voice trailed off. Mayumi was saying something but he was no longer listening. As he stood there, the soft hum coming from the *hibutsu* died away. Tokuda's eyes widened in horror. The statue's golden glow faded as he watched, and its fragrance disappeared. Panicked, he looked around.

What's wrong?" Mayumi asked.

"Your mother! Where is she?" Tokuda croaked in a strangled voice.

"She's in Tokyo...why..."

A chill passed through the drafty hall. Mayumi pulled her yellow gloves back on.

Tokuda stumbled backward, staring at Mayumi, the realization washing over him that he had been wrong again. It wasn't Kon, and it wasn't Nagiko. Kon had been at all the temples while filming the documentary—but so had Mayumi. And Kanshinji? Nagiko had taken the child along with her. Tokuda had even seen them together, but he hadn't understood—again. The floor seemed to drop out from under his feet. What was she saying now? That when she inherited Metcalfe's letters, she had gone on the Shikoku pilgrimage, but in reverse, and hadn't made it very far. But she'd obviously made it to Shidōji. And the others. It was now growing very dark. Tokuda's ears detected a rumbling sound, growing louder as if something was rushing forward with great speed. Mayumi seemed unconcerned. Didn't she hear it? Now the glow was coming from Mayumi herself, her golden arms, the perfume—a sharp cool scent that he had once smelled long ago.

Always amazed at how much two teenage boys could eat, Nora was piling up the empty plates from Sunday lunch, oblivious to the Taepodong-2 missile passing almost directly over Maizuru from the west. At the same time, Bertrand Maigny was peering out the window of Air France flight 1370, hoping to catch a glimpse of Mt. Fuji. An unearthly glow filtered up through the fog. The captain's voice came over the intercom. They were diverting the plane to Taipei. No explanation.

Deep on the cedar-forested slope of Mt. Kōya, the monkeys ceased chattering. An eerie wind arose and the skies darkened. As the earth shook, the massive cedar beams holding up the tile roof of the Hall of Lanterns groaned. A young monk was thrown to the ground. The door to the Inner Sanctum cracked open, and the light of a thousand lanterns spilled out, illuminating the roiling gray clouds.

Tokuda had fallen to the ground. Mayumi was holding his head up off the cold stone floor. He felt the warmth of her lap cradling his shoulders. His five senses were overwhelmed—the light, the sound, the warmth, the fragrance. And then a sweetness began at the tip of his tongue and flooded his body. It was as if his lifelong reaction to a *hibutsu* had been magnified to a point where he no longer existed—only the sensations. The sixth sense, consciousness, suddenly shot through him like a lightning bolt. The Womb! Nagiko Kiyowara was the womb! Mayumi was the Diamond! They had reconciled. The world was ready. He understood that the secret transmission was at an end. He looked up at Mayumi and saw the face of Miroku.

Acknowledgments

My husband, Michael Dalby, and my children Marie, Owen, and Chloë have been enthusiastic and supportive sounding boards always. To them I give deepest thanks. I am also grateful to Mark Blum who first led me to Mt. Kōya and showed me Kūkai's tomb in 1998, planting the initial seed of curiosity; to Nagako and Shinobu Koide who arranged a special opening of the hidden buddha at Ōkannonji; to Reiko Nakamura, Chiaki Kato, and Yoko Nishina who came along to explore temples with hidden buddhas; to Alfred Eberle who generously showed me notes from his visit to the Hall of Dreams. My character Philip Metcalfe's shuddering reaction to seeing this *hibutsu* belongs, in real life, to Alfred. I also thank beekeeper Drew Lehman of Arlington Skeps who taught me bee lore, and Sarah Kliban who kindly corrected my French. I am grateful to Head Priest Shinku Matsuo of the Shingon temple Matsuodera in Maizuru for his hospitality and conversation. Susan Matisoff read early drafts with encouragement, as did Dave Barbor, Peter Ginsberg, Martha and Mary Grisier, Jeffrey Hantover, Jane Rosenman, Cathleen Schwartz, John Stevenson, and Shirley Stewart. Their suggestions were invaluable. Artist Michael Hofmann provided many helpful insights as well as the illustrations, and I am grateful to Peter Goodman for his editorial acuity and for giving me the opportunity to be a Stone Bridge Press author.

LIZA DALBY
Berkeley, California, 2009

www.lizadalby.com
www.hiddenbuddhas.com
www.mayumimode.com